FIND THEM DEAD

Peter James is a UK number one bestselling author, best known for writing crime and thriller novels, and the creator of the much-loved Detective Superintendent Roy Grace. Globally, his books have been translated into thirty-seven languages.

Synonymous with plot-twisting page-turners, Peter has garnered an army of loyal fans throughout his storytelling career – which also included stints writing for TV and producing films. He has won over forty awards for his work, including the WHSmith Best Crime Author of All Time Award, Crime Writers' Association Diamond Dagger and a BAFTA nomination for *The Merchant of Venice* starring Al Pacino and Jeremy Irons for which he was an executive producer. Many of Peter's novels have been adapted for film, TV and stage.

www.peterjames.com
@peterjamesuk
peterjames.roygrace
@peterjamesuk
peterjamesPJTV

FIND THEM DEAD

PETER JAMES

PAN BOOKS

First published 2020 by Macmillan

This paperback edition first published 2020 by Pan Books
an imprint of Pan Macmillan
The Smithson, 6 Briset Street, London EC1M 5NR
Associated companies throughout the world
www.panmacmillan.com

ISBN 978-1-5290-0432-8

7 9 8 6

A CIP catalogue record for this book is available from the British Library.

Map artwork by ML Design
Typeset by Palimpsest Book Production Ltd, Falkirk, Stirlingshire
Printed and bound by CPI Group (UK) Ltd, Croydon, CR0 4YY

TO JULIAN FRIEDMANN

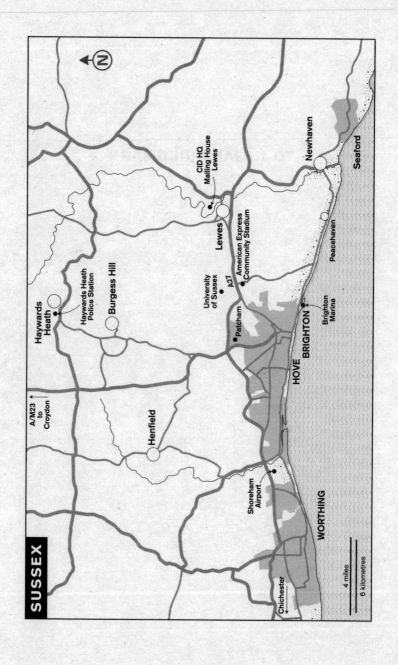

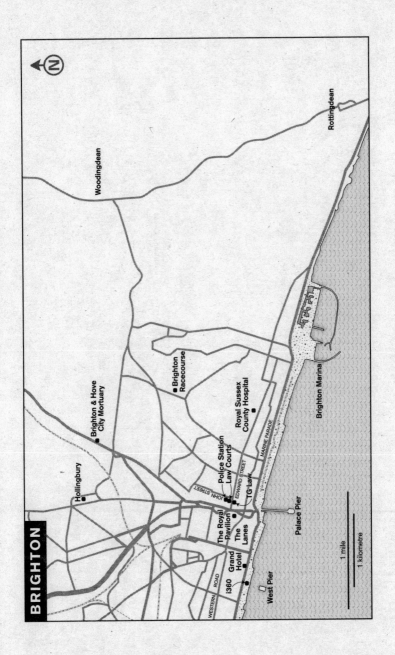

BRIGHTON

N

Woodingdean

Rottingdean

Brighton & Hove
City Mortuary

Brighton
Racecourse

Hollingbury

Royal Sussex
County Hospital

Police Station
Law Courts

JOHN STREET

EDWARD STREET

TG Law

MARINE PARADE

Brighton Marina

The Royal
Pavilion

The Lanes

WESTERN
ROAD

i360

Grand
Hotel

West Pier

Palace Pier

1 mile

1 kilometre

1

Monday 26 November

Mickey Starr gazed into the night, feeling restless and apprehensive. And afraid. It wasn't fear of the darkness but of what lay beyond it.

Going to be fine, he tried to reassure himself. He'd done these Channel crossings before without a hitch, so why should this one be any different?

But it was. No escaping the fact. This *was* different.

Fear was something that had never troubled him before, but throughout this trip he had been feeling a growing anxiety, and now as the shore grew closer, he was truly frightened. Terrified, if it all went pear-shaped, what would happen to the one person in his life who had ever really meant anything to him and who loved him unconditionally. Whatever bad things he may have done.

Wrapped up against the elements in a heavy coat and a beanie, roll-up smouldering in his cupped hand, the muscular, grizzled, forty-three-year-old stood on the heaving deck of the car ferry, braced against a stanchion to keep his balance.

In prison, some eighteen years back, his cellmate, an Irishman with a wry sense of humour, had given him the nickname *Lucky Starr*. Mickey should feel lucky, he'd told him, because he had a spare testicle after losing one to

1

cancer in his teens, a spare eye, after a detached retina in one had put an end to his boxing career, and a spare arm for the one he'd subsequently lost in a motorbike accident.

It was 4 a.m. and he was fighting off seasickness. He wasn't feeling particularly *lucky* at this moment, out here in the middle of the English Channel, in this storm. He had a bad feeling that maybe he'd used up all his luck. Perhaps he should have found someone else to come with him after his colleague had pulled out at the last minute due to sickness. He always felt less vulnerable and conspicuous when he had a female companion with him. Maybe the Range Rover he was driving was too shouty?

Put it out of your mind, Mickey, get on with the job.

The sea was as dark as extinction. The salty spray stung as he squinted through the bitter wind and driving rain. His confidence in tatters, he was wondering if he was making the most stupid mistake of his life.

Calm down. Pull yourself together. Look confident. Be lucky!

Be lucky, and soon he would be home, back with his younger brother, Stuie, who totally depended on him. Stuie had Down's Syndrome and Mickey affectionately referred to him as his 'homie with an extra chromie'. Many years ago, Mickey made a promise to their dying mum that he would always take care of him, and he always had. His 'differently-abled' brother had taught Mickey how to see life in other ways, more simply. Better.

He wouldn't be doing any more runs for the boss after this. He'd talked with Stuie about setting up a business with the cash he'd stashed away – nice money from the small quantities of drugs he'd pilfered from his boss on each run, too small for him to ever notice. Although this time he'd added substantially to the cargo, and a very nice private deal awaited him. Big proceeds – the biggest ever!

But now he was riddled with doubt. All it needed was one sharp-eyed Customs officer. He tried to shake that thought away. Everything was going to be fine, just as it always had been on each of these trips.

Wasn't it?

Stuie liked cooking and constantly, proudly, wore his 'special' chef's toque Mickey had bought him for his birthday last year. Mickey had planned to buy a chippy as close to Brighton seafront as he could afford – or in nearby Eastbourne or Worthing, where prices were lower. But with the money he stood to make now, he'd be able to afford something actually *on* Brighton seafront, where the best earnings were to be made, and he had his eye on a business in a prime location near to the Palace Pier that had just come up for sale. Stuie would work in the kitchen preparing the food and he would be doing the frying and front-of-house. All being well, in a few days he'd have the cash to buy it. He just had to get his load safely through Customs and onto the open road. And then – happy days!

He swallowed, his nerves rattling him again, breathing in the noxious smells of fresh paint and diesel fumes. The boss had patted him on the back a few days ago, before he'd headed to Newhaven, and told him not to worry, all would be fine. 'If shit happens, just act normal, be yourself. Be calm, take a deep breath, smile. Yep? You're *lucky*, so be lucky!'

The 18,000-ton, yellow-and-white ship ploughed on through the stormy, angry swell of the English Channel, nearing the end of its sixty-five-nautical-mile crossing from Dieppe. Ahead, finally, he could now start to make out the port and starboard leading lights of the deep-water channel between the Newhaven Harbour moles, and beyond – spread out along the shore even more faintly – the lights of the town.

A short while later a tannoy announcement requested, 'Will all drivers please return to your vehicles.'

Starr took a final drag on his cigarette, his fifth or sixth of the voyage, tossed it overboard in a spray of sparks and hurried through a heavy steel door back inside, into the relative warmth, where he made his way down the companionway stairs, following the signs to Car Deck A.

No need to be nervous, he told himself yet again. He had all the correct papers and everything had been planned with the military precision he had come to expect of the boss's organization, after nearly sixteen years of working loyally for him. Well, pretty loyally.

The boss had long ago told him this was always the best time of day to pass through Customs, when the officers would be tired, at their lowest ebb. He glanced at his watch. All being well, he'd be home in two hours. Stuie would still be asleep, but when he woke, boy, would they celebrate!

Oh yes.

He smiled. It was all going to be fine. Please, God.

2

Monday 26 November

At 4.30 a.m., Clive Johnson sat in his uniform dark shirt, with epaulettes and black tie, in the snug, glass-fronted office overlooking the cavernous, draughty Customs shed at Sussex's Newhaven Port. The Border Force officer was sipping horrible coffee and thinking about the beer festival at the Horsham Drill Hall next Saturday – the one light at the end of the tunnel of a long, dull week of almost fruitless night shifts and big disappointment among his team, so far.

An average height, stout man of fifty-three, with a friendly face topped by thinning hair, Johnson wore large glasses which helped mask the lenses he needed for his poor eyesight, steadily deteriorating from macular degeneration. Coincidentally and helpfully, his wife owned a Specsavers franchise in Burgess Hill. So far he'd kept his condition from his colleagues, but he knew to his dismay that it would be only a year or two, as the ophthalmologist – who worked for his wife – had informed him, before he would have to give up this job he had come to love, despite its frequent unsociable hours.

Rain lashed down outside, and a Force 7, gusting 8/9, was blowing. One of the sniffer dogs barked incessantly in the handler's van at the far end of the building, as if it sensed the team's anticipation that maybe, after a week of waiting on high alert, acting on a tip-off from a trusted intel source, this might be their night. Although 'trusted' was a questionable term. Intelligence reports were notoriously unreliable and often vague. It had indicated that a substantial importation of Class-A drugs was expected through this port imminently, concealed in a vehicle, possibly a high-value one, and coming in on a night ferry this week. Which was why tonight, as for the past six days, they had a much larger contingent of officers than usual present here at Newhaven, backed up by Sussex Police detectives and an Armed Response Unit waiting on standby. All of them growing bored but hopeful.

The roll-on, roll-off *Côte D'Albâtre* had just docked after its four-hour voyage and was now disgorging its cargo of lorries, vans and cars. And there was one particular vehicle on its manifest emailed earlier from the Dieppe port authority that especially interested Clive.

Apart from real ale, his other passion was classic cars, and he was a regular attendee at as many gatherings of these around the country as he could get to. He never missed the Goodwood events, in particular the Festival of Speed and the Revival, and he had an encyclopaedic knowledge of pretty much every car built between 1930 and 1990, from its engine capacity to performance figures and kerb weight. There was a serious beaut arriving off this ferry, one he could not wait to see. Bust or no bust, it would at least be the highlight of his week.

One problem for the officers was in the definition of 'high value' vehicle. The source of the report was unable to be any more specific. Dozens of cars came under that category. They'd been pulling over and searching many vehicles that might match the description, including a rare Corvette, to date without any success. All they'd found so far was a tiny amount of recreational cannabis and a Volvo estate with a cheeky number of cigarettes on board – several thousand – all for his personal consumption, the driver had said. On further questioning he'd turned out to be a pub landlord, making his weekly run, turning a nice profit and depriving HMRC and thus the British Exchequer of relatively small but worthwhile amounts of cash. They'd impounded the Volvo and its cargo, but it was small fry, not what they were really interested in. Not what they were all waiting for.

As the week had worn on, faith in the intel was fading along with their morale. If tonight came up goose egg too, Clive would be losing most of his back-up.

The first vehicle off the ferry to enter the Customs shed was a camper van with an elderly, tired-looking couple up front. Clive spoke into his radio, giving instructions to the two officers down on the floor. 'Stop the camper, ask them where they've been, then let them on their way.'

Body language was one of Clive Johnson's skills. He could always spot a nervous driver. These people were just plain tired, they weren't concealing anything. Nor was the equally weary-looking businessman in an Audi A6 with German plates who followed. All the same, to deliberately make his target nervous if he was behind in the queue of cars, he ordered two officers to pull the Audi driver over and question him, too. The same applied to another elderly couple in a small Nissan, and a young couple in an MX5. The lorries would follow later. Some of these would be picked out at random and taken through the X-ray gantry, to see if there were any illegal immigrants hidden among their cargo.

Clive had heard the period between 3 a.m. and 5 a.m. called the *dead hours*. The time before dawn when many terminally ill people passed away. The time when most folk were at their lowest point. Most, maybe, but not him, oh

7

no. Just like an owl, he hunted best at night. Clive had never set out to be a front-facing Customs officer because he had never been particularly confident with other people in that way, too much small talk and pretence. He used to prefer back-room solitude and anonymity, the company of tables, facts and figures and statistics. When he'd originally joined Customs and Excise, before it was renamed Border Force, it had been because of his fascination – and expertise – with weights and measures. He had an excellent memory which had served him well as an analyst in the department before he had, rather reluctantly, accepted a move a few years ago to become a frontline officer, after his superiors had seen in him a talent for spotting anything suspicious.

Over these past seven years he had proved their judgement right. None of his colleagues understood how he did it, but his ability to detect a smuggler was almost instinctive.

And all his instincts told him that the driver of the approaching Range Rover towing an enclosed car trailer unit looked wrong. Nervous.

Nervous as hell.

He radioed his two officers on the floor.

3

When anyone asked Meg Magellan what she did for a living, she told them straight up that she was a drug dealer. Which she really was, but the good sort, she would add hastily, breaking into a grin. In her role as a key account manager for one of the UK's largest pharmaceutical companies, Kempsons, she sold and merchandized their range of over-the-counter products into the Tesco store group.

She also tried, mostly unsuccessfully, to augment her income by betting on horses. Never big stakes, just the occasional small flutter – a love of which she'd got from her late husband, Nick, whose dream had been to own a racehorse. The closest he'd got was to own one leg of a steeplechaser called Colin's Brother. She'd kept the share after Nick's death, as a link to him, and followed the horse in the papers, always putting a small bet on and quite often being pleasantly surprised by the nag getting a place – with even the occasional win. Whenever the horse ran at a reasonably local meeting, she would do her best to go along and place a bet and cheer him on, along with the two mates, Daniel Crown and Peter Dean, who owned the other three legs between them. She'd become so much closer to them both since Nick died. In a small way they kept Nick alive to her and she could see his humour in them.

At 4.30 a.m., Meg's alarm woke her with a piercing *beep-beep-beep*, shrieking away a dream in which Colin's Brother was heading to the finishing post but being strongly challenged, as she shouted encouragement at the top of her voice.

Avoiding the temptation to hit the snooze button and grab a few more precious minutes of sleep beneath the snug warmth of her duvet – and continue the dream – she swung her legs out of the bed and downed the glass of water beside her.

She had to get up now. No option. At 9 a.m., in less than five hours, she was presenting her company's latest cough-and-cold remedy to the Tesco buying team, seventy miles of stressful traffic to the north of here. Normally, she'd have stayed at a Premier Inn close to the company's headquarters. A ten-minute drive instead of the three hours facing her now, if she was lucky with the traffic. But this wasn't a *normal* day.

Today, her daughter – and only surviving child – Laura, was heading off to Thailand and then on to Ecuador as part of her gap year. She and Laura had rarely been apart for more than a few days. They had always been close, but even closer since five years ago, when they'd been driving back to Brighton from a camping holiday in the Scottish Highlands.

Always car-sick, Laura sat in the front. After Nick had done a long spell at the wheel of their VW camper van, Bessie, Meg had taken over from her husband, who then sat in the back with their fifteen-year-old son Will, and had slept. As she'd slowed for roadworks on the M1, an uninsured plumber, busily texting his girlfriend, had ploughed his van into the back of their vehicle, killing Nick and Will instantly. She and Laura had survived, and their injuries had healed, but their lives would never be the same again – there was no going back to normal family life. Meg would have given anything to have even the most mundane day with her family one more time. Of course, friends and relatives had rallied around her and Laura in the days and months after the accident, when it felt as if they were living in a surreal bubble, but eventually and inevitably life went on, grief had to be dealt with, and as the years passed people stopped talking about Nick and Will.

Not one day went by when she didn't think of them and what might have been.

Meg had stayed home to be with her daughter on what was to be their last night together for several months. This summer, Laura had saved up for this gap-year backpacking trip, with her best friend, before she went off to study Veterinary Science at the University of Edinburgh.

Nick, who had worked for the same company as Meg, had often jokily discussed with her what life would be like one day as empty-nesters when Will and Laura eventually left home. A positive man, they'd made all kinds of plans – perhaps to take a gap year themselves, which neither of them had done in their teens – and head off to travel Europe, and maybe beyond, in their beloved Bessie.

Laura was a good kid – no, correct that, she thought – a *great* kid. One of the many things she loved about her bright, sparky daughter was the way she cared about animals. Meg was charged now with looking after Laura's precious pet guinea pig, Horace, and her two gerbils, as well as her imperious Burmese cat, Daphne.

When she came back home tonight to their small, pretty, mock-Tudor semi close to Hove seafront, Meg was painfully aware she would be truly alone. Home to a new reality. A real, lengthy period alone. And when Laura returned from her gap year, she'd then be getting ready to move to university. No more music blasting from Laura's bedroom. No more questions on homework to help her daughter with. No more running commentaries on who was going out with who, or the geeky boy who had been trying to chat her up. A big, lonely, empty nest.

God, she loved her daughter so much. Laura was smart, fun and incredibly streetwise. Above all, Meg always knew she could trust her to take care of herself when she went out into town with her friends. Every night, apart from when she had to spend time away from home, travelling on business, they would sit down and have supper together and share their days.

But not any more. Tonight, she'd be alone with her memories. With Laura's beloved pets – hoping and praying none would die while she was away – and with the photographs around the house of Nick and Will with her and Laura when they were a family of four. *You have children?* people would ask. Meg would reply, 'I have two.' It wasn't true, but she did, back then.

'I am a mother of two children, and I am a wife. But my son and my husband are dead.' She never found those conversations any easier.

And to add to her concerns, her employer for the past twenty-odd years, ever since she had left uni, would be moving next year from nearby Horsham just forty minutes' drive from here, up to Bedfordshire – a two-and-a-half-hour grind. No date had been fixed yet but, when the time came, she would have to make the choice either to stay on or take the redundancy package on offer.

Meg showered, got herself ready then went down into the kitchen to make some breakfast and a strong coffee. Daphne meowed, whingeing for her breakfast. She opened a tin and the cat jumped up onto the work surface, barged her arm and began eating, though she had barely started scooping the fishy contents out. 'Greedy guts!' Meg chided, setting the bowl on the floor. The cat jumped down and began to scoff the food as if she hadn't been fed for a month.

Moments after Meg sat at the table, beneath a large framed photograph on the wall of Colin's Brother passing the finishing post at Plumpton Racecourse half a length ahead of the next horse, she heard soft footsteps behind her and felt Laura's arms around her. Laura's face close against hers, wet with tears. Hugging her. She ignored the five earrings cutting into her cheek.

'I'm going to miss you so much, Mum.'

'Not as much as I'm going to miss you.' Meg turned and gripped both of her daughter's hands. Laura's dark hair was styled in a chic but strange way that made her think of garden topiary. She had a scrunchie on one wrist and a Fitbit on the other and was dressed in striped paper-bag trousers and a white T-shirt printed with the words, in an old-fashioned typeface, YOU MAKE ME WONDER.

Meg smiled through her own tears and pointed at it. 'That's for sure!'

Her daughter had changed so much in these past few years. And recently seemed to be changing week on week with new piercings appearing. From nothing a year ago, she now had, in addition to her ears, a nose ring and a tongue stud, and, horror of horrors, she'd had her first tattoo just this past weekend – a small hieroglyphic on her shoulder which Laura said was an ancient Tibetan symbol for protecting travellers. Meg could hardly argue with that.

Laura's expression suddenly darkened as her eyes darted to the right. Freeing her hands, she pointed at a pile of plastic carrier bags. 'Mum, what are those?' she chided.

Meg shrugged. 'I'm afraid I'm not Superwoman, I forget things sometimes, OK?'

Laura shook her head at her. 'OK, right, we're meant to be saving the planet. What if everyone forgot to take their own bags to the supermarket every time they went shopping?'

'I'll do my best to remember in future.'

Laura wagged a finger at her then leaned forward and kissed her. 'I know you will, you're a good person.'

'What time are you leaving?' Meg choked on the words.

'Cassie's mum is picking us up at 6 a.m. to take us to the airport.'

Cassie and Laura had been inseparable for years. She'd been the first to get a piercing and of course Laura had to follow. Now Cassie had three tattoos – God knows what Laura was going to come back with after their long trip.

'You'll keep in touch and let me know when you've landed?'

'I'll WhatsApp you every day!'

'You're all I have in the world, you know that, don't you, my angel?'

'And you're all I have, too, Mum!'

'Until you meet the *right person*.'

'Yech! Don't think there's much danger of that. Although maybe when we get to the Galapagos next year, I might kidnap a sea lion and bring it back.'

Meg smiled, knowing she was only half jesting. Over the years, Laura had brought all kinds of wounded creatures into their house, including a fox cub, a robin and a hedgehog. 'Be careful in the water, won't you – don't forget about those dangerous rip tides and currents?'

'Hello, Mum! Didn't we grow up on the seaside? I'll be careful! You'll look after all the animals – don't forget the gerbils?'

'I've got all your instructions.'

Laura had written a detailed list of their food and the times they liked to be fed.

'And special hugs and treats for Master Horace?' She was struggling to speak now, her voice choked. 'Don't be sad, Mum. I love you so much and I'll still love you just as much when I'm over there.'

Meg turned her head and looked at her daughter. 'Sure, I know you will,' she said.

And the moment you get on that plane, you will have forgotten all about me.

That's how it works.

4

Monday 26 November

Shit, Mickey thought, his nerves shorting out as he obeyed the two Border Force officers' unsmiling signals to pull over into the inspection lane. This wasn't supposed to happen. *Shit shit shit.*

Be calm. Deep breath. Smile.

That was all he needed to do. But at this moment there was a total disconnect between his mind and his body. His ears were popping and his armpits were moist. A nerve tugged at the base of his right eye; a twitch he'd not had for years suddenly returned at the worst possible moment imaginable.

Stepping out of the office, Clive Johnson continued to observe the driver's body language as the vehicle and trailer came to a halt. The man, who was wearing a black beanie, lowered his window, and Johnson strode up and leaned in. He smelled the strong reek of cigarette smoke on the man, noticing his badly stained teeth; the tattoo rising up above his open-neck shirt. He was wearing leather gloves. His skin had the dry, creased look of a heavy smoker, making him appear older than he actually was – probably around forty, he thought.

'Good morning, sir, I am with the UK Border Force,' Johnson said with consummate politeness.

'Morning, officer!' Mickey said in his Brummy accent. 'Bit of a ride that was. Good to be on terra firma!'

The man had almost comically thick lenses, which made his eyes look huge, Mickey thought.

'I'll bet it is, sir. I'm not much of a seafarer myself. Just a few questions.'

'Yeah, of course, no problem.'

The man's voice seemed to have risen several octaves, Clive Johnson noticed. 'I will need to see the documentation for your load. Have you come from anywhere nice?'

'Dusseldorf, in Germany.'

'And where's your destination?'

'Near Chichester. I'm delivering a vehicle for LH Classics.' He jerked a finger over his shoulder. 'They've purchased this vehicle on behalf of a client and they're going to prep it for a race in the Goodwood Members' Meeting.'

'And what is the vehicle you are transporting?'

'A 1962 Ferrari – 250 Short Wheelbase.'

'Pretty rare. Didn't one of these sell at auction recently for nearly £10 million, if I'm correct?' Clive Johnson said.

'You are correct. But that had better racing history than this one.'

Johnson nodded approvingly. 'Quite some car.'

'It is, believe me – I wouldn't want to be the guy responsible for driving it in a race!'

'Let's start with your personal ID. Can I see it, please?'

Starr handed him his passport.

'Are you aware, sir, of the prohibitions and restrictions of certain goods such as drugs, firearms and illegal immigrants for example?'

'It's only the car and me!' Starr said cockily, pointing his thumb towards the trailer.

Johnson then asked him a number of questions regarding the placing of the vehicle in the unit and its security on the journey, which Starr answered.

'Can I now see the paperwork for the vehicle?' Johnson said.

Mickey lifted a folder off the passenger seat and handed it to him. Johnson made a show of studying it for some while. Then he said, 'I'd like to see the vehicle, please, sir.'

Immediately he noticed the man's fleeting hesitation. And the isolated beads of perspiration rolling down his forehead.

'Yeah, sure, no problem.'

Mickey got out of his car, butterflies in his stomach, telling himself to keep calm. Keep calm and all would be fine. In a few minutes he'd be on the road and heading home to Stuie. He went to the rear of the trailer unit, unlocked it and pulled open the doors to reveal the gleaming – almost showroom condition – red Ferrari.

Clive Johnson ogled the car. Unable to help himself, he murmured, 'Ah, but a man's reach should exceed his grasp, or what's a heaven for?'

'You what?' Mickey said.

'Robert Browning. That's who wrote it.'

'Oh,' Mickey said, blankly. 'I think you're mistaken. David Brown – he was the man who created Aston Martins. DB – that stood for David Brown.'

'I know my cars, sir,' Johnson said, still inscrutably polite. 'I was talking about Robert Browning.'

'Dunno him, was he a car designer, too?'

'No, he was a poet.'

'Ah.'

Clive Johnson stepped back and spoke quietly into his radio. Moments later a dog handler appeared, with an eager white-and-brown spaniel on a leash with a fluorescent yellow harness.

'Just a routine check, sir,' Johnson said. And instantly noticed a nervous twitch below the man's right eye.

'Yeah, of course.'

The handler lifted the dog into the trailer, then clambered up to join it. Immediately, the dog started moving around the Ferrari, occasionally jumping up.

'Make sure it don't scratch the paintwork, I'll get killed if there's any marks on it,' Mickey said.

'Don't worry, sir,' Clive Johnson said. 'Her claws are clipped regularly, her paws are softer than a chamois leather.'

The handler opened the passenger door and let the dog inside. It clambered over the driver's seat then, tail wagging, jumped down into the footwell and sniffed hard.

Its demeanour and reaction were a sign to its handler that the dog had found something.

Mickey watched it, warily. His boss had told him not to worry, they'd used new wrappers, devised by a Colombian chemist, that would stop sniffer dogs from finding anything. He hoped his boss was right. Certainly, the dog seemed happy enough – it was wagging its tail.

5

As the dog handler led the spaniel back down from the rear of the trailer, he exchanged a knowing glance with Clive Johnson, who climbed up and peered into the car. Looking at the spoked wood-rim steering wheel. The dials. The gear lever with its traditional Ferrari notched gate. He opened the door and leaned in, sniffing, and that was when his suspicions increased. Authentic classic cars had an ingrained smell of worn leather, old metal and engine oil.

This car did not smell right.

He removed a wallet stuffed with £50 notes from the door pocket. Sniffer dogs were trained to smell not only drugs but also cash. Was it going to turn out to be just an innocent wad of cash in a wallet, after all this? Hopefully not.

He jumped back down onto the shed floor, turning to Starr. 'I'm seizing the wallet and its contents pending further investigation as the cash could be evidence of criminal activity.' He sealed the wallet into an evidence bag in front of him.

Mickey could feel his anger and anxiety growing. 'What are you doing, is that really necessary?'

Johnson ignored the question. 'Is the car driveable?'

'Yes,' Mickey said, pointedly.

'Good. What I'd like you to do, please, is reverse the car onto the floor. I need to weigh it.'

'Weigh it?'

'Yes, please.'

The butterflies now raised a shitstorm inside Mickey's belly. He tried not to let that show. 'No problem.' He began removing the wheel blocks.

The sound of a classic Ferrari's engine starting was more beautiful than any music to Clive's ears. It was a sound that touched his heart and soul. Poetry in motion. But the engine noise resonating around the steel walls of this shed had little of that music. Just like the smell of the Ferrari's interior, the engine noise was also not quite right. He stood behind, waving the car down the ramp, watching the wheels, the tyres. The way the car sank on its haunches as the rear wheels reached the concrete floor.

He walked around the car, having to force himself to focus on his task and not simply be blown away by its sheer animal beauty. Yet the more he looked at it, the more something else did not seem right. He guided the driver, smiling pleasantly all the way, along the shed and over to the left onto the weighing platform built into the floor. He made the driver back up, move over further to the left, go forward, reverse again then stop and get out of the car.

Clive looked at the readout. And his excitement began to rise. He had checked earlier, when he'd received the manifest, the kerb weight of a proper 1962 Ferrari 250 SWB. It should be 950 kilograms.

This car weighed 1,110 kilograms.

Why?

Many classic cars were rebuilt, or even faked from new, some using chassis numbers from written-off wrecks while other rogues brazenly copied existing numbers. And not always with the original expensive metals. Some were rebuilt for an altogether very different purpose. Was he looking at one now?

In a few minutes he would find out.

He walked over to the driver's side of the Ferrari, smiling, giving the impression that everything was OK. Instantly, he could see the change in the driver's demeanour.

Mickey smiled back, relief surging through him. *Got away with it! Got away with it! Yesssss!*

He was so gleeful that he wanted to text Stuie. He would be with him in a little over an hour, on the empty roads at this time of morning. But he decided to wait until he was well clear, to get out of here as fast as he could in case the officer had a change of mind.

Then the Border Force officer stepped up. 'Just before you go on your way, sir, I'm going to have my colleague drive it through the X-ray gantry.'

Mickey felt a cold flush in his stomach. *Be calm, deep breath, smile.*

Clive Johnson stood in front of the X-ray's monitor, watching as the vehicle was driven through the scanner, until he had the completed black-and-white image. Almost immediately, he could see an anomaly: the tyres should have been hollow, filled with air as all tyres normally were. Instead, the scanner showed they were solid.

Johnson was excited, but still mindful of the value of this car if it was genuine, despite his suspicions. The least intrusive place to start, from his past experience, would be with the spare wheel.

He opened the boot and, joined by two colleagues, removed it. They lifted it uneasily out of the vehicle, alarm bells ringing at the weight of it. One of the officers rolled and bounced it. He then spoke to his colleague, who produced a Stanley knife.

Mickey watched in horror as the man ripped through it.

'For God's sake, that's an original that came with the car!' Mickey shouted, desperation in his voice. 'Do you have any idea what you might be doing to the value of this Ferrari?'

'I'm very sorry, Mr Starr, the car's owners will of course be compensated for any damage done during the examination if the car proves to be in order,' Clive Johnson said.

'Can I have a smoke?'

'I'm afraid this is a no-smoking area.'

'Well, can I go outside then?'

'I'm sorry, sir, not at this moment,' Johnson said. 'We need you to be in attendance to observe what we are doing.'

There was no *hiss* of escaping air as the officer sliced the blade deep into the tyre wall. For some while he worked the blade around in an arc, until finally he pulled away a large flap of rubber.

In the gap it left, a plastic bag filled with a white powder was clearly visible. The officer reached in to pull it out and held it up, showing those present what he had found.

'Most people fill their tyres with air, sir.' Johnson moved forward towards Mickey. 'I believe this package contains controlled drugs and I'm arresting you.'

Mickey stared at him for a fraction of a second in complete blind panic. Trying to think clearly. A voice inside his head screamed, *RUN!*

Mickey shoved the officer harshly sideways, sending him stumbling into the wall, and sprinted forward, racing through the shed. He heard shouts, a voice yelling at him to stop. If he could just get out of here, out into the dark streets, he could disappear. Hole up somewhere or steal a car and get back to Stuie.

His foot hit something painfully hard, a fucking wheel brace, and he sprawled forward. As he scrambled desperately back to his feet, someone grabbed his right arm, his prosthetic arm.

He twisted, kicked out backwards with his foot, felt it connect and heard a grunt of pain.

His arm was still being held.

He spun. Two men, one with the big glasses. He lashed out with his left arm, punching Four-Eyes in the face, straight in the glasses, sending him reeling backwards, then he lashed out at the other, much younger man who was still holding his arm. Aimed a kick at his groin, but the officer dodged it and Mickey lost his footing, tripping backwards, falling, his entire weight supported now by the man holding his arm.

As he staggered back, trying desperately to keep on his feet, he picked up the wheel brace and registered the momentary shock on the officer's face. Then he rushed him, headbutting him with all his strength, and heard a *crunch* as he did so.

The officer, blood spurting from his shattered nose, fell to the ground. Mickey sprinted again, past a parked van with amber roof lights, and out through the far end of the shed into chilly early morning air and falling rain, into darkness and towards the lights of the town beyond.

Safety.

A voice yelled from the darkness, 'Stop, Police!' Flashlight beams struck him, and an instant later two police officers, one a man-mountain, hurtled from seemingly nowhere towards him. Mickey swung the wheel brace at the big one's head but too late; before it could connect, he felt like he'd been hit by a fridge. A crashing impact, the momentum hurling him face-first to the ground. An instant later there was a dead weight on top of him. A hand gripped the back of his neck, pushing his face down hard onto the wet road surface.

Instantly, using all his survival instincts and martial arts training, Mickey kicked out backwards, catching his assailant by surprise, and in the same split-second reached up, curled his left arm round the man's thick neck and gave a sharp pull. With a startled croak, the man rolled sideways as if he was as light as a sack of feathers.

Freeing himself, Mickey rose to his feet and, before the startled officer could react, slammed his powerhouse of a southpaw fist into the man's jaw. As the officer staggered backwards in agony, Mickey sprinted again towards the lights of the town. He overtook several foot passengers and reached the junction with the deserted main road.

Thinking hard and fast.

Glancing over his shoulder.

In the distance, he saw bobbing flashlights. People running, but a good few hundred yards behind him.

He was about to cross the road when headlights appeared. Hesitating in case it was a police car, and ready to melt back into the darkness, he saw it was an Audi with German plates. The driver clocked him and slowed to a halt, putting down his window.

Mickey stared in at a serious-looking man in his thirties in a business suit. In broken English, the man said, 'Hello, excuse me, I've come from the ferry but think I have taken a wrong turning. Would you know the direction towards London?'

Mickey slammed his fist into the side of the man's neck, aiming it directly at the one place that would knock him unconscious instantly. He opened the door, unclipped his belt and shoved him, with some difficulty, across into the passenger seat. Then he jumped in, familiarizing himself in an instant with the left-hand driving position, and accelerated hard away, ignoring the insistent pinging of the alarm telling him to fasten his belt.

Something more insistent was pinging inside his head. *Get home to Stuie before the police get there.*

In his red mist of panic, he figured so long as he got home, everything would be all right. He and Stuie, they were good. They were a team.

'I'm coming,' he muttered. 'Stuie, I'm coming. Going to scoop you up and we'll head north up to Scotland, lie low for a bit. I got friends there on a remote farm. We'll be safe there.'

And maybe safe in this car. Had anyone been close enough to see him taking it? He'd have to chance not. He'd call Stuie, who always slept the sleep of the dead, and tell him to get up, pack a bag and be ready to leave the moment he arrived. The way to get him to move fast would be tell him it was a game and that he could bring his chef's hat!

He put his hand down to the front pocket of his jeans to tug out his phone.

It wasn't there.

6

Monday 26 November

Shit, Mickey thought, trying to concentrate on driving, panic rising again. *Shit. What numbers did the phone have on it?* It was a burner he'd bought a couple of weeks before the start of the trip.

There was a groan from the passenger seat, which he ignored as he concentrated on navigating through the outskirts of the town, away from the harbour and towards the A26.

A couple of minutes later, driving like the wind, he shot out of the industrial area and onto the long, twisty, rural part of the road, checking his mirrors constantly. There was nothing so far. Just more of that darkness.

A bus-stop lay-by loomed up ahead. He braked hard and swung into it. Then he ran round to the passenger door, bashed the German unconscious again and dragged him, out of sight, into dense undergrowth. Not great but the best he could do, short of killing him. Returning to the car, he drove on at high speed. Thinking.

What a mess.

All his great plans down the toilet.

Jesus.

The boss was going to be furious – but that was the least of his problems right now.

He carried on, flat out up the winding country road that he knew well, 70 . . . 80 . . . until he reached the roundabout at the top. Right would take him towards Eastbourne. Left towards Brighton on a wide dual carriageway taking him directly to Stuie in Chichester. They would head north towards London and the circular M25 around it. And then towards Scotland. Find a service station and steal or hijack another car there.

He turned left, checking his mirrors again. Nothing. Only street-lit darkness. Wide, fast, empty road ahead now for many miles. He floored the accelerator and the car pushed forwards – 80 . . . 90 . . . 100 . . . 120. He slowed, approaching a bend, aware of the roundabout ahead. Right would take him through the Cuilfail tunnel into the county town of Lewes, straight on along the fast road, past the University of Sussex. He carried straight on over the roundabout, accelerating hard, still nothing but darkness behind him. Thinking.

Suddenly a sliver of blue appeared in his mirrors. Like the glint of a shard of broken glass. Had he imagined it?

Then it appeared again. More insistently.

What?

He drove on as fast as he dared, crossed another roundabout, then accelerated along a fast, straight stretch, the needle passing 130 then 140 kph. He only slowed a fraction as he took a long right-hand curve and powered up a hill.

The slivers of blue in his mirror were getting brighter. Gaining. Strobing in all his mirrors.

Shit, fuck, shit!

Cresting the top, he raced down the far side. In two miles or so was another roundabout, off a slip road to the left. That would give him three options – towards Brighton, towards the Devil's Dyke or towards London.

Which would they be expecting him to take?

He held the accelerator to the floor.

The lights behind him were gaining. Closing.

Then, to his horror, just ahead of him, blocking off two of his options – to go straight on or take the slip road – there was an entire barrage of blue lights.

Taking his chances, he powered straight on.

As he shot through, between all the flashing lights, he heard a series of muffled pops and the car suddenly began to judder, snaking right, then left, then right again. Out of control. He'd driven over a fucking *stinger*, he realized.

The car was shaking violently. Swerving right towards the central reservation, then left, towards the verge. Somehow, he got it straightened out and carried on, with a loud *flap-flap-flap* sound.

The blue lights were right up his rear now and the interior of his car was flooded with blazing headlights.

He ploughed on, wrestling with the steering wheel in sheer panic, the car slowing despite keeping the pedal to the metal.

More headlights in his mirror now. A marked police estate car suddenly pulled level with him on his right, then darted in front of him, replaced seconds later by another identical car on his right.

The one in front braked sharply.

He stamped on his brakes, too, swerving left, right, left, the Audi totally unstable again. As he pulled away from the verge on his left, he banged doors with a loud, metallic *boom* with the car to his right.

Headlights in his mirror dazzled him. Flashing. Flashing.

Right up his jacksie.

He was totally boxed in, he realized. Fucking T-packed.

Trying to think.

Running on what felt like four flat tyres. Maybe even just rims now.

The car in front was slowing. He rear-ended it, then slewed to the right, banging doors once more with the police BMW alongside him.

Slowing more.

He looked desperately right, then left, for a gap. Something he could swing through.

His brain raced.

Had to get away. Take them by surprise?

He wrenched the steering wheel hard right. Banged, with a loud clang, into the BMW again, and an instant later, with no time to brake, slammed into the rear of the police car which had halted in front of him.

Before he could even unclip his seat belt, his door was flung open and a police officer in a stab vest loaded with gear was standing there, joined a second later by a colleague. He was yanked, unceremoniously, from his seat and pushed, face-down, onto the road surface.

'Michael Starr?' a male voice said.

He twisted his head to look at the man, and retorted in what he knew was a futile act of defiance, 'Who are you?'

PC Trundle of Sussex Road Policing Unit introduced himself, then arrested and cautioned him.

'Save your breath, I know the law,' Starr retorted.

'Do you?' said Trundle's colleague, PC Pip Edwards. 'Then you should know better than to be driving with four flat tyres. Tut, tut, tut! You could get a big fine for that.'

'I'm guessing that's not why you've stopped me.'

'Really?' Edwards retorted. 'That's pretty smart thinking. Ever thought about going on *Mastermind*?'

'Very funny.'

FIND THEM DEAD

'There's someone at Newhaven Port wants a word with you, matey boy. Because we're kind, obliging people, we're going to give you a lift back there – so long as it's not inconveniencing you?'

7

Monday 26 November

As dawn was breaking outside, Clive Johnson sat in his office with the bag of white powder he'd removed from the spare tyre, listening on his borrowed police radio to the update from the Road Policing Unit. He was wearing forensic gloves, video recording what he was doing and ensuring that he was protecting possible traces of DNA, fibres and finger-prints. He slit the bag open and performed a brief chemical analysis on a sample of the contents. It tested positive for cocaine – and a very high grade.

He knew that the current street value of this drug in the UK was around £37,000 per kilogram. Which meant, if he was right in his calculation, judging from the weight of the Ferrari, there could be close to six million pounds' worth of drugs inside that beautiful vehicle, maybe even more.

And the car wouldn't be looking quite so beautiful by the time every panel had been removed and its bare entrails exposed.

Twenty minutes later, cuffed to an officer, Mickey was frog-marched back into the shed and up to the Ferrari where the Border Force officer who had first questioned him was now, once again, standing. He had a piece of sticking plaster on his bent glasses, one lens of which was cracked, and was not looking as friendly as before. 'Decided to come back, did you? Very obliging of you.'

'Haha,' Mickey said, sourly.

'I won't keep you too long, Mr Starr,' Johnson said. 'But as a formality I do need you to witness our continued examination of this vehicle.'

Much too late, Mickey knew, he tried reasoning with the man. 'Look, see – I just got hired to transport the car – I didn't know there was nuffin' in it.'

'Is that so?' Johnson said. 'Did you not have the slightest inkling?'

'Honest to God, no. I'm just a driver, right, hired to transport the car. I don't know about any drugs. I'm totally innocent.'

'Which is why you assaulted me and ran away, is it?'

'I – just got scared, like.'

'I suppose I do look a bit scary, don't I?' There was a hint of humour in the Border Force officer's voice. But not much.

Clive Johnson stared hard at Mickey. 'Mr Starr, I believe these packages contain controlled drugs. I am also arresting you on suspicion of being knowingly concerned with the illegal importation of a Class-A drug.' He cautioned him. 'Is that clear?'

'Clear as mud. I need a fag. Can we go outside so I can have one?'

'I'm afraid not, and I'm not one to preach,' Clive Johnson said, 'but you really ought to think about quitting. Smoking's not good for your health.'

'Nor is being arrested. You should try prison food.'

'Well, if it's not to your taste, have you ever thought about making better career choices?'

8

It had been many years since Roy Grace had gone out on patrol – being a proper copper, as he called it – and he was loving it. It was all part of the learning curve on his six-month secondment to London's Met Police. And he was finding front-line policing in one of the most violent areas of London to be a real baptism of fire – and a million miles from the very different vibe of his usual patch, the county of Sussex.

The Violent Crime Task Force had been set up by the Prime Minister, in conjunction with the Mayor of London and the Commissioner of the Metropolitan Police, to curtail the knife crime epidemic in the city. The unit worked hand in hand with the specialized Metropolitan Police units, fighting Serious and Organized Crime. Knife crime was directly linked to one of their top priorities, tackling the vast and brutal so-called 'county lines' drug-dealing empires, which now had a near monopoly on Class-A drugs throughout the UK.

'County lines' was the generic name given to gangs – or Organized Crime Networks – bringing drugs on a large scale into different regions of the country. Their principal method of operation was to coerce children and vulnerable adults, either through bribery or brutalizing violence, into hiding, storing and distributing drugs, weapons and cash.

These disposable human couriers were equipped with untraceable pay-as-you-go phones – deal 'lines' – giving no link back to their direct bosses if they were caught. They would travel, largely by train, often dispatched to different counties, moving quantities of cocaine and heroin to the local county line 'lieutenants'. These lieutenants would break the drugs down into individual 'wraps' for the street dealers, who would regularly carry the drugs in their body cavities.

Much of the current wave of street violence, Grace knew, came from turf wars between county lines gangs. The gangs themselves were modelled on the Mafia structure, with a ruthless capo, known in street parlance as the 'Diamond', at the top, and a lieutenant beneath him, known as the 'county line head'. And like the Mafia, they were highly efficiently run businesses, willing to torture and kill anyone stepping on their toes.

It was a former boss in Sussex, Alison Vosper – then an Assistant Chief Constable, now Deputy Assistant Commissioner of the Met – who had offered him this six-month posting in the role of Acting Commander. He had accepted it, liking the challenge and thinking he might learn a lot from it, which he could apply down in Sussex. And as an added sweetener, it put him on level ranking with his current boss there, ACC Cassian Pewe.

He missed the camaraderie of his team in Sussex, despite being only a few weeks into the posting. But he was determined this unit would make a difference to the appalling murder rate in London.

Earlier this week, Alison Vosper had phoned, sounding him out about extending the posting for another six months, but Grace was not at this moment enthusiastic. The job up here was taking him away from home too much; he'd barely seen his family during the last month. Added to which, back in Sussex he had two separate murder trials coming up of suspects he had arrested, one starting next spring, set down for Lewes Crown Court. He was going to need time to prepare for them.

This evening, he was sitting in the back of an unmarked, innocuous-looking Vauxhall Astra with burly, experienced PC Dave Horton at the wheel and Detective Inspector Paul Davey in the passenger seat, cruising the dark streets of Camberwell in South London, during another of their regular blitzes. Hunting anyone who might be carrying a knife or drugs, as well as moped gangs who were currently plaguing the city, snatching bags and phones.

The car's interior had the familiar rank smell of most operational vehicles, of junk food and the odour of unwashed villains, but he didn't mind. He peered out of the window, studying the body language of everyone they passed, while Davey watched the ANPR camera mounted on the dash, which would pick up the registration plates of any car with a previous history of association with any criminal activity.

All three of them were wearing jeans and T-shirts and bulky stab vests beneath bomber jackets, with brand-new, expensive trainers, issued by the Met. Fresh kicks were the principal status symbols of the new wave of young street criminals, and the easiest way for them to spot a copper was by the old and shoddy trainers they usually wore. Not any more. This had been one of Grace's first initiatives since taking on his new role, to spend a tiny portion of the £15 million budget the Task Force had been given on kitting out his team with the latest drop of trainers.

They were travelling along a main road lined with shoddy shops and restaurants on both sides. As Grace watched a dodgy-looking group of youths on the far side, some in trainers, some in their casual, insouciant street footwear of sliders and black socks, Dave Horton suddenly shouted out, 'Him!' and swung sharply left into a side road, unclipping his belt and stamping on the brakes. As the car squealed to a halt, all three opened their doors and jumped out.

Grace sprinted after Horton and Davey, back onto the main road, just in time to see someone in a Scream mask, puffa jacket, gloves and trainers pedalling a bike hard along the pavement towards them.

Shouting, 'Police!' Paul Davey put his hands out wide to stop the cyclist, while Horton side-stepped into the road to stop the bike swerving past. Roy Grace braced himself to grab the rider if the other two failed.

The cyclist halted as the Inspector held up his warrant card. An aggressive youth in his late teens raised his horror mask and glared at the three men. 'Yeah? What you want? You stopped me just because I'm black, right?'

Before either of the other officers could say anything, Roy Grace stepped forward, holding up his own warrant card. 'So, we're psychics, are we?'

'What?'

'Are you telling us we're psychics?'

'Ain't telling you nothing. You stopped me because I'm black. That's what you do.'

'What's your name?' Grace asked him, pleasantly.

'Darius.'

'Darius what?'

'Yeah, Darius *What*. That's my name. Darius What.'

Grace nodded. 'OK, Darius. Do you want to tell me how, before we stopped you, any of us knew you were black?'

The cyclist frowned. 'That's why you stopped me, innit?'

Grace shook his head. 'You're wearing a mask, a jacket zipped to the neck and gloves. You could have been a Martian inside that lot for all we knew. Riding a bike on a pavement is an offence, but that's not why we stopped you. Your ethnicity doesn't come into it, but if you go around wearing a mask that scares and intimidates people, we are going to stop you. It's early evening, don't you think it might be frightening for any young children to see that?' Grace smiled. 'The way you're making us feel, we should be the ones in the mask. We're the monsters and you are OK. Is that right?'

'What you mean?'

'What I mean, Darius, is that I care about one thing only, and that's that ordinary folk can walk down the street – any street they choose – without being afraid, without being intimidated, without someone in a terrifying mask hurtling down the pavement towards them. Am I being racist for wanting that?'

Darius looked at him as if trying to figure him out.

'Well?' Grace pressed. 'I'm not going to search you, I'm not booking you for riding on a pavement, or for riding after dark without any lights, which I could. I'm going to let you go on your way, on one condition.'

'Condition?'

Grace nodded. 'One condition.'

'And that's, like, what?'

'That when you get to wherever you are going, you give your mates a message. Will you do that, Darius?'

'What message?'

'That not all cops are bastards. Tell them we are your cops, too. We care for everyone, regardless of their colour, their gender or their faith. Tell them to stop mistrusting us and work with us, instead, to help make this city better. Go on your way and give them that message. Tell them we didn't search you and we didn't ticket you for riding on the pavement, OK?'

Darius looked at him, warily, as if still waiting for the sting.

'Tell them what my mum used to tell me,' Grace said.

'Huh?'

'My mum used to tell me: *If you're ever in trouble, go to a policeman.*'

'In your fucking dreams.' He lowered the mask and raced off, pedalling like fury.

Grace turned to his colleagues with a shrug. 'Win some, lose some.'

Paul Davey patted him on the back. 'A *ten* for effort, boss.'

'And a *one* for results, sir,' Horton added.

And the whole enormity of what they were up against, this vast clash of cultures, hit Roy Grace yet again.

An instant later, Horton inclined his head to listen to the radio in his breast pocket. Then he looked up. 'We're on!' he said, gleefully, and sprinted back towards the car, followed by Grace and Davey.

9

Horton accelerated as Grace and Davey struggled to clip on their seat belts, then turned the car around, racing back down to the intersection with the main road, where he waited. 'Little fucker on a red moped, green helmet, just threw acid in a man's face and grabbed his mobile phone. Heading north down this road. Part index, Charlie Alpha Zero Eight—'

At that moment, a bright red moped raced across their path.

'That's him!'

In a long-rehearsed move, Paul Davey, in the front passenger seat, leaned forward and punched on the blue lights and siren, as Horton pulled out in front of a line of traffic and accelerated hard. The car, *whup-whup-whupping*, raced past several vehicles, gaining speed, seemingly oblivious – to Roy Grace in the rear seat – to the oncoming traffic, which melted away as Horton swerved through an impossible gap between a bus and a taxi.

The moped rider appeared ahead between a van and a minicab, a hundred metres or so in front.

They were gaining on him.

Horton swung out, overtaking the van. A red traffic light was against them. The moped ran it. Taking a risk that Roy

Grace would not have done in Brighton, Horton barely slowed, following it straight over the lights, cars braking sharply to their right and left. Grace held his breath. His buddy Glenn Branson's driving used to scare the shit out of him, but Glenn drove like a dawdler compared to this guy. Although he had to admit, Horton was a brilliant driver.

They were gaining.

Twenty metres behind the moped now.

Of all the methods employed by muggers, those using acid – mainly sulphuric, car-battery acid – were the ones Grace hated the most. The young guy, whoever he was, who had just had the hideous stuff thrown in his face for nothing more than the pathetic value of a black-market mobile phone, was now going to be facing life-changing injuries. Perhaps blinded. Years of agonizing plastic surgery. Whatever looks he might have once had destroyed. And probably terrified to ever go out in public again.

Still gaining.

Ten metres.

'There's an alleyway coming up in five hundred metres, guv,' Horton cautioned, and Paul Davey nodded in confirmation. 'He swings left down that and we've lost him. Permission to take him down?'

Like an armed officer faced with a gunman, who had a split-second to decide whether the gun pointing at him was real or fake, Grace was aware he had only seconds to make the call.

A few months ago, the Commissioner of the Met had given an instruction to her officers to go ahead and knock riders off their bikes if there was no other means of stopping them, but this was not universally supported. Protests in the papers and all over social media. Poor little moped riders should be free to throw acid in people's faces without having the nasty big bully police knock them off and scrape their little knees. And the Independent Office for Police Conduct (IOPC) had recently issued a statement questioning the morality of the Commissioner's decision.

Morality? thought Roy. Some people had a damned skewed idea of morality.

The car accelerated, drew level with the moped's rear wheel. Roy could hear the rasping of its exhaust. Saw the rider's green helmet with some jagged motif on it. His blood boiled as he saw the arrogant stance of the rider, glee in his body language. Glee at what he had done.

'Knock the bastard off, Dave,' he commanded.

'Knock the bastard off, with pleasure, sir.'

Horton swung the car sharply left, striking the centre of the moped's rear wheel hard. The effect was instant and catastrophic for the machine and its rider.

The rear kicked out hard left, hitting the kerb in front of a Kebab House, catapulting the rider several feet through the air before he struck the ground with his helmet, somersaulted and lay still.

Horton pulled the car up in the middle of the road beside him and the three officers leaped out. Two black youths were racing up to the motionless figure. One of them shouted out at the police, 'You fucking racist murderers!'

The rider was already stirring, and climbed up onto his knees.

'What did you do that for, you filth?' the other youth shouted.

Horton, followed by his colleagues, ran up to the rider before he could get to his feet, silently relieved he wasn't seriously hurt – to avoid the inquiry that would go with any injury. He grabbed the rider's right arm, pulled it behind his back and snap-cuffed him. Then he yanked back his left arm and cuffed that, too. Paul Davey, wearing protective gloves, shoved up the rider's tinted visor and said, 'You're nicked, mate.'

Davey began to pat him down, carefully, aware of the youth's hostile eyes peering out from under his helmet. An instant later, the Inspector pulled out of a pocket a small glass bottle containing a clear liquid, half of which had gone. Shaking with fury, he held it up to the youth. 'Thirsty? Like a swig, would you?'

The rider was shaking his head, wildly.

'What's your name?' the Inspector asked him.

'Lee.'

'Lee? Lee what?'

'Lee Smith.'

'So, it's all right to throw this in someone else's face, is it, Lee? But you don't want any yourself? Why's that? Want to tell me?'

The rider stared in sullen silence.

Horton placed the bottle in an evidence bag, then wrapped it up in a cloth and placed it in the boot of the car before returning to the rider to read him his rights.

Grace walked over to the two youths on the sidelines, aware that a considerable crowd was now forming. He could hear sirens approaching – an ambulance and back-up, he assumed. 'Would you like to be witnesses as you seem so interested and saw everything? Care to give me your names and addresses?'

Both of them hesitated, glanced at each other, then sprinted off, shouting abuse as they did so.

10

On the second and third floors of a shabby terraced building above a Chinese takeaway on a main road close to Brighton's Magistrates' Court, a stone's throw from the police station, was the law firm of TG Law, Solicitors and Commissioners for Oaths. For over twenty-five years its eponymous proprietor Terence Gready and his associates had practised criminal law, specializing mostly in legal aid cases.

Occasionally the firm took on a rape case, or a GBH, or murder, but its bread and butter was an endless procession of impaired drivers, small-time drug dealers, shoplifters, sex workers, muggers, burglars, domestic abusers, sex offenders, pub brawlers and the rest of the flotsam of low-life criminals that plagued the city and endlessly stretched police resources.

Terence Gready was a short, neatly presented and scrupulously polite fifty-five-year-old who had a sympathetic ear for every client. He always put them at ease, however hopeless he considered their case might be. With his conservative suits, club ties, immaculately polished shoes and beady eyes behind small, round tortoiseshell glasses – which had been in and out of fashion during his thirty years of practising law and were now back in again – a client had once described him as looking like the twin brother of

44

the late comedian Ronnie Corbett – but with smaller glasses and flappier hands.

Gready presented to the world a family man of seemingly modest ambition, for whom the pinnacle of success was to avoid a custodial sentence for a drug addict accused of shoplifting thirty pounds' worth of toiletries from an all-night chemist. A good husband and devoted father, a school governor and a generous charitable benefactor, Terence Gready was the kind of person you would never notice in a busy room – and not just because of his lack of height. He exuded all the presence of a man standing in his own shadow, perfectly fitting Winston Churchill's description of 'a modest man with much to be modest about'.

'Gready by name but not by nature,' the solicitor would never tire of telling his occasional private clients, when informing them of his fees. On the wall behind his desk was a framed motto: NO ONE EVER GOT RICH BY GOING TO JAIL.

Terence Gready could have added to it that no one ever got rich by defending clients on legal aid. But he seemed to make a decent-enough living from it. A nice four-bedroomed house in a des-res area of Hove, with a well-tended garden – mainly due to his wife's green fingers – and a holiday timeshare in Devon. They always had nice cars, recent models, although never anything remotely showy. The only thing about him that could in any way be called flashy was his proudest possession, his vintage Rolex Submariner watch. But, at over sixty years old, it did not look anything special to anyone other than real watch collectors.

His wife, Barbara, had sold her small orchid nursery and was much in demand as an orchid competition judge, which frequently took her abroad. Any free time she had, she spent choreographing for the local amateur dramatics society.

They had privately educated their three children, who were all doing well on their chosen career paths, the eldest of whom, their son, Dean, was a successful accountant with a firm in the City of London and married to a colleague, who was soon to produce their first grandchild. Their two daughters were both working more locally, one as a mortgage broker and the other for a domestic abuse charity.

After her husband's arrest, Barbara Gready would tell everyone that she had absolutely *no* idea, none at all, about all the offences he was accused of, and simply would not – could not – believe it. There'd been a big mistake, they had the wrong man. Completely. They *must* have.

11

'*The French Connection*, yeah?' DI Glenn Branson said into the phone, seated at his workstation in the empty Major Incident Room at Sussex Police HQ.

'French Connection?' Roy Grace replied, mildly irritated by the early-morning phone call interrupting his routine of stretches. He was standing in the field next to his cottage, at the end of his five-mile run. Humphrey, his rescue Labrador-cross, was running around sniffing the ground hard, on the scent of something – probably a rabbit, he guessed.

Grace was taking a rare weekday off, because he would be at work most of the weekend, overseeing a major stop-and-search operation in South East London on Friday and Saturday night. He was happy to enjoy this unusual time at home with no commitments whatsoever.

Glenn Branson and some of the team from Major Crime were working with the Regional Serious and Organized Crime Unit on the investigation of a Ferrari busted for drugs at Newhaven earlier that week. Glenn had been appointed SIO, heading up a multi-agency team as the RSOCU had a number of high-profile jobs running simultaneously.

'I'm not with you, Glenn – you mean because the Ferrari came in from Dieppe?'

'Duh! Surely you remember that movie? It was about your vintage!'

'It's ringing a faint bell.'

'Nah, that's the sound of the dinner bell in your old people's home! Off you run, you don't want to let your soup go cold – isn't that what they give you, cos you can't really chew any more?'

'Cheeky bugger! *The French Connection*?'

'Gene Hackman and Roy Scheider.'

'Wasn't he the cop – the Chief of Police – in *Jaws*?'

'Now you're getting there.'

'Yep, I remember now, vaguely. *The French Connection* – didn't it start with Gene Hackman in bed with some bird in handcuffs?'

'Trust you to remember that bit. What I'm talking about is the car, the Lincoln Continental that the villain, Fernando Rey, shipped over to New York from Marseilles.'

Branson paused to nod greetings to some of his team, who'd entered the room for the morning briefing which was due to start in a few minutes. 'Gene Hackman had it weighed and realized it was wrong – it weighed more than a proper Lincoln should have.'

'Got it, yes! I remember now, good movie!'

'It was well brilliant. Yeah, so that's how the Border Force officer rumbled the Ferrari, because it weighed more than it should have.'

'Not surprised, with six million quid's worth of Class-A stashed inside it.'

'Top-quality cocaine.'

'Don't I get any credit for the tip-off?'

'I suppose so, since you asked so sweetly.'

'Sod you! How's the investigation going?'

'Slowly, thanks to the silence of our courier.'

'The one who's been potted?'

'Yep. Michael Starr. Went *no comment* in all interviews. So far, the Ferrari's a ghost car that was en route to a suspect company. LH Classics appears to have no formal management structure. The staff there, one full-time and two part-time mechanics, have all been interviewed. The company computers and phones have been seized. The company's owned by a Panama shell with nominee directors and a CEO listed as a Swiss citizen, Hermann Perren – but so far the only person of that name we've been able to trace was killed in a climbing accident on the Matterhorn nearly thirty years ago.'

'I presume you're following the money?' Grace said. 'Any progress on the info we've given you on Mr Big – the *Diamond*?'

'I think we're getting close to an arrest. We're all over it, like a rash. Emily Denyer from the Financial Investigation Unit has been seconded to the team.'

'Smart lady – that's great.'

'She's super-smart – very glad she's on our side! She's already done some useful background work, finding out the details on LH Classics. Oh, and there is one possible breakthrough: a member of the public off the same ferry handed in a phone he found lying in the road outside the Customs shed. It's a burner with Starr's prints on it, and Digital Forensics have put in a cell-site analysis request on it.'

'Didn't he have gloves on at the time of his arrest?'

'Ever tried dialling a mobile when you're wearing a glove, boss? Oh no, on second thoughts, you're probably still using a rotary dial phone.'

'Haha. Well, I'm not planning on any sort of phone today; I'm actually having a day off.'

'Oh yeah? Up to much?'

'Cleo's going to work, Bruno's at school. I'll have Noah to myself this morning, there'll be toys everywhere, it'll be brilliant. I've got Kaitlynn coming this afternoon to look after him so I can do all sorts of important stuff like wash the car and then satisfy my obsession.'

'Which is?'

'Cataloguing the latest additions to my vinyl collection. Don't judge me! And remember trashing my music collection when you were my house guest?'

There was a brief silence as Glenn, slightly embarrassed, thought back to when he'd split up with his wife, Ari. Roy had let him stay in his house – then had gone mental when he'd found he'd put some of his precious collection into the wrong order. 'I try not to! So, how's Cleo doing this time round?'

'She's good, thanks, almost three months in – a bit of morning sickness but she's a trooper. We're trying to prep for having a newborn in the house again. Talking of preparations, how are yours going? You should have been married by now.'

'Yep, we've just been way too busy. We're fixing a date for summer next year now, there's no mad rush. I'll let you know as soon as we have it so you can book time off! Siobhan is mega busy so I'm part-time wedding planner at the moment and, honestly, I'm enjoying it, you know? Getting in touch with my feminine side, sorting the cake and flowers.'

Grace had a momentary image of Glenn, six foot two inches tall, solid muscle, black and bald. 'I'm trying to imagine that – it's not pretty.'

'Yeah, yeah. Hope you're working on your speech?'

'Every minute of every day – thinking of how I can trash you.' Grace paused. 'Cake and flowers. Nice! Very exciting for you.'

'This is the modern world.'

'I have to say, one positive about being in the Met, I'm not missing your daily insults. So, about this Ferrari and the French connection, if you need any help from me, let me know. Gotta go now, I can hear that dinner bell again – don't want the soup going cold.'

'Make sure there aren't any lumps in it.'

'Lumps?'

'Don't want you choking to death.'

'Haha!'

Then he heard a scream. Cleo's voice from inside the cottage.

'Roy! Oh God, ROYYYYYYY! ROYYYYYYYYYY!'

The sound pierced his heart.

He killed the call without saying anything, let himself in through the gate and, without waiting for Humphrey, sprinted towards the house.

12

Five minutes later, Glenn Branson checked his notes and addressed his assembled company of detectives, including Kevin Hall, Jack Alexander and Velvet Wilde. They had been joined by two members of the Financial Investigation Unit, led by civilian Emily Denyer, a dark-haired woman in her early thirties.

'The time is 9 a.m., Thursday, November 29th. This is the seventh briefing of Operation Farmhouse – the investigation into the attempted importation into the UK of six million pounds' worth of cocaine, discovered in a faked rare classic Ferrari at Newhaven Port early last Monday morning, November 26th.'

He glanced at his notes. 'Our prime suspect, Michael Starr, the driver of the car and enclosed trailer bringing the Ferrari into England, is currently on remand in Lewes Prison. As you know, we believe Starr is a major player in the bigger investigation. The National Crime Agency intelligence, together with information from the Met regarding this route and details around LH Classics, has come up trumps, and I believe, thanks to further information from London, we are close to nailing the mastermind behind the entire operation.'

Branson continued. 'OK, we've searched Starr's home in

West Sussex and removed a computer which Digital Forensics are now examining. Living in the house with Starr is
his younger brother, Stuie, who has Down's Syndrome and
needs help with day-to-day living. A neighbour had been
keeping an eye on him whilst Mickey Starr was away on his
– ah – business trip. Velvet has an update on him, I believe?'
He looked at her.

'Yes, sir,' DC Wilde said, in her Belfast accent. 'As he is
close to independent living, I've arranged with social
services for an appropriate adult to call daily at the house
until the immediate future of his brother is ascertained.
Starr's solicitor is appealing to have him released on bail,
so he can look after Stuie.'

'That's not going to happen,' Branson said. 'Not with
the charges facing him for the value of the drugs, and his
assaults at the time of his arrest.'

'I agree with you, sir.'

'Has the younger brother given any useful information,
Velvet?' Jack Alexander asked the DC.

'Not so far, no. He's angry that Mickey hasn't come home
because he'd promised they were going to buy a chippy and
he would have a job as the food preparer.'

'Well, that promise is fried!' Hall said and chuckled,
looking around.

'If I could *chip in*,' Wilde said, 'his future has gone down
the pan!'

'People!' Branson admonished. He turned to the Financial Investigators. 'Emily, I understand you have some fresh
information for us?'

'Yes,' she said, scrolling through the digital information
on her screen. 'As we always do, we've been tracking the
financial trail, and I'm very pleased to say we may have a
breakthrough. Our devious crime lord has been very careful

to hide his tracks, and he's done it very ingeniously – but we may have found a crucial chink.'

'Yes?' Branson said.

'We've found a bank account in the Seychelles which appears linked to the company LH Classics. The Seychelles used to be completely secretive about all financial transactions, but recently they've had a policy change and are now cooperating with government agencies over money laundering. They're sending us over statements showing all transactions since the account was set up. It's interesting to see there are numerous cash payments originating in Brighton going into this account.'

'Nice work, Emily!' the DI said.

'Thank you.'

Branson's mobile rang. He glanced at the display and when he saw who it was from, Aiden Gilbert of Digital Forensics, he raised an apologetic hand. 'This might be something of interest, excuse me a sec,' he said to the team and answered it. 'DI Branson.'

'Glenn,' Gilbert said. 'I thought I'd call you right away. I've just had the cell-site analysis report back from the phone company for the burner with Starr's prints all over it. It's quite interesting.'

'Yeah?'

'We've a plot of the phone's movements for the ten days since it was activated, and a log of the calls made on it. The day before we know that Starr took the car and trailer across the Channel, en route to collect the Ferrari, he visited a location in Brighton, where he spent just over an hour. Cell-site doesn't usually enable us to pinpoint an actual building in cities, but there were two phone calls made, over the next four days, to a firm located within the area pinpointed.'

Branson sat upright, excited. 'Yes? You have its name?'

'Yes, it was simple. I rang the number and the switch-board answered.'

'You're a star! What's the firm?'

Gilbert told him.

As he heard the name, Glenn beamed. 'Brilliant, Aiden,' he said. 'Just brilliant!'

'Yes?'

'Christmas has come early.'

13

Six million pounds' worth of cocaine seized, and along with it the Ferrari, taken apart at Newhaven Port, every panel of its bodywork, every pillar and post dismantled, some of it opened up like a tin can – violated – by Fire and Rescue officers using tools more normally used for cutting victims out of wrecked cars. All thanks to the dumb greed of a one-armed minion he'd thought he could trust.

The Ferrari was a fake, a copy, but an expensive copy and still worth big money in the hands of a dealer turning a blind eye to the more questionable areas of its history. And there was one particular dealer that had shifted plenty of his high-end classic cars, all with seemingly squeaky-clean provenance. He had also brokered a number of the cars built by LH Classics over the last sixteen years.

Now the car had been seized under the Proceeds of Crime Act, and his one meagre crumb of comfort was the knowledge that, with the damage that had been done to it, as well as it being exposed as a fake, neither Customs and Excise nor the police were going to be able to sell it.

Since the early days of his career as a legal aid solicitor, Terence Gready had been living behind an elaborate and scrupulously maintained facade. The seeds of the idea for his empire had been planted after listening to the stories

– and aspirations – of an old lag called Jimmy Pearson whom he'd defended early on in his career.

The world of drugs offered riches beyond anyone's wildest dreams, but most of the people who chased those dreams, like Jimmy Pearson, were ultimately losers who played the blame game the way so many cons and ex-cons did – *I was fitted up . . . it was a bent copper . . . my brief was on the take . . .* Few were ever smart enough to avoid, finally, getting caught. And what often nailed so many offenders were their sudden, uncharacteristic spending sprees. The flash new car, clothes, holidays, boats, homes. The law-enforcement agencies had one dictum in their eternal hunt for the major players: *Follow the money.*

But Terence Gready was smart enough – and going very nicely, thank you, twenty-five years on – thanks to his entirely fortuitous career choice. Being a solicitor practising legal aid, criminal law had presented him with both the perfect opportunity – and the perfect cover.

He'd realized that every day in his work he would be encountering criminals, and occasionally some with wide networks of connections. From talking to the brighter ones, it hadn't taken him long to build up a picture of how the drug supply chains in England operated, the ports where drugs entered the country, the areas for distribution that were carved up between the crime families and the hotspots where there were gaps in law enforcement.

Distributors and dealers were the low-hanging fruit of the drugs world – they were easy for the police to catch. And even easier for someone like himself to replace, because there was always going to be a never-ending supply of lowlife wanting to dip its snout in the rich pickings of the drugs trough. He defended dealers every day of the week, most just small-beer street runners, but others a rank or two higher up the food chain. Some of them talked openly to him. And he listened. Made notes. Crucially, he made decisions about who he could trust.

The Mr Bigs of the drugs world ran their empires, mostly out of metropolitan London, in a tight, businesslike manner, with an accountant, a lawyer and a manager operating a group of foot soldiers – mainly teenagers coerced through drug dependency or fear. Most of the bosses originated from the criminal fraternity in South London or the Caribbean and more recently Eastern Europe, and they were raking in fortunes. Dealing half a kilo at a time, mostly of cocaine or heroin, buying it 40 per cent pure then cutting it, reducing it to 10 or 15 per cent for onward sale, they could earn £50,000–£100,000 in a very short time.

A large amount of the drugs trafficked into England, Gready had learned, originated from countries in Central and Eastern Europe, with supplies for the South East, his manor, coming mostly through the Essex and London docks – and just occasionally through Liverpool. It was one particular network of Eastern Europeans, from Albania, who had begun to interest Gready.

They were universally feared for the brutality of their retribution to anyone who crossed them, but, as he learned, they were also the best people to buy from, good businessmen, and that was rare in a flaky trade. They would deliver on time, always top quality, and if you weren't happy – just like a wholesale version of Marks & Spencer – they operated a no-quibble returns policy. And, of course, he took very special care to look after any of them should they come to him with their legal issues.

The secret of success, Gready had figured, was to buy top-quality Class-A drugs and remain totally remote from those selling it on the streets, for two reasons. Firstly, to avoid getting into turf wars with any of the existing crime families – if they didn't know who was behind a new supply on the streets, it was much harder for them to muscle in and stop it – especially if the quality was better than their own and the price cheaper. Secondly, whenever a street dealer was arrested, there was no way of linking it back to him. He had organized his own empire by placing Mickey Starr as its nominal head. Whilst he made all the decisions, Starr was the operational contact for the importation and distribution. He made sure he had no involvement in this part whatsoever and could not be connected to it.

But now, for the first time, he was really worried. A big fly in the ointment.

Lucky Mickey Starr.

Lucky. Why the hell had that fool ever been called *Lucky*?

The television was on, an episode of *Endeavour*, one of the few crime dramas Terence Gready bothered to watch, because he liked its accuracy. But tonight, to him, it was all blurred images and noise. The volume up so damned loud. 'Barbs, can't you turn it down a little?' he said to his wife, who was perched on the sofa opposite.

'I've already turned it down once. Any more and I won't be able to hear it,' she replied.

He peered at her, fresh out of humour. 'You need to get your ears tested – maybe you need a hearing aid.'

'My hearing's fine,' she laughed.

Gready had been seething with rage for the past four days and still seethed now. He sat in the living room of his home, his glass of whisky empty, just a few partially melted ice cubes in the bottom rattling in his shaking hand. Scarcely able to believe the greed of the man he'd always paid so well. What a fool. Stuffing the tyres of the Ferrari with drugs. Hadn't he realized the X-ray would pick them up?

Now Starr was banged up on remand in Lewes Prison, but could he trust him to keep his trap shut? The stupid idiot was looking at around fifteen years, minimum. Would Mickey Starr do anything to lessen his sentence? Gready thought he was loyal, but he couldn't be sure.

And what if he did squeal?

For the past two decades, Gready had so very carefully covered his tracks, hiding behind the cover of his law firm, never been remotely ostentatious in any way and was ever diligent.

Nicked for drink-driving at 3 a.m. and in urgent need of a solicitor? Terence Gready was your man! He would always obligingly rock up to the custody suite to advise you. Unfailingly polite to police officers, custody sergeants and to his clients, he had earned grudging respect from most police officers, who as a general rule intensely disliked lawyers, especially his grubby kind.

The firm of classic car dealers, LH Classics, to which the Ferrari had been consigned, was, to anyone investigating, owned by a Panama company, with nominee directors. A money-laundering front – and a method of importing drugs – which he had successfully used for several years. No way could the police connect it to him. He'd doled out enough cash to his international lawyers to ensure that. Just like the Chinese takeaway below his office and the twenty others around Sussex, who were laundering drugs cash. All of their proprietors had big gambling habits, spending thousands weekly at the local casinos and never raising any suspicion. The Chinese community was well known for being big gamblers. No one had ever suspected it was mostly his money they were playing with. Oh yes, he had been so clever, so many tentacles to his business!

Barbara suddenly pointed at the screen where a BMW

was being dismantled. 'Look!' she said. 'Smuggling drugs hidden in a car, a bit like that Ferrari that was just in the news.'

'Yes, that was quite a bust at Newhaven; I don't imagine that was just somebody operating on his own. There's bound to be a Mr Big behind it,' he said. 'What do you think?'

'I hope he gets bloody nailed,' she said, vehemently. 'You know my views on drugs, my love. And how much it upsets me when you get some dealer off who you're pretty sure is guilty. Any drug dealer who uses kids should be lined up against a wall.'

'I agree,' he said quietly.

'What's up, Terry?' Barbara asked suddenly. 'Please tell me. You've not been yourself for days now.'

Endeavour was over, the credits rolling. He looked at her. 'I'm fine.'

'How did it go at the doctor's today? You've not said.'

'Yes. All good. He said I've got the heart of an ox.'

Terence Gready's mum and dad had been greengrocers in South London. His dad, Godfrey, had been a meek man, short and with a permanently sad, brow-beaten expression, as if the world bewildered him. Gready had memories of him up at the crack of dawn, and later, outside in all weathers, croaking out the prices of his wares: *Bananas half price today! Special offer on greengages!*

His dad had his dreams and his plan. To sell up at sixty and buy a place in Spain's Costa del Sol, whilst the two of them were still young enough to make the move and enjoy their life. Their flat above the shop was always littered with brochures about Spanish properties. Often his dad would hold up one of the brochures, with a sunny villa or condominium on the front cover, and say to Terence, 'Always have your dream, lad, and make sure you get to live it. Pity the man who dies with all his dreams still inside him.'

He'd dropped dead at fifty-four, holding up a bag of satsumas. His last words had been, 'Cheap at twice the price!'

His mum had died two years later, from cancer.

Sod all that. Terence had gone to university and then to law school. And then had rapidly realized there was no money to be made in criminal law legal aid work. But there was a great – a very great – amount to be made dealing drugs. The clients he ended up defending were the losers. The expendables. The bottom feeders. They were the ones who were always caught, whilst their bosses, quietly and under the radar, amassed fortunes.

And he had always been very happy to live under the radar. He didn't feel any need to show off. The bang for Gready was knowing just how much money he had stashed away.

Biding his time.

He had his aspirations, of course. His dreams. A hankering for the good life. And one day soon, he planned, he would make the move and start to live it, doing all the things with Barbara he'd ever wanted. She could cultivate rare orchids to her heart's content. They could live in style in the sun! Do a world cruise. Visit the Antarctic. Perhaps buy a yacht. A plane. Buy houses for the kids and set them up for life.

But for now, there was one obstacle he had to deal with: Mickey Starr. Shouldn't be a problem. He had plenty of contacts inside Lewes Prison. Perhaps someone could have a quiet word in Mickey Starr's ear. A gentle warning. But would that be enough?

Perhaps not.

He knew the man's one weakness. His love for his brother.

'Are you sure you're OK, Terry? You just keep looking so worried,' Barbara said. 'I know you too well. What is it?'

'We're good,' he said. And thought, *Yeah, we are, we are good.* 'Honestly, I've got a lot of cases on, that's all. Trying to do my best for my clients.'

'Well, I'm off to bed,' she said.

'I'll be up later.'

She kissed him and went out of the room.

He waited until he heard her footsteps upstairs, then hit a stored number on his latest burner phone.

When it was answered, he kept it short. 'Nick, Mickey Starr's kid brother, Stuie. Find someone to have a word with Mickey, tell him if he knows what's good for his brother, he'll keep his trap shut. Know what I'm saying? Just have someone give him a friendly reminder. Oh yes – and see if he needs anything and send him my regards.'

14

Friday 30 November

It was just gone 11 p.m. on Friday. Roy Grace sat beside Cleo's bed in the tiny, stark single room adjacent to the maternity ward at the hospital. He was holding her clammy right hand, even though she was now asleep, her face an unnatural chalk white.

Hail thudded against the pitch-black windowpane; a steady, icy draught from the relentless wind outside blew in through the thin glass, onto his face. He should have been up in London tonight, out in the area car supervising the operation he was running from Croydon to Newham, but he'd delegated the task to his second-in-command, so he could be with Cleo.

A sudden light pressure on his hand. She was squeezing it. He looked down, tenderly, and moments later she opened her eyes. 'I just can't believe it,' she said, her voice weak and raspy from the breathing tube that had been removed only a few hours earlier. 'I can't help thinking I could have stopped this happening.'

He bent down and hugged her gently; both had tears rolling down their cheeks. 'It wasn't your fault, you've been doing everything right.'

'No, I was stupid – we had a whopper brought into the mortuary on Wednesday – a woman weighing thirty-four stone. I helped Darren lift her – and immediately didn't feel right afterwards.'

He shook his head. 'We've already discussed that.'

She looked puzzled. 'We have?'

'Yesterday, with the consultant. He said lifting something is extremely unlikely to cause a miscarriage – unless there was some underlying problem with the pregnancy.'

She looked puzzled. 'I – don't – remember.'

He stroked her cheek, gently. 'I'm not surprised, you've been through a lot in the past day and a half – a blood transfusion and a general anaesthetic. I had a long chat with the consultant earlier. He explained miscarriages are very common – something like one in five. And he said that fifty per cent of miscarriages are because of a genetic problem.'

The door opened and Craig Comber, the consultant gynaecologist, peered in, then entered. A tall, smiley man in scrubs and a blue mop hat, surgical mask hanging below his chin, he said, 'Good evening, just thought I'd check on how Cleo is doing before I head home.' He looked down at her. 'Good to see you're awake – how are you feeling?'

'A little tender.'

He smiled again. 'I'm afraid we had to do a rather invasive surgical management of the miscarriage. There was a lot of tissue stuck near the lower end of your uterus – in the cervix – causing you more pain than usual and making you bleed heavily. You did right not to stay at home and miscarry, as you were in cervical shock – that's when what's happening causes a rapid drop in your blood pressure and heart rate, leading to collapse. But you're out of any danger and you'll be feeling much better in a couple of days. The nurse will be in shortly to give you something to make sure you sleep. I'll come and see you in the morning, Cleo, and, all being well, you'll be able to go home.' He looked at Roy. 'Will you be able to drive her?'

'Yes, of course,' Roy said. He smiled down at her then turned to the consultant. 'We're devastated by what's happened, Mr Comber, and we'll have to come to terms with it. Will it affect our chances of having another baby in the future?'

'Not at all, you've nothing long-term to worry about, Mr – sorry – *Detective Superintendent* – right?'

Grace nodded distractedly.

The consultant looked at Cleo. 'You should feel better in a few days, Cleo. I'd advise you to have iron and folic acid at a higher dose, as we know it can help prevent some abnormalities of the baby. I would say to wait a couple of menstrual cycles to let the lining of the uterus recover – and both of you emotionally – then try again. That time will also help raise the level of folic acid in your body.'

After Comber had left, Cleo sighed.

'How do you feel about what he said?' Roy asked her.

'Crap, to be honest. I'm going to have to deal with all the sympathetic well-wishers. I know they'll all have the best intentions, but I don't think I can face anyone. I know what they'll all say. *Better it happened now . . . How far along were you? . . . Ever thought of adoption?*'

'Darling, just remember everyone will mean well. What could they possibly say in this awful situation?'

'Just that they're *sorry*, that's all.' She was silent for a moment then she said, 'Maybe we *were* lucky with Noah.'

He gave her a questioning look. 'We'll be lucky again.'

'We will be,' she said. 'We will.'

'Yes.'

She lapsed into silence, staring down at her bedclothes, her face sad.

'Penny for your thoughts,' he said after a while.

She gave a wan smile. 'I was just thinking how bloody random life is. How unpredictable. One moment you're all excited, you're going to have a baby, and the next you've got blood pouring out of you and you're in a hospital bed.'

Roy nodded. 'Coppers see the random nature of the human condition all the time, just like you see every day at the mortuary.' He gave a wry smile. 'One moment someone's having the time of their life, the next, a pathologist's working out the time of their death.'

15

Saturday 1 December

In Terence Gready's dream Lucky Mickey stood in front of the desk in his office, all apologetic, telling him the bastards at Newhaven Border Force had planted the coke in the Ferrari's tyres.

'I'm innocent, honest!'

And in his dream, he was disbelieving him.

'Fitted up, I was. I'd never screw you over, Terry, you know that, you've been good to me.'

'You think I didn't notice there was always a shortage in your previous runs? Always just a tiny bit missing. Just a few grams and a nice little earner for you. Who do you think I am, Mickey, *Mr Potato Head*? I let you get away with it because it was your little perk. Your little bit of *cabbage*, as they call it in the rag trade. But then your greed got to you, didn't it?'

As Mickey began to protest his innocence again, Gready heard the sound of a bell. An insistent ringing. Like an alarm clock but not like an alarm clock.

Barbara was nudging him. 'Someone's at the door.'

The bell rang again. Followed by a loud *rat-a-tat-tat*.

Instantly, he was awake.

Heard the bell again. The knocking.

He looked at the alarm clock: 4.45 a.m.

Who the hell?
But he had a horrible feeling he knew just who.
More knocking.
Pounding.
Pounding like his heart now.
BLAM, BLAM, BLAM.
Then a shout, 'POLICE! THIS IS THE POLICE!'
From the outside, the house looked nothing special. But all the doors and window frames were reinforced, and the glass was bulletproof. Ready for an eventuality like this.

All the same, he was in the grip of panic as he slipped out of bed, hands flapping wildly, telling Barbara not to worry, taking deep breaths to calm himself down as he switched on the light. He found his glasses on the bedside table, pulled on his dressing gown, jammed his feet into his slippers and hurried into his den across the landing.

He unlocked the drawer below his laptop, pulled out his micro SD card, on which he had his entire network of contacts and all his records, removed his three current burner phones, then ran through into a spare bedroom.

This one had an ornate brass bedstead with four short bedposts. He'd had the bed specially commissioned, some years ago, at considerable expense – Barbara, of course, was not aware of this, just like she wasn't aware of the reinforced doors and windows. The posts, to anyone looking, appeared solid. He went to the nearest one, gave the top five hard turns, then removed it, like a cap, dropped the micro SD and phones down it, and replaced the top, ensuring it was tightly screwed.

BLAM, BLAM, BLAM.
Downstairs, at his front door, he heard more shouting.
'POLICE! THIS IS THE POLICE!'
'Coming!' he called out, hurrying down the stairs.

'Good morning,' he said, politely, opening the door. 'Can I help you?'

An authoritative, good-looking black man came in through the doorway holding up what looked like a police warrant card. 'Terence Arthur Gready?'

With a nervous smile, he answered, 'Yes, that's me. What on earth do you want at this hour?'

'I'm Detective Inspector Branson of Surrey and Sussex Major Crime Team. I'm arresting you on suspicion of importing Class-A drugs. You do not have to say anything, but it may harm your defence if you do not mention when questioned something that you later rely on in court. Anything you do say may be used in evidence.'

'You will allow me to get dressed?' he answered calmly.

'You may,' Glenn Branson said. 'One of my officers will accompany you while you do so.'

'I hope you know what you are doing, officer. I am a solicitor, I think you have got something badly wrong here.'

Another police officer entered the house with a spaniel on a leash. 'Does anyone in your house have an allergy to dogs, sir?' he asked.

'We don't like dogs.'

16

'For the benefit of the recording,' Kevin Hall said, glancing up at the video camera in the small interview room at the Brighton and Hove custody centre, behind the former CID headquarters on the Hollingbury Industrial Estate. 'The time is 3.30 p.m., Saturday, December 1st. Detective Constable Kevin Hall and Financial Investigator Emily Denyer interviewing Terence Gready in the presence of his solicitor, Nicholas Fox. Will each of you say your names, please.'

All three of them, in turn, did so.

Fox was a tall, leonine, silver-haired Londoner specializing in criminal law. Now in his mid-fifties, he had been Terence Gready's solicitor for over twenty years and knew where the bodies were buried. Gready trusted him implicitly and had long ago nicknamed him 'King of the Jungle'. Over the years, Fox, a bruiser behind his smart veneer, had taken enough bungs from him to ensure his loyalty – and silence – with which he had created a very nice nest egg in an overseas bank account.

Gready was bleary-eyed, dishevelled and unshaven, and unhappy in police custody issue plimsolls. His suit and shirt were crumpled after the sleepless few hours he'd had earlier on a hard bunk, in a cell.

He'd already been through several interviews about the

71

alleged offences for which he had been arrested, which included the importation of drugs and his apparent links to LH Classics, with DCs Hall and Wilde, in the presence of his solicitor. This interview was being held as an initial enquiry under the Proceeds of Crime Act.

Emily Denyer, smartly dressed and looking fresh, had a sheaf of forms in front of her. 'Mr Gready, I just need to establish with you some information about your income and expenditure.'

'Of course.' He blinked several times. 'Fire away.'

'You have a rental flat in Marbella in Spain, for which you paid £272,000 in cash, no mortgage, eight years ago. Is that correct?'

His blink rate increased, and his hands jigged. 'Yes, from memory I believe that was the amount, yes. But we have never stayed there, it is permanently rented out.'

She shuffled through some of the papers. 'I have here the past ten years of your company accounts, filed at Companies House – TG Law. That is your company, of which you are the owner?'

'It is.'

She looked down at the documents. 'After paying the salaries of your staff as well as bonuses, and yourself taking drawings of approximately £80,000 each year, you have a net retained profit of approximately £20,000 year on year. Is that correct?'

Gready hesitated and glanced at his solicitor, who looked impassive. 'More or less – I can't remember the exact figures.'

'I have them here, in case you'd like to check them?'

'No, I'm sure they are accurate.'

'What I'm struggling with is this, Mr Gready,' she said. 'Out of your salary, net of tax, you are paying off the mortgage on your house in Hove, yet you and your wife were able to put all three of your children through expensive private schooling, at a cost for several years of over £95,000 a year. Where did that money come from?'

'Our parents helped out.'

Emily Denyer nodded. 'Good money in the greengrocery business?'

'There was, yes, back in my father's time. He stashed away a lot of cash.'

'Enough to pay all those school fees and to pay for the flat in Marbella? He must have sold a lot of bananas.'

Out of the corner of her eye she caught both Kevin Hall and Nick Fox concealing their smiles.

'It was all different back in my dad's time,' Gready said, defensively.

'And in your in-laws' time too?' she pressed. 'Your wife's father was a travelling sales agent for a number of handbag manufacturers – his patch was the North of England, wasn't it? Are you saying he salted away enough cash to let you buy the Marbella flat?'

'He was a very canny man, investing every spare penny he earned on the stock market. He died a very wealthy man.'

'That's odd,' Denyer said, shuffling through more documents. 'I have a copy of his grant of probate, filed with the Probate Registry. It showed he left a net of £177,532, to be divided between your wife, Barbara, and four other relatives. I'm struggling at the moment, Mr Gready, to get to the £272,000 you paid for your Marbella flat.'

'Yes, well, I'm sure you are,' Gready said, testily. 'I'm afraid what the will isn't showing you is all the money he had placed, quite legitimately, abroad. He was an extremely good salesman and his customers loved him and supported him strongly. There is a lot of money to be made in handbags.' He hesitated. 'Look, I'm an ordinary guy, this is all hugely embarrassing. I'm struggling to keep my legal practice afloat thanks to the ridiculously low fees we get these days. So, my wife and our parents stashed away a bit of cash – good on them. You've also not mentioned the money my wife inherited from her mother, close to £300k. What's your problem?'

Emily Denyer went through a number of documents and spreadsheets regarding his financial accounts and background over the next hour.

'Have you now all the answers you need, Ms Denyer?' Fox asked.

Gready glanced at his wrist, forgetting his watch wasn't there – it had been taken off him for safekeeping after his arrest. He glanced at his solicitor's watch. 4.53 p.m.

Emily Denyer produced a clear plastic exhibits bag, with an Envoseal tag securing it and a signed exhibit label. Inside was his beloved Rolex.

Sounding much more friendly, she said, 'Nice watch! My dad's got one very similar. Can I have a look?'

'Yes, please do!' he said proudly, thinking that maybe this could be the icebreaker between them.

She made a play of peering closely at it, through the plastic. 'Am I right, it's a Rolex Submariner?'

Gready nodded eagerly. 'Yes.'

'A vintage one? Looks vintage to me.'

Gready nodded again. 'Yes, you are right. Circa 1955!'

'Very nice, must be worth a few bob.'

'It's insured for £50,000.'

'Very sensible,' she replied. 'I'd make sure it was well insured if it was mine.' Then, seamlessly, before Terence Gready was even aware what she was doing, she dropped the watch into her briefcase. 'I need to retain this.'

'Hey,' he said. 'What are you doing? You can't take it!'

'Don't worry, I'll give you a receipt for it – I have one here. Your watch will be part of our investigation. If everything is fine, you'll get it back. You will just need to prove to us that the money to purchase it came from a legitimate source – that it was honestly purchased.'

'This is outrageous. I'm a solicitor, I bought it out of my earnings. You can't take my watch, give it back to me, you bloody bitch!'

She smiled at him, and at the ruffled face of his solicitor. In a calm voice she said, 'Don't worry, it's fine. I've been called a lot worse.'

17

When the interview with the detective and the Financial Investigator terminated, Terence Gready, only too well aware of his rights, requested that he stay on in the interview room for a private conference with his solicitor.

For many years, despite Gready's own extensive knowledge of the law, he had always listened to Fox's wise counsel. After the others had left, he looked up warily at the wide-angle CCTV camera. 'Want to check that's off, Nick?' he said.

Fox shook his head. 'It'll be off – and even if it wasn't, you know anything we discuss now would be inadmissible evidence. We're good.'

'I don't feel that good. My big worry is Mickey – he loves that brother of his. Fucking dotes on him. I've been worried ever since he was arrested that he might try to make a deal with the prosecution – and rat me up. What do you think? One of your colleagues is acting for him, has he said anything to you?'

Gready was paying Fox's firm to act for Mickey. But it wasn't out of altruism, it was so he would know what Starr was thinking.

'A chain is only as strong as its weakest link, Terry. Starr is your weak link. You're smart to be concerned. He asked my colleague yesterday if he thought he'd get a lesser sentence by pleading guilty.'

'Understandable. As long as he doesn't grass me up, it's OK.'

Fox raised a calming hand. 'He's got the message not to go there.'

'And?'

'He's sore. He's blaming his arrest on you.'

'On me? If he hadn't been so damned greedy and packed all the Ferrari's tyres with coke – the fucking stupid idiot – we'd have been home free.'

'That's not what he thinks, Terry. From what he's said, he reckons you knew your operation was under surveillance and you let him be the fall guy.'

Gready shrugged. 'Let him be the fall guy? Does he seriously think that if I had the remotest intention of doing that, I'd have lost six million quid's worth of cocaine in the process? It doesn't make any sense, Nick. Shit, if I had any inkling – any at all – I'd have halted everything until the heat had blown over. Tell him that.'

'I'll tell him, but you need to look at it from his perspective. He's bang to rights. Caught red-handed trying to import six million quid's worth of cocaine. Looking at the wrong end of fifteen years, at best. Whilst you might, just might – in his mind – wriggle away free.'

'Well, if I did manage to get out of this shit, I'd be his best chance of getting him out, too.'

'You really think that, Terry?'

'Don't you?'

'Sure I do. But we've a PR job to do on Mickey.'

'Nick, whether he pleads guilty or not, whatever happens, I need him in the witness box telling the jury he doesn't know me, and we've never met. I need him backing me that this is all a stitch-up by rival drug dealers.'

Fox looked at him, dubiously. 'Well, that's going to depend, there might be a big difference in his attitude if he does plead guilty.'

Gready narrowed his eyes at Fox. 'Well, you tell him there's another big difference, that it's not the fall that kills you, it's the sudden stop. Tell him if we're both going down, I'll be the one with the parachute.'

Fox stood up and patted him affectionately on the shoulder. 'Don't worry, I'll sort him.' He grinned. 'Trust me, I'm a lawyer.'

Gready managed a weak smile back.

FOUR MONTHS LATER

18

Wednesday 20 March

A tailback, caused by a minor crash on the M25, delayed Meg Magellan's journey home from the Tesco headquarters in Welwyn Garden City by nearly two hours. When she finally arrived back in Hove and pulled onto the driveway alongside Laura's grimy old Kia, in front of what had once been the garage until she and Nick had converted it into an extension of the living room, she was exhausted and ravenous.

And feeling lonely and heavy-hearted about again going into the empty house.

She lugged her briefcase off the passenger seat and let herself in the front door. The day's post was scattered across the floor – the usual assortment of bills, fast-food flyers and a couple of official-looking letters. Daphne sat in the midst of the mail.

She knelt and stroked the cat. 'Are you hungry? You must be – sorry I'm so late! I'll get you food in a minute.'

The hall and staircase walls were lined with black-and-white photographs in black frames. Nick had been a keen amateur photographer, and loved taking photos of his family and of Brighton scenes, especially the beach, beach huts and the piers. When he had died, she and Laura at least had a detailed photographic record of their family activities and, crucially for Meg, of Will and Laura growing up.

What was Laura doing today, she wondered? Four months since she'd left with Cassie. And another five months before she would be back. The last communication she'd had was a Whats-App photograph of her and Cassie inside a thatched mud hut, standing beside a toothless man in a felt trilby and traditional striped cape and a small, grinning boy in a grey hoodie, who was holding up a stack of brightly coloured friendship bracelets. All around them on the straw-covered floor were dozens and dozens of guinea pigs. It was captioned by Laura:

> **This is a guinea-pig farm, can you believe it, Mum? Horace would not be impressed!!!**

Meg knelt and scooped up the bunch of letters, carried them through to the kitchen and plonked them on the table. Daphne meowed.

'Dinner is coming!' She tore open a packet of a new, supposedly highly nutritious cat food she was trying out, but which Daphne didn't seem wild about, squeezed its stinky contents into the bowl and put it on the floor. The cat walked around it, peering at it warily, and then, dismissively, walked away.

'Great! What do you want? Beluga caviar?'

The cat reached the kitchen door, gave a disdainful *miaowww*, then jumped out through the flap.

'Go find yourself a takeaway out in the garden!' she said. 'Chinese? Pizza? Thai? Maybe a Mexican?'

The creature had always been Laura's pet, sleeping with her on the bed. Ever since Laura had gone, it seemed to Meg that the cat held her responsible for her daughter's absence, and kept its distance – apart from when it was hungry – despite all her efforts to befriend it.

She switched on the oven, then went upstairs to Laura's room, where the smell of sawdust greeted her. She opened the window to air the room, before checking on the precious creatures in their cages. Relieved as she was every day that none of them had died, she topped up their food and water then took a few photos to send to Laura – she demanded them every few days. Horace, his little face twitching, actually looked like he was posing for his close-up.

Back downstairs, she opened the freezer and took a desultory look through the options. Like the cat, she wasn't hungry, but she knew she needed to eat. She removed a vegan curry, which she'd bought as an experiment, read the instructions, removed the packaging, put it on a baking tray and bunged it in the oven. Then she sat down to tackle the post.

The first envelope she opened, which was for Laura, had an Edinburgh postmark. It was from the Royal School of Veterinary Studies, giving Laura the dates of the autumn semester, starting 2 October. Meg was so proud her daughter had got in, against stiff competition. She immediately messaged her with the date.

Then she opened the buff envelope addressed to herself. And felt a strange frisson as she read the contents.

It was a very formally worded letter on pink paper summoning her for jury service at Lewes Crown Court – in seven weeks' time. Within the letter were options to delay, should there be a reasonable cause.

In exactly six weeks' time she was taking voluntary redundancy from her employer, Kempson Pharmaceuticals, due to their move further north. The timing was almost perfect. She could do it, although it might interfere with interviews for a couple of other positions she'd applied for.

But it might be interesting, she thought. Perhaps a distraction from how much she missed Laura.

As she read the letter and conditions more carefully, a reply beeped in from Laura with another photograph, this time a close-up of a seriously ugly reptile.

> Can I bring him home, Mum?

Grinning, Meg tapped out,

> So long as you are not inside his belly!
> Remember the song?
> She sailed away on a sunny summer day, on the back of a crocodile . . .
> At the end of the ride, the lady was inside, and the smile was on the crocodile!

The reply came back,

> I'm serious, Mum! I soooo want one!

Meg responded,

> Go for it!

Then added,

> Are iguanas allowed in Edinburgh?

Laura replied,

> You need to come here, Mum. It is A-MAZ-INGGG!

Meg smiled. Pleased that Laura sounded so well and happy, enjoying her trip of a lifetime. Then she returned to the jury service letter, studying it carefully.

It might make a really great transition between Kemp-sons and wherever she moved to next. And, hey, it would be a civic duty done!

She signed her name and placed the reply slip in the postage-paid envelope that came with the letter.

19

Lewes Crown Court was an imposing presence on the town's High Street. Its classically handsome colonnaded facade of Portland stone gave it an air both of timelessness and of gravitas, but once you were inside, past the security counter and metal detector, it wasn't so timeless any more, Terence Gready thought.

The furnishings and decor of its common parts and rooms were dated, as was the layout of the building and its courts, some more than others, but especially Court 3, which he would be going up to soon. Modern courts were designed with the benefit of hindsight and experience. Witnesses, the accused, their family and friends, and jurors entered and left via separate entrances and were segregated throughout. And in modern courts the jurors were out of the line of sight of the public gallery. But not here. Everyone came in and left through the same entrance and mingled, however reluctantly and unpleasantly, in the lobby.

Terence Gready knew the building inside out. He'd appeared here countless times with clients and had always liked the faded grandeur and sense of history and importance of the place. But now, to his humiliation, for the first time ever he had not entered through the front entrance. Instead, handcuffed and accompanied by two security guards, he had been driven round to the back in a prison van and unceremoniously marched straight down to the holding cells.

He now sat on a thin blue cushion on the hard bunk, staring around at the windowless room, his thoughts as stark as his surroundings. To add to his despondency, his wife had bought him a brand-new white shirt, which she had delivered along with his blue suit to High Down Prison last night. Why, he cursed, hadn't she checked the shirt first? The collar had been creased, carelessly, in the wrong place, so no matter how he had arranged his tie, the starched collar rode up the back of his neck. And the shirt itched.

Mickey Starr was in another of the cells, close by, but Gready didn't know which one. He glanced at his watch – the shitty one that no one would steal, replacing his Rolex that bitch Financial Investigator had seized. It was approaching 10 a.m. They would be going up soon for the Plea and Trial Preparation Hearing.

God, after all he'd done for Mickey over the years, the man owed it to him to stick by him now, so they had a chance of getting through this crisis. If Mickey did anything other than plead guilty, and failed to stick to the script Nick Fox had given him, Gready knew his entire defence could be scuppered.

His last meeting with Fox, two days ago at High Down, had not left him feeling confident. Quite the reverse – he'd had the sense that Fox was being evasive when he'd asked him about Starr.

His thoughts were interrupted by the sound of his cell door opening, and the voice of a uniformed female dock officer. 'You're on parade, sunshine.'

As he stepped out, he saw Mickey, dressed in a suit for the first time in all the years he had known him, and looking distinctly awkward in it. It seemed at the same time to be both too big and too small for him, with his shirt collar all rucked up and his dark tie stopping halfway down his chest.

With a stern dock officer behind him, he followed the first one up the steps and emerged into the glassed-in booth that was the dock of the wood-panelled Court 3. Countless of his clients had stood here previously, but it was his very first time and he felt like a caged animal in a zoo. Both defendants sat down, separated by a dock officer and with another officer also remaining. Mickey was staring resolutely ahead.

They were at the same level as the wigged judge, His Honour Richard Jupp, with the rest of the court benches below, the empty jury box to his left, the press box, half full, over to his right. He recognized some of the journalists, one in particular – the smart, attractive senior *Argus* crime reporter, Siobhan Sheldrake, who had doorstepped him during a number of previous trials. He could see her looking at him now, as if somewhat bemused to see him in his reversed role.

A handful of people sat up in the public gallery, among them his wife, son and one of his daughters. He caught Barbara's reassuring smile and returned it with a discreet nod. Down below in the well of the court sat his barrister, Primrose Brown QC, gowned and wigged, and a short distance along the same row was another wigged brief, representing Mickey Starr.

Seated at the far end of the same row, in the sparsely attended hearing, was a Crown Prosecution Service barrister, a woman he'd not seen before. Some greenhorn cutting her teeth on the easy part of a trial.

Behind Primrose Brown sat his trusted Nick Fox, and next to him was Anu Vasanth, the solicitor from the same firm looking after the interests of Mickey Starr. The mere sight of Fox instilled confidence and optimism in Gready. During the coming difficult months, Gready knew there wasn't a better man to handle the situation. Fox was a force of nature. So long as they could keep Mickey Starr in his box they would, almost certainly, be OK.

The black-gowned clerk of the court stood, holding a sheaf of papers. 'Terence Arthur Gready, please rise.'

Gready obeyed.

Reading from the papers, she asked, 'You are Terence Arthur Gready of Onslow Road, Hove, Sussex?'

'Yes, I am.'

'Terence Arthur Gready, you stand charged on this indictment containing six counts. Count One is being knowingly concerned in the fraudulent evasion of a prohibition on the importation of goods, contrary to section 170(2)(b) of the Customs and Excise Management Act 1979. The particulars of the offence are that you, between the 1st day of January 2018 and the 26th day of November 2018, in relation to a Class-A controlled drug, namely 160 kilos of cocaine, were knowingly concerned in the fraudulent evasion of the prohibition on importation imposed by section 3(1) of the Misuse of Drugs Act 1971. How do you plead?'

Gready spoke loudly and clearly: 'Not guilty.'

The clerk read out to Gready four further counts of importing cocaine, covering four similar significant incidents between 3 February 2013 and 26 November 2018. To each of them he again stated, 'Not guilty.'

Finally, the clerk finished with: 'Count Six statement of offence: conspiracy to supply a controlled drug to another contrary to section 4(3)(a) of the Misuse of Drugs Act 1971. The particulars of that offence are that you, between the

10th day of January 2003 and the 26th day of November 2018 conspired together with others unknown, to unlawfully supply a controlled drug of Class A, namely cocaine, to another, in contravention of section 4(1) of the Misuse of Drugs Act 1971. How do you plead?'

'Not guilty,' he said without hesitation. He glanced down at Nick Fox and caught his nod of reassurance, and wink.

'Please sit down, Mr Gready,' the judge commanded.

As he complied, the clerk said, 'Michael Rodney Starr, please stand.'

Starr stood, looking even more gawky, his collar seemingly bursting out of the top of his jacket. The clerk read out an identical first charge to the one she had for Gready.

'How do you plead?'

'Guilty.'

Mickey Starr then pleaded guilty to the further five counts that had been put to his co-defendant.

He also pleaded guilty to counts of assaults on two Border Force officers, two police officers, a member of the public and, in addition, a number of driving offences. Starr sat down.

A discussion followed between the counsels about the various trial dates before they were able to fix a date in early May.

His Honour Richard Jupp, addressing Starr, said, 'Stand up.'

Starr obeyed.

'I intend to sentence you at the end of the trial of your co-accused, which is likely to be late May. You may sit down.'

Gready had to wait, patiently, for the next twenty minutes, while the court dealt with a number of administrative matters. Finally, the judge addressed the dock officers.

'You can take the defendants down.'

Gready followed Starr to the rear of the dock. Then, as they descended the steps and he was out of sight of the judge, he grabbed Starr's shoulder.

'Mickey, a gentle reminder not to talk to the cops – you've got nothing to say.'

20

Accompanied by a dock officer, Nick Fox went down to the holding cells beneath Lewes Crown Court, to where Terence Gready was sitting. Fox entered and the door clanged shut behind him.

Gready shook his head. 'Mickey's got an agenda. You already told me he was asking about what kind of reduction in his sentence he could get by pleading guilty. I bet his next step will be to see what he'd be offered by turning Queen's evidence. Don't you think?'

Fox was silent.

'Nick? Don't you think?'

'It's a possibility.'

'My defence relies on Starr saying he doesn't know me, and he's never met me. He needs to be in the box for *me*, not the prosecution. It's time to play hardball. Even with all the reductions he might get, he's still going to be inside for a few years. You'd better tell him that if he wants his brother protected, properly protected, then he'd better keep his trap shut. Time to teach him a lesson. Get the boys to go and see Mickey the day before the trial starts, to keep it fresh in his mind. Tell them to go and have a little chat with Stuie, know what I'm saying? That way it'll get back to his brother.'

Fox smiled. 'Smack him about a little?'

'Yep. Smack him about good and proper. Then let Mickey know that's just the beginning. If he thinks he's giving evidence against me, life for Stuie is going to be hell. Proper hell.'

'Understood.'

'And make sure Mickey understands, gets the message loud and clear.'

'I know just the right people to do it.'

'Of course you do.'

21

Roy Grace's last day in his post as Acting Commander of the Metropolitan Police Violent Crime Task Force, began much the same as his first day had. With his job phone ringing in the middle of the night.

Grabbing it and hitting 'answer' as quickly as he could, to try to avoid disturbing Cleo, he slipped out of bed and went through into the bathroom, closing the door behind him. 'Roy Grace,' he said, instantly awake and alert.

'Sorry to disturb you, boss,' said the familiar voice of the on-call SIO, Detective Inspector Davey. 'We've a fatal stabbing in north Croydon.'

'Thanks, Paul. What details do you have?'

'Sketchy at the moment, but it sounds like a wrong-time, wrong-place. A young lad walking his girlfriend home. From what we have from her, so far, they were surrounded by a bunch of youths making sexual innuendos and he answered them back. The next thing she knew, he was lying on the ground, bleeding heavily from the neck, and they all ran off. She phoned in hysterics and stayed with him whilst the operator talked her through staunching the blood loss and CPR, but he died at the scene. I know it's your last day, but I thought you might want to attend as usual, so I've dispatched a car to collect you. It can be with you in thirty minutes, if you want to come up?'

'I do. Where's the girl now?'

'Being treated for shock at the hospital, but she's a plucky kid and has given us some good descriptions. We've a pretty good idea who one of the offenders is. I know it's early, but I've already got uniform officers there doing house-to-house and we are sitting on the suspect's home.'

Despite the tragedy of the situation, Roy Grace knew that when he returned to Sussex, one thing he would miss was the sheer number of officers the Metropolitan Police were able to deploy to a crime scene – and the speed at which they could do it.

Another thing he would miss was having a driver at times like these, he thought. Especially after last night, when he'd had farewell drinks at a pub with his team. He'd grown fond of them all in the short time he'd been in London and would miss them.

Thanking Davey, he started collecting his thoughts about this murder and the day ahead, as he showered and shaved. He needed to be looking sharp for an 8 a.m. break-fast meeting with Alison Vosper – which she had requested, somewhat to his surprise.

He waited downstairs, dressed in his uniform, sipping a strong coffee as he was eyed by a half-awake Humphrey, licking his paws. When he heard the sound of a car pulling up outside, he went upstairs, finding Cleo awake now and sleepily putting on a T-shirt. He apologized for waking her, held her head in his hands and gave her a big kiss. Then he hurried back down, grabbing his laptop and go-bag, and climbed into the back of an unmarked Audi.

Too wired to go back to sleep, he spent the thirty-minute,

high-speed, blue-light journey on his laptop, going through the case files of the trial of Dr Edward Crisp.

'This is as close as we can get, sir,' his driver announced, bringing the car to a halt.

Grace looked up, surprised they were here already. A street-lit residential road. A couple of low-rise apartment blocks and post-war semis on both sides. Ahead, through the windscreen, he could see a blaze of blue flashing lights, and just beyond, with a uniform scene guard, police tape sealing off the road. It was a hive of activity. A large number of police vehicles, including a marked Transit van and a Crime Scene Investigation truck.

Leaving his laptop on the rear seat, he climbed out with a heavy heart. Every knife-crime murder that happened under his watch he considered to be a failure. A failure down to him.

Opening the boot of the car, he pulled out a protective oversuit, shoes and gloves from his go-bag, wrestled into them, then walked towards the cluster of vehicles and a group of people, mostly youths, hanging around the outer cordon. He showed his warrant card to the scene guard, signed the crime scene log and ducked under the tape.

A short distance ahead was a group of people similarly attired to himself, standing in the glare of temporary flood-lights around a tent, the generator powering them rumbling close by. Several POLSA, in blue gloves, were on their hands and knees on the pavement doing a fingertip search, taking advantage of the so-called 'golden hour'.

The words of the Murder Manual were ingrained in his brain, if not his soul, playing to him as he approached.

Who? What? Why? When? Where? And very importantly – How?

Davey turned to greet him as he approached.

'What do you have, Paul?'

'Only what I told you, boss. Nothing more at this stage, I'm afraid. Pathologist is on his way.' He opened a flap in the tent and stepped aside to give Grace a view of the victim.

A black kid, eighteen years or so old, with a massive wound in his neck. Vacant eyes wide open. Short, bleached dreadlocks. A white, blood-soaked tank top. Dark tracksuit bottoms. Brand-new trainers. A large stain of pooled, drying blood on the pavement.

'He wanted to be a doctor, his girlfriend told the first officers who attended,' Davey said.

Anger flared in Roy Grace. Anger against the perpetrators, whoever the hell they were. The same anger he had felt so many times during the past six months. Anger at his impotence. Yes, he had made a difference. During his time here in this role the number of knife-crime deaths had reduced. But there were still far too many.

Just *one* was too many.

It was easy to look at statistics and feel smug about them. Hide behind them. Much harder to look at a dead teenager who had wanted to be a doctor, murdered for trying to walk his girlfriend home. Murdered, most likely, by a group of youths so dispossessed by society that this was their vile, pathetic way of achieving some kind of status.

Murdered, by default, by a succession of governments whose politicians were just not interested in understanding the different strata of society they were responsible for.

The pooled blood was black beneath the harsh glare of the lights.

Black like the dead youth's skin.

Black would give the politicians all kinds of mealy-mouthed excuses to explain about divided communities.

Bollocks.

This dead young person, with his £200 trainers and his ambition to be a doctor, deserved better than the hand he'd been dealt.

Failure. He looked at the boy, thinking, *Failure by all of us to create a society that recognized your ambition and talent.*

Shit. Grace knew how awful it was to tell a parent that their child would never come home again. A dreadful thing.

He turned away, his eyes stinging with salty tears.

22

Friday 3 May

Many criminal law barristers worked long hours for a relatively modest living, frequently alternating between prosecuting and defending. But some, like Primrose Brown, had carved a niche for themselves through winning high-profile trials for their clients against the odds – clients who were only too aware that no price was too steep to pay for freedom.

Brown was a QC – a Queen's Counsel, or 'silk' as they were colloquially known – with an impressive track record. A short and ferociously bright woman of fifty-five, her fair hair pulled tightly and severely back and gripped by an ornate hairslide, she had a penchant for voluminous, sombre dresses, chunky jewellery and expensive shoes.

For many years Terence Gready had regularly entrusted clients to her when he needed the services of a QC, and they could afford her, and she seldom disappointed, either in the eye-watering size of her fees or in the evisceration of the prosecution's case. At an age when many of her colleagues had opted for less stressful, but also less lucrative, positions as judges she had made the career decision to remain at the Bar, because she loved the work and was endlessly fascinated by the characters she encountered. But during these past months it was Gready himself who was now dependent on her skills of advocacy – and at the mercy of her fee notes.

At 11 a.m., seated opposite him at the metal table in the cramped, grotty interview room at High Down Prison – away from his home patch of Brighton and Hove – Primrose Brown brought a rare dash of glamour into the numbing drabness of the place, Gready thought, and the fragrance of her scent made a welcome change to the cheesy ingrained smell in the room. To her left was her junior barrister, a smartly turned-out man in his late thirties called Crispin Sykes, who spoke little but had made copious notes at every meeting since Gready's arrest. Primrose would not normally attend this type of meeting, leaving it to her junior counsel, but she had made an exception today due to her long history with Terence Gready.

To his left was Nick Fox. This was their last meeting before the trial.

Primrose Brown's voice over the years had refined from a Yorkshire accent into London legal posh. But a trace of the gravelly North Country still remained. 'I have to level with you, Terry, it's not looking good,' she said, peering at him through half-frame glasses.

And he wasn't looking good, either, she thought. He'd lost weight and looked a decade older than when he'd first been incarcerated, just over five months ago. Prison did that to people, she was well aware; the diet, the drugs, the lack of fresh air – and perhaps all the other mental stuff, including loss of self-esteem, that went with the territory of being banged up. She'd met plenty of recidivists who looked twenty years older than their real age, but all the same she was shocked this change had happened so quickly.

'Tell me about it, Prim,' he said. 'The police seized my

laptop and phones. They took all the office computers, and the Law Society have closed me down. All my cases and colleagues have gone to other firms. In addition, all the proprietors of every takeaway I've helped set up, out of my community spirit, have suffered the indignity of being questioned, and it's affected their trade for some months. Not to mention the effect this has had on my family.'

'I'm sorry to hear that,' she said. 'Luck doesn't seem to be going our way on this case, at the moment. We've got Stephen Cork as lead prosecutor.'

Gready started at the mention of the name, as did everyone else in the room. 'Shit,' he said.

There were good and bad prosecutors, and Cork was renowned as one of the toughest. He was an experienced criminal barrister with a chip on his shoulder because he'd never become a QC. While training for the Bar, his pupil master had been disbarred for manipulating evidence – and while Cork had never been accused of taking part or having any knowledge, the taint of that episode had dogged him throughout his career. He blamed it as the reason why he had never taken silk.

Brown peered hard at her client. 'Look, Terry, I'm sorry to have to ask you this, but you'll understand why I have to.' She gave him a quizzical look.

Gready shrugged. He sat on the hard chair opposite her, hunched but defiant. 'Go ahead.'

'Despite all your bank accounts being frozen, you've been able to come up with my original retainer, which was not insubstantial. You've met all my fees during these past months, and you've now been able to pay a further substantial retainer for my estimated fees for your trial. I need to know where this money has come from.'

'It's a loan from a mate who believes in my innocence,' he said, guilelessly.

She glanced down at her files. 'Mr Jonathan Jones, who resides in Panama?'

'Yes. I helped him out years ago when he was in financial trouble. He's since made a fortune in property out there and he's repaying an old mate.'

Silently, she jotted down a note and slid the pad over to him for a signature. As soon as he had complied, she said, 'Good, that's out of the way. And my next question is, your instructions to me are that you still wish to proceed to trial having entered "not guilty" pleas on all counts, is that correct?'

He stared back at her levelly. 'As I've maintained all along, Primrose, I've been fitted up. You understand better than most how much the police loathe us lawyers. Give them any opportunity to hit back and pot one of us and they'll seize it with open arms. I'm a victim. An innocent victim. This is all a huge embarrassment for me.'

She glanced down and made another note, then looked back up at Gready and their eyes locked.

Her expression was deadpan, but there was the hint of humouring him in her bright blue eyes.

They both knew the score. Two pros. Fighting on the same side. No moral judgements. The trial that began next Tuesday in Court 3 of Lewes Crown Court, in Sussex, like all jury trials, was never going to be about delivering justice. It was going to be a game where personality ran roughshod over evidence. It was going to be about convincing twelve ordinary citizens that the family guy standing in the dock with a pleasant smile in the dark-blue suit and nice tie could not possibly be guilty of the allegations.

It was about those *one* or *two* words the foreperson would read out after the jury had retired to deliberate their verdict. Quite binary, really.

Guilty.

Not guilty.

Or in a barrister's more colloquial terms –

Win.

Lose.

Fox remained behind after Brown and her junior barrister left the room. He gave Gready a reassuring smile. 'We'll sort it, Terry,' he said.

'What's the update on Mickey Starr?'

'No news – a lot depends on the outcome of your trial. If you were found guilty – heaven forbid – you'd both be sentenced together.'

'And he's kept schtum?'

'Appears to have done. He doesn't feature in any of the trial documents. Want him as a character reference?'

'Funny,' Gready said, bitterly.

Fox was silent.

Gready went on. 'You said a while back he's looking at the wrong end of fifteen years plus?'

Fox nodded again. 'For that amount of drugs, yes, plus his violence at Newhaven. He'd likely serve half actually inside, less what he's done already on remand, the rest out on licence.'

'How much reduction do you think he'd get for ratting me up?'

The solicitor was evasive. 'Depends. You know the score, Terry, you've been in that situation with clients yourself.'

'I know – but I'm finding it hard to think straight some-times, at the moment. Depends on what?'

'On how valuable the prosecution thinks what he has

to say is. He could be looking at a substantial reduction in sentence.'

Gready smiled. It was a while since he had last smiled. But Nick Fox would sort it, he knew. They had their plan. *King of the Jungle.* He always sorted everything.

23

'You look tired, Roy. Are you OK?' Alison Vosper asked.

They were in a booth of a hotel on the Embankment, close to New Scotland Yard.

'I'm good, ma'am,' he said, grateful for the strong but bad coffee that had been poured into his cup. He sliced open a poached egg, the yolk running across the toast and avocado. 'Just sad about the stabbing victim I saw earlier.'

The Deputy Assistant Commissioner of the Met shrugged. 'I know how well you've picked up on the fact there are huge cultural differences between communities. Not all our officers get it, but you do. I'm really impressed with what you've achieved in your short time with us – and it hasn't escaped the attention of my boss and the Home Office. You've done what I thought was impossible when I took on this role.'

He smiled. 'What is it they say, ma'am? The impossible we do immediately, miracles take a little longer?'

She reached across the table and gave his right hand a supportive pat. There had been moments, back in the time when she was his ACC in Sussex, when – despite her sweet and sour approach – he'd seen her with her guard down and sensed her affection for him. He was sensing the same thing now. She withdrew her hand and dug a fork into her scrambled eggs but maintained eye contact with him for some moments.

'You've established stronger community links. You've done great work in education, outreach, youth services. And your stick-and-carrot campaign has gained strong support. I like your work on the minimum three-year sentence for first conviction for anyone carrying a knife, and your "three strikes and you're out" initiative.'

'Thank you, ma'am.'

She locked eyes with him again. 'You have an opportunity here to make a real difference. Are you sure you don't want to stay and at least see some of this through?'

He ate a mouthful of egg, toast and avocado, using the time to compose his reply. 'The Met response from a murder point of view is excellent. I feel I've done my bit, adding my SIO head. Everyone here knows what they have to do, but my family needs me home – and there's a lot of work to be done in Sussex.'

She stared back at him.

'You and I make a great team. Stay in London, Roy, and I'll give you a Commander's job, crime-related so you can still do the things you love. I'm going to be around for a long while – this offer doesn't have a shelf-life.'

'That's very generous of you, ma'am.'

'I'm serious. If you want to leave Sussex at any time, ring me. You have my personal number. My offer isn't going to go away, I'd give you a job as a Commander tomorrow.'

24

'Nice epaulettes, Roy,' ACC Cassian Pewe commented, slightly mocking as Grace entered his office. 'But not for much longer, eh?'

'Actually, Cassian, I've been offered an extended Commander posting to the Met,' he said. On their current equal ranking there was no requirement to call him by the respectful title of *sir*. For this week, at least. Next week, when he returned to his former rank in Sussex, it would be different, as he dropped back down to Detective Superintendent.

'So why don't you take it, Roy?' Pewe asked. 'Although I'll tell you the truth, we're missing you here.'

'Really?'

He nodded. 'We are. We're short on the Major Crime Team. I hope you've felt your time in the Met has been worthwhile?'

'I do, I think what I've learned will be of invaluable help in the future here.'

'Sounds very worthy, Roy. Jolly good. But is there another reason why you wanted to see me?'

Grace told him his concerns about Dr Edward Crisp.

'You seriously think the doctor is going to do a runner from court?'

107

'If he was capable of escaping from a French prison then I do, yes. That's why I want to upgrade the security for the trial.'

'What do you have in mind?'

'Extra security for his transportation to and from prison to court. Two security guards posted on each court door and at least one police officer, if not two, at the street entrance, for the duration of the trial.'

'I'm not sure the cost of extra policing would be justified.'

'A lot less than the cost of a manhunt for an escaped murder suspect. Not to mention the egg on our faces in the eyes of Joe Public.'

Pewe shook his head. 'I don't have the luxury of spare police officers to pull off frontline duty to use as doormen. Perhaps in your Met you do, but not here. It's not going to happen. Relax. If the CPS want more security, they can liaise with the security providers. I'm not using my resources on someone who's already in our prison system.'

Roy held his counsel for a few seconds before replying. 'All security discussion aside, Cassian, Sussex Police kick off the promotion procedure for Chief Superintendents next week. It's something I need to think carefully about – I may be throwing my hat in the ring.'

Pewe looked at him for a few seconds. 'Really? Are you expecting me to support your application?'

'Not expecting, but if you value me as much as you say, then I'd like to think I can count on your recommendation?'

Pewe smiled. 'Look, Roy, I know you and I have our differences. And history. And I don't want to lose you, I genuinely don't. I want you back on my team. I have the greatest respect for you.'

'Really? You've a strange way of showing it sometimes, Cassian.'

Pewe stood up, opening his hands in a gesture of friend-ship, and walked round his desk. He put an arm round Roy's shoulder and steered him over to the L-shaped sofa. 'Sit down – can I get you any tea or coffee?'

As he sat, Grace shook his head. 'I'm fine, thank you.'

Pewe sat a short distance away. 'OK, let's start again. Bury the hatchet?'

'How deep? Beneath sonar range?' Grace said it with a smile like dry ice.

Pewe winced, visibly stung by the reference to his previous time in Sussex, when he had been on equal rank to Roy Grace. Prompted by the parents of Roy's missing wife, Sandy, who had long suspected Roy of murdering her, Pewe had taken it upon himself to have a sonar scan done of the back garden of the house where he and Sandy had lived.

Grace had never forgiven Sandy's toxic parents, nor Pewe for this outrage, although he had been marginally more forgiving of Pewe for acting on information, albeit unsub-stantiated, given by her parents.

'I didn't have any choice, Roy,' Pewe said. 'You know that, you'd have had to do exactly the same if the roles had been reversed.'

Grace resisted the urge to say he would have had the courtesy to let Pewe know first, and not done it behind his back. But if the ACC was genuinely offering him an olive branch, he didn't want to throw it back in his face. Not yet. 'Sure,' he replied, flatly.

'So,' Cassian Pewe sat up, brightly. 'You'll have my support for your application for the Chief Superintendents boards. And we start afresh from next Monday, maybe not as bosom buddies but as colleagues who respect each other?'

'Sounds good,' Grace said, guardedly.

Pewe beamed. 'Right then, get out there and move the needle on Sussex's crime statistics. Know a negative feedback loop when you see one.'

Grace looked at him, wondering as he always did where the hell Cassian Pewe got all this corporate gobbledygook from. 'Absolutely,' he replied.

Pewe patted him on the shoulder and jumped up again. 'Are we done?'

'We're done.'

'Good man! Good to have you back.'

25

When people encountered Richard Jupp for the first time, away from his work environment, most of them assumed the tall, thick-set, teddy bear of a man in his late sixties, with thinning grey hair and a beard verging on the straggly, was a teacher or perhaps an environmentalist, or maybe even some kind of local politician. No one would have put him down as the country's longest-serving Crown Court judge.

But beneath his cuddly exterior was a man who could, when needed, be as hard as nails or as kind and humane as your favourite uncle. He was one of three judges in Sussex who were 'ticketed' – as it was called in legal parlance – to sit on murder trials.

He liked to be in very early on the morning of a major new trial, to review the key documentation and be fully prepped. At 7.45 a.m. he sat in his chambers adjoining Court 3 of Lewes Crown Court. He loved this Victorian building – the four law courts it housed had a grandeur and sense of occasion that he felt was missing in most modern courts. And compared to modern judge's chambers, this room was wonderfully old-fashioned and spacious, with more the feel of a suite in a grand but tired hotel, rather than an office.

Its ochre walls were relieved by uninspired framed

prints of Lewes landscapes; there was a patterned lavender carpet and imposing drapes hung from an elaborate pelmet atop an almost impossibly tall window. The furniture was just old, rather than antique. A spacious L-shaped desk was cluttered with a photocopier, conferencing laptop, box of tissues and a row of legal tomes, with a short meeting table attached. There was a wardrobe, a pastel armchair, a handful of purple-upholstered conference chairs and some desultory potted plants. On a shelf sat a black-and-gold tin with a brass handle, containing his wig. He had forgotten it on a couple of occasions when he had been distracted by something on a case and had sent his clerk scuttling out of court to fetch it. But in all other respects, he was sharp as a tack.

Jupp stroked his black-and-white spaniel, Biscuit, comfortably seated on his lap, whilst his other dog, Charlie, snored in his basket on the floor. 'Lock-'em-up Jupp' was the moniker that His Honour Judge Richard Jupp had long been given by his colleagues and by all the barristers, local and from afar, who had ever come before him, whether prosecuting or defending. He liked it, well aware his repu-tation was as a judge to be feared, but one who was fair.

In the courts over which he presided, the accused, their briefs and the jury would always know where they stood when they were in front of him. If clearly guilty, in his view, from all the evidence presented, he'd always done his best to get that message across to even the most dim-witted of juries in his summings-up and directions. And, boy, while many were good, he'd had more than his share of seriously dim-witted ones! And if there was proper doubt about the person in the dock's culpability, he would try equally hard to direct the jury towards that coveted two-word verdict:

Not guilty.

The problem was, in his long experience, that whilst many juries were highly competent, the jury system itself had flaws. It was a lottery what jury you got.

Frustratingly, on a few occasions juries got it very wrong. So much could sway a bunch of inexperienced people, of mixed backgrounds and views, to go either way. And occasionally they made a totally incomprehensible decision. All it took was a group of malleable jurors and a passionate – but misguided – one to sway them.

In Richard Jupp's view, formed after forty years of appearing in court, on both sides of the bench, juries often convicted or acquitted on emotions rather than on facts. He likened juries to a lucky dip – you never knew quite what you were going to get.

The system wasn't as bad as portrayed in a television show many years ago, with the late comedy genius Tony Hancock, whom he had loved. One episode featured an unemployed Hancock doing jury service. Hancock had discovered that jurors got paid a daily rate equal to an entire week's dole money, so every time the rest of the jury reached a verdict, one way or the other, he would convince them to reverse it in order to prolong the trial and increase the meagre amount of his earnings.

Although a fiction, there had been genuine instances of bizarre behaviour in jury rooms which made it seem not so far-fetched. For example, after the trial of a double murderer, here in Sussex, had ended, it was revealed that drunk members of the jury had resorted to consulting a Ouija board in the hotel where they were sequestered, to communicate with the spirits of the murder victims, to help them with their verdict.

It was not surprising there were occasional instances of odd behaviour when a group of total strangers, generally lay people, were put into a daunting environment and had to reach decisions that would make or destroy many people's lives – the lives of both the accused and of the victims or their loved ones.

And despite what some tabloids screamed on their front-page splashes, prisons were not holiday camps. In Jupp's view, most UK prisons were brick shithouses, filled with bullies. Nasty, scary places where you were confined with total strangers, a percentage of whom were likely to be violent. A place where you were not simply deprived of all the liberties and luxuries you'd previously taken for granted, but a horror hotel, where there was no pillow menu, no breakfast list to hang on your door, no privacy – frequently an open toilet where you had to perform your functions behind a plastic curtain, inches from your cell-mate's face – and scant relief from the relentless tedium and the constant threat of being brutalized by other inmates. One wrong look or ill-chosen word and your face could be slashed open, boiling porridge poured on your genitals, or worse.

Sure, there had been inmates who'd boasted how they ruled the roost in luxury, past villains like East End crime overlord Reggie Kray, who'd had his own phone, kettle and toaster in his cell, and the officers in his pocket. But seldom any more. Although, today, plenty of prisoners made big money forcing others to buy drugs. If you were locked up for a long period, even if you'd never before taken a drug in your life, there would be strong pressure from others inside, and in some instances from officers on the take as well, for you to start on the slippery slope.

When Jupp did send a first-timer down, he knew it was likely to be the beginning of a downward-spiralling life. An attempt at prison reform was something he planned to work on in his retirement. And that ominous day was looming faster than he liked.

As he continued stroking Biscuit, whilst reading through today's very straightforward list of cases in other court-rooms, mostly plea hearings and a couple of sentencings, he was reflecting on just how good life was at this moment. After a divorce, he'd finally found happiness again with his new lady, Frances, twenty years his junior. She shared his love of dogs and his other passion, sailing his 39-foot yacht, *Banged Up*, out of Brighton Marina whenever the opportun-ity arose.

He'd actually lived on the boat for three years during the split-up from his wife Madeleine and had enjoyed the somewhat bohemian lifestyle – in total contrast to his outwardly conformist duties as a Crown Court judge. But now he was almost conventional again, living in a barn conversion a few miles outside Brighton.

He was more content than he had felt for a very long time. Perhaps, if he thought about it, more so than at any time before he had become a judge. His early career as a criminal barrister had for a long time been one of low pay and constant stress. Taking any job, going for the pittance legal aid work paid, being given his brief the night before a trial if he was lucky, but more often than not, an hour before it started.

He'd built up a good reputation, and the quality of work that came his way did improve, but after serving the minimum fifteen years as a junior at the Bar he took silk to become a QC, lining himself up for the next stage in his career plan, for what seemed to him the more stable and less stressful life as a judge.

But now there was an issue looming. On his next birthday, in just four months' time, he would be seventy, which was the compulsory retirement age for a judge, although it was possible to get a one- or two-year extension. He was fit, as alert as ever and had no desire at all to retire. He loved his job. Human nature fascinated him. He was endlessly intrigued by, above all, two things. The first was the legal question of whether the person in the dock had actually done the crime they were being accused of. Followed by the much bigger social, anthropological question after a guilty verdict: *why had they done it?*

Love. Jealousy. Greed. They were the front-runners.

Behind them came pure, irrational hatred.

During his career, the prison population in the UK had risen by 70 per cent and was still rising, thanks to deeply flawed social welfare and justice systems. But every now and then, along came a total scumbag, to whom none of the mitigating factors could apply. Someone who had decided to take the wrong path to instant riches by whatever means required – even torture and murder.

One such name was today's headliner. The case had been listed to start two days earlier but, much to his annoyance, as sometimes happened, had to be delayed as the previous case in Court 3 had overrun. The trial was set down to last for two weeks. It might even be his own swansong, Jupp thought, ruefully. His last really big case.

What a swansong. Regina v Terence Arthur Gready. By all accounts, from what he had read so far, Gready appeared to be a bent solicitor. Very seriously bent.

After the previous court hearing several weeks ago, Jupp was still curious as to why Gready wanted to be tried at one of his home Crown Courts – Lewes. Normally his barrister would have applied for the case to be heard elsewhere in order to ensure impartiality. Jupp knew from previous dealings with this sharp solicitor never to underestimate him, but he couldn't see what advantages for Gready there might be. Regardless, he was confident that he would ensure the whole judicial process would remain scrupulously fair.

But if there was one thing he loathed even more than a bent copper – of which he'd encountered a few in his time – it was a member of his own profession gone rogue.

26

It was the first week of her new life having left Kempsons for the last time the previous Friday. Meg was free! No longer a slave to her alarm clock and the big corporate world – for a while at least. And although it was only 8.25 a.m., the day was already feeling warm beneath a cloudless sky – and full of promise.

And she was boosted even more by a sweet WhatsApp message from Laura that had come in yesterday afternoon.

> You'll be a great juror, Mum, you believe in
> decency – doing the right thing. Do it and enjoy
> and stick to your guns!

As she drove her little black BMW convertible towards the tunnel beneath the cliff on the outskirts of the county town of Lewes, loving the sunshine, she sang along to the words of 'We Will Rock You' blasting out from Radio Sussex.

But the instant she entered the sudden darkness of the tunnel, she had a frisson of apprehension, partly about the day ahead but also, and more significantly, her career.

She'd taken the redundancy package that Kempson Pharmaceuticals had offered, including buying her company car on very fair terms, but leaving was a big gamble, she knew. Sure, she had plenty of experience, but would she get another job at the same salary level? The recruitment agency she'd signed up with were confident, but the two job interviews she'd had through them so far had not appealed.

At least she wouldn't be spending all of her first week of unemployment sitting at home, finding things to fill her time. Reading, gardening, lunching with friends and watching daytime TV. Wondering if she had the temerity, as the HR woman at Kempsons had suggested she should, to sign up for Jobseeker's Allowance. But for the moment that was on hold, and she was on her way to begin her stint of jury service, albeit later than she had expected. This was due to a trial that had overrun, she'd been told.

More importantly to her, she hoped these coming weeks might be a welcome distraction from her worrying about Laura. She was a good girl, constantly updating her on where in Ecuador she and Cassie were and what they were doing. But if Meg didn't hear from her for longer than a day, she started to fret. There had been a major story in all the papers only last week about two girls on their gap year, of similar age to Laura and Cassie, who had disappeared while backpacking around Thailand over six months ago, and their mutilated bodies had just now been found in a dense forest.

Meg's best friend, Alison Stevens – who had helped her through that terrible time after Nick and Will died – had coincidentally done jury service herself a few months ago, and had been on a nasty child-abuse case, which had sickened her, all the more so as she'd got a one-year-old daughter – a late and unexpected addition to her family. And a work colleague had done jury service last year, which had been the trial of a conman who'd gone around Surrey posing as a gas-meter reader, stealing stuff from elderly people's homes. Meg hoped she might get something less distressing than child abuse and more interesting than a phony gas-meter reader, today. And she had something to look forward to at the weekend. Colin's Brother was running in a steeplechase at Plumpton Racecourse on Saturday, where he had won once before. She would be going along to cheer him on with the two partners Nick had shared the horse with. And to have a punt on him.

The music ended and she heard the voice of the presenter. 'A big trial starts at Lewes Crown Court this morning,' he said. 'Brighton solicitor Terence Gready faces charges in connection with one of the most valuable drug hauls ever seized by Sussex Police. Six million pounds' worth of the Class-A drug cocaine concealed in a vintage Ferrari at Newhaven Port in November last year.'

Meg listened intently. That sounded interesting. As she headed towards the station car park, she wondered if she was going to be on the Terence Gready jury. It would be great to be on something juicy, one she could be excited to tell Laura about – and that Laura would be keen to know all about – although she'd read the jury service bumph she'd been sent and had noted she was not permitted to speak about the trial or discussions between jurors to anyone, not even to close family. But hopefully she'd be able to give Laura a flavour at least.

Ten minutes later, as she crested the steep hill leading from the railway station to the High Street, panting with exertion, the imposing building of Lewes Crown Court loomed above her on the far side of the road. A disparate mass of people, some in suits, many in casual clothes, were in a queue that stretched along the pavement from the steps to the columned entrance. Several photographers and reporters milled around.

Meg walked behind a parked white van, and as she did

so, heard the ping of an incoming WhatsApp message. Hopefully from Laura. She hurried across the road and joined the back of the queue, eager to check her phone. Like everyone else, she paid no attention to the white van, signed HALLIWELL PLUMBING with a motif of water spiralling down a drain, parked outside the elegant facade of the historic White Hart Hotel.

But Jeff Pringle, concealed in the back of the van, was paying close attention to her, and to everyone else in the line. Very close – through the telephoto lens of his camera, the peephole masked by the black epicentre of the fake company's logo. He was snapping each person in turn. This was just for back-up, in case anything happened to the photos that would be taken inside. Belt and braces. That was how his boss always operated.

The ponytailed sixty-two-year-old was one of Terence Gready's longest-serving and most trusted associates, managed by Mickey Starr. His normal role in the operation was organizing the drugs distribution network out of London. He handled, through a sterile corridor, the fifteen youngsters who travelled daily by train to the South Coast, distributing drugs, and replaced any of them who were busted – a regular occurrence. Gready's solicitor, Nick Fox, had delegated him this role today because of his hobby as a twitcher – photographing rare birds – and, equally importantly, because of his IT skills.

He tightened focus on the lady who had just joined the queue. Shoulder-length brown hair nicely styled, cool sunglasses, a smart, dark two-piece. Probably a lawyer, he decided, watching her pull her phone out of her handbag, peer at it for a short while and smile. *Nice smile*, Jeff thought.

Then, suddenly, she turned her head and appeared to be staring straight at him. 'Lovely, darling!' he murmured and snapped away. Perfect! A full-on frontal view was always best for the Google facial recognition software.

He glanced at his watch: 8.55 a.m. All the jurors for the trial starting today should be either in the building or the queue. They would have been told to arrive by 9 a.m. If he had missed any, he'd pick them up later, no problem. Right now, he was anxious to get to the public gallery quickly, to secure a front-row view if possible, before too big a crowd gathered. He didn't want to risk having to wait outside.

He emailed the photos to Rio back at the office, climbed into the front and drove the van off to a car park. As he locked it and began making his way towards the court, he had on his person a much smaller camera. So small and well disguised, no dumb security officer would spot it in a million years.

And nor would the judge.

27

When Meg finally reached the front of the queue and entered the building, a world-weary security officer, on the far side of an airport-style conveyor belt, instructed her to put any metal or electronic devices into a tray. She walked through the scanner and had her phone and car keys returned to her.

Her nerves jangled as she found herself standing alone in the wide, maroon-carpeted hall, along with a bunch of other slightly lost-looking people. She was rescued by a smiling, fair-haired young man brandishing a clipboard, who approached her, limping slightly. 'Are you here for jury service?' he asked.

'Yes,' she answered.

'Do you have your summons?' he asked.

Meg removed the pink document from her handbag and showed it to him. He flipped over a couple of pages on his clipboard, looking through a list, then ticked her off. 'I'll be taking you all up to the jury room in a few minutes,' he said, indicating a group of around thirty people standing a little awkwardly, all total strangers but all here for a common purpose, many busy looking at their phones. Meg smiled at a woman and got a friendly shrug back.

She watched the steady procession of people passing

through the scanner with interest, trying to guess what they were all doing here. A complete mix. Fellow jurors, defendants and their lawyers and friends and family, witnesses, police officers, reporters or just curious members of the public?

Finally, the man with the clipboard announced brightly to the group, 'Right, jurors, this way please!'

Meg followed him, amid the throng of fellow jurors, up two flights of ornately balustraded stairs, then along past a wooden bench into a cavernous room with the feel of a school assembly hall, filled with rows of green chairs, the walls lined with noticeboards.

'Can you all please take a seat!' he said, pleasantly but firmly.

Meg sat down next to a man in a checked shirt, who smelled unpleasant. A young man in skinny jeans, with a precious hairstyle and a nervous tic, took the seat to her right and immediately began studying his phone.

She had dressed smartly for the occasion, but from what she had seen of the others in here, she was in the minority. There were a couple of older men in suits and ties, and one strange-looking woman who appeared to have dressed for a garden party, but most people were in casual attire. She needn't have bothered going to such an effort, she realized. Maybe she'd come in more comfortable clothes tomorrow.

Some moments later, the man who had led them up stood in front of them and said, loudly, 'Hello, jurors, I'm Jacobi Whyte, your jury bailiff. Thank you for your patience with the delayed start of this trial. I'm going to show you a video which will tell you what to expect today – you will all be handed a form which has everything on it, including how to claim your expenses, but it is very important you pay attention.'

Meg paid attention.

'You have all been summoned for jury service randomly by a computer. If your name is called you will be one of fifteen people, and your names will be called at random. This is done in case any of you jurors are objected to. If you are not called, or objected to, an usher outside the court entrance will escort you back here.' He paused. 'Is everyone with me so far?'

Meg added to the sea of nods. The bailiff continued to spell out the obligations and the restrictions, and explained that, if they had employment, they would be paid £64.95 per day. Next, he reminded them that googling a defendant's name carried a potential jail sentence and listed all the other dos and don'ts. He pointed to the room behind and up a couple of steps, telling them there were drinks vending machines in there, and informed them they would be hearing announcements shortly. He reminded them that it was an offence to take photographs in court, and that all phones taken into court must be switched off.

Then he played the video, which showed the courtroom they would be in and pointed out the places where everyone would be seated and who they all would be. When it ended, anxious to get away from the body odour of the man beside her as soon as she could, Meg grabbed a form, then went through to the rear and got herself a coffee from a machine. Then she took a seat and read through the form, which was titled WELCOME TO NEW JURORS, and began to fill in the details it required.

When she had finished, she handed it in to Whyte, then sat down on her own and looked again at a new WhatsApp that had just pinged in from Laura. It was a photograph of her and Cassie, both in shorts, T-shirts, sunglasses and baseball caps, standing with legs straddling either side of a narrow, paved path behind a red-and-yellow sign which read:

ECUADOR IN THE MIDDLE OF THE WORLD

LATITUDE 00° 00′ 00″

CALCULATED WITH G.P.S.

Laura was leaning sharply to the right, Cassie to the left. The message read:

> **Mum, we are actually standing on the Equator!**
> **One foot in the Northern Hemisphere, one in**
> **the Southern. And the water really does go down**
> **the plughole clockwise in the Northern and**
> **anti-clockwise in the Southern, we just tried it!**
> **And I got an egg to stand upright on a point,**
> **but Cassie couldn't do it!**

Meg smiled, wistfully. She was glad for her daughter, glad to see the genuine happiness in her face, and that she seemed finally to be over all the horror of the loss of her father and brother. But she was sad, at the same time, that they were currently so far apart.

She checked her emails, just in case there was any communication from the recruitment agency – there wasn't. She took the novel she had brought with her and began to read.

But she only got a few pages in before she suddenly heard her name called out.

28

Richard Jupp sat at his desk in his chambers, sipping a strong coffee he'd brewed himself, both his dogs lying at his feet. The coffee was supplied by a criminal law solicitor called Gerry Maye. Maye was smartly – in Jupp's view – diversifying from his law practice into coffee importing. Due to reductions in legal aid rates, a large number of law firms had gone to the wall during the past couple of years. It made him gladder than ever that he was a judge, on a comfortable salary and with a good pension ahead.

The round clock on the wall read 9.55. Five minutes to the start and the defendant's QC, Primrose Brown – a clever barrister who he knew and liked – had just informed him via the clerk of the court, Maureen Sapsed, that a new financial report had only just been received by the defence counsel. More evidence linking Gready to offshore accounts.

Maureen, garbed in the traditional black gown and now nervously standing in front of him, was efficient in the extreme, and always did her very best to keep all court business flowing. But, like himself, she was often driven to distraction by the inefficiencies that dogged the entire legal system. Like all major public services, the court system had been affected by the austerity measures brought in over a decade ago.

The under-funded and therefore under-manned Crown Prosecution Service was in a constant state of false economy. The cost of putting together any major trial was immense. Getting all the witnesses, police officers, prosecution advocates and defence counsel together for a specific date was always a nightmare of scheduling. With a never-ending backlog of trials waiting in the wings, adjourning a case was never a simple matter of putting it back a few days. All the players involved had myriad other commitments. An adjournment would often mean months before all the elements could be assembled again. And with it came another problem. If the accused had been remanded in custody, they could be kept there, by law, for a maximum of six months. There had to be good grounds for an extension.

Sometimes, he said, only partly in jest, that he felt like a shepherd trying to herd cats. It was a major headache to hold all the different, diverse and moving pieces of a trial together.

For all these reasons, the decision facing Richard Jupp, just five minutes before the start of Regina v Terence Arthur Gready, was whether to go ahead or adjourn due to the late arrival of this new evidence. He knew that obtaining financial information from overseas was an imprecise science, but that was a problem for later. There were two elements to the trial – the first being whether Gready was involved in the importation of six million pounds' worth of cocaine and four similar importation charges, as well as a much wider network of county lines drug dealing.

But the second element and the main focus of this trial was whether Terence Gready was actually the mastermind behind a vast drugs empire.

A major factor for any judge was whether any decision

he or she made would leave an opening for an appeal. But in his opinion, there would be ample time during the following days for the defence to study the late financial documents. It wasn't enough to justify an adjournment of probably many months. And the defence counsel, if they were sensible, wouldn't challenge this. The trial had already taken long enough to come to court, with the defendant locked up on remand. Everyone wanted to get going.

Jupp looked up at the clerk. 'We start, regardless of this, Maureen. But I want a written explanation from the SIO for the lateness of this evidence.'

'Yes, Your Honour.'

'How's the audience looking?'

He was referring to the public gallery. There was a general rule-of-thumb about the numbers attending court cases out of pure interest. The 'chart busters', as he liked to call them, were Death by Dangerous Driving cases, which always attracted the biggest crowds, often filling the courts to capacity. Next came murder trials. And a long way third were sex cases.

'Pretty full,' she said. 'The case has had a lot of local media coverage.'

Jupp didn't like a full gallery. Dozens of strangers staring at him and, more importantly, at the jurors. Intimidating them. Especially during trials when a large contingent of the public gallery was made up of family and friends of the accused. Which this one almost certainly was.

He glanced at the clock. 'OK, let's rock and roll!'

29

Moments after the clerk left Richard Jupp's chambers, an usher knocked and entered. Thirty-year-old Matt Croucher, neatly turned out in a grey suit beneath a black cloak, his ID card hung on a lanyard around his neck, said, 'Ready, Your Honour? Don't forget your wig!'

Jupp grinned a thank-you, removed the short, grey wig from the tin and, checking in the mirror, aligned it on his head, then followed him out of the room and up the short flight of carpeted stairs to his entrance door to the court.

Croucher knocked loudly, twice, as was the tradition, then opened it with a bold sweep, announcing, 'All rise!'

As everyone stood, silent, Jupp walked past the screened-off area for vulnerable witnesses, revelling in the expectant atmosphere, the same as at the start of every major case. It often felt to him similar to the moment the curtain rose at the start of a play, and indeed in his view, to some considerable extent, court cases *were* theatre. Both in the antiquated costumes worn by some of the players, and the fact that many barristers were, in secret, frustrated actors.

But courts were theatres where, unlike make-believe tragedies such as *Hamlet*, the bodies on the stage were often all too real. A theatre where, when the final curtain descended, there were no bows. Just the grim reality of the sometimes-crushing verdict. Theatre in which a legally innocent person – at the time of the trial – might be fighting for their reputation, career and liberty.

As was the defendant facing him now, in the enclosed glass dock, accompanied by a security guard. A short, harmless-looking man, wearing a blue suit, white shirt and dark tie – no doubt as instructed by his barrister, Jupp thought with a smile. Ensuring clients dressed in a manner to make them look as innocent as possible was something he had always emphasized during his time at the Bar, when briefing clients for their court appearance. Navy blue was the friendliest suit colour. Theatrical costume, again.

In the front row below Jupp was the formally wigged and gowned prosecutor, Stephen Cork, with his junior, Paul Williams, behind. The other side of the court there was Primrose Brown QC, and her junior, Crispin Sykes, behind her. A formidable QC from the same Inn of Court as himself, Primrose and he once both belonged to the same chambers. But their friendly acquaintance would play no part in this trial.

Immediately behind them was a suited woman sitting on her own, the Crown Prosecution solicitor, and separated by a wide gap, a woman in her thirties conferring earnestly with a tall, silver fox of a man in his fifties – the defence solicitors. Seated again, all of them on both benches were busy with last-minute preparations, checking through files or jotting notes. And the defence, no doubt, dealing with the late arrival of the financial report.

To Jupp's left were a number of reporters in the press box and, below them, to the side of the dock, the usher was seated, with two police officers in smart business attire behind him – the Senior Investigating Officer who he recognized as DI Glenn Branson and another detective, the Exhibits Officer, one or the other of whom would be present for much of the trial.

Behind the dock was the public gallery, full but not packed, and to Jupp's right were the two empty rows of the jury box, soon to be filled by a motley crew of people who had received their summons and were now here, reluctantly or otherwise, to carry out their civic duty. They sat currently at the rear of the court, with the jury bailiff.

Jupp cast a brief eye over his potential jurors. Fifteen of them waiting, some looking expectant, some nervous, some bored. Twelve, plus three spares in case of valid objections by the defendant. He spent some moments logging on to the computer in front of him, as well as checking his printed notes, before nodding to the clerk to begin the proceedings.

Maureen Sapsed stood up, just below him, and addressed the man in the dock. 'Are you Terence Gready?'

His voice was quiet but calm. 'I am.'

Jupp then said to the clerk, but addressing the whole court, 'May we have the jury panel in, please.'

Meg, along with the other fourteen jurors who had been called, sat waiting. Keeping her fingers crossed that she made the cut. But a little jittery at the same time.

The clerk addressed the defendant again. 'Terence Gready, the names you are about to hear called are the names of the jurors who are to try you. If you wish to object to any of them, you must do so as they come to be sworn, and before they are sworn, and your objections shall be heard.'

Gready gave a single polite nod in response.

Then Jupp addressed the would-be jurors, as he liked to do to help put them at ease. 'Ladies and gentlemen, twelve of you will be selected randomly from the fifteen of you present. When you hear your name called out, answer "yes" and make your way to the jury box.' He pointed to it. 'Fill the front row first and then the rear.'

The jury bailiff, Jacobi Whyte, at the rear of the court, shuffled the fifteen cards he held, each bearing the name of a juror, selected one from the pack and read out the name: 'Sophie Eaton.'

A casually dressed woman in her mid-thirties replied a hesitant 'Yes,' then stood up and walked self-consciously to the box, taking the far end position.

'Edmond O'Reilly Hyland.'

A charismatic man in his fifties, with a big, open face, dressed like a lawyer himself in a chalk-striped three-piece suit, said, 'Yes,' stood up and strode confidently across towards the jury box as if he owned the place.

'Megan Magellan.'

It took her a second to realize it was her name.

She jumped up like a startled rabbit. *No need to be nervous,* she tried to calm herself. *You are here out of civic duty. Relax. Enjoy!* 'Yes,' she said, trying to project, but the word seemed to catch in her throat. She was blushing as she walked the short distance to the jury box, well aware that every eye in the court was on her at this moment.

She took her place next to the man who smelled, not unpleasantly, of aftershave, unsure where to look. She shot a glance first at the judge, who was studying his computer screen, then at the dock at the defendant, a wretched, miserable-looking man who didn't look like he was capable of committing any crime. He caught her sympathetic eye and gave a wan smile back.

The next name was called. 'Hari Singh.'

A tubby Indian man in a smart suit and tie and with a

nervous, almost apologetic smile, made his way to the box, seating himself beside Meg.

Another name was called and an instant later the older woman she had exchanged a smile with earlier sat down on the bench.

'Maisy Waller.'

'Yes.' It came out as a timid squeak. A tight-faced, terrified-looking mouse of a woman in her fifties with limp grey hair and wearing an old-fashioned floral-print summer frock followed, approaching the jury box as if it were a cage full of lions, then almost tiptoed to her place.

Next up was Harold Trout, a rather intellectual-looking man in his early seventies, in a tweed suit and a golf club tie.

The litany of names continued, whilst Meg looked around the court, trying to figure out what the roles were of everyone present, occasionally shooting glances at the dock, but each time quickly looking away as the defendant was staring directly at them. She glanced up at the sea of faces in the nearly full public gallery, almost all of whom were looking down towards her and her fellow jurors. In the front row, she clocked a denim-jacketed, ponytailed man, who looked like a rough diamond, sitting a little stiffly and too far away for her to have noticed the pen clipped to his breast pocket. He seemed to be taking a particularly keen interest in them all, and she wondered if he was perhaps a relative of the defendant.

When the two rows were filled, three potential jurors remained behind, looking like lost little Billy-No-Mates.

Maureen Sapsed then turned to the jury box. 'Members of the jury, the defendant, Terence Arthur Gready, stands charged on this indictment containing six counts.'

She proceeded to read out all of the counts in full, before

pausing for a moment to glance down at her notes. Then she looked at the jury again. 'To each count the defendant has pleaded not guilty, and it is your charge to say, having heard all the evidence, whether he is guilty or not.'

She paused to let this sink in. Then she looked at the three jurors left behind in the selection area. 'Would those remaining jurors who have not been selected please leave now with the jury bailiff.'

There was a brief, expectant silence as they filed out.

Meg looked back at the defendant, who was sitting impassively, staring ahead, with a guard behind him. The dock looked like the loneliest place in the world. It was a very strange feeling being here, being a juror. This wasn't some party game. Over the coming days – weeks – she and the other eleven randoms would be deciding on this man's future. The charges sounded very serious, and no doubt would not have been brought without good reason, she assumed. The trafficking of the drugs particularly revulsed her. But could that mild little man really have been behind all that?

Then she thought about Harold Shipman, the harmless-looking bearded and bespectacled family doctor who was estimated to have murdered over three hundred of his patients. Appearances sure were deceptive.

Richard Jupp studied the twelve jurors in the box, privately assessing them. Eight men and four women. A few of them looked quite bright. One man looked to him like a cop – or a retired one. And the fellow in the suit with the grand name looked like a man used to being in charge. No doubt he would consider he should be the foreman.

He addressed them the way he always did, to try to put them at ease, leaning towards them with a warm, avuncular smile. 'I'd like to welcome you all to the jury,' he said. 'It's you and me who will be trying this case together. The first thing I'd like to say to you, as I see many of you have your pens out, is please do not be distracted by taking notes.'

He paused then went on. 'Of course, some details and timelines will be significant and may be complex, but I'll be doing a thorough summing-up at the end of the trial before you go out to consider your verdict, and you'll have a full recap then. What is important for you as jurors is to concentrate on listening to all the arguments for and against the defence of the man standing in the dock. It is your assessment of the evidence that is crucial. Will you believe the evidence of the prosecution against this man, or the evidence of the defence? You twelve people alone will have to make that decision. I want you to arrive at your decision based on what you see and hear, on body language and on the verbal evidence. I don't want you distracted by feeling you must write down notes – and perhaps in doing so miss something crucial.'

He paused again. 'I do also want to emphasize that, as jurors, you are forbidden to talk about this case to anyone other than your fellow jurors. You must not say a word to your wives, husbands, partners, friends or business colleagues. And you must not attempt to google the defendant. If any of you have any concerns about the trial, if you realize you know the defendant personally, or have had any professional dealings with him, please send me a note via the clerk of the court.'

He stopped to sip a glass of water. 'The most important thing for you as jurors is your eyes and ears. You must watch and assess for yourselves each person giving evidence for or against the defendant. I want to remind you that under English law this man standing before you, accused of these crimes, is currently innocent until – and unless – proved guilty. That is the question for you alone. It is not a question of *maybe* he did it, or even that he *probably* did it. You need to be sure that he committed these offences, in order to convict. So, your role, as fellow human beings, is to assess both the credibility of the defendant and the witnesses both for and against him. I hope that is clear.'

30

'Very clear, Your Honour!' Rio Zambrano said loudly, with a grin.

Sixty miles away from Lewes Crown Court, on the tenth floor of a high-rise office building in Hoxton in East London, Zambrano, a thirty-eight-year-old computer programmer, originally from Quito in Ecuador, sat in front of his large computer screen. He was listening intently to the court proceedings being relayed to him through his headphones by Jeff Pringle's concealed video camera. He had pulled off stills of each of the faces of the twelve jurors, which he saved into individual files.

Beside him sat Paul Constantinidi, a private investigator and disgruntled former Met Police detective who had been forced into early retirement following an accusation – not for the first time – of excessive violence during an arrest. He had been for some months in the lucrative pay of Mickey Starr and, as it appeared now, ultimately the top boss, Terence Gready. Paul Constantinidi had retained many friends within the Met, one of whom was proving particularly helpful in checking the backgrounds of each of the jurors as he relayed them to him, whilst at the same time – along with two techies who ran the county lines network for Starr – doing a google search on each of them.

Juries, if they could not agree a unanimous verdict, could reach a majority verdict as directed by the judge either on an 11–1 or 10–2 basis. If a jury could not agree then they would be discharged by the judge and, in normal circumstances, there would be a retrial. But the clear plan, outlined by Gready's solicitor, Nick Fox, was to do better than that. Much better.

So far three names had produced hits. The first was potentially interesting: Mike Roberts, a retired Hampshire Police Detective Superintendent and former Senior Investigating Officer on the Major Crime Team. A stocky, silver-haired man of sixty-two, who left the police a decade ago as part of the government's A19 programme. Highly unpopular, it had forced officers to retire at thirty years' service, regardless of their rank or experience, to be replaced with new recruits, so the government could claim the salary saving and at the same time claim they had kept police numbers up. He could be a potential, Paul Constantinidi thought. An aggrieved former cop, like himself?

The second was an obese guy, Hugo Pink. His search showed that he was in deep financial trouble. Definitely a potential target. Terence Gready would be more than happy to bail him out.

The third was very interesting. A forty-two-year-old widow, Meg Magellan. Her husband and teenage son had been killed in a car crash five years ago. Now her teenage daughter, Laura, was on her gap year, backpacking through South America, and from her latest posts, currently near Quito, in Ecuador.

He turned to Rio. 'You must have friends back in Ecuador?'

'Sure, many. Why?'

Paul Constantinidi nodded. 'Good to know. Might be useful.'

31

In the court, Richard Jupp gave the jurors another *we're all in this together* smile of reassurance and silently hoped that was the case. Then he shot a glance at the defendant. Terence Gready sat behind the glass shield, all nicely shaven, with his neat blue suit and butter-wouldn't-melt-in-his-mouth expression. *Wrongfully accused. Fitted-up. The police getting their own back on the legal profession. Only the flimsiest circumstantial evidence to link him to any of the crimes for which he was standing trial.*

Jupp had read through all the documents, every word. He'd read the evidence stacked against the accused solicitor and studied the defence's arguments. He was confident Stephen Cork, the prosecutor, would drive a coach and horses through those.

He gave Gready, who was staring, deadpan, straight ahead, another quick look. The man disgusted him. Not only a traitor to his profession but actually, in doing what he was accused of, in many ways a traitor to his country. In Jupp's view, laws were the glue that held civilized society together. When legal practitioners perverted them, they were committing a far worse sin than lining their pockets through greed. They were threatening the very fabric of the nation they fed off. They were like leeches that attached themselves to their host.

That leech in the dock, Jupp had a feeling, by the time this court had finished with him, would not be harming anyone again for very many years. With luck, maybe even forever. Just so long as, he hoped fervently, this wasn't going to turn out to be a jury dominated by numpties.

32

Roy Grace was hoping he would get a bright, attentive jury, and not a bunch of numpties, too. Next week, Brighton's biggest ever serial killer, family doctor Edward Crisp, was in Court 2 at Lewes Crown Court facing seven counts of murder and a host of other offences. From all he had done, the doctor deserved never to see the outside of a prison cell again. And Grace was determined to make sure that happened.

As part of the pre-trial preparations, he had called a meeting at Sussex Police HQ to discuss aspects of the evidence with key members of his team, Norman Potting and Jack Alexander, who were assisting him as case officers. Alexander was not required at court for the Terence Gready trial yet – he had been excluded at the request of the defence, as he was giving evidence against the suspect.

The three of them were seated at the conference table on the first floor of the Major Crime wing discussing a variety of responsibilities. The top of which on Grace's list was security, because the wily doctor, in his late fifties, had a past history of cunning escapes from custody.

Roy Grace had been Crisp's arresting officer – nearly losing a leg in the process thanks to being shot by the doctor – so this was personal. For Crisp's trial, as SIO, he needed to ensure the Exhibits Officer was set up and that the Family Liaison Officers were working with the agencies to support all of Crisp's surviving victims and the families of the deceased. He wasn't leaving anything to chance.

He checked with the two detectives about the witnesses the prosecution counsel intended calling to give live evidence, and that all of them were ready. One of their key prosecution witnesses was a plucky lady called Logan Somerville, who had very luckily survived being abducted and imprisoned by Dr Crisp. Another was forensic archaeologist Lucy Sibun.

'Boss, don't forget Bobby the dog, who's going to present the bitemark and DNA evidence,' Alexander said.

They all laughed. But, as they well knew, it had been Bobby's barking that had saved another victim's life, and his bitemark that gave them the breakthrough DNA evidence identifying Crisp.

Grace moved on to the subject of court security. Edward Crisp was one of the most devious criminals he had ever encountered, a man who would have given the legendary Harry Houdini a run for his money. Crisp had a mole-like ability to tunnel his way out of captivity. His sumptuous home in Brighton was riddled with secret passages he had dug. And after evading captivity by Sussex Police and fleeing to France, he had again escaped from a high-security prison near Lyon.

Crisp would be appearing before a High Court judge who was visiting Lewes Crown Court to hear this important trial. Due to the case involving multiple deaths, the criminal justice system required such a figure to preside over the hearing.

Court 3, where the dock was inside a glass enclosure, was already in session. Court 2, where Crisp's case was listed, had an antiquated open dock. Defendants had escaped from this court's dock before, and once out of the courtroom there were only a couple of security staff, who would be too preoccupied checking people coming in to prevent any absconder from running out into the busy street and away. Short of bringing the doctor in chained with manacles – which his defence counsel would never have allowed – the court security would be hardly adequate at best, with just two security staff in the dock with Crisp – and that worried Grace.

33

A modern, neat-but-soulless red-brick housing estate, opposite a garage, on the outskirts of Chichester. Carer Denise Clafferty, doing her daily round, rang the doorbell of number 23, a small three-bedroom detached house, dropping in on sweet Stuie Starr.

The thirty-eight-year-old, with Down's Syndrome, had been living on his own for nearly six months since his brother had been arrested and was currently in prison on remand, awaiting sentencing. Stuie couldn't understand why his brother hadn't come home since travelling to Germany to collect a car, a Ferrari that Stuie had been excited to see.

Every day when Denise visited him, to check on his welfare and the state of the house, Stuie persistently asked her the same question: 'Is Mickey coming home today?' Then he would add, proudly, 'We are starting a fish and chip shop!'

Some days, the way he said it broke her heart. She had tried to explain that it would not be for a while, to manage his expectations, but nothing she said could dim his sunny enthusiasm. Every day when he opened the door, he was all smiles for an instant, all expectant, then he would burst into tears when he saw it was her – or on occasions one of her co-workers – and not his brother.

At least the trial of Terence Gready, Mickey's alleged co-conspirator, was now under way. Sentencing was just weeks off. Hopefully the judge would take into consideration that Mickey Starr had pleaded guilty, that he'd already served six months and that he had a brother who needed him.

There was no response to her ring.

She rang again. Waited.

Still no response. Unusual. Normally, Stuie opened the door within seconds. He had been coping pretty well, ordering his groceries and essentials and getting them delivered, and he kept the house scrupulously, obsessively tidy. For Mickey, he said.

Maybe he was on the loo, she wondered. Or asleep. She rang again and waited. Several minutes passed. She glanced at her watch. Another six appointments today. Reluctantly, using the key she had – much preferring for his self-esteem for him to let her in himself – she unlocked the front door and entered.

'Stuie!' she called out.

Silence greeted her.

A silence she did not like.

'Stuie! It's Denise!' she called.

There was no response.

'Stuie, OK if I come in?'

She waited for some moments, then closed the front door behind her. 'Stuie?'

The silence made her uncomfortable.

'Stuie? You OK?'

There was a handful of post on the floor. Ignoring it, she walked through into the kitchen-dining area and saw what looked like the remains of breakfast on the table. Stuie always left the kitchen immaculate in preparation, he told her, for the fish and chip restaurant he was starting with his brother.

'Stuie?' she called out again. 'Stuie, it's Denise!' She peered out through the window at the small, neat rear garden but there was no sign of him out there.

She went through into the lounge. The television was on, the sound low, a presenter she vaguely recognized standing on a cliff in a stunningly scenic location, talking earnestly to camera about erosion.

She went out and stood at the foot of the stairs. 'Stuie!' she called out. 'Stuie! Are you up there? It's me, Denise!'

No response.

'I'm coming upstairs, Stuie, is that OK?'

She waited, then climbed up the short steep staircase and stood on the landing. Three doors were closed and a fourth was slightly ajar. She called out his name yet again. And again, no response.

She pushed on the door that was ajar and peered in. Stuie, in a T-shirt and tracksuit bottoms, was curled up in a foetal position on the floor, beside the bed. The room looked like a bomb had detonated. A chair was upended and half the duvet was on the floor. The dressing-table mirror was smashed. One of the curtains had been pulled off and the rail hung down at a lopsided angle.

She ran across to Stuie and looked down. His hair, and the white rug on which his head lay, skewed sideways, were soaked with blood. There was blood on the walls and ceiling. His right arm was at a strange angle and his hand was covered in blood, too. She knelt and felt his wrist for a pulse.

Shaking, she stood up, backed away a few paces, looking wildly around, then pulled her phone out of her bag and dialled 999.

34

It wasn't since his more junior days that Roy Grace had been among the first to arrive at a murder scene. Mostly, as head of the Surrey and Sussex Major Crime Team, by the time he got there, the well-oiled machinery was well under way.

This was the case now, as he approached the modern, bland red-brick housing estate, across the road from a garage, on the outskirts of the historic cathedral city of Chichester. The familiar assortment of marked and unmarked police vehicles, the large, square CSI truck, the cordon of blue-and-white police tape, and the usual cluster of media, the curious and the ghouls gathered beyond it.

For many, it would have been a profoundly disturbing sight. But not for the ones holding up their phone cameras, snapping and videoing away. Much though he disliked them – and much though he did not want to admit it – he was a bit of a ghoul himself. Murder fascinated him and always had, like all of his colleagues in Major Crime – he wouldn't be doing this job if it didn't.

The one thing that separated him from the onlookers was his reason for being here – and at any murder scene. It was both a privilege and a heavy burden. To do all he could to deliver justice to the victims and closure to their loved ones.

Norman Potting, who was temporarily in the role of Acting Detective Inspector for this case, parked their unmarked Mondeo estate at the rear of the cavalcade. They walked round to the boot and Grace opened it. As he did so, he noticed something silent, high up in the sky towards the edge of the city. A glider. He nodded at it. 'Ever done that?'

Potting craned his neck. 'Gliding?'

'Always looks so beautiful. Must be amazing, to be up there in total silence. Like sailing without the waves.'

His colleague looked dubious. 'A plane without an engine? Not for me, chief. Not sure I'd want to be at the mercy of updraughts, downdraughts, thermals, or whatever they call them. Like riding a horse – did that once and it scared the shit out of me. I don't like anything that doesn't have an ignition switch and a brake pedal.'

'Thought you were a farm boy. Didn't you grow up in rural Devon?'

'Arable, we didn't have livestock other than pets, a few hens and some pigs. Pigs are all right and a lot safer than horses.'

'Unless you're the wrong end of a Mafia hit and get fed to them?' Grace said with a grin as he reached in and opened his go-bag, pulling out his protective suit, overshoes and gloves.

'Pigs,' Potting said. 'They're very efficient. If I was going to murder someone that's what I'd do, chop 'em into bits and feed 'em to pigs.'

'Remind me never to get on the wrong side of you, Norman.'

Potting nodded, thoughtfully. 'Very wise, chief.'

A few minutes later, attired all in blue outer clothing, they made their way across to the scene guard, ignoring a few shouted questions. They signed the log and greeted the

Crime Scene Manager, Alex Call, who had come out to meet them, along with DC John Alldridge, who had been the first Major Crime Team officer at the scene.

'What do we have?' Grace asked the two men.

'It's not pretty, boss,' tall, burly Alldridge said, leading them under the second tape cordon across the front door. 'A thirty-eight-year-old man with Down's Syndrome – looks like he's been beaten and kicked to death.'

Grace saw the post and mail shots scattered on the floor. He knelt and glanced at the name that was on all the letters. *Michael Starr.* He frowned. Over to his right, through an open door, he heard the sound of a television. A voice he recognized, the presenter Angela Rippon, talking about a consumer issue.

'Who've you got here, Alex?' he asked Call.

'A POLSA and four search officers doing a finger-tip search in the gardens and pathways, James Gartrell is doing the photographs and video,' the CSM replied. 'Two CSIs checking for prints and DNA in the house, but excluding where the body was found. The Home Office pathologist should be here in the next hour – he wants to see the body in situ before it's moved to the mortuary.'

'Any early indicators of the time of death?' Roy Grace watched a search officer through a downstairs window, in protective clothing and blue gloves, inching forward on her hands and knees across the main garden path.

'It was called in at 11 a.m. by his carer – Denise Clafferty, from social services. She normally visits every day to check on him, make sure he's looking after himself and hasn't done anything careless like leaving the gas on. But for once, she didn't come yesterday because of a family emergency.'

'He's got Down's Syndrome but lived on his own?' Grace quizzed.

'He lived with his brother, who looked out for him, but the brother was nicked last November and has been on remand in Lewes ever since.'

'Mickey Starr?' Grace asked.

Call nodded. 'Yes.'

'Glenn's case,' Potting added, helpfully.

'Does Glenn know, Norman?' Grace asked.

'Shall I tell him, chief?'

'Yes.'

Pulling out his phone, Potting stepped outside. Grace and Call went up the stairs, across a short landing into a bedroom, where a scene of utter devastation greeted them.

The room was totally trashed, items of furniture upturned and the curtains torn down. Blood spatters all over the walls and carpet – and even the ceiling. The victim, in a T-shirt, tracksuit bottoms and trainers, lay like a fallen sack on the floor, his head on what must have been a white rug but was now mostly red from the massive wound at the rear of his head. It had stained his thinning fair hair. His face had been beaten – or kicked – into an unrecognizable pulp. There was more blood across his white T-shirt on which a legend was printed.

Grace read the words, with a lump in his throat.

DOWN'S SYNDROME AWARENESS!
I'M A HOMIE WITH AN EXTRA CHROMIE!

Poor bloody sod, he thought, anger welling up inside him. Who had done this? What bastards could have come in here and done this – to such a vulnerable person?

His mind was spinning. Was there a connection with his brother being in prison? All his experience and instinct told him there must be. He turned to the Crime Scene Manager. 'Any idea how they got in, Alex?'

'No, sir. None of the door locks were forced and there are no broken windows. The victim must have opened the front door and let his killers in.'

Grace nodded. 'That fits with what I know about Down's Syndrome from a previous case – some years ago. They are lovely, trusting people. He'd have probably opened the door and welcomed them in.'

'So why would anyone have wanted to kill him?' Call asked.

'His brother's on remand, charged with one of the biggest drug importations in Sussex history. Maybe his associates or rivals came here looking for cash or drugs and got surprised by Stuie?'

Grace paused, thinking, looking down at the body that was like a broken, bleeding rag doll. 'If they were surprised by him, Alex, they might have knocked him out or tied him up. Why would they have done this?'

'I agree with you, sir. This isn't how you'd deal with someone who surprised you.'

Grace shook his head. 'No, it isn't. This was savage, way over the top.'

'Do you think they might have killed him to stop him from identifying them?' Call ventured.

'Possibly, Alex. That's one hypothesis. But maybe there was something else going on.'

Grace turned and looked out of the window, which overlooked a small, fenced-in garden, with a recently mown lawn and a shed at the far end. There was a basketball net on a post, with a white ball lying in the grass.

He walked across the room, over the landing and into the room opposite, which was a similar size. The bed sloppily made, the counterpane pulled over unevenly. On the bedside table sat the memoirs of Muhammad Ali. On a shelf was a row of books on boxing, and a photograph of a man in his late twenties in a boxing ring, gloves raised, head down. Hanging from a hook on the wall opposite was a pair of boxing gloves.

Grace went back out and into a third, much smaller room which appeared to be a den. There was a laptop dock on a table, with an ergonomic chair pulled up to it. Below was a set of drawers. Nothing in here looked like it had been touched. Next, he went into the bathroom. Two towels lay on the floor, another was draped over the side of the bath. The showerhead lay in the bath, at the end of its metal hose.

What had been cleaned up in here? Or who?

He went downstairs and checked out the kitchen, noticing a plate with congealed egg on it and a partly drunk mug of tea, then the little dining room and the living room, where he noticed a tall, empty glass jar on the coffee table. It stood a good two feet high and was at least six inches in diameter. He wondered what it was for. Then, as he looked around, he realized. There was a photograph of Stuie and another male, probably his brother, he assumed, as there were other photographs of this person in the house. They were standing behind this same jar, which was crammed to the brim with banknotes. There must have been hundreds, possibly even thousands of pounds in it. The money had gone. A laptop, an amount of cash. Burglars?

And suddenly, Roy Grace realized what it was he had missed the most during the past six months in the Met. Much of his work there had been about policy and politics, with the occasional adrenaline rushes, chasing and catching small-time villains and getting them off the streets. But they were nothing compared to the mental challenge of a murder scene. Especially not a potentially high-profile one like this.

35

At 6 p.m., in the conference room of the Major Crime suite, Roy Grace addressed his small, hastily assembled team around the oval table. They included Jon Exton, Norman Potting, John Alldridge, Emma-Jane Boutwood, the Crime Scene Manager, Alex Call, as well as an indexer, a new HOLMES analyst, Luke Stanstead, and joining them for this investigation, a local community officer, Kerry Foy.

'This is the first briefing of Operation Canoe, the investigation into the murder of Stuart – Stuie – Robert Starr, in the house owned by his brother, Michael Starr,' Grace said. 'DS Alexander is currently attending the postmortem on Stuie Starr at St Richard's Hospital, Chichester, and we will have more information in the morning. As we know, Stuie's brother is currently on remand in Lewes Prison, having pleaded guilty to a number of offences relating to the importation of six million pounds' worth of cocaine through Newhaven Port on November 26th last year, together with other drugs offences.'

He pointed at a group of three whiteboards in front of the flat-screen, wall-mounted monitor. On one were several photographs taken by a crime scene photographer, showing Stuie Starr on the floor, and the blood around him. Two other photographs showed the trashed state of his bedroom.

The second whiteboard showed a photograph of Mickey Starr along with a series of photographs of the Ferrari being dismantled in the Newhaven Customs shed. Pinned to the third was a family tree of the Starr family and, next to it, an association chart. Grace stood up and walked over to the whiteboards.

First, he talked his team through the visible injuries inflicted on Stuie, working from what he had witnessed himself at the crime scene, and from the preliminary thoughts of the pathologist. Next, he pointed at the photograph of Mickey Starr, making reference to his past history as a suspected drug dealer, arrested but then subsequently released on appeal due to a chain of evidence issue. Grace made it clear that although he had been acquitted by a clever brief, in the view of the police, back then, there was no doubting the man's culpability. He then went on to the family tree and the association charts. Both were fairly threadbare.

'The big question is why Stuie Starr was killed,' he said. 'It is possible that this was a random house burglary gone wrong. Whilst at the scene I noticed a jar that I believe may have contained a substantial sum in banknotes, and it appears a laptop is also missing. There were signs of a ransacking type search. But, despite these indications of a burglary, I think we need to look deeper. What reason would anyone have for harming a thirty-eight-year-old with Down's Syndrome?' Grace paused. 'Pure sadistic pleasure – or some other, darker reason? I am looking at a connection to Glenn's large drugs case. Particularly at Mickey Starr's alleged co-conspirator, Terence Gready.

'Let's say Mickey Starr has enough evidence to completely kibosh Gready's defence. Mickey Starr has already pleaded guilty to get a reduced sentence. If I was Terence

Gready and – pure supposition – Mickey Starr was my wingman, I'd be worried about him making a deal with the prosecution.'

Potting frowned. 'Good point.'

'And . . . if I was Terence Gready on trial and facing incarceration for a good chunk of the rest of my life, I'd bust anyone's balls to get off the charges. Whatever it took.'

Potting nodded. 'If I'm reading you correctly, chief, you are suggesting that Stuie Starr might have been murdered on Terence Gready's instructions?'

'Exactly,' Grace replied. 'My primary hypothesis is this: could Terence Gready have become worried about his colleague, friend, right-hand man – Michael Starr – doing a plea bargain of some kind against him? Gready arranges to put the frighteners on Starr by having his brother roughed up a bit? And the thugs he hired went a bit too far? There is evidence of a burglary, but was that staged to throw us off the scent? I can't see any other reason why a seemingly harmless man like Stuie should be so brutally attacked. Do you have any ideas?'

'Except,' EJ chipped in, 'in our sick modern world, it could be someone or a group targeting Stuie because of who he is. There have been cases here where teens have targeted and attacked vulnerable people, usually with tragic consequences.'

'What about a revenge attack?' Jon Exton suggested. 'And it was mistaken identity?'

Grace nodded. 'It's another possibility, Jon. But if it's a revenge attack on Mickey for some past quarrel, I doubt from these photos anyone could mistake his brother, Stuie, for him, and besides, everyone would know Mickey is in prison.' Thinking hard, he noted down *Kids* in his Policy Book. But he doubted that was the scenario here.

The dead man's brother had pleaded guilty to very serious drugs importation charges on a scale rarely encountered in Sussex. His – as yet unproven – associate Terence Gready was currently on trial for his part in those offences of drug importation and distribution. The two men were suspected of running a major county lines distribution network. The masterminds of these networks were brutal people. They would stoop as low as it took, and they were operating in waters teeming with rivals. They could have any number of enemies, all after the same lucrative business. And any of these, knowing the two men were currently out of action, might be behind the break-in. Stuie could simply have been collateral damage. Getting in the way of their search of the house.

Could it be that whoever had done this had gone into the house to look for cash, or drugs, or maybe even Starr's contacts list, and had been disturbed by Stuie? They'd had a fight with him and then, when they realized he was dead, they did a runner, in panic? He wrote that down too, as a third hypothesis.

'Is there any CCTV in the area of this house?' he asked the team.

'The nearest was on a garage forecourt opposite, but we don't know yet if it was actually working,' EJ said. 'We've been running an ANPR check on all vehicles picked up within twenty-four hours prior to the discovery of the body, but so far nothing. We can extend that time frame if necessary. We've also carried out a house-to-house, but so far nothing from any of the neighbours.'

'I see.' In his mind, Roy Grace intended to make his first priority to look for any evidence that might implicate Terence Gready orchestrating the attack on Stuie Starr. He would have known where to find him.

EJ continued. 'Apparently the two brothers kept a very low profile. They have one neighbour, an elderly lady, who regularly kept an eye on Stuie whenever Mickey was away. She looked in on him yesterday morning around 9 a.m. before going out for the day. She may well have been the last person to see him alive.'

'Away for the day, of course she was,' Grace said, sounding more cynical than he had intended. But throughout his career in homicide investigation, it seemed that a gremlin was constantly at work, ensuring that the one key potential witness was always otherwise engaged at the crucial moment. He smiled, not wanting to give the impression to the team that he was a tired old cynic.

And hoping, privately, that he really wasn't.

'I plan to hold a press conference tomorrow and make a public appeal for any witnesses to come forward. I will make sure they understand the vulnerability of the victim and the truly horrendous nature of this crime.'

'Playing the emotional card, are we, chief?'

'Yes, Norman, the bastards who did this to poor Stuie didn't hold anything back. Neither will I.'

36

Friday 10 May

In the tenth-floor office of the building in Hoxton, with venetian blinds permanently angled so no one could see in from any of the buildings opposite, twelve whiteboards lined the walls.

Attached to them now were photographs of each of the jurors in Terence Gready's trial, along with growing details of their home and workplace addresses, a brief bio, names of close family members and known associates, interests and details of car driven, if any.

The whiteboards were getting increasingly covered in names and information as more research results came in from the team of Rio Zambrano, the former Met detective, Paul Constantinidi, and the two techies.

Constantinidi glanced at his watch. Coming up to mid-day. So far there had been no activity involving the jurors since they'd been sworn in. The prosecution and defence counsel were locked in legal dispute.

At close of play yesterday, the judge had sent them home for the weekend so the counsels for the prosecution and defence could clear the deck of any legal arguments. The trial would start in earnest on Monday.

It gave Constantinidi and his team useful extra time and they were making the best of it, assembling very detailed information. He read through the whiteboards, checking for any updates he might have missed.

Juror no. 1: *Sophie Eaton.* A streaky blonde, thirty-six-year-old specialist nurse. Quite a thoughtful-looking young woman.

Difficult to read this one and he had already decided Juror no. 1 could be too principled and dangerous. A large black cross had been marked on the board.

Juror no. 2: *Hugo Pink.* A portly, self-assured-looking man in his late forties, with a foppish hairstyle much too young for him. Married twenty-three years. Two children, late teens. His only social media presence appeared to be a Facebook page in the name of his company, Pink Solar Systems.

A former mobile phone salesman, Pink had cashed in on the growing demand for solar energy. His sales patter was obliging his customers to help save the world. Their research showed the company was in dire straits and was heading for bankruptcy. Terence Gready would gladly bank-roll them out of trouble. Definite potential. A tick was on his board.

Juror no. 3: *Megan Magellan.* Definite potential also. Currently top of his list. The forty-two-year-old widow. Nice-looking, too, not that there was a huge chance she was going to jump in the sack with him. But there was more work to be done, more due diligence on Meg Magellan – and she was not the only one with potential. He just needed to be beyond 100 per cent certain that when they made their move on any of them, they would capitulate. There would be no second chance.

If they misjudged the integrity of a juror and that person either informed the clerk of the court or sent a note to the judge, it would be game over. Any attempt at nobbling a juror that came to the judge's attention would result, instantly, in one of two situations, both equally bad. The first would be a new jury which would be sequestered at nights and weekends in a hotel, under close guard and scrutiny for the duration of the trial, and with no communication with the outside world. The second, if the prosecution counsel could make a suitably convincing case, would be that the trial be heard by the judge alone without a jury.

Juror no. 4: *Maisy Waller. Miss Drabby*, Paul Constantinidi thought. A timid creature, fifty-four years old, with thin, tight lips. Lived alone in the Portslade area of Brighton and Hove with her elderly mother who was suffering from dementia. Worked as a payroll clerk for a local insurance company. No social media engagement. Member of a book group. A volunteer at a charity for the homeless. A question mark on her board.

Juror no. 5: *Rory O'Brien*. Thirty years old. Born in Ireland. Single. Geeky-looking with shouty glasses, wearing a blue jumper over a grey shirt and chinos. Project manager. Marathon runner. Member of a happy-clappy charismatic church. On a variety of social media, regularly posting contrary political views. Trouble written all over him. A black cross against his name.

Juror no. 6: *Harold Trout*. Seventy-one years old. Married thirty-seven years. Four children. Seven grandchildren. Resided in Hove. Retired insurance actuary. Rotarian. Former local golf club captain. Weakness: limited at this stage.

Juror no. 7: *Mike Roberts*. The retired, silver-haired, distinguished former Hampshire Police Detective Superintendent, who he had already studied with some interest, as a potentially aggrieved former cop, like himself. But risky. All the same, he warranted a question mark.

He continued on through the list, which included an actor called Toby DeWinter, a posh middle-class do-gooder, an Uber driver called Mark Adams, an Indian chef, and finally the property developer Edmond O'Reilly Hyland. All of them needing more research. By late afternoon he had come up with a plan. Five names of potentials that he would discuss this evening when he met up for dinner with Nick Fox, in a secluded room they had booked in a private members' club in Mayfair. Fox had briefed him at the start that among the jurors they needed to find one who was a sure-fire *banker*.

He was pretty confident he had identified just that person.

37

A briefing room at Chichester police station was being used for the press conference. Roy Grace sat in the centre of a row of chairs that had been placed facing the healthy turnout of local media that he had anticipated, flanked on his right by the local district commander, Chief Inspector Emily Souders, and on his left, PC Kerry Foy, the community officer; to her left sat Tony Morgan from the Sussex Police comms team.

In the two rows of chairs facing them were Siobhan Sheldrake from the *Argus*, as well as reporters he recognized from the *West Sussex Gazette*, the *Chichester Observer*, the *Bognor Regis Post*, Radio Sussex and Radio Solent, a camera operator and presenter from Meridian TV, and a student reporter from the Southampton media school.

Some police officers, in Grace's experience, viewed all press and media with suspicion and hostility. But he had always found that if you handled them in the right way, far from being the enemy they could be not only a good ally, but could play a key role in getting that vital public engagement. And right now, when all their investigations had so far drawn a blank on Operation Canoe, hopefully today's conference might just lead to a member of the public coming forward with a piece of information that could unlock the puzzle.

He began with a restrained smile, friendly but serious. 'Thank you all for attending today, we are hoping, through your coverage, you may be able to help us solve a very nasty crime. Stuie Starr was a thirty-eight-year-old man with Down's Syndrome, who shared his home with his brother, Michael, who is currently on remand in Lewes Prison.' He coughed to clear a frog from his throat.

'By all accounts, Stuie was a sweet, trusting man, who loved everyone he met and had one dream, which was to run a fish and chip shop with his brother. Yesterday, local police were called to a house, at 23 Smithgreen Lane, Chichester, following a call from Stuie's carer, who looked in on him daily to check he was all right. They found his body, very savagely beaten, with multiple injuries including kicks to his head – a number of which, according to the pathologist's report, were inflicted with sufficient violence to have been fatal on their own.' He paused to clear the frog again.

'I do really want to emphasize the savageness of this murder. There is no indication Stuie put up any defence – this was an act of gratuitous violence against someone we believe had no enemies. The time of this attack is estimated at somewhere between the morning of Wednesday the 8th of May and the following morning. We are keeping an open mind on the motive, but we are aware his brother is currently awaiting sentence on drugs charges. We are also aware that property may have gone missing from the house, so one of our key lines of enquiry relates to whether the motive was burglary.'

Grace paused again, then continued. 'If this was burglary, we are considering whether it might have been opportunist thieves who did not realize the house was occupied, or whether whoever did this was searching for a cache of drugs or cash. We believe this attack was the work of at least two people. Stuie's home was just off a busy main road and opposite a garage. Someone must have seen the perpetrators arriving or leaving. I'm appealing for anyone who was in the area at the relevant time to come forward. You might just have seen something you did not think was significant at the time. Were you driving or cycling through this area with a dashboard or helmet-mounted camera? Or walking past?

'I want to stress that Stuie Starr was an extremely vulnerable man. If this *was* a burglary, the level of violence was completely disproportionate and unnecessary, and we are looking at the actions of at least two callous and sadistic individuals who put no value on human life. I would now like to introduce my colleague, PC Kerry Foy, to talk about the community impact of this murder.'

Foy, a short, friendly-looking officer with an empathetic nature, said, 'I knew Stuie and often saw him around. He was well known in the local community and loved by everyone. He often attended local events, and he was always dressed in his trademark T-shirt emblazoned with the legend I'M A HOMIE WITH AN EXTRA CHROMIE, or else in one of his chef outfits. He was friendly to everyone – I just cannot imagine why anyone would have wanted to harm him.' She glanced down at her notes. 'Until the offenders have been apprehended, I would ask the local community to be extra vigilant over locking their doors and who they let into their homes. But I would like to stress we believe this is very likely to be an isolated incident and that risk to the community at large is low.' She turned to Chief Inspector Souders.

The District Commander nodded. 'I have to agree with PC Foy. It makes no sense that anyone would have wanted to harm such a warm and loving person. It is my strong view that in all likelihood this was a one-off attack, carried out by villains who knew that Stuie's brother was in prison, and who may have been looking for drugs and cash. However, I have put extra patrols and a visible police presence in the area. And I would like to reiterate that Chichester is a safe place to live and work.'

'We'll now take a few questions,' Roy Grace said.

Several hands immediately shot up. Siobhan Sheldrake called out to Emily Souders. 'Commander?'

'Yes?' she answered.

'You've just said the perpetrators might have been looking for cash or drugs concealed in the house. Are you implying that the police team who must have carried out a thorough search of the house after the brother's arrest might have missed these?'

Roy Grace stepped in quickly with a reply. 'The search team were highly professional and experienced and it is highly unlikely they would have missed anything of significance following Michael Starr's arrest. The point being made is that if this was a burglary, the offenders were clearly ignorant of the depth of search that would have been done.' He shot a glance at Souders.

She nodded. 'That is correct.'

Another voice shouted out, the reporter from the *West Sussex Gazette*. 'Detective Superintendent, do you have any suspects?'

'We are working on a number of leads but at this time, no, we have no prime suspects. But we are confident we will find the offenders and bring them to justice.'

He fielded a number of further questions, then brought the conference to a close. 'I would like to again thank you all for attending, and to remind you that how you report this could, ultimately, be the make or break in bringing these vile people to justice. Someone will know something or have seen something. Anyone with basic human decency must be repulsed by this attack. I would request that you publicize the number of the Incident Room from the sheets you have been given and stress that alternatively they can call Crimestoppers, in complete anonymity, the number of which is also on the sheet. Thank you again.'

Along with the others, Grace hurried out of the room, then followed Souders along to her office for a quick debrief. He was, as usual after press conferences, sodden with perspiration, knowing he had done his best, but aware, as always, he could probably have done better.

38

Friday 10 May

For some inmates, spartan though it was, prison was home, a way of life. They had their friends, three meals a day, television and their board and lodging all found – and jobs within the prison where they earned pin money. Many of those persistent reoffenders considered the times when they were released on licence to be their holiday. Freedom to do drugs, sell drugs and shag. Then back inside again until the next time.

A smaller minority – much smaller – used their time to learn a trade or craft, or even to read and write – with the intention of going straight once they were released. And an even smaller – depressingly small – percentage would succeed in doing just that.

But many lived in morose silence, relieving the boredom by working out, body-building, doing drugs, or just drifting around, sometimes in the library, sometimes anywhere. Thinking. Sometimes daydreaming.

The common factor for most of them was the numbing tedium. *Doing time* was the right expression. Waiting for time to pass. Welcoming any distraction, however small – a phone call, a visit, a work-out, when they weren't confined to their cell for days on end because of a shortage of prison officers.

Mickey Starr, in Lewes Prison, was in his third consecutive day of being locked in his cell this week, due to staff shortages, and was literally going up the wall with frustration, most of all because this prevented him from making his daily phone call to Stuie. And neither he nor his cellmate had been able to have a shower or a change of clothes for three days.

The previous occasion he had been in prison was eighteen years ago, after being arrested and convicted for possession and dealing cannabis on Brighton's seafront, down under the Arches. His then solicitor had turned up one day and told him about an associate, Terence Gready, whom he had never met, who 'knew people inside the police'.

Gready had offered him a deal. He could get him acquitted on appeal with the help of a bent detective who would testify that the chain of evidence was unsafe. This happened and Starr walked free. He developed a relationship with Gready over the next eighteen months and one day Gready told him he wanted to make him an offer. Partly in return, but also because he needed someone he could trust, Starr would work for Gready as his trusted confidant in the various drug operations that he was looking to set up.

It had been the start of a friendship – and bond – between the two men. Starr had trusted Gready implicitly ever since. And despite his current predicament, he still had faith that the legal team would pull some kind of a rabbit from a hat and get him out of this shit.

But he had been here now six months and there was no sign of it yet. Gready was himself in the dock and Mickey knew that part of Gready's defence was that there was no connection at all between the two of them and that they did not know each other.

It was both Nick Fox's team and the barrister he had got him, who had advised him – out of kindness to him and Stuie – that if he pleaded guilty, he would get a lesser sentence and be reunited with Stuie sooner. So long as Mickey kept up his story that there was no connection between him and Gready, it would be fine.

Mickey knew how stressed his brother always was when he was away, and couldn't imagine quite how Stuie was feeling with him being absent for this length of time. He was desperate to get out and carry on doing what he had done before his arrest, giving his little brother the best life he could.

And prison was even more shit since the smoking ban had come into effect. In the daytime, anyhow. After evening lockdown he shared cigarettes, which he got on the prison black market, with his cellmate.

Mickey had always been a good listener and was helping the poor sod, Charles Nelson – a posh guy of twenty-nine, an insurance broker who'd been privately educated and never in trouble with the law before – to cope with the nightmare he was currently living through. Nelson was in bits, facing a potential life sentence for one stupid, drunken moment.

Six months previously, Nelson had been with his girl-friend in a bar in Brighton, late night, after a dinner out to celebrate a bonus much bigger than he had been expecting, when another drunken guy had hit on her. Nelson had remonstrated and received a punch for his troubles, which somehow, according to him, had been missed on the bar's CCTV. In return he'd decked the guy, who had struck the back of his head on a table on the way down. And died.

Charles Nelson, facing a manslaughter charge, was now

on remand in prison and was looking at probably four to six years' imprisonment, and he wasn't even sure that his girlfriend, whose honour he'd been trying to defend, was still there for him. Her visits were becoming less and less frequent.

The two of them smoked and talked every night in the semi-darkness. With frequent interruptions while his friend just sobbed. They also talked about Stuie. Mickey told Nelson of his plans to open a fish and chip shop, with his brother working in the back room, mostly preparing the fish and slicing the potatoes. It turned out, to Mickey's surprise, that Charles Nelson had recently inherited a property on Brighton seafront, close to the Palace Pier, with three shops on the ground floor. One of them was vacant – if Mickey wanted it after his release, he was sure they could agree a deal.

Finally, today, the days of lockdown came to an end. Just as he'd returned to his cell having eaten breakfast and was about to head off to his current job in the prison laundry, one of the more pleasant screws appeared in the doorway. 'The Governor wants to see you,' he said. 'She's free now.'

Mickey's hopes rose. Throughout his time here he'd been careful to behave, to be, as much as he was able, a model prisoner. So he could get home to Stuie as soon as possible. Maybe the Governor had good news for him? That perhaps, as he had requested, he was going to be allowed to have a special visit from Stuie accompanied by an appropriate adult.

Ten minutes later, accompanied by the screw and trying to look as dignified as his ill-fitting, prison-issue tracksuit and crap plimsolls would allow, he entered the Governor's small, surprisingly cluttered office.

The Governor, Susan Ansell, held out her hand and

shook Mickey's, then pointed at two chairs in front of her desk.

'Please have a seat, Mr Starr. Mickey, yes – or is it Michael?'

'Mickey.'

He sat and the screw left the room, closing the door.

Ansell's demeanour changed and she suddenly looked very serious. 'Mickey, thank you for coming to see me.'

Like I had any option, he thought. *And hey, this was a better gig than doing laundry.* He shrugged.

'Your brother, Stuie – I understand you have been his carer for some years?'

'It was a promise I made to our mum when she was dying.' Alarm bells were ringing.

She nodded. 'Mickey, I'm sorry but there is no easy way to tell you this. I'm afraid your brother is dead.'

'Dead?' He stared at the woman, the word not fully sinking in. '*Dead?*'

Ansell looked back at him with genuine sympathy in her face.

'What – what do you mean? He's only thirty-eight. He . . .' His voice tailed off. He felt gutted. 'What – what's – what's happened?'

'From the police report, it looks like he was murdered.'

'Murdered?' Mickey rose from his chair then sank back down into it and lowered his head into his hands. 'No, please tell me – please tell me it's – it's not true.'

'I'm so very sorry,' the Governor said.

Mickey stayed for some while, head in his hands, crying uncontrollably. 'It's not true. It can't be.' Finally, when he had composed himself a little, he looked back up, dabbing his eyes with a corner of his top. 'What do you know – about – what happened? Who did it? How?'

'I don't have much information, Mickey. Do you – or your brother – have any enemies?'

'How the hell could Stuie have any enemies? He's the sweetest person. He wouldn't harm a fly. He loves everyone. He makes people smile. It's not possible. Please tell me – there must be a mistake.'

'From what I've been told he seems to have put up a spirited fight. His room was wrecked.'

Mickey Starr sat still, in silence. Trying to absorb what he had been told. Trying to make sense of it. He shook his head, then dabbed his eyes again. 'Who? I mean, why? Was it burglars? Did some bastards know I was in prison and decide to burgle my house – and Stuie disturbed them?'

'The police told me that there is evidence of property having been stolen and there are some signs of ransacking. It's also possible your brother may have been the target. Could he have upset anyone?'

'With respect, ma'am, that's bloody ridiculous. As I said, Stuie loves – loved – everyone.'

'I will, of course, give you leave to attend his funeral, after his body is released – accompanied by officers from here. And we will respect, if we can, any wishes you have regarding the funeral.'

'That's very big of you,' he replied, bitterly. 'What do you mean, he was the *target*?'

'I understand he was beaten up pretty badly.'

Starr buried his face in his hands again.

'Do you have any idea at all who might have done this?' the Governor asked.

Starr shook his head.

'We've contacted your solicitors, and I understand someone will be coming to see you later today. If there is anything we can do for you at this difficult time, please ask one of the officers to let me know.'

Mickey sat in silence for a long while. Finally, he answered, 'There is something.'

'Yes?'

'Find the bastards who did this.'

39

After her earlier thrill at being selected for the Gready trial, so far serving as a juror had turned out to be a bit of an anticlimax, Meg was thinking. But hey, hopefully next week would be more exciting. For sure it would be *interesting*.

She looked down at the list of names of her fellow jurors and a brief description of each of them to help her remember them. A disparate group of people, none of whom seemed to have anything much in common with any of the others. They'd spent much of Thursday closeted in the jury room, apart from being allowed to leave the court building and go into town during the lunch period. Most of them passed the time reading, doing emails, some with headphones listening to music or watching films or television on their hand-helds. As well as talking, some of them increasingly argumentatively. A recurring complaint had been the lack of convenient parking in Lewes.

One particularly annoying juror, a woman in her early fifties, Gwendoline Smythson, told them she cycled the five miles to court from her country home. She had suggested they all do that and then they would have no problem with parking.

Meg had pointed out that would have meant a

fourteen-mile cycle ride each way, much of it along perilous main roads. Another juror, who lived near Hastings, indignantly said it would mean a thirty-mile trip each way – again, much of it along main roads.

The one juror who made Meg smile was Hari Singh, a chef. He worked in a modern Brighton restaurant. He'd arrived on Thursday morning with a bag full of samosas, one for each juror. It had amused her to see the stiff, hesitant reactions from the two crusties on the jury to his act of generosity and kindness.

Late afternoon on Thursday they were informed by the jury bailiff that the trial would resume on Monday morning. But by then tensions were rising among the jurors, firstly over whether the person they elected as foreman should be called, as they were now known, the foreperson. And secondly – and more vociferously – over who should have the role.

The retired cop, Mike Roberts, a former Hampshire Police senior homicide detective, had volunteered to take it on. In Meg's view, he would be good: he had both experience of the law and a calm authority about him. But Hugo Pink, with his arrogant self-importance, had thrown his hat in the ring. So had the retired actuary, Harold Trout, who was insisting he had the best credentials.

For God's sake, Meg thought, *what the hell did it matter?* She hadn't as yet put herself forward and was slightly disappointed none of the other female jurors had. Maybe she should enter the fray herself on Monday. Laura would have fought like hell to have been in that position if she was one of the twelve, she knew.

But at this moment, swigging her second or perhaps third glass of Taittinger champagne and finishing a sumptuous seafood lunch in the owners' enclosure at Plumpton

Racecourse, feeling decidedly – and very pleasantly – tipsy, all of that was forgotten.

She was enjoying the company of Nick's mates and their partners who shared the ownership of Colin's Brother, and looking forward to the race, the Butler's Wine Cellar Hurdles, due to start in just over a quarter of an hour, at 3.35 p.m. A short while earlier they'd stroked the horse and chatted to the jockey, who was bullish. He'd ridden to victory in this same race last year and said the thoroughbred was on peak form. The going – good to soft – was the one in which Colin's Brother performed best.

Knocking back the rest of the contents of her glass, she said to her friends, 'Just going to check out the odds on our nag with the bookies.'

'I'll come with you,' Peter Dean said. 'I've a good feeling about our chances today.'

'Me too!'

Dressed like a true racegoer, in her smart Barbour, designer jeans and ankle boots, and accompanied by Dean, sporting a trilby hat, his enclosure pass hanging from his neck along with binoculars in an ancient leather case, they walked out into a cloudy, blustery afternoon with the threat of rain in the air. As they hurriedly threaded their way through the crowd of people, many similarly garbed themselves, holding race cards or folded copies of the *Racing Post*, kindly Peter Dean asked, 'So how are you doing?'

The former family doctor had, for some years, been the Coroner for Suffolk. He understood the pain of bereavement like few others of Meg's circle of friends.

'I'm OK – looking forward to a new challenge, whatever that might be. But I'm really missing my baby!'

'When is she coming home?'

'Not until the end of August. Then in October she's off again to Edinburgh Uni.'

'To study to become a vet, right?'

Meg nodded.

'Must be tough to have to let her go. But you're lucky, you know, Meg. She's a good kid.'

She gave him a wan smile. 'She is.'

'Listen, this summer you must come out for a day on our boat on the Thames!'

'I'd love to.'

They reached the bookmakers, each of them with a line of punters queuing to place bets. 'See you back in the enclosure?' she said.

'I'm going to go up in the grandstand to watch the race with Daniel,' he said.

'I'll find you guys there.'

The first stall bore the name PHIL HOMAN at the top of a tall board. The names and odds of each horse in the race were listed below, and at the bottom were posted the words EUROS TAKEN.

The bookie, a tall man in a flat cap and greatcoat, was taking a bet from a punter, whilst shouting an instruction to his clerk sitting out of sight behind him. Meg looked at the list of runners. Colin's Brother, no. 3, was showing odds of 2:1. She could see that the next stall, headed WILLIAM HILL, was showing only a marginally better 5:2. The next one along showed the same. Clearly, she thought, she wasn't going to make a fortune on this race if the horse did come good.

As she continued walking along the bookies' stalls, looking at the constantly changing odds they were posting, she was alarmed to see the next two were also shortening the odds to 2:1.

Then, to her pleasant surprise, she saw that the last one, JACK JONAS, was showing no. 3 at 4:1.

She joined the back of the queue, digging her purse out of her handbag and watching his board. It was an extravagant bet she was about to place, but last year she'd got back over £1,000 on the win, so if she lost a little of that today, what the hell. Nick would have been proud of her boldness. And if she won, she had decided, she would put the money into Laura's bank account to help with her start at uni.

Jonas, a wiry, chirpy man in his fifties in a pork pie hat, was taking cash, handing out tickets and calling to his clerk behind him as each bet was placed. She stared at the posted odds, nervous they would shorten before she could put her own bet on, and she was relieved when she finally got to the front of the queue.

Before attending to her, he turned to his board and shortened the odds on two horses, but to her relief, left Colin's Brother still showing 4:1.

'Yes, darling?' he said, turning back to her.

Holding out the wad of banknotes she'd withdrawn from a cashpoint yesterday, she said, boldly, 'Number three, one hundred and fifty pounds to win.'

'Number three, Colin's Brother, one hundred and fifty to win,' he shouted briskly to his clerk and gave her a betting slip. 'There you go, darling!' Instantly, his attention was on the next person in the queue.

She turned away and headed back through the throng. After showing her pass to the steward on the gate for the private enclosure and entering, she stopped to tuck her ticket, headed JACK JONAS, in her purse. It was only then she noticed there was a second, flimsy slip of paper beneath it.

A receipt, she presumed at first, but then she saw the shadow of handwriting on the reverse. She turned the slip over and read the words, written in ink in very neat handwriting.

Then stood, stock-still, shaking.

40

Saturday 11 May

Is your daughter having a great time in Ecuador with her friend, Cassie? Laura is such a pretty name. I really hope she stays safe.

Meg had to read the note twice. Was she dreaming? Had the bookie written it? What did he mean by it?

Her stomach heaved with sudden fear. She turned, barged past the steward, back out of the enclosure gate, then knelt and threw up on the grass.

'Are you OK, madam?' a kindly male voice behind her asked.

'God,' said a disgusted, haughty female voice. 'Don't people know how to behave any more these days? I mean, *really*. This is a race meeting, not a chavs' day out.'

Ignoring both, and the commentary over the speakers announcing they were under starter's orders, she ran, stumbling her way back through the crowd towards the bookies.

'It's Spartan from Blue Dancer, Alcazam, Made of Honour, then Colin's Brother, Gemini, What-a-Boy, Gunslinger.' The commentary rang out, echoing, across the entire racecourse. Increasingly, people were stopping whatever they were doing and listening.

'Made of Honour is a faller. It's now Spartan from Blue

Dancer, Alcazam making ground, then Colin's Brother, What-a-Boy, Gunslinger on the rails.'

To Meg, as she hurried on, it was just noise, it meant nothing, her bet forgotten. To her relief there was no queue now for Jack Jonas. The bookie was tapping an electronic device.

'Excuse me,' she said, breathlessly, as she reached him.

He looked up at her, blankly.

'I placed a bet with you a few minutes ago,' she said.

He shook his head. 'Sorry, darling, no more bets, the race has started.'

'No, that's not what I want to talk about. I placed a bet – £150 – on Colin's Brother, do you remember?'

'I'm sorry, darling.' His tone was turning increasingly unpleasant. 'Don't think you heard me the first time. I said, *no more bets.*'

'I don't want to place another bet. I want you to explain this.' She held up the slip of paper.

'Look, clear off, lady, I'm busy.'

'You gave it to me, underneath the betting slip,' she persisted.

He made a show of studying it for some seconds then shook his head. 'Never seen it before in my life.'

'I'm telling you, you gave me this – with my betting slip.'

'And I'm telling you, darling, I ain't never seen this in my life. Are you sure you placed your bet with me?' He stared hard at her and jerked a finger to his right. 'Wasn't with any of them?'

She stared equally hard back at him. 'No.' She produced the ticket bearing his name. 'I put a £150 bet with you on Colin's Brother. Don't you remember?'

'Darling, I'm a bookmaker, not a bleedin' circus Memory

Man.' He looked back down at his electronic device and tapped keys on it.

Conversation over.

Meg continued to stand there, fighting off tears. 'Please help me. Maybe it was your assistant – the guy sitting behind you?'

'Beg pardon?' he said, without looking up from his device.

'Someone put this note with the betting slip – ticket – whatever. Could it have been your colleague? Shall I ask him?'

Jack Jonas looked up, suddenly, his face full of menace. 'Colin's Brother you bet on?'

'Yes.'

'Each-way or win?'

'To win.'

'Wouldn't have mattered.' His expression morphed into a smug smile. 'Came fourth, you'd have lost anyway. Now stop bothering me before I call security.'

'Call them,' she challenged, standing her ground.

'You sure?'

'I'm very sure.'

'Before I do, darling,' he sneered, 'let me just tell you that vomit down the front of your jacket really doesn't become you . . . Not a good look at a nice race meeting.' He nodded at her badge. 'Had a fancy lunch in the owners' enclosure restaurant, did you? A bit too much of the posh sparkles? Happens all the time. Know what I suggest?'

She faced him off.

'You're pissed. I suggest you get out of here, before I get security to throw you out. That would be really undignified.'

41

Shortly after 6 p.m., as they were on their way back to Brighton from the racecourse, the rain had finally begun. The grey sky and the *screech-clunk* of the wipers contributed to Meg's gloom, as she sat in the rear of the Prius behind Peter Dean and his girlfriend, a concert violinist, whose name she, embarrassingly, couldn't remember. They'd picked Meg up earlier and were now kindly giving her a lift home before heading up to London, where they both lived.

Dean turned into Meg's street and pulled up outside her house. He politely declined her invitation to come in for a coffee, explaining he had a complex and harrowing inquest starting on Monday and had to get back to read through a ton of paperwork in preparation, and that Jonquil was playing a new piece tomorrow night and needed to rehearse.

She walked up to her front door, waved them goodbye as they drove off then entered the house. Daphne greeted her with a glare.

She knelt and stroked her. 'Hungry? I'll get some food in a minute, OK?'

Meg was still going over and over in her head the encounter with the vile bookmaker earlier, and fretting about the note. A note passed along with a betting slip. The bookmaker, Jack Jonas, had to have known, it must have been deliberate. To give him the benefit of the doubt, maybe it was his clerk, or someone else at the race track who had given it to him to pass to her? But it was still completely creeping her out.

She'd not said anything to Peter or Daniel about it – not really sure what to tell them. Much of their conversation after the race had revolved around how their jockey had got himself boxed in on the rails. Daniel had said, darkly, that it smacked of race-fixing between the jockeys, which did sometimes happen at the point-to-point level of racing in order to get the odds higher on a future race. But she hadn't really been able to focus on what they were saying.

Just what the hell had that note been all about? Who had written it? For what reason? How did they know about Laura and where she was? How had they known she was going to place a bet with them?

Deep in thought, she slung her jacket on the Victorian coat stand inside the front door, made her way into the kitchen and went straight to the fridge. Removing a bottle of sparkling water, she took a large gulp.

The cat gave a loud *miaowwwwww*.

'OK, I hear you, patience!' She walked over towards the cupboard where she kept the cat food and was about to pull out a tin when something on the kitchen table, lying near *Sussex Life* and some other magazines, caught her eye. A photograph.

It had not been there when she left the house this morning. Had it?

Puzzled, she stepped over to the table and looked down at the 5 x 3, brightly coloured picture of Laura and Cassie on the Equator. The one Laura had WhatsApped her.

The two girls in shorts, T-shirts, sunglasses and baseball caps, laughing, carefree, legs straddling either side of a narrow, paved path behind a red-and-yellow sign.

ECUADOR IN THE MIDDLE OF THE WORLD

Meg hadn't printed it out. So who had? She picked it up and turned it over, but the reverse was blank.

She knew the girls had set up a WhatsApp group for their trip. In a wild thought, she wondered if one of Laura's friends had done it and brought it round as a gift. A surprise gift. But surely they would have left a note with it?

And how would they have got in? The only person who had a key was her Latvian cleaning lady, Vesma, and she was the last person on earth she could imagine being on social media. Besides, she only came on Fridays.

Then she remembered the hidden spare key beneath a flowerpot in the garden shed. Laura used it regularly as she was always forgetting her key. Probably half her friends knew where it was. But all the same, she thought, it was very odd there was no note with it.

Suddenly, looking at the photograph again, she was struck by something. Curious, she pulled her phone out of her bag, opened WhatsApp and went to the photograph Laura had sent on Thursday. Then she compared it to the one on the kitchen table and, with a trembling hand, put her phone down.

They were different.

Both must have been taken at almost the same moment, but the one Laura had posted was face-on, with other tourists clearly visible in the background and trees beyond. The printed one was angled, high quality, and must have been taken from some distance away. The girls were clearly not aware of the photo being taken as they were so far away and not looking at the camera at all. Her heart sank as she realized it was most definitely not the same photo.

There was a creak from out in the hallway and she spun round. Shivers rippled through her. Someone had come in whilst she'd been at the races and put this on the table. Could that person still be in here?

Another creak. It was drowned out a moment later by the cat miaowing.

'Hello?' Meg called out, a dark unease coiling through her. 'Is someone out there?' She turned sharply, her eyes hunting in every direction.

Miaowwwww.

'Shut it,' she hissed. Then listened. The house was old, 1930s, it creaked all the time. She waited a full minute, the thudding of her heart echoing in her ears like drumbeats – *boomf . . . boomf . . . boomf . . .* A few feet away were a bunch of kitchen knives in a wooden block. She strode over, grabbed the largest then walked to the doorway to the hall. 'Hello?' she shouted and marched through, brandishing the knife.

There was nothing there.

She stood for some moments, wondering. Should she call the police? And say what? That someone had broken into her house and left a photo of her daughter in the kitchen?

The thought suddenly occurred to her that she hadn't checked to see if anything had been taken. Still holding the knife and still scared, she went from room to room. Nothing seemed to have been touched. Laura's menagerie was all fine. She was topping up the water for the gerbils when she heard a phone ringing downstairs.

Might it be Laura? She raced back down and into the kitchen, and realized it wasn't her own phone as she saw another one on the sideboard that she didn't recognize. A cheap-looking one. Whose was this phone – Vesma's?

She answered it, tentatively. 'Hello?'

'Hello, Meg!'

A male voice. Confident. Pleasant, with the rasp of a heavy smoker. Almost like they were best buddies. Salesy. These kinds of calls really pissed her off. 'Who am I speaking to?' she asked, coldly.

'A very good friend, Meg.' He sounded so hurt that, for an instant, she thought she must know him, and the fault was with her for not recognizing who it was.

'Really?' she said. 'I'm sorry but your number hasn't shown up, so I'm not sure who I'm talking to.'

'Do you like the photograph?'

'Photograph?'

'The one I left on your kitchen table. By the way, that's a nice photograph of your racehorse – I presume it's yours, the one on the wall. Did your late husband take it?'

She could scarcely believe her ears. 'You've been in my house while I was out? What? How dare you? Just who the hell are you?' She began screaming at him. 'What do you want? What the hell do you want?'

'She's a lovely girl, your daughter, Laura. Having the time of her life backpacking in Ecuador with her friend Cassie, isn't she?'

She was silent for a moment, her mind spinning for traction, trying to make sense of what she was hearing. 'Laura? Did you say Laura?'

'That's a cute tattoo she has on her left shoulder. A Tibetan symbol to keep you safe when travelling – very appropriate.'

'Who the hell are you? How dare you come into my house? How – how do you know – my daughter?'

'Let's just call me her *guardian angel*.'

His tone was still cloyingly pleasant.

'Where did you get that photograph?'

'There's a guy there all the time, snapping tourists and trying to sell photos to them. Just out to make himself a buck. Actually, that photo was of someone else that day, he just got lucky to have caught Laura and Cassie in the background.'

'Was it you – did you write that note the bookie gave me?'

'The thing is, Meg, I know how much Laura must mean to you. After the terrible loss of your Nick and Will, she really must be so precious to you.'

She said nothing. Her mind was churning, trying to make sense of what she was hearing. He was silent for a moment, too, before he went on.

'Meg, you need to trust me. Laura's in danger and I want to help you – we really need to make sure she is safe, don't we? South America's a wild and dangerous place, it's not like England. Life is cheap, people get killed or vanish there all the time. Laura and Cassie are very vulnerable, they need someone to keep them safe. Make sure they don't get anything stolen, you know what I mean?'

'Oh God,' she said, scared. 'What do you mean? Please, please, do not hurt them. What do you want?'

Ignoring her comment and her question, he went on. 'I can keep Laura safe, Meg, no charge, I've got contacts there. They're already looking out for her, for me. I'll ping you a photo they sent me this morning so you can see. Coming through now!'

Almost instantaneously, the new phone pinged with a text alert. It was a photograph of the girls sitting on the veranda of a large wooden shack, each holding a wine glass and what looked like a cigarette. Again, it was taken from a distance and the girls were not looking at the camera.

Beneath was the geomapping time, date, location.

She stared at it. 'Why did you send this? Did you leave this phone here? Are you following them?'

'Like I told you, Meg, I just want to make sure your daughter stays safe, and to show you how we are watching her all the time. We've left you this pre-paid mobile to keep in contact with you.'

She stood there, unable to think clearly, feeling like a rabbit frozen in headlights. Anger was rising through her fear. 'Stop it, just stop it. Get away from those girls.'

'I'm afraid they need me, trust me. I'm phoning to offer you a deal, and I think you should accept it for your daughter's sake.'

'Really? What *deal*?'

For the first time, she could sense a tone of real menace in his voice.

'Firstly, just in case you're thinking of warning Laura, or telling her to come back home right away, then all bets are off. You do understand me, don't you, Meg?'

'What is this all about?' Meg demanded.

She had a nasty feeling that she already knew.

'I just need you to do something for me, Meg. Something very simple. It's not rocket science in any way. But you do need to understand my rules if we're going to work together, if you want me to keep your daughter safe. Am I clear?'

She was shaking, her voice trapped in her gullet, momentarily unable to speak.

'My first rule, Meg, is you tell no one. No one at all. You don't breathe a word to any of your friends. We will know, trust me. You tell any friend or go to the authorities and you will find them dead. The phone is to be kept on you at all times, it's how we'll contact you. If you try to get a message to the judge, or tell your fellow jurors, or alert anyone who could get the trial stopped, then I'm afraid it's game over for little Laura. At least when your husband and son died, you were able to go to their funerals. But you wouldn't have that luxury with Laura – you might not even get her body back. You would never see her alive again. Are you absolutely clear?'

Raging with anger, but paralysed by shock at the same time, she was unable to speak. She let out the tiniest, high-pitched sound.

'Good, so we understand each other, Meg. As I said, it is very simple. If you ever want to see Laura again – alive – all that has to happen is your jury foreman, at the end of the trial, has to say just two words – and repeat them five times, for each of the counts on which Mr Gready is indicted.'

She did not respond.

'You know what they are, don't you, Meg?'

She remained silent. She knew.

But he said them all the same, his voice lowering to a whisper. It grated like a wood saw.

'*Not guilty.*'

42

After his evening meal, which he had barely touched, Mickey left his cell to go for a walk around before lockdown. He didn't notice anyone on the way, didn't want to talk to anyone. He returned, finally, and perched, heavy-hearted, on the edge of his bunk, staring at the photograph of Stuie on the wall beside him. The photo that had always made him smile, the last thing he saw at night and the image that greeted him each morning. Stuie in the set of chef's whites he'd bought online, ready for his duties in the fish and chip shop.

Stuie was always online, looking at items on Gumtree, eBay and Catawiki mostly, but rarely actually buying anything. For him, the excitement – and challenge – was always to see how long he could stay in the auction without getting caught out and ending up as the final purchaser.

But this chef's outfit was something he'd hankered after ever since Mickey had first told him their plans for the chippie. And it was the full monty. Toque, double-breasted white tunic, apron, black and white houndstooth-checked trousers, and he had taken to wearing it whenever he went into the kitchen. In this photograph he was standing upright, proudly posing, the tall white hat as lopsided as his happy grin.

Once again Mickey was fighting back tears. Who the hell had done this? When he found them, he would rip their heads off – after he had torn off every other appendage first. He punched the wall in frustration, then punched it again.

'Do you want to talk, Mickey?' said his cellmate, from the bunk above him. Mickey hadn't even noticed he was there.

'No, I don't want to talk, I want to fucking do something. I've gotta find out who did this – find out and—'

He was interrupted by a figure stepping in through the open doorway. It was one of the officers he liked, and who had been sympathetic towards him. 'You've got a visitor, Mickey,' he said.

Starr frowned. It was 7.30 p.m. and visiting time had ended several hours ago. 'It must be the solicitor,' he said.

Maybe, he thought, with more information on how Stuie had died. Or perhaps with the news that they'd caught the bastards who had done this. Not that he really wanted to see anyone or talk to anyone. He just wanted to be on his own with his thoughts. He didn't want people to see him crying.

Mickey followed the officer, almost blindly, along the gridded landing, down the stairs, through the maze of stark corridors, through one double door after another – assiduously unlocked and locked by the officer – and finally into the large visitors' area. Normally, most of the brightly coloured chairs, facing each other across a table, would have been occupied and it felt strange to Mickey that tonight they were deserted. Everything felt strange at the moment, badly strange, as if the world he knew had been kicked over onto its side, into shit.

A tall figure rose over on the far side of the room. Nick Fox.

'I'll leave you to it,' the officer said. He jerked a thumb towards the observation platform. 'I'll be over there – have as long as you need.'

Starr thanked him and walked over to the solicitor. Fox clasped Starr's right hand and held it for some seconds, looking deeply upset, too. 'Mickey, I'm so sad for you. What a terrible thing to have happened. I know how much Stuie meant to you and how you cared for him.' He shook his head. 'I just can't believe it.'

They sat, facing each other. Mickey nodded. 'I don't know what's happened – do you know anything? Are there any suspects?'

Fox raised his arms. 'Not so far – it's early doors. There's a CCTV camera on the garage forecourt opposite your house. The footage is being looked at, I'm told, but I think it's the wrong angle to be of much help.' He was silent for a moment. 'Is there anyone you might have upset – on the outside or in here?'

'Upset? You mean enough that they'd go and kick my brother to death?'

'Yes.'

Mickey shook his head. 'No way – I mean – absolutely *no way*. OK – I decked a couple of cops at Newhaven, but—' He shook his head again.

'No one you've pissed off in here? Done over? Tucked up?'

'I've followed your advice, Nick. You know how badly I've been wanting to get out – for Stuie. I've kept my head down, stayed clear of any trouble, been respectful to the screws, even the bastard ones.' He buried his face in his hands. 'Oh, Jesus. I guess I've had one thought – Stuie was always online on the internet. He loved chatting to strangers. He's not always the most tactful person, know what I'm saying?' He looked up. 'He doesn't always know what words mean, or realize, sometimes, when he's being rude. Maybe that's a possibility – that he upset someone online?'

Fox looked at him, dubiously. 'Enough that they would kill him – do you really think so? The police are also looking at whether it was a burglary gone wrong.'

'I dunno what I think. Nothing else makes any sense. Shit, I need a fag.'

The solicitor smiled. 'I'm sure they're not hard to get hold of in here.'

Starr barely acknowledged the comment. 'Make me one promise, Nick.'

'What's that?'

'When they get the bastard – or bastards – who did this, you'll give me ten minutes alone in a room with them.'

'Won't you let me join you?'

Both men grimaced at each other.

'Think hard, Mickey, is there anyone, anyone at all who has reason to be upset with you?'

Starr was silent. Then he said, 'There's only one person I can think of – but I've always trusted him like he's one of my family.'

'Who's that? Who do you mean?'

'Terry. I got his message about keeping my mouth shut – surely he wouldn't have killed my brother. He's a bastard, but he wouldn't have killed Stuie.'

As he said the name, he noticed the very faint upwards curl of Fox's eyebrow.

And suddenly he knew for sure.

'Terry?' Fox replied. 'No way.' He shook his head. 'Never!'

Mickey let it drop, and they chatted on. But all the time he was thinking silently, burning inside as if the blood in his veins had turned into a corrosive acid.

After Fox left, promising to update him the moment he had further news, Mickey was escorted back to his wing. He was deep in thought, replaying over and over in his mind that twitch of Fox's eyebrow when he'd suggested Terence Gready might be behind this. Had he touched a nerve? Did Fox have the same suspicions?

For sure he did. That twitch was the giveaway. Maybe he even *knew*?

Hiding behind the carefully constructed artifice of respectable citizen, family man, champion of the under-privileged and charitable benefactor, Lucky Mickey was aware, better than anyone, what an utterly ruthless man Gready was. The invisible mastermind behind a string of children and vulnerable young adults, many with mental health issues, coerced through drug addiction – engineered by him – into acting as his dispensable foot soldiers. He had cuckoos in towns across the South Coast – addicts forced by the threat of withdrawal of their drugs into using their residences to deal from. Mickey knew this because he ran the whole operation on behalf of Terry.

Just as Gready had used a bent copper in his pay to get him acquitted eighteen years ago – and to ensure his ongoing loyalty – perhaps the solicitor had his eyes and ears throughout the police and prison system today. Had word got back to Gready that he had been in discussions about grassing him up to further reduce his own sentence?

Although he'd been using a different brief to broker this, had he or someone else told Fox? They were both from the same firm, after all.

By the time he was back in his cell, which stank of shit, and the door had banged shut behind him, he had convinced himself.

'Sorry,' his cellmate said, from the other side of the plastic curtain which screened off the toilet. 'Got the runs.'

But Starr barely heard him. He perched back down on his bunk. Terence fucking Gready. There was no one else. He'd seen it in the twitch of Fox's eyebrow. He was certain.

And he knew the one thing he could do to take revenge.

43

Meg stood in the kitchen, staring at the photograph, still holding the planted phone. Laura and Cassie.

ECUADOR IN THE MIDDLE OF THE WORLD

At the far end of the world, it seemed at this moment.

She was shaking. Shivering. The room felt icy as if a ghost had entered. Rain tapped hard on the windows and the glass of the conservatory off the kitchen. Her eyes darted around.

Someone had been in here. They might come back at any time. She hurried, stumbling up the stairs and into her den. Then she googled 'Hotels in Brighton and Hove'.

Twenty minutes later, having fed the animals, Meg left the house with a few things in an overnight bag, including her own phone and the new phone, and checked into a budget hotel she had found just off the seafront, a mile from her house. The interior was as gloomy as the exterior was drab, the room furnished with a small double bed, a side table, an ancient television, a clock radio and a Corby trouser press, and there was barely enough light from the feeble bulbs to be able to read.

She sat down on the hard bed with her things beside her, shaking and crying, a terrible sick feeling in the pit of her stomach. *What to do? God, what to do? Go to the police? And risk Laura's life?*

She had never missed her husband more than at this moment. What would her lovely sensible Nick have done, she wondered?

So often he used to quote an old saying of his father's – that life could turn on a sixpence. He was also fond of quoting, 'Live every day as if it's your last, because one day you'll be right.'

And he had been right. The day their lives had turned on a damned sixpence, or rather on that sodding van driver's mobile phone screen, and whilst he would be out of prison in just eighteen months, for causing death by dangerous driving, she and Laura were doomed to a life sentence.

Yes, my darling, darling Nick, you were so right. And, God, I need you here now so badly. I need to talk to you. I need your advice. What would it have been? You were always so wise, you'd have found a solution, the one I hadn't thought of. I know you would.

She eventually undressed and went to bed, but sleep for a long while was impossible. The clock radio filled the room with a green glow and there was a loud, persistent *drip-drip-drip* from a broken pipe or gutter just beyond her window.

The night ticked by, one slow minute at a time. Finally, she dozed off, only to wake with a start and a terrible feeling of dread.

3.38 a.m.

Then 3.39 a.m.

What to do? What the hell should she do?

She and Nick had tried to instil in their children always to do what they felt was the right thing, despite what anyone might think or say to the contrary. Will and Laura had been very close. He had been a huge champion of the issue of climate change, which was why Laura now, bless her, had become almost messianic in her zeal to stop the use of plastic bags and any single-use plastic items, among other things she tried to do for the environment. She cared, really cared, about her fellow human beings and all animals, and Meg loved that about her. She was proud of the kind and thoughtful young woman Laura had become.

But now she was faced with a dilemma she just could not get her head around. A dilemma that so wracked her with fear she struggled to think straight. It felt as if her brain was revolving like a tombola drum, tossing all her thoughts around like the raffle tickets inside. The only good way out of this situation would be if Terence Gready was so obviously innocent of all charges that the verdicts on every count could not be in doubt.

And what were the chances of that? She'd be better able to assess the trial after the next couple of days, when they'd heard the prosecution's opening case on each of the counts, and the defence's response. But they were very serious offences, and she doubted she'd ever have received that phone call if the defence had felt truly confident.

Earlier in this endless night she'd done an internet search to see how juries worked, and found out that a majority jury verdict of 10–2 would normally be accepted by a judge. So, regardless of the evidence, she was going to have to coerce at least nine of her eleven fellow jurors into giving the verdicts she needed on each count.

Just how morally wrong was it to potentially let a major criminal, whose drugs probably killed dozens of people every year, according to the indictments, go free? In order to save her daughter? And in doing so to go against every principle she believed in and had instilled in her kids?

And she knew exactly how Laura would react if she knew. She'd be livid if she believed her mother was prepared to do anything to pervert justice. Which was why, if she succeeded – and at this stage, God only knew how – Laura must never ever find out. This dilemma she faced struck at the heart of her conscience and her very being. What would anybody do in this situation?

She so badly needed someone she could talk to, confide in.

You tell any friend or go to the authorities and you will find them dead.

4.01

4.02

Through the curtains, the sky was now starting to show the first signs of daylight. Outside, the first tentative chirrups of the dawn chorus began, like first arrivals in an orchestra pit tuning their instruments.

You tell no one. No one at all. You don't breathe a word to any of your friends. We will know, trust me.

Was he bluffing or would they really know?

If so, how?

The man who had put the photograph on the kitchen table had been in her house, and she had no idea for how long. It could have been less than sixty seconds, or he could have spent hours there. Perhaps with colleagues? Planting bugs in every room? In her computer? In phones?

Meg reached for her own phone and went to the Google app. Was it dangerous typing anything? Would they have some way of knowing what she was looking for? Was even just doing this putting Laura's life in danger? But she had to do something. And, she reasoned, her mind suddenly very clear, the power Terence Gready's people had over her at this moment was the threat to Laura. If she did something that angered them, they would let her know. They weren't going to harm Laura all the time there was a chance she would comply with their request.

She entered: *How to find hidden electronic bugs.*

After she had done that, she did another search, this time for local locksmiths.

Then she made the decision that she could not stay here, it was too depressing. And besides, what could she achieve by becoming a fugitive from her own home?

44

Sunday 12 May

The rain had cleared overnight and it was now one of those rare, glorious, early-summer mornings, full of promise, with a cloudless sky and not a breath of wind. Roy Grace had worked in the incident room until late last night and was going back after lunch with Potting holding the fort this morning. He ran down the side of the steep field, exhilarated and excited.

Almost intoxicated by the sheer beauty of the rolling Sussex countryside in which he always felt he was lucky to live, he sprinted the last couple of hundred metres back down to the cottage as the ground levelled out. Humphrey, unusually, was dragging behind, to Grace's surprise. Entering the gate into their garden, feeling pretty all-in after his run, he stopped to get his breath back and to do his stretches. Humphrey caught up with him, limping a little.

Grace stroked his head. 'You're not knackered, are you, boy? You're just warmed up! The thing is, you've got four legs against my two, so it's like you have four-wheel drive up those hills, right? Unfair advantage!' Humphrey cocked his head and Grace stroked him again. He adored this creature, envying him, as he so often did, the apparent simplicity of his life.

When he went inside, he saw Bruno seated at the

breakfast bar, glued to the television, on which a documentary was playing. The logo of the Discovery Channel was in one corner of the screen. Noah was sitting in his high chair, banging a spoon, a mess of food all over the tray and on the floor around him. Cleo, cracking eggs into a bowl, turned round with a smile.

'How was your run?'

'Eight miles!' He kissed her.

Humphrey sat in front of her, head up, expectant.

She popped half an eggshell into his mouth, and he crunched on it contentedly for several seconds before it was gone, then looked up for another. 'Eight miles – brilliant!'

'How did you get on with the lots we've bid on at the auctioneers?'

'Someone from Bellman's left a message to say we've won three bids – two paintings and a runner for the hallway! I've arranged for Kaitlynn to collect them for us.'

'Fantastic!' He hesitated. 'You've a PM tomorrow with Frazer, right?'

She nodded. 'A woman in her thirties brought in yesterday. Looks like she fell from a balcony.'

He looked at the pile of mashed bananas on the wooden board beside her.

'Are you making banana bread?'

'Nope, a new recipe I saw in the paper. Banana *pancakes*! Less than 150 calories a serving. One banana and two eggs, with some berries on top.'

'Sounds delicious,' he said, a tad dubiously.

'Well, as we're having a blow-out fish and chips lunch on the pier, I thought a light breakfast made sense.'

'Anything I can do?'

She touched his face tenderly with one hand. 'Yes, have a shower and be prepared for a taste sensation!'

'I'm ravenous!'

He was about to head upstairs when a face he recognized appeared on the television screen. A pensive, good-looking man in his thirties, with dark, wavy hair and a side parting, wearing a beige jacket and open-neck shirt. Chin resting on his hand. A clipped American accent.

He knew that face and not in a good way.

Born Theodore Robert Cowell, the man had at some point early in his life changed his last name to Bundy. A former law student, Ted Bundy had become America's most notorious ever serial killer.

Why was his eleven-year-old son watching this, and looking so absorbed? And why was Cleo letting him, or had she not noticed?

He gave her a look and pointed at the screen. She gave him an *I know* shrug back.

'Enjoying the programme, Bruno?' he asked.

His son nodded. 'This guy's ace! I mean, a douche bag, but ace!'

'Really?' The boy's enthusiasm worried him.

'Sure, like he confessed to thirty victims on his deathbed, but the FBI detective, Bill Hagmaier, reckons his total could be loads more – isn't that awesome?'

'Awesome? Why do you think that, Bruno?'

'It's – like – sick!'

The more time he spent with his son, the more Roy Grace thought the boy's moral compass was a little skewed. But at the same time, he was aware he needed to tread carefully to avoid further alienating the boy. 'What about all the victims? And their families?'

Without taking his eyes from the screen, Bruno said, 'You can choose to be a victim, or not. It's Darwinian, yes?'

'Darwinian?' Grace frowned.

'Ted Bundy was an innocent victim of *natural selection*. Don't you agree?'

Grace was struggling to get his head around the boy's logic. 'Want to tell me how you arrive at that conclusion, Bruno?'

'Aren't we all prisoners of our genes?' he said, again without turning from the screen. 'Don't you think so, Papa?'

'No, I don't, Bruno. We are all born with the capacity to do evil, but whether we do or not is a choice we make – a conscious choice.'

Bruno shook his head. 'That's not what Mama told me.'

Grace glanced at Cleo, who was listening with interest. 'What did your mother tell you?' he asked.

'That sometimes the choices are already made for us.'

'And have any choices already been made for you, Bruno?'

For some moments his son concentrated on the screen. Bundy was talking to the camera and he realized, uncomfortably, that Bruno was echoing what this monster was saying. He was tempted to grab the remote and switch the television off, but he held back. Let him continue and he would try to engage with him after the programme was over. He turned to Cleo again. 'How long till breakfast?'

'Ten minutes.'

'I'll go and jump into the shower.'

'Yes, one choice has been made,' Bruno said, suddenly. 'What I can and cannot eat, apparently.'

'What you can and cannot eat?' Grace asked him.

'*Jah.* I'm blood-type A positive, which Mama told me was a meat-eaters' group. Now my new mother tells me she was wrong. I should be eating vegetarian – and vegan.'

'Well, we're all trying to eat more healthily, Bruno.'

'You're making a value judgement based on an unproven hypothesis,' Bruno said.

Grace glanced at Cleo, who caught his eye with a silent *what?* Both of them were constantly startled by the very adult expressions and opinions Bruno regularly came up with. Was this the result of things he had picked up from his mother Sandy – Grace's former and estranged wife – in the first ten years of his life, or was it how kids his age were today, Grace wondered?

As he went upstairs, he was thinking back to a parents' evening at Bruno's school last autumn. To something the bemused headmaster had told them. He'd said that when asked what he wanted to be when he grew up, Bruno had replied, 'Either a chemist or a dictator.'

They understood the peripatetic upbringing Bruno must have had with his erratic mother, before coming to live with them in England after her suicide.

Both he and Cleo hoped that by introducing him to a stable, loving family environment, they could, in time, change him. But so far there was little sign of that happening. It probably hadn't helped that he'd been a largely absent father during these past six months, and he determined now that he was back down in Sussex to spend more time with him.

They had an ally in a forensic child psychologist called Orlando Trujillo, who had been giving them advice on how to handle Bruno. Trujillo had warned them against trying to intervene too much at this stage, but rather to simply observe and gradually try to instil in Bruno new values. They were doing their best, but God, it was hard. And to compound their difficulties, with one major trial running at Lewes Crown Court starting tomorrow, and a murder investigation he was leading, in addition to all the preparations he needed to do for the Chief Superintendent boards, he was going to be desperately squeezed for time.

He was about to step into the shower when his job phone rang. Although not on-call today, he glanced at the screen and saw it was Glenn Branson. 'Hi,' he answered. 'What's up?'

'Not sure if you're going to like this or not, boss. Your good buddy, Edward Crisp, has been attacked in Lewes Prison. Stabbed in one eye with a ballpoint pen by a fellow inmate who apparently doesn't like men who hurt women.'

'Well, I'll be a monkey's uncle. Was the pen damaged?'

'I didn't ask, boss!'

'How badly injured is he?'

'He's being taken under guard to Moorfields Eye Hospital in London. The prison doctor thinks he may be permanently blinded in that eye. So, it doesn't look like the trial's going to be starting tomorrow after all.'

'How many officers are with him?'

'Dunno, boss.'

'Make sure he's properly guarded, it could be another of his ruses to escape.'

'Not from what I hear – the pen's still stuck in his eye.'

'Too bad the bastard didn't push it further, into his twisted brain, and spare us all a lot of wasted time in court,' Grace said.

'You really are sick, aren't you?'

'Just a realist, matey. You'll get there one day, after you've dealt with as many shitbags as I have. Keep me posted. Want me to send him a *get well soon* note?'

'What a lovely gesture, I'm sure he'd appreciate it.'

'So long as he can read it.'

45

Meg sat in her place on the wooden front row seat in the jury box, with tired eyes from two virtually sleepless nights.

The jurors had bundles of documents in front of them, with coloured, marked tabs sticking out. There was one bundle between two.

She looked up at the packed public gallery, where several people seemed to be staring at her and her fellow jurors, then at the defendant seated in the glassed-in dock, with a guard beside him. As she watched him, Gready suddenly looked straight in her direction. Was it her imagination or did he catch her eye?

She shivered. Had his henchmen already got the message to him? *Juror no. 3, she's your pal, she's your get-out-of-jail-free card?*

Quickly glancing away, she focused on the two rows of lawyers, some wigged and gowned, trying to work out which was the prosecution and which the defence. Several people sat in the press box over the far side. The judge was seated; she could see the top of his shiny blue chair, and the stalk of the black microphone on his bench, alongside a laptop, video monitor and conference telephone. The royal coat of arms, fixed high on the wall behind his seat, was a reminder of the gravitas of this place.

She felt nauseous. It was daunting being here, actually being part of these proceedings rather than a mere spectator. And not just *part* of it. Clandestinely *taking control* of it. Pulling the strings. Perverting the course of justice – if she had the strength; courage; ability. Everything felt so overwhelmingly real and purposeful. And powerful. Crown Court. A criminal trial presided over by a senior judge. It didn't get any more serious than this.

There was an air of expectancy, everyone waiting for the drama to unfold. But there was no curtain about to rise, no lights about to dim for a movie to start. This was real, Meg was thinking. This was about the law of the land, a blunt iron fist under which human beings could be deprived of their liberty for years – sometimes even forever.

The enormity of what she had to do had been sinking in gradually over the past day and a half. She knew she had to do what they had told her; she had the burner phone on her at all times. Her eyes were raw and her brain foggy and she was struggling to even think straight. But she had to. Had to hold it together for Laura. The biggest question she had been churning over relentlessly in her mind ever since that phone call was whether the man's threat was real or a big bluff.

But no way could she gamble with Laura's life by risking calling it – in case it wasn't.

She had few other options. She could send a note to the judge, as he had instructed them last week, or go to the police to see if the British Embassy in Ecuador could intervene and helicopter Laura out of trouble and bring her home.

But at what risk to her daughter with either?

If you try to get a message to the judge, or tell your fellow jurors, or alert anyone who could get the trial stopped, then I'm afraid it's game over for little Laura.

The most convincing evidence that he had not been bluffing was the photographs. The one at the Equator and the one outside the hacienda. Later on Saturday, Laura had sent her an almost identical photograph of her and Cassie – plus two more – on WhatsApp, as well as posting them on Instagram. These photos had clearly been taken with their consent. All smiles into the camera.

Meg's attempt to debug the house yesterday – if indeed it was bugged at all – had not gone well. She found a ton of stuff on electronic surveillance devices on the internet, and watched several YouTube videos on how to detect them. Many of the latest bugging devices were almost microscopic in size, barely even visible to the untrained human eye. There was a range of detectors, at an affordable price, but the fastest delivery any were offering was two days. So instead, in the early hours of yesterday, she'd begun her own search, using the assortment of tools in Nick's box and beginning with the most obvious places.

She removed the covers of the smoke detectors in each room, checking inside before replacing them; similarly the light fittings and all the electrical sockets and plugs. But after two hours, she'd started to realize the hopelessness of her task. She wasn't tech-savvy enough to risk opening her computer, phone or the phone they had given her – and she wouldn't have had a clue what to look for if she did.

There could be something concealed in one of the televisions, in the speakers in the ceiling, inside a radiator or in so many other potential hiding places. She'd seen bugs online that were even disguised as small pieces of electrical flex and computer cables. Some extra-powerful ones didn't need to be in the house at all but could pick up conversations from outside in the garden. They could be hidden behind vents in her car. Anywhere.

She'd had some respite later in the day, when she was coaxed out of the house by her best friend, Alison Stevens, to share a picnic with her on the beach. They'd sat in glorious sunshine, demolishing a bottle of cold Sauvignon Blanc. Several times during the afternoon, the more the alcohol kicked in, she'd been increasingly tempted to confide in Ali.

Despite Alison constantly asking her what was wrong, sensing that something was clearly troubling her, Meg said nothing about the situation, not wanting to put her friend's life at risk.

You tell any friend or go to the authorities and you will find them dead.

She thought about the indictments Terence Gready faced. These weren't for parking infringements or shoplifting, or some other kind of minor misdemeanour. He was in the dock accused of being a drug dealer on an organized-crime scale – a criminal mastermind.

While they were closeted in the jury room last week, the retired cop, Roberts, had helpfully and somewhat gleefully informed his fellow jurors what the sentences could be for each of the counts if Gready was found guilty. And it was very clear to Meg from the way he spoke that he'd already made up his mind that the defendant was guilty of the entire lot, and faced being locked up and having the key thrown away.

Not a happy prospect for a man at the still relatively young age of fifty-five, who might not see the outside of a prison again until he was a septuagenarian – if he lived that long. A mobster with a criminal empire, with everything to lose, would surely do everything he could to stay free, wouldn't he?

Although the judge had expressly instructed the jurors not to google the defendant, Meg was so terrified about the situation that she had gone to Brighton Library and done so, anonymously, on one of their computers. But there was not much to interest her about him. Just the name of his law firm. He did not appear to have ever had any social media engagement. She found a few bits relating to his personal life. He had a wife and three children. There was an article showing him and his family at a charity event and a lifestyle piece in the local paper about his wife's interest in orchids. She appeared to be some sort of expert on them.

Had he deliberately spent years under the radar, or could they possibly have arrested the wrong person? Was it wishful thinking, that they had an entirely innocent man, she wondered? Or the new mindset she was going to have to adopt?

Two loud knocks as loud as gunshots startled her out of her thoughts. They were followed by a stentorian command.

'The court is in session!'

46

Monday 13 May

Richard Jupp took some moments to adjust the mic in front of him, then the position of his water glass. Continuing to take his time, as if in doing so he was further asserting both his stamp of authority and his power over his domain, he peered around, observing who was here and staring for quite some while at the jury, to Meg's discomfort. 'I want to apologize that you have been kept waiting for this trial to begin properly until this morning. The reason for this is that I had to deal with a number of legal and evidential issues that needed to be discussed without you present. These have now been resolved and the trial can start.'

He paused for a few seconds, then went on. 'Members of the jury, you may have seen in the media over the weekend reports regarding the tragic death of a man called Stuie Starr. I can tell you he is the brother of the co-defendant in this case, Michael Starr. You should not take any account of what you have read during this trial or when you make your deliberations. You will not discuss anything about this amongst yourselves or in the jury room.'

He then nodded at the prosecuting counsel. 'Mr Cork, you may proceed.'

'Thank you, Your Honour,' Stephen Cork said very

formally and gravely, rising to his feet and turning to the jury, and, as he did so, turning on the charm.

A slim man in his fifties, with horn-rimmed glasses which, combined with his wig and gown, gave him a distinctly learned look, he appeared completely at home in the grandeur – and formality – of this room. He exuded all the confidence of a lion in its natural habitat confidently stalking its prey. He leaned towards the jurors, addressing them in a warm and friendly tone. There was nothing patronizing about his manner, it was more in the style of a compere at the start of a stage variety performance.

'Ladies and gentlemen of the jury, this case is about conspiracy to smuggle and distribute millions of pounds' worth of cocaine. My name is Stephen Cork and I will be presenting the case for the prosecution. I will be assisted by my learned friend, Mr Paul Williams.' He turned briefly to look at the defence counsel, a wigged and gowned woman seated close by. 'My learned friend Primrose Brown QC appears for the defendant, Terence Gready, assisted by Mr Crispin Sykes.'

He turned back to the jury, all smiles, theatrically removing his glasses, momentarily, so they could all see his kindly eyes, then replacing them. 'Before we come to the evidence, it is my task to give you an outline of the prosecution case.'

He glanced down at the bundle of notes in front of him, then back up at the jury. 'The counts you have heard represent conspiracy to import and distribute significant quantities of a Class-A drug. This first charge relates to conspiracy to import into the country drugs worth, at street level, up to six million pounds.'

He paused again, removed his glasses once more and then looked profoundly apologetic. 'I'm afraid you may hear some rather disturbing information during the course of this trial, but I will endeavour to ensure that you only see what is strictly necessary in helping you to arrive at your decisions.'

He replaced his glasses. 'Nearly six million pounds' worth of cocaine weighs over 160 kilos. The method of importing it cannot be via a drugs mule or postal system. Something far more sophisticated must be deployed. Such as a 1962 Ferrari car. At approximately 4 a.m. on Monday November 26th of last year, such a car arrived on the *Côte D'Albâtre* ferry, transported in an enclosed car trailer from Dieppe to the Port of Newhaven. Nothing unusual about that.' He smiled again. His *trust me, I'm on your side* smile.

'You have before you a folder of documents. The counts on the indictment are behind Tab D. If you turn to Tab F of the bundle you will see a photograph of that car. You may know something about cars or not, but for this case, you do not need to know anything. The essential point is that, as with much of this case, not everything is as it seems. A genuine Ferrari of this type would be worth in the region of five to ten million pounds.'

Cork paused to let that fact sink in. 'It may therefore be inferred that the last thing anyone would do is tear it apart and use it as a Trojan Horse, cramming as many packages of cocaine into every available nook and cranny. But that is exactly what was done. Because this car is a fake. It was designed to closely resemble a 1962 classic. But it is actually a confection of fibreglass laid on the chassis of a VW Beetle.'

He removed his glasses again and smiled at the jurors, as if to say, *I know, incredible, I'm with you on that!*

'Rather fortuitously, the Border Force officer on duty had a particular specialist interest in classic cars. And unlike the Trojan Horse, there was no one to persuade him that everything was fine, or to allay his suspicions. If you could turn to Tab Z, please.' He waited while they all did so, the rustle of pages turning the only sound in the courtroom for a brief while. Each folder was shared between two jurors. Meg shared hers with Maisy Waller.

'There you will see images of the drugs in situ, and gradually being removed. This took some time.' He smiled again, waiting for them to study the photographs.

'None of this is in dispute,' he went on. 'We know when the fake Ferrari arrived, we know where it was loaded, we know the weight and value of the drugs. The question you need to consider, and the answer you need to be sure of is this: to whom did the drugs belong? We will ask you to be patient when we call the evidence of ownership, it is complex – and we say *deliberately* so. There are a number of shell companies and offshore holdings used to muddy the waters. The prosecution will call experts to help you navigate through them. But having done so, you will see there is clear evidence that the car and drugs were ultimately owned by the defendant, Terence Gready.'

Again, he smiled at the jurors. 'I appreciate that what I've told you might sound a little dry, so I'm going to give you a flavour of what happened in the Port of Newhaven Customs shed at approximately 4.30 a.m. on Monday November 26th last year.'

He stated in detail the events that unfolded leading up to the search of the Ferrari.

Cork gave the jurors a theatrical gesture of shock with his arms. 'But in the early stages of the examination of the vehicle, after suspicious packages were found concealed inside the car's spare tyre, Michael Starr assaulted the Border Force officer by punching him in the face and breaking his glasses, as well as assaulting a second officer, and then ran off.' He looked around the court, pausing for a moment. 'You will hear shortly afterwards he was detained by the police, hardly *The Great Escape*!'

The jurors looked among themselves, unsure at this early stage if they should laugh. Meg glanced at the judge, who was not smiling.

Jupp, his voice heavily laced with sarcasm, said, 'Mr Cork, I'd be grateful if you could reserve your jokes for when you are at the other kind of bar.'

Cork momentarily turned towards him. 'I apologize, Your Honour, it just slipped out. It won't happen again.'

As he turned back towards the jury, Meg watched the prosecutor's face closely. There was something very measured about the man. She didn't think he was the kind of person who would let anything *just slip out*. Everything he said would be for a reason. The joke, which he must have known would bring a reprimand, was clever. He was trying to win the jury over by showing them he was a regular guy beneath his wig and gown, that he had a good sense of humour. And she realized what he had just so cleverly done. By getting the big bad judge to chastise him for a seemingly harmless joke, he had got most of the jury on his side.

Cork continued. 'The details of that run for freedom are that Starr made his move, two police officers attempted to apprehend him a short distance on and he assaulted both of them with a wheel brace, before hijacking a car and escaping. Following a high-speed pursuit, Starr was subsequently stopped and arrested just over an hour later.' He paused again, glad to see that he had a reasonably attentive jury.

'One important thing I would like you all to bear in mind is that throughout his interviews with the police, the defendant, Terence Gready, has strenuously denied that he had any connection with Mr Starr. He has denied that he had any knowledge of the classic car company, LH Classics, which had employed Mr Starr for nearly sixteen years. He has denied that at any time he has ever met Mr Starr. During the course of this trial I will be endeavouring to prove to you that not only had the defendant met Mr Starr, but that he actually employed Mr Starr! And to give you a further flavour of the denial by the defendant of having any knowledge of Mr Starr, I will be showing CCTV images of Starr actually entering the offices of Terence Gready, from which you can draw your own conclusions.

'The two men worked together through a very cleverly set up chain of shell companies around the globe established for one reason and for one reason only, which was to put as much distance as possible between himself and LH Classics in an attempt to hide from the authorities the fact that he did actually own one hundred per cent of this company himself. And you will also hear about evidence seized by the police linking the defendant with Michael Starr and again you will be able to draw your own conclusions.'

Once more, Cork looked at the jury. 'I suggest that the defendant, Terence Gready, who purports to the outside world to be a simple legal aid solicitor, is in fact an immensely cunning and dangerous man, the criminal mastermind behind a vast and highly lucrative major drugs importation business. We will show that for many years he has been methodically distributing Class-A drugs within Sussex. More recently that drugs network has been modelled on the so-called county lines drug supply network.

'During the course of this trial I will endeavour to show you just how clever Terence Gready has been, and just how far-reaching the network of dealers he controls really is.' He paused again.

'However much you may have heard or read about the drug cocaine, it is classified as a Class-A drug and therefore I cannot overestimate the seriousness of this crime. Of course, if you are not sure on any of these counts, you must acquit. The learned judge will give you directions on the law in due course, but you may already know the prosecution brings this case and it is for the prosecution to prove each charge. The defendant does not have to prove anything. And for the prosecution to prove its case, you must be satisfied on the evidence so that you are sure of the defendant's guilt and that he committed the acts described.'

Cork made eye contact again with the jury. Meg felt a shiver as his eyes bored into hers.

'One thing that may surprise you during the course of this trial is that not all evidence will come from live witnesses. That makes for good television, but it is not how things work in reality. There are Admissions, facts which are not disputed. To keep this trial focused on the relevant issues, these have been agreed by the prosecution and defence.'

Meg was unsure what he meant by this. But there was no opportunity at this moment to question the statement.

'There are the interviews with the defendant, who when questioned went *no comment* which he was entitled to do. You will be hearing from the police officers involved in the investigation and, finally, the financial experts, who will unpick the trail of ownership of the fake Ferrari, behind Tab X, to companies based in Panama, the Seychelles, the Cayman Islands and Liechtenstein, and finally back to the man before you in the dock today. Terence Gready.

'You will also hear detailed evidence about items that were recovered from the defendant's home address including a key to a safety deposit box with the company Safe Box

Co. These items and documents provide extensive details to support the evidence against this defendant. The police, during these searches, also recovered a large quantity of cash.'

Meg, although listening intently, was thinking about her fellow jurors. If she was going to have to manipulate them, would she have more sway as just a straightforward juror or by being elected the foreperson? Before the start of the proceedings this morning, they had agreed between them that during the lunch break they would go out and get sandwiches, then return to discuss and decide on who it should be.

She would be up against Roberts. The retired cop had made it plain he felt he was best suited to the role. Hugo Pink also clearly believed he should do it, as did Harold Trout, the retired actuary who had turned up today in a bow tie.

Yesterday evening she was checking her jury list. She couldn't remember most of their names, but she was able to visualize their faces. What a microcosm of Little England this bunch was, she thought.

Meg had always been a good salesperson and she knew one of her strengths was in being persuasive, something she had always relished in her senior account manager role at Kempsons. She could, when she wanted, be extremely forceful – something Nick had noted when he was her line manager, long before they had started dating. Over the coming days she was going to have to use that ability to maximum effect.

She would start this lunchtime, getting them to agree, come hell or high water, to giving her the foreperson role.

47

They've elected me foreperson, but that's all I'm allowed to tell you – actually I don't think I'm even supposed to tell anyone that. But I guess in deepest Ecuador you can probably keep a secret :-) Sending this from the train. Love you and miss you. Mum XX

Meg sat in her seat in the packed carriage and read through the WhatsApp message as the train rolled past the remains of the former Lewes Racecourse, then sent it. She'd realized the train from Hove station, a twenty-minute walk or five-minute drive from her home, was a lot easier than driving to Lewes – and she knew it would please Laura to know she was doing something more environmentally friendly than driving. Silly, she thought, that she should be doing something to seek her daughter's approval, but it was another small way of creating a bond with her over this vast distance separating them.

God, she so wished she could get a message to her to get the hell out of that damned country and on a plane back home, but she knew that wouldn't necessarily make her any safer from these evil people. She did a mental calculation. Ecuador was five hours behind the UK, so it would be midday for Laura. She wondered where she and Cassie were right now.

A reply came back just a couple of minutes later. With it was a photograph of a roadside cafe with what looked like small animals cooking on a rotary grill outside.

> Wow, does that mean you get to wear a wig
> when you deliver the verdict? Or is that just the
> judge???!!! Respect, Mum! See this pic?? Am
> totally grossed out – did you know guinea pig is
> the local delicacy? Yech. How cruel. Good for you
> taking the train – my mum saving the planet!
> I'm so proud of you, luv uuuuuu XXXXX

Meg smiled, her eyes moist. There was so much to be afraid of in Laura's big adventure, quite apart from the bastards who were threatening her. The standards of driving in South America; the crime in a place where life was cheap. Two young girls travelling alone. Such damned easy targets.

She tried to put those worries from her mind and thought back to lunchtime today. To her surprise it had been Hugo, the one she'd thought would be the biggest problem, who had turned into her ally. He'd done it in a crass, patronizing way, which had included patting her thigh, suggestively, but she didn't care.

'Women have better intuition than us men, this lady wants the role and, in the interests of demonstrating gender equality on this jury, I vote we seriously consider Mrs Magellan as our foreperson,' he'd said. Then he'd gone on to really annoy her with his comment, 'At home, She-Who-Must-Be-Obeyed is almost always right.'

In different circumstances she might have brained him with the closest weapon. But at lunchtime today she could have kissed him. Except he was gross, sweaty and a lech. It didn't matter, she had what she wanted. And 'Bat Out of Hell' was blasting out of the radio into her headphones, lifting her mood fleetingly as the train rolled into Brighton station.

At 4.30 p.m. they'd been released for the day and were required back for a 10 a.m. resumption tomorrow.

A quarter of an hour later, Meg left Hove station in bright, warm, late-afternoon sunshine and walked down towards her house. She passed a row of large, terraced Victorian houses. In one front garden she passed, a couple were sitting on a bench in shorts with a bottle of wine in a bucket on the table in front of them, soaking up the rays. A little further down the street she smelled smoke from a barbecue. Normality. Everyone seemed to be having a pleasant afternoon, going into a pleasant evening. Just doing normal stuff.

Everyone except herself. She walked with fear curling in her stomach, enveloped in a darkness blacker than her shadow that glided beside her.

The forecast was good for the next few days, getting increasingly warm, maybe an early summer heatwave. Usually, she'd have made plans. Maybe changed into her swimming cozzie and taken a book down to the beach. Or called Ali and suggested meeting at their favourite seafront bar for a cocktail. But she just wanted to be home, indoors with her thoughts, all the doors bolted.

Thank goodness the house would be more secure now. Last night she'd had the locks changed by an emergency locksmith who'd charged her an outrageous amount. But she didn't care. At least that evil bastard who had called her on Saturday evening wouldn't find it quite so easy to invade her home now.

She opened the front door and was greeted by Daphne, who looked at her like she would have called the RSPCA if

PETER JAMES

she knew how to dial a phone. On the floor, among a couple
of envelopes that looked like bills, was a brown Amazon
package.

Closing the door, she knelt and stroked the cat. 'Hey,
beautiful! What's your problem?' Then she prised open the
package and saw it was an old movie she'd ordered after
one of the jurors had mentioned it last week. *Twelve Angry
Men.* What had particularly interested her about the film,
when she'd looked it up online later, was its subject. It was
about a juror who had, one by one, changed the minds of
all his fellow jurors from a guilty to an innocent verdict. She
would watch it this evening.

'You hungry, Daffers? Let me get you some food. Your
mummy has had a busy day. Want me to tell you about it?
They made me foreperson. Impressed?'

As she walked across the hall, Meg continued chatting
to the cat. 'We heard the opening statement from the
prosecution this morning. Then all afternoon we were
sequestered in the jury room, because there were more legal
arguments going on in court. I'm not really sure what *legal
arguments* are, but I guess they're important and hey, it
meant I got to leave the court a little early. I'll bet you're
glad about that, aren't—'

She stopped in mid-sentence as she entered the kitchen.
Her flesh crawled. On the table was a new photograph, a
typed note beside it.

She ran over to it and stared down.

The photograph, again taken with a telephoto lens, was
of Laura and Cassie, taken from behind as they boarded
a tiny, archaic train with just two carriages. At the top in
small print was the word *Alausí* followed by the date.
Yesterday.

The note read:

> Laura and Cassie having a great time on the
> Devil's Nose railway! All the animals fed and
> watered. Smart thinking, changing the locks.
> Nice try. Well done on becoming foreperson.
> Keep our phone with you at all times. You are
> doing well. Just don't try a silly stunt like
> changing your locks again, otherwise we'll have
> to hurt Laura. Nothing life-threatening, but a
> nasty wound. One which in that heat could turn
> septic very quickly. Hospitals in that part of
> Ecuador are a bit scarce and a bit shit. I'm sure
> you understand me.

Moments later her new phone rang. She answered, warily, and heard the familiar male voice from before.

'You are doing well, Meg, apart from that faffing around with the locks. That won't stop us. Please don't underestimate us. I really want your daughter to be safe, believe me, I've a little girl almost exactly her age and I know how I'd feel if I knew her life was in danger. So, let's just behave like adults, shall we?'

'You bastard,' she replied, the words coming out before she could stop them.

'Attitude is not going to help you, Meg. I'm sure you don't like me at this moment, but when I return Laura safely home, you will thank me and realize I'm your best friend in the world.'

'In your fucking dreams.'

'Tut, tut, I hope you don't use that language with your fellow jurors. What you need to understand is that we're both on the same side here.'

'Oh yes? Like one of us is on the side of the Devil and the other on the side of the Angels?'

'You really need to calm down, Meg. Focus. Think just one thing. You want to see Laura again, don't you?'

She said nothing.

After some moments, he went on. 'Of course you do, she's all the family you have left in the world. How would your life be without her? With her dead, like your husband and son? Think about it, Meg. Think what it would be like to go to the airport and sign a receipt for little Laura in a coffin. Go on, think really hard. What kind of wood would you choose for it? What lining inside? Brass handles?'

'Stop it,' she blurted, choked. 'Please stop.'

'Meg, you know what you have to do. We are very aware some of your fellow jurors could be a problem, but don't worry about them – we'll do what we can to take care of it.'

The line went dead.

48

At 7 p.m., in the Hoxton office, computer programmer Rio Zambrano, former Met detective Paul Constantinidi and Gready's solicitor, Nick Fox, sat at the conference table with the large computer monitor on the wall in front of them displaying an image of Hugo Pink.

'OK, guys, we got to first base,' Fox said. 'This gentleman was only too happy to take our offer to help him out of his financial hole. What he said in the jury room today worked. So now we need to turn our focus on the other potential problem jurors – and witnesses. Let's start with the jurors.'

He clicked a button on his mouse and the image changed to the silver-haired man in his sixties.

'Mike Roberts,' Fox said. 'Retired former Detective Superintendent with Hampshire Police. All we really know about him is that he was forced to take early retirement. There's a good chance he's bitter about that, but we need more information on him – I'm working on it.'

He clicked the mouse again. A photograph appeared of a slender man with rimless glasses, his fair hair fashionably styled. Moments later, more images of him came onto the screen in sequence, and then a Wikipedia entry.

Toby DeWinter, 31, Actor. Married to Michael – né Davenport.

PETER JAMES

'What do we know about him, Nick?' Paul Constantinidi asked.

'Gay, left wing, LGBT+ activist, very involved in Brighton Pride. Intellectual. Couldn't call which way he would decide. But he might take the side of the underdog.'

Constantinidi nodded. 'I'll see if I can dig up anything on him.'

Both men grinned. Rio Zambrano, getting their gist, grinned also.

Next up was tight-faced Maisy Waller, with a silver cross on a chain around her neck.

'Single,' Constantinidi said. 'Attends a High Anglican church. Lives with her elderly mother incapacitated with dementia. A good Christian, she's a likely forgiveness merchant. "Not guilty" should be an easy win.'

They carried on through the list of jurors.

The one that all three agreed was another potential problem was the horsey woman, Gwendoline Smythson, who, from the sound relayed back to them via the bug implanted in Meg Magellan's burner phone, had already decided Gready was guilty from the prosecution's opening statement.

What they needed to be wary of, Nick Fox cautioned the two men, was getting a hung jury. They needed an out-and-out 'not guilty' verdict on each count. Anything less could result in a retrial. Which meant it was going to be down to Meg Magellan's powers of persuasion, along with any influence they could bring on dissenting jurors.

She would have her work cut out. And Fox knew very well, from his reading of the disclosure documents, that some of the evidence against Gready was extremely damning. Therein lay the big difference between having a jury trial and not. Judges wanted facts; juries wanted to listen to stories. Winning or losing a case was in large part a question of who told the jury the best story, the prosecution counsel or the defence. They could not take the risk of this trial ending up in front of a judge, solo. Absolute care was needed. And he had found generally throughout his career that if you wanted someone silent, the next best thing to killing them was to frighten them – frighten them like they'd never known fear before.

When they had finished identifying the potential problem jurors, Nick Fox next looked at the witnesses who would be presenting evidence for the prosecution. Several would be a problem. There were a number of 'expert witnesses' – people with the credentials to be an acknowledged authority in their field. He had read all of their statements. And the facts supporting them.

And the witness they were about to hear was going to be Meg Magellan's first big challenge.

49

The judge entered and everyone remained standing until he was seated. Then Stephen Cork stood, his collar and bands looking freshly laundered and crisply white against the black of his gown. He was a picture of elegance. The jury entered the court and took their seats.

'Ladies and gentlemen of the jury, yesterday I outlined the Crown case to you in broad terms. I will remind you of one key fact, which is that the defendant, Terence Gready, has strenuously denied knowing – or indeed ever in his life meeting – a gentleman by the name of Michael Starr. I will remind you also that Michael Starr was the driver of the vehicle and trailer transporting the fake Ferrari car in which was found six million pounds' worth of the Class-A drug, cocaine. Please do remember this very important thing. Terence Gready has denied *ever* meeting Mr Starr.'

Cork engaged friendly eye contact with members of the jury, before continuing. 'It is now my task to bring out the evidence for you to consider. Can we please call my first witness, Ray Parker.'

An usher brought in a man in his sixties, holding a thick folder.

Meg watched him with interest, thinking he looked uncomfortable in his suit and white shirt. His tie was too

232

short, as were his trousers. He looked like a man who had dressed up for the occasion because he felt he ought to but would have been happier in jeans and a T-shirt.

'Please say your name,' asked the clerk.

He said loudly, but falteringly, 'Raymond Parker.'

'Will you take the oath or an affirmation?'

The man blushed, beads of perspiration popping on his brow. He looked like he was out of his comfort zone in every way. Instead of addressing the clerk, he looked up at the judge in answer. 'Affirmation, please, My Lord – I mean, Your Honour.'

Jupp smiled. The clerk handed him a card.

In a gruff voice, Ray Parker read the words on it. 'I solemnly and sincerely declare and affirm that the evidence I shall give will be the truth, the whole truth and nothing but the truth.'

Jupp turned to the prosecutor. 'Please proceed with your witness.'

'Thank you, Your Honour.' In a calm, measured voice, Cork asked, 'Can you give your name and occupation to the jury, please?'

'Raymond Parker. I work for the Sussex Police Digital Forensics Unit.'

Meg felt for the man. He was clearly a back-room boffin. The sort of person who was not comfortable talking to strangers – especially not under this kind of close scrutiny.

Cork responded. 'So, you have worked there for three years, and prior to that you were employed for eleven years in British Telecom's Digital Forensics Department, liaising with police forces around England, with your speciality being what is termed *cell-site analysis*, is that right?'

'It is, yes.'

'And in addition are you also an expert in identifying

the location of mobile phones through their connectivity with local Wi-Fi installations?'

'Yes, sir.'

'You are in fact an expert witness in such matters?'

'I am, sir.'

'Can you please explain what work you do in the Sussex Police Digital Forensics Unit?'

Parker half turned towards the jury. Meg studied him hard. He looked a decent man, she decided, if a bit nervy. She would have been, too, in that box, in front of everyone. He stumbled over his first few words before he got into his stride.

'Well, I'm sure many people in this court have heard that boast, by the phone companies, that even the most basic handset today contains more computing power than NASA had in 1969 when they put a man on the moon. But really, it's no idle boast. Not only are phones getting more powerful by the day, they contain more and more data about their owners.'

Blinking hard, he stopped, pulled out a handkerchief and dabbed his forehead, before continuing. 'This began as a cunning ploy by the phone companies to learn more about their customers, to find out their travel habits, their likes and dislikes, the purchases they made, to help target them for future sales. Technology is evolving rapidly. Today, people are carrying around in their handsets computers that will record an astonishing amount of data about who they contacted, what they said, where they were. A forensic download of that information can paint a detailed picture of their life.' He was looking more confident now, Meg thought, comfortable expanding on his world. He managed a sly smile at the jurors.

'That information is of immense value to companies

such as Facebook, Twitter, Instagram, WhatsApp, as they can use it in all kinds of commercial ways. But –' he smiled again – 'it is also of great value to the police when they want to trace someone's movements. I'm sure you've all heard of the expression *digital footprints*. Most of us who own a mobile phone leave digital footprints wherever we go. I don't mean just to a town, or even a particular street. The technology today is accurate enough to give us an address. Sometimes even the number of a particular apartment in a block of flats.'

Stephen Cork prompted, 'It is not in issue that you prepared a report on this matter for this trial. Could you turn to Tab A in the bundle and confirm to the jury what that is?'

Parker took a few moments to leaf through the papers in front of him, then again addressed the jurors, looking even more confident. 'Mobile phones, just like their owners, tend to be very sociable creatures – they like to find friends wherever they are!'

That brought a smile to most of the jurors' faces, but not Meg's; she was frozen in concentration.

'It's a bit like that Steven Spielberg film, *ET,*' he continued. 'They constantly send out signals, looking for friends. They get a signal back from the nearest mobile phone mast to them. Like a lot of neurotic people, they need constant reassurance, so they carry on sending out signals – like, *Hello, I am here!* – until a second mast responds. Then, because they are still neurotic and unsure of themselves, they try for a third mast!'

'And these conversations of an *ET* nature,' Cork asked with a good-humoured smile. 'What do these phones and the masts chat to each other about? The weather? Politics? Football?'

Parker smiled nervously. 'The *chat* is all through electronic signals; it is possible to interrogate and establish from them the location of a specific phone.'

'And what were you tasked with in this report?'

'I was tasked with providing an account of the movements of the mobile phone belonging to Mr Michael Starr between the dates of January 1st and Monday November 26th of last year.'

'What can you tell us about Mr Starr's movements?'

'During this period, Michael Starr made trips most days from an area identified as his home, in Chichester, West Sussex, to an area which includes the offices of the classic car dealership, LH Classics, just outside Bosham. By further interrogation of Wi-Fi signals, I was able to establish that the precise location Mr Starr attended was indeed the offices of LH Classics.'

'Apart from weekends and holidays, were there any variations to this routine? Any other places Mr Starr visited occasionally other than the Bosham premises of LH Classics?' Cork queried.

'Yes, on occasion during the past year – which were the records I checked, and the dates are marked by Tab N – Mr Starr attended premises in the city of Brighton and Hove.'

'Are you able to give us, accurately, the address of these premises?'

'Yes. Number 176A Edward Street, Brighton.'

'Would I be correct in saying that the premises at 176A Edward Street is in a row of terraced buildings which include a vintage women's clothing store, a Chinese takeaway and three other law firms?'

'That is correct.'

'And is it correct that the ground floor of 176A Edward

Street is occupied by a Chinese takeaway called Sun Yip Lee?'

'Yes, sir.'

'And is it also correct that the three floors above Sun Yip Lee are occupied by the premises of TG Law, legal aid law practice?'

'That is correct.'

Cork paused before continuing. 'A further question: are there any other premises occupying this same address in Edward Street, Brighton, where Sun Yip Lee is located? Somewhere else in the same building that Mr Starr might have visited?'

'The rest of the building is occupied by the law offices of TG Law. They would be the only other possibility.'

'Thank you.' Cork continued. 'Mr Parker, could you please explain to all of us in this court how the process of identifying the specific location of a mobile phone works in more detail, to help us all understand this better?'

Ray Parker turned back to face the jurors directly and went into *expert* mode. 'I need to point out that triangulation between three phone masts gives an indication of the location of a phone but rarely the precise location.' He drew a large imaginary triangle with his finger as a diagram for the jurors. 'The phone will be somewhere in the centre of this triangle.'

'So, you could not be certain which address, precisely, the defendant visited the morning of November 21st?' Cork asked.

'Well, yes, I can be, and I will explain how. It is hard to pinpoint an exact location in a rural environment, where several square miles could be covered by triangulating mobile phone masts. But in an urban situation we can be a lot more precise, partly due to the density of masts and partly due to other aids available to us, such as Wi-Fi and CCTV. In this case in particular we can be accurate to within two hundred square yards. That is still quite a big area, including Brighton and Hove Magistrates' Court and Brighton Crown Court, the premises of Sun Yip Lee, a ladies' vintage clothing shop, Dig For Victory, the law offices of TG Law, and also the premises of Latest Television and the *Argus* newspaper, as well as a substantial number of residential addresses. However, we have other tools available to us, as I mentioned, to pinpoint the location more precisely.'

He paused to mop his brow again. 'The first is all the Wi-Fi that the phone logs on to in an attempt to connect. In this particular instance I have obtained the Wi-Fi logs of six premises within the immediate area of 176A Edward Street, including those of Sun Yip Lee and TG Law, which put Mr Starr, on each visit, to a location within two square metres of 176A Edward Street.'

'Thank you.' Cork smiled, the very picture of confidence, at the jury. 'Wednesday November 21st. Perhaps the jury would like to take note of that date, as it will be important in due course.' Meg realized that this was just a few days before the car arrived at Newhaven. 'We will now look at this address and the link between Gready and Starr. I will start by playing you a video from a CCTV camera across the road from the premises of TG Law.'

He gave a signal to the clerk.

50

On the monitor screen, to the left of where the judge was seated, angled so that everyone in the courtroom would see it, a colour, low-resolution video began playing. It showed a wide urban street, with traffic passing. On the far side were three firms of solicitors, shoulder-to-shoulder, a Chinese takeaway, Sun Yip Lee, with the name TG LAW across a first-floor window, and a small fashion store next door. A clock in the top right-hand corner of the frame showed 11.17 a.m.

An elderly woman walked along the far pavement, pulling a wheeled shopper. Then a man appeared, wearing a bomber jacket, jeans, dark glasses and a beanie. He was walking determinedly, on a mission, passing the premises of the first three firms of solicitors, then the takeaway restaurant, and stopping just beyond it, at a doorway. Reaching out his left arm, he pressed what was, presumably, the entry-phone bell. The door opened shortly after and he went in.

As the video ended, Stephen Cork asked, 'Mr Parker, are you able to identify the man in the footage we have just seen, who entered the premises of TG Law?'

'No, the quality of the footage doesn't allow me to identify who that is for certain, but whoever it is was carrying Michael Starr's phone.'

239

Cork thanked him.

Primrose Brown QC stood up. 'Good morning. I appear for the defendant. I believe that eleven people worked in the law offices of TG Law: four other solicitors, in addition to the defendant, one paralegal, two legal executives, two legal secretaries and an accounts clerk. You can't be certain he was visiting TG Law, can you?'

'No.'

'Or, if he did, that he wasn't visiting one of the ten other people who worked there?'

'No.'

'There's nothing to show that he met anyone at all, is there?'

Parker replied, 'No.'

'Mr Parker, you have mentioned the subject of Wi-Fi connectivity. What margin for error in these connections might there be? Are they completely accurate or could there be doubt – by which I mean sufficient doubt to allow for the possibility of error within the criteria of this court? Can you really trust the accuracy of the Wi-Fi?'

Meg watched Parker shift uncomfortably. *Good*, she thought. Good question!

Parker answered. 'We don't rely solely on Wi-Fi records – we always try to support these, where possible, with CCTV footage, and in this instance, we have obtained footage from the camera of Brighton Law Courts, located directly opposite number 176A Edward Street. Significantly, we have footage on the date of the last recorded visit of a male in possession of Mr Starr's phone in the vicinity of 176A Edward Street on Wednesday November 21st of last year, which clearly shows the male entering the door to the side of Sun Yip Lee, which is the entrance to the offices of TG Law.'

Brown continued. 'You have no evidence that the two men met. Is that correct?'

Parker replied reluctantly, 'That is correct.'

'Mr Parker, is there CCTV footage showing that same male leaving the premises?'

'No, this is all we have.'

'So we don't know if it was Mr Starr who was there, if he met anyone, or even, on the CCTV evidence, if he ever left?'

Parker replied a grudging, 'No.'

'Then I have no more questions.' Brown sat down.

Cork told the court he also had no further questions and Judge Jupp told Parker that he could stand down.

'I would now like to call my witness Haydn Kelly,' Stephen Cork said.

Defence Counsel Primrose Brown rose. 'Your Honour, can I ask for a short adjournment of no more than twenty minutes? I have arranged for an expert witness to listen to the evidence that this next witness for the prosecution will be giving to the court. I understand his train this morning was delayed but he is on his way to court as I speak.'

Richard Jupp responded, 'Very well, Ms Brown, we will adjourn for twenty minutes.'

51

Meg, along with her fellow jurors, filed out of the court and into the jury room. It was furnished with a long, plain, rectangular table taking up much of the space, with reasonably comfortable chairs upholstered in purple and a blue carpet. There was a fan on a tall stand, a dehumidifier, a monitor, a whiteboard with a selection of coloured marker pens, tea and coffee-making facilities, as well as male and female toilets. The solitary, curtained window looked out at a blank wall. There was nothing, she had noted previously, to distract them from their purpose for being here.

And on one wall was a stark warning notice.

It is contempt of court punishable by a fine or imprisonment for a juror to disclose to any person any particulars of statements made, opinions expressed, arguments advanced or votes cast by members of the jury in the course of their deliberations.

Everyone took their seat, in the same order as earlier today, with herself, now she was foreperson, given the one chair with arms at the head of the table.

'Are we going to be long? Shall we get refreshments?' Gwen asked in her affected accent. 'Or is there someone who will bring drinks?'

Harold Trout – Meg remembered his name – said, 'I'm afraid it's self-service. I'll put the kettle on.'

The woman frowned, as if never before in her life had she had to stoop so low as to make a drink herself. 'Well,' she said. 'I hope we can get rid of this beastly business before Royal Ascot. Can anyone imagine the disappointment of missing it – especially Ladies Day – because of some horrid little drug dealer?' She looked around, her face a mask of contempt.

From the blank expressions around the table, it didn't seem to Meg that anyone else could imagine it.

'I mean to say, the man is obviously guilty,' she went on. 'I think we've already heard quite enough to reach a verdict, don't you all?'

'Well,' Trout said, standing up and pottering over to the kettle, 'I don't think I can agree with that.'

Meg looked at the woman. 'Mrs Smythson—'

'Oh, Gwen, please, Meg,' she simpered then added, 'As we are all becoming such good friends here.'

'Very well, Gwen,' Meg said. 'I really don't see how you can have formed a verdict when we have only heard the opening statement by the prosecution counsel and the first witness. And we've barely heard anything yet from the defence.'

'Really?' Gwen retorted. 'Well, I think I've heard quite enough, and we could all save a lot of time and unnecessary expense by agreeing to an early verdict, don't you think?'

'No,' Meg said, firmly. 'I don't.'

To her relief, from the expressions and nods of her fellow jurors, they did not either.

'I think it would be extremely inappropriate not to hear out the full trial,' said Maisy Waller.

'And unbalanced,' Meg said, emphatically. 'It would be a complete dereliction of our duty.'

Mike Roberts chipped in. 'Gwen, we might have our private opinions of the defendant at this stage – and as a former detective who has dealt with plenty of Terence Gready characters in my time, I do understand where you are coming from – but as the judge has reminded us, persons on trial under English law are innocent until proved guilty. I agree with our foreperson and Maisy, we need to hear all the evidence from both sides.'

'Huh,' Gwen said with a scowl. Then she turned to Trout. 'I'll have an Earl Grey, with just a touch of milk and two sweeteners.'

He smiled at her politely. 'I think it's best if we all make our own drinks.'

Gwen gave a *what's this world coming to?* shake of her head.

'I really don't think we have enough information at this stage to even begin to discuss what we've heard so far, Gwen,' Meg said, sternly.

'Really? Well, let me tell you, the hat I've had made for Ascot this year has cost me a fortune.'

'Would you like me to ask the judge if he will excuse you from this jury on the grounds of what your hat has cost?' Meg asked her.

There were some smiles around the table.

The woman looked at them all, partly in disgust and partly in bewilderment. 'Well, surely none of us wants to miss it, do we?'

'I'm afraid I've never been,' Meg said. 'And to be honest, Ascot is the least of our worries.'

52

Under blazing hot, cloudless sunshine in Guayaquil's Seminario Park, Laura knelt, smiling happily, beside a large iguana, as Cassie took a video. They had both been a little subdued after thinking they might have had their drinks spiked last night. Two very sleazy guys had been hitting on them in a bar, and they had both felt very drunk after just two small beers. They'd asked the barman to call them a taxi, and drunk a lot of water, at Cassie's suggestion – she'd read about it somewhere – when they got back to their room. But Laura perked up at the sight of the camera.

'Hey, everybody!' Laura said to the camera. 'When I marry, I'm going to marry an iguana! Aren't they beautiful? Did you know, here's an interesting fact for you . . . they have two penises.' She paused. 'It's true!'

Cassie snorted and ended the video laughing. 'Seriously?'

'Seriously!' Laura replied. 'They're called *hemipenises*. One works with the left testicle and the other with the right. It gives them two shots at impregnating the female.'

'Are you sure it's not so the female has a choice of sizes? I mean, how cool would that be?' She put on an affected accent. 'Eow, Rodders, I think tonight I'll go for the big one.'

Laura laughed. 'And if he can't raise one, well, hell, he's got backup!'

The crazy-paved paths through the small park in the centre of the busy city were teeming with iguanas of every size, a sanctuary the creatures had made their own. Tourists, many backpackers like themselves, were posing with them and the iguanas seemed quite happy.

Suddenly, Cassie looked serious. 'Let's go and sit down.' She pointed to an empty bench.

They eased their heavy backpacks off their shoulders and sat, placing them on the ground in front of them, watching the interaction between the people in the park and the prehistoric-looking creatures in silence for some moments. Both of them took several photographs. Then, still holding her phone up and without looking at Laura, Cassie said, quietly, 'Someone is following us.'

Laura replied, 'Oh yes? Is he fit?'

'I'm serious.'

Laura gave her a sideways look. Her friend wasn't smiling. 'One of the guys from last night?'

Cassie shook her head. 'No, but I've got a feeling I've seen him before. Creepy. Don't look now, he's on that bench, the far side of the tree in the middle of the path, with the turquoise building behind him.'

Laura waited a few seconds, then with her head still tilted towards her friend, her eyes safely concealed behind her sunglasses, glanced in the direction Cassie said. A man, maybe in his forties though it was hard to tell his age from this distance, wearing a blue baseball cap, sunglasses, T-shirt and jeans was sitting alone on a bench, seemingly absorbing the atmosphere. A camera with a long lens lay on his lap.

'Blue cap?' she queried.

'Maybe I'm being paranoid, but I swear I've seen him before. And more than once. I wasn't going to say anything, but it's very weird that now he's here.'

'We're following a pretty common tourist route, C. Maybe he's just in sync with us?'

'Maybe,' Cassie said, dubiously.

'Maybe he has two penises?'

Cassie grinned. 'Now, that would make him more interesting!'

'Shall I go over to him and ask him how many he has?'

'No way!' She hesitated. 'Oh, shit.'

'What?'

'Don't look. He's taking a photograph of us.'

53

A sturdy, confident-looking middle-aged man, with close-cropped hair, was led into court by an usher. He was dressed in a navy-blue suit, white shirt and burgundy tie and had a friendly demeanour. He entered the witness stand, stated his name when requested and took the oath as if well used to doing this.

Stephen Cork stood up. 'Haydn Kelly, could you please tell the court your professional qualifications.'

'Yes, of course.' He turned to the jury. 'I was elected Dean of the Faculty of Podiatric Surgery completing a full three-year term of office. I still have supported links with the University of Plymouth where I initially qualified before undertaking and completing my Fellowship in London. I have received university accreditation as an expert witness. I was also the founding chair of a forensic podiatry group. I have contributed to book chapters and written and compiled a textbook on Forensic Gait Analysis.'

Cork remained standing. 'And in 2000 you created Forensic Gait Analysis. It was during July of that same year when it was first admissible as expert evidence in criminal law, at the Old Bailey, London. Is that correct?'

'Yes, it is.'

Cork continued. 'Could you tell the court in your own words what is Forensic Gait Analysis?'

'In the general context, Forensic Gait Analysis is the application of gait analysis knowledge to legal matters or problems. More specifically, the identification of a person or persons by their gait or features of their gait, usually from closed-circuit television – CCTV – footage and comparison to footage of a known individual.'

Kelly cleared his throat and went on. 'We must also appreciate that all forms of identification are based on probability and this should not be misunderstood.'

'Thank you for clarifying that with the court. Is it also the case that you have provided expert evidence on numerous occasions, receiving instructions by counsel for the prosecution and the defence, in the UK and overseas?'

Kelly answered in the affirmative.

'And you have given expert evidence in medico-legal matters of clinical negligence and personal injuries to the civil courts for many years. Is that also correct?'

'Yes,' Kelly replied.

'And this is in addition to you having treated many thousands of patients in your years of practice, with the diagnosis and treatment of a wide variety of foot, lower limb and musculoskeletal-related problems, which often involves gait analysis and biomechanical assessments?'

'Yes, that is correct.'

'I would now like to come, if I may, to the video footage that you have studied, and as detailed in your report provided for the court. In particular, the video CCTV footage taken in Edward Street, Kemp Town, Brighton, on the morning of Wednesday November 21st of last year, which has been shown to this court. Could you please tell us what you are able to establish from this?'

'Firstly, the CCTV footage was examined, followed by that of the custody suite video footage. Both are of a quality that is suitable for the purpose of Forensic Gait Analysis to be undertaken. The unknown person displayed on the CCTV footage is seen walking along Edward Street and stopping at the doorway to the premises named TG Law. The person rang the doorbell and some moments later entered the premises. That individual seen on the CCTV footage displays the same distinctive and unusual features of gait as seen on the comparative footage taken of the person made known to me as Michael Starr, filmed walking in and around the police custody centre in Brighton.'

'So, in your professional opinion as an expert in Forensic Gait Analysis, you are of the view that the person shown in the CCTV footage in Edward Street has the same distinctive features of gait as those displayed by the defendant Michael Starr recorded on the custody suite footage?'

'Yes.'

'From the material provided to you, is there anything that indicates otherwise?'

'No.'

Primrose Brown rose to her feet, turning to Kelly. 'You expect the jury to believe that the poor-quality CCTV footage, and your analysis of it, is proof that Mr Starr went into those premises that day?'

Jupp tilted his head towards the expert.

Kelly responded calmly but pointedly, a true expert witness and impartial as always, addressing first the judge, then the jury. 'Your Honour, I'm unable to comment on other areas of expertise beyond my own – such as the field of facial recognition. In my opinion the CCTV footage and the custody suite footage are both suitable for the purposes of Forensic Gait Analysis, as I have outlined and as detailed in my report. The report provided by the defence's gait expert also confirms the material is suitable for such purposes.'

Primrose Brown shuffled some papers. 'Sir, you have presented your evidence that Mr Starr entered the premises of TG Law, but referring back to my earlier statement that there are ten people employed at the firm of TG Law, in addition to the defendant, are you able to tell this court, from your *Forensic Gait Analysis*, which of these eleven people he might – assuming you are correct in the first place – have gone to see?'

Kelly shook his head and politely replied, 'No, madam.'

Brown looked at the witness intently. 'Mr Kelly, is this not really pseudo-science? I suggest you are only interpreting what you have seen to support your findings. How can you be sure of its accuracy?'

Kelly replied, 'With the greatest of respect, that is not the case, madam. Forensic Gait Analysis has and is being used in court cases. I have no doubt that by recognizing the distinctive and unusual features of gait as those displayed by Michael Starr, he is the person entering that premises.'

As Brown sat, Cork immediately stood. 'Thank you, no further questions.'

54

Meg walked home from Hove station through drizzle, beneath a sky as dark and heavy as her heart. A seriously shit day in court. Her hopes had risen after the defence counsel's attempted grilling of Haydn Kelly and the Forensic Gait Analysis evidence, but it went nowhere. Throughout the rest of the day Stephen Cork read through a stream of witness statements made by Gready's work colleagues from November 2018.

With each one in turn denying, all equally convincingly, that they had ever met Michael Starr, the evidence against Gready was growing increasingly strong. During the lunchtime recess, and again during a brief adjournment in the afternoon, the opinionated woman juror, Gwen, had insisted that Gready must be guilty. An alarming number of her fellow jurors concurred, despite Meg's strenuous argument that it was still far too early in the trial to form any opinion, and that there were many more witnesses to come. The arrogant woman was a real problem, she thought. A ghastly snob but, incredibly, she had the ear of most of the jury.

It was already becoming clear to Meg – without the help of Mrs Smythson – that Gready's defence was foundering on the rocks.

What to do?

God, how she wished Nick was around. They could have discussed this together and he would have helped her to come to the right decision. He'd always been such a positive person and so full of wise words. One of her favourite sayings of his was, 'Stay away from negative people – they have a problem for every solution.'

That was how it felt on the jury. All but Hugo Pink, who, resolutely maintained, as she did, that it was far too soon to come to any judgement, and that they were doing the whole notion of justice a great disservice by jumping to early conclusions.

As she opened the front door, the cat looked at her.

'What is it, what do you want to tell me? You need food? Water? Biscuits?'

Then, as she entered the kitchen, she felt a tightening in her throat and stopped, staring. At something on the table that hadn't been there this morning when she'd left.

Another photograph. What now? She went, warily, over to the table and stared down at the print. Laura and Cassie on a park bench, in shorts and T-shirts, with iguanas all around them. The two girls had big grins on their faces but were seemingly oblivious to the camera.

Someone had been in here again.

Were they still here?

She held her breath. Listened. Looked around. Then finally called out, 'Hello?'

Silence.

She checked every room in the house.

The burner phone rang. She jumped. Everything made her jump right now. Her anxiety was so high she felt completely wired.

ID withheld. Of course.

'Hello?' she answered.

The same smug, creepy voice as before. 'Not good today, was it, Meg?'

She looked around, shaking. 'Not great.'

Where are you?

'Meg, you need to know there is another juror on your side. And there is one very negative juror we are going to take care of. Keep the faith.'

'What do you mean *take care of*?'

'Tomorrow Laura and Cassie are doing a zip wire across a gorge. Crazy, if you ask me. Can you imagine the wire breaking? Laura halfway across? I don't even want to think about it.'

'Don't. You. Dare. Please, please,' she implored. 'I'm doing everything I can.'

'I'm sure you are, but it's not enough, is it?'

'What more can I do?' she asked, then broke into a scream. 'What FUCKING MORE?'

'We'll give you all the assistance we can, but you have to be stronger, Meg, more assertive.'

'How?'

'That's for you to figure, Meg. You know what the score is. You know what you have to do.'

There was a long silence.

'How?' she shouted. 'Please tell me how, you bastard!'

But the line was dead.

55

Trembling, Meg put the phone down on the table, fed Daphne, then poured herself a large whisky, really worried where all this was going and how much danger she, her daughter and Cassie and God knows who else that she cared about were in.

She sat down at the table and drank a large gulp. Thinking. Staring at the photograph of the two happy girls. Feeling so desperately alone and scared. And aware that anything she said might either be listened to, live or recorded. She sipped some more, then stared in surprise at her empty glass.

Did I just drink that?

Sod it. She refilled her glass and sat back down. Feeling emboldened, suddenly, she picked up her own phone and dialled Laura. Hell. They hadn't spoken in over a week, she was entitled to call her daughter, damn you, you evil shit.

To her relief, Laura answered almost immediately. 'Hey, Mum!'

'How are you, darling?'

'Oh my God, Mum, it's so good to hear you! I sort of shouldn't tell you this cos I know you will worry but we were a bit freaked out. Don't panic though, we are totally fine now, I promise.'

'What, darling, what on earth has happened to you?'

'Oh, honestly, Mum, chill, it's nothing major. We just had a couple of beers and we were both out of it – I mean after just two beers. We think they were spiked – apparently you have to be really careful about that here. We're on the lookout from now on. We both felt really strange until this morning. Thank God we got back to our rooms OK and just slept it off. Apart from that, we are having the best time!'

For some moments Meg felt in the grip of fear. She desperately, desperately wanted to tell Laura to come home. But she couldn't, and even if she did plead, Laura wouldn't agree. Instead, lamely, she said, 'Please, please, be careful, Laura. It's really important you look after each other. Promise me you will.'

'We will, we will. We're fine, Mum.'

And she really sounded as if she was. From her voice, she seemed so happy, so carefree. They chatted for several minutes, as Laura wanted to know how all her pets were. Then she asked, 'So, how's jury service? Have you got a really nasty villain?'

Meg hesitated before replying. 'Well, I can't really talk about it, I'm not allowed to.'

'Is it a murder trial?'

'I can't say, darling. So, what are your plans?'

'We're going to this place tomorrow everyone says is amazing – a gorge that goes into rapids – and we're going to do a zip wire right over the rapids!'

'Zip wire? Isn't that dangerous?'

'Mum! Honestly!' There was reproach in her tone. 'If it was really dangerous, would I do it?'

Yes, you probably would, Meg wanted to say. Instead, she said, 'Please be careful. Check everything, especially your harness. And if you don't want to do it, just don't do it, OK?'

'I'm always careful,' Laura said, solemnly. Then, her voice brightening, she said, 'Mum, we saw hundreds of iguanas in a park today. A public park where you can just walk through, and the iguanas are literally all around you! It is amazing.'

Meg had to bite her tongue not to give away she'd already seen the iguanas. She had always loved Laura's passion for animals. 'So, I'm guessing the next addition to your menagerie here is going to be an iguana?'

'That would be so cool!' Then the tone of her voice changed. 'Cassie reckons there's a guy following us around. This creepy-looking man with a big camera taking pictures of us. We both saw him in the park this morning. She reckons she's seen him a couple of times before. She doesn't think he had anything to do with the spiked drinks because he wasn't in that bar. We've decided if we see him again, we're both going to challenge him.'

'No,' Meg cautioned, alarmed. 'Just ignore him, don't encourage him.'

God, she so wanted to warn Laura. To tell her to take a flight back home, today if possible. She'd happily pay for their fares. She felt so damned helpless.

'The bus is arriving, gotta go, Mum!'

'I love you, darling. Be safe.'

'I love you, Mum. Cassie says hello!'

'Hello back!'

Meg put the phone back down and sat, deep in thought.
Not guilty.

How?

Gwen was having a toxic influence over the jury.

The trouble was, based on what they had heard so far,

the bloody woman was right. All the evidence they had heard against Terence Gready was compelling. She sat for a long time at the kitchen table, deep in thought.

Who was the juror on her side? Coerced like herself? Pink? And who was the one about to be *taken care of*? Please God, make it Gwen.

And then?

The remaining nine.

Hopefully one of the witnesses still to be called, or Primrose Brown, would come up with something. Something strong and convincing enough for her to be able to persuade her fellow jurors that there was reasonable doubt.

Her thoughts went back to the voice of her caller. Then the voice of her daughter.

She shook with fear.

Zip wire.

56

Laura was going to go first. But as she stood at the top, the gorge looked a long way down and she felt scared. Beautiful and sinister, it looked like an open wound slashed through the midst of the dense forest. A brutal torrent of fast-moving river, foaming through jagged rocks before plunging over rapids. It was fed by one stream of clear water, cascading in forked rivulets down an escarpment, and by another that was muddy, like brown volcanic lava, pouring from a cave-sized hole halfway down.

A packed, rickety-looking open-cage cable car was making its way across to the far side, swaying precariously. A short distance from it, a zip wire stretched out across the gorge, sharing the landing platform on the far side with the cable car station.

The two girls had been standing for some while in the searing morning heat, in the queue for the zip wire, licking their ice-cream cones and feeling grateful for the faint breeze that rose from the gorge.

'I'm worried about Mum,' Laura said, suddenly. 'She doesn't sound right when we speak.'

'How do you mean?'

'You know, she doesn't sound herself. She's normally all excited to get my news. After Dad and Will – we've been really close. But there's something in her voice recently. I have a feeling there's something she's not telling me.'

Cassie licked her ice cream, with a studious expression. 'Maybe she's just missing you. First time you've been away on your own – apart properly – since – you know.'

Laura nodded. 'I hope so. But she had a mammogram just before I left – she has one regularly because my nan died of breast cancer. Maybe it wasn't good news.' She closed her eyes, momentarily. 'God, I just couldn't bear to – to lose her. I love her so much. I couldn't cope, I just couldn't cope.'

'You won't lose her, L, and you're just being morbid. Your mum probably sounds down because she's missing you. She's all alone. Snap out of it!' As if to drive home her remark, she snapped off the end of her cone with her teeth and crunched the wafer.

An instant later, they were distracted by a scream.

'Yaaaaaaa-orrrrrrrr-hrrrrrrrrrrr-eeeeeeeeeee!' a Japanese man cried, either in terror, or elation – or perhaps both – as he was launched, suspended in the harness, screeching all the way down and across to the platform on the far side. He would return, like everyone else, on the cable car.

'You sure you want to do this, C?' Laura asked. 'Looks pretty scary.'

'Wuss!'

'I'm so not a wuss!' she said, indignant. 'I'm just not that crazy about dying.'

'It would be quick – the piranhas would eat you the moment you hit the water!' Cassie replied.

'Shut up!' Then she looked at her friend, concerned. 'Piranhas? Do they have them in this river?'

'They're indigenous to South America, aren't they?'

'Yech!'

'They start with the soft bits – they'd strip your face in seconds.'

Laura looked down again. 'Really not sure I want to do this after all.'

'Come on, don't be a wuss – it's not the fall that kills you, it's the sudden stop!'

'Great. And then the piranhas get to eat you.'

'I'll go first and then you can follow if I live,' Cassie said, grinning, and shot a brief glance over her shoulder, before looking back down at the gorge and inching closer to her friend. 'Don't turn around, L,' she hissed. 'But Mr Creepy is watching us again. God, he's weird.'

'What?'

'Seriously. He's on the viewing platform.'

'The same guy?'

Cassie nodded.

'The one that was in Guayaquil?'

'It's him, I promise you. The one that has no neck. Our stalker.'

'Let's go over to him and say hi! Embarrass him!'

'Not worth losing our place in this queue.'

Laura pulled a handkerchief out of her bag and dropped it on the ground. Kneeling to pick it up, she turned and shot a glance behind her, catching the glint of a lens in the sunlight. Standing up again, she said, 'You're right. It is him.'

Cassie pursed her lips. 'Why's he taking photographs of us, L?'

Putting on a phoney South American accent, Laura replied, 'Because we iz ze best-looking broads on the trail!'

Cassie giggled. Then she looked serious again. 'Maybe we should let him know we're aware of him?'

'Or make a real effort to give him the slip?'

'And how do we do that, with the tour bus waiting for us, L?'

'Plan B!'

'Which is?'

'Haven't figured that one out yet!' Then she added, 'But why's he following us?'

'He's probably on the same tour trail we're on. It's the regular circuit, he's probably just some saddo – got his bedroom walls lined with pictures of girls and lies there tossing off to them.'

'Gross!'

The queue moved forward. There were now just three people ahead of them. Laura peered down and the gorge looked even deeper and scarier. She wouldn't admit it, but she was quite glad her friend was going first.

'Heard from your mum today?'

Laura shook her head and glanced at her watch. 'Three thirty p.m. in the UK, she's probably still in court.'

'Sounds a cool trial, shame she can't talk about it.'

'Yep. When did you last hear from home?'

'Over a week ago.'

'You're lucky, not having such a worrier of a mum.'

'I guess because there's four of us – you're all your mum has in the world.'

There was another loud scream as a kid in a bumblebee-striped T-shirt shot down the wire; they moved up another place.

'Think she'll find someone else one day and remarry?' Cassie asked.

'Yuck.' Laura shook her head. 'Maybe, I don't know. I don't like the idea.'

'Would you rather she was alone for the rest of her life?'

'No – I guess – I want her to be happy. But the idea of her – you know – being with a man. That's just like – yuck.'

The couple in front of them suddenly shook their heads, wimping out, and stepped away.

'Shit, we're on!' Laura said.

Two young men in green T-shirts beckoned a suddenly very reluctant Cassie forward and began clipping her into the harness.

'Get some photos, L!'

'On it!' She was setting her phone camera to video. Then she stepped forward onto the viewing platform and braced herself against the guard rail. She raised the phone and started recording Cassie's terrified face. 'Here's Cassie, moments before the piranhas eat her!' she announced for the recording.

Moments later, Cassie was launched, shrieking. She hurtled down the wire and low over the gorge. But then, suddenly, to Laura's shock, instead of continuing on to the platform on the far bank there was a loud *TWANG*.

Cassie stopped dead, for an instant. She plunged down into the water then bounced back up. Then down again.

All around, people were screaming.

Her insides feeling hollowed out, all Laura could do was watch in horror as her friend dropped back down into the foaming water, then rose up again, then dropped down again, staying submerged for several seconds before springing up again, dangling and bouncing like a marionette.

If the wire snapped and she was swept along the rapids, she would be over the rocky gorge in seconds.

Shaking and feeling utterly helpless, all she could think for a moment was: *This could have been me.*

Then she turned to the two operators who were shouting at each other. One, looking bewildered, was stabbing buttons on a control panel. 'Do something!' she screamed at them, then looked back at her friend, who was now dangling, legs flailing, in obvious terror, perilously close to the raging water.

A door opened behind the operators, revealing a large cog. A bulky man in overalls and covered in grease came through holding a crank and yelling at the two younger men. He gave the crank to one of them, opened a metal cabinet cover and began throwing switches inside it. Laura looked back, fearfully, at her friend.

Suddenly the wire tightened. Cassie rose a few feet, then a few more, away from the water. Laura looked back and saw all three men were turning the crank, which had been inserted into part of the apparatus close to the open door.

Steadily, slowly, inch by inch, they wound Cassie up in the air. The wire was tight now and she'd at least stopped bouncing. Staring at it, Laura was thinking, *Oh God, please don't break. Don't snap. Don't. Please don't.*

Slowly, agonizingly slowly, seemingly inches at a time, Cassie was cranked back towards them. Laura suddenly realized she was still filming. She shoved her phone in her pocket, anxiously holding her breath.

Please don't break.

The three men were shouting at each other again. Arguing about something. But, mercifully, sweating heavily, they were still working the handle. Cassie was coming closer.

Closer.

Now she was just a few feet from the launch platform.

'You're going to be OK, C!' Laura yelled.

To her astonishment, her friend was laughing.

'Nearly there!' Laura called out.

And a minute later, to Laura's desperate relief, Cassie was back over the platform and out of danger.

Laura ran towards her as the two younger men were freeing Cassie from the harness and apologizing profusely to her. All the time, she was giggling and laughing.

Laura looked down at her friend, who was now lying on the ground, alternating between crying and laughing.

'You OK, C?'

But her friend was unaware of her presence. She was in the throes of a total fit of hysterics.

57

Meg was struggling to concentrate this morning because she was so worried about her daughter.

All night she had been fretting about Laura doing the zip wire today. How many other dangerous sports were she and Cassie engaging in on this trip that they weren't telling her about? All the time with someone watching them? Laura had promised to text her after she'd done it, to let her know she was safe.

It was 10.45 a.m. when Stephen Cork called the final witness who worked for Terence Gready's firm, an intelligent-looking woman in her late twenties, with long, layered brown hair. Her name was Sophie Butt.

Watching her closely, Meg could see, from her body language, that she was both a determined character and a loyal employee.

'Mrs Butt,' Cork said, 'could you tell us the capacity in which you were employed by the defendant?'

She spoke with clear diction and had quite a posh accent, Meg thought.

'I was Mr Gready's secretary and the receptionist at TG Law.'

'And how long had you been employed in this capacity?'

'Over eight years.'

'To what extent were you aware of Mr Gready's day-to-day activities?'

'Well, very aware, I kept his diary,' she answered stiffly.

'And in keeping his diary, you were aware of his daily appointments and meetings?' Cork asked.

'I was, yes.'

'All of them?'

'All of them,' she said, resolutely.

'On the morning of Wednesday November 21st last year, do you recall Mr Gready meeting at any time with a gentleman by the name of Michael Starr? Quite a distinctive-looking man, it would seem, with a prosthetic right arm.'

'No, I don't,' she said.

'Does the office have a visitors' book where guests sign in and out?'

'No,' she answered.

'Is it possible Mr Gready could have met with him without your knowledge?'

She shook her head. 'No.'

'Would there ever be meetings Mr Gready held that might have escaped your notice?'

'Not during business hours, certainly not. Mr Gready was a busy man, much in demand – he relied completely on me for keeping his schedule.'

'Would you organize his meetings, court appearances and such?'

'I would keep a diary of his commitments.'

She was clearly thinking carefully each time before she spoke. Meg wondered if she had been coached for this grilling.

'And you would ensure he was not double-booked, was in the right place at the right time, and keep his diary up to date?'

'Correct.'

'Did you always know exactly your boss's movements, or did he ever do some things himself without informing you?'

'We always worked closely as a team,' she replied.

'Was there any flexibility in your working arrangement for Mr Gready to meet anyone without your knowledge?'

'I would say not really, no.'

Meg, in the jury box, wondered exactly where this was going. She rather liked this woman, who stood with her head held very high, her body language telling Stephen Cork she was not going to be intimidated by him.

There was a sudden, expectant hush in the court. All eyes locked on Cork. Clearly some kind of sucker punch was coming.

Without taking his eyes off the woman, he said, 'In Tab M of the bundle you will find a statement that you gave to the police, shortly after Terence Gready's arrest.' He turned to the jury, indicating for them to check their bundles. Then Cork's assistant counsel, Paul Williams, handed him a document, marked with fluorescent tags.

'Mrs Butt, do you recall giving a statement to the police on the 11th of December 2018?'

'Yes,' she replied.

He then asked the usher to pass the statement to the witness.

'Mrs Butt, do you recognize this document?'

'Yes, it's the statement that I made to the police.'

Cork said, 'Might I ask you to read paragraphs 12, 13 and 14 just to yourself?'

After a short time, she looked up and said she had done so.

Cork said, 'In your evidence you stated that Mr Gready

would not meet anyone without your knowledge – that is what you said just now, isn't it?'

'Yes.'

Cork continued. 'But that isn't quite what you told the detectives in your statement on the 11th of December?'

For the first time, Sophie Butt looked flustered. 'Well – not exactly, no. I was confused and frightened when speaking to the police.'

'Your exact words were: *My boss is mostly pretty good at keeping me filled in, but he's a very busy man, much in demand, and does sometimes forget to tell me about appointments.*'

Cork had just the hint of a predatory smile on his face. 'This is what you told the police. In light of this, can you assure this court categorically that your boss did not meet Michael Starr on the morning of Wednesday November 21st last year? Can you be absolutely certain that Mr Gready and Mr Starr did not meet?'

She wavered. 'Well, not completely certain I suppose, no. But there is no client file on a Michael Starr.'

'And would there be files on clients, generally?'

'Without exception.'

Cork nodded. 'So, can we safely say from that, Mr Starr is not a client of TG Law?'

'Yes, you can.'

'So, if indeed a meeting took place on that day between the defendant and Mr Starr, it would have been of a personal or private matter?'

'Quite possibly.'

'Something they might not have wanted recorded, which was why no file was opened?'

Primrose Brown jumped up, indignantly. 'Your Honour, that is mere speculation on my learned friend's part.'

Nodding, the judge turned towards the jury. 'You will please ignore that last remark by the prosecution.'

Shit, Meg thought. Cork was cunning. Just by making that suggestion, however wrong he was to have made it, the damage was done. It would stick in the rest of the jurors' minds. He had successfully driven a locomotive through Sophie Butt's credibility.

'Thank you, Mrs Butt, no more questions.' He took his seat.

Primrose Brown rose. Her junior barrister, Crispin Sykes, passed her a sheet of paper, which she in turn handed to Sophie Butt.

'Mrs Butt,' she said, 'I would like you to tell this court what this page is.'

The woman studied it for some seconds, then said, 'It is a copy of Mr Gready's diary page, from November 21st last year.'

'Would it be Mr Gready's office diary?'

'Yes.'

'Containing his appointments?'

'That is the function of office diaries.'

Her response provoked several smiles. But not from Cork.

'You are certain?'

'Yes, I am.'

'Thank you.' She addressed the witness again. 'Mrs Butt, could you please read out to the court the entries for the morning of Wednesday November 21st?'

The woman studied the sheet, then began. 'At 8.30 a.m. I was going through three case files relating to forthcoming court appearances with Mr Gready. At 9 a.m. he had a client meeting with a lady charged with DUI.' She paused and smiled at Ms Brown. 'Driving under the influence of alcohol,' she said, by way of clarification.

'Thank you, Mrs Butt, I am familiar with the term.'

Butt continued. 'At 10 a.m. he met with a gentleman charged with possession of stolen goods. At 10.45 a.m. he went out to a dental appointment. He returned to the office at 11.30 a.m., where he had a sandwich delivered, to enable him to work through the lunch hour, preparing for a court hearing in the afternoon.'

Primrose Brown continued. 'So, Mrs Butt, in checking the diary for that day it appears that Mr Gready was busy throughout and only left the office for a dental appointment.'

'That is correct,' Mrs Butt replied.

'Does your boss have a separate diary for private events?' the QC asked.

'Not to my knowledge, no.'

Brown thanked her. 'I have no more questions.'

Stephen Cork stood. 'One last question for you. The court has heard evidence indicating that Michael Starr entered the premises where you worked, having been buzzed in. Do you recall seeing him that day?'

'No, I do not.'

'If you did not see him, where would he have gone in the building?'

'I don't know.'

'Thank you. No more questions.'

Mrs Butt was instructed to leave the witness box and she walked calmly out of the courtroom.

The rest of the day was taken up by the prosecution reading a number of statements from witnesses. These had been agreed in advance with the defence, and included evidence of the arrest of Gready, provided by a number of police officers. There was also additional evidence from Border Force officers who had been deployed at the port at the time of the attempted drugs importation. The jury then heard evidence from the forensic laboratory confirming that the white powder, seized from the vehicle, was cocaine and was analysed to be of high purity.

Primrose Brown rose and addressed Jupp. 'Your Honour, there is an issue I need to raise with you without the jury present.'

The judge looked at the clock. It was coming up to 4.15 p.m. He turned to the jury. 'As you have just heard, there is an issue we need to sort out. I will adjourn court and we will recommence at 10 a.m. tomorrow.' He looked at Cork, then at Brown. 'Come to my chambers in five minutes.'

58

'It is what it is!' Nick used to say. All the time.

It used to irritate her, Meg remembered. So damned much. The phrase had gotten into his head like a mantra. *The electricity bill's more expensive this month than last! It is what it is.*

It was his answer to any piece of bad news, however insignificant.

Now she would give everything she had in the world to hear him say it one more time. And that was never going to happen.

Daphne, she thought back sadly. A feisty little nine-month-old kitten when Nick and Will died. Only the day before, Will had confessed that he'd never liked cats before Daphne. They'd had a real bond together.

How did you explain death to a cat?

How did you explain to a kitten that its owner had been wiped out by a man in a van busy texting his girlfriend?

You didn't.

You just got on with life. You climbed back on your horse, your bike or whatever the hell it was you had fallen off and you got on with it. Until another death of someone you loved felled you again.

Who was it – Max Planck – who said, 'Science moves forward one funeral at a time'?

As life does, too.

But maybe not cats.

There were some days when Daphne sounded like she had been to cats' choir practice. Even before Meg had reached the front door, she could hear the creature meowing on the other side.

She had been sick with anxiety but trying to pull herself together on her journey home as she mulled over the evidence they'd heard. Sure, that forensic podiatrist had been convincing in the details he had given that it was, beyond doubt, Michael Starr who had entered the premises of TG Law on that November day last year.

But Gready's diary clearly showed him to have been out of the office at the exact time Starr was supposed to have been in his office. If that evidence was upheld, then despite the forensic gait expert's evidence, there was no certainty Gready and Starr had met. She was anxious to see how that played out tomorrow, because it seemed to be the first possible chink in the prosecution case. Along with Cork trying to force the point to the jurors that there had been a clandestine meeting between Gready and Starr, which was why it was not in the diary and why no one in the office had been aware of it.

Checking her phone, she was worried there was still no message from Laura. She unlocked the front door and entered, glad to see there were only a couple of flyers on the floor, no post, no bills. Daphne stared up at her, meowing like some tortured creature.

'Hey, cool it!' She scooped the cat up into her arms and cuddled her. 'What's your problem, little one?'

Daphne began purring as she stroked her head then

chest. After a short while she started to wriggle and Meg set her back down, gently.

She dutifully fed all of Laura's pets and headed back down to the kitchen, hoping a glass of wine would numb some of her fears. She would bung something from the freezer into the oven then have an early night and try to get some sleep. She again checked her phone. Just gone 6 p.m. That would make it 1 p.m. in Ecuador. Laura said they were doing the zip wire in the morning. *This* morning. And that she would text her straight after. So why hadn't she?

Meg was about to message her when there was a ping, indicating a new WhatsApp message, on the phone that bastard had left for her.

Check this out, Meg!

There was a blank screen with a black arrow inside a white circle in the centre. Hesitantly, she clicked on it.

A jerky video began playing, showing images of Laura and Cassie standing in a queue. They were wearing vest tops and shorts, Cassie with a baseball cap and Laura with a straw trilby-style hat at a jaunty angle. Both were licking ice-cream cones. They turned, almost synchronized, and stared in harmony for several seconds directly at the camera, before turning away, clearly giggling.

Then, from a different angle now, she saw a close-up of a terrified-looking Cassie strapped into a harness. Seconds later, she hurtled down a zip wire towards a gorge, heading towards a platform across the far side. Suddenly, to Meg's horror, Cassie jerked to a halt and, as if the wire had snapped, she plunged into the fast-moving water. An instant later she rose up, dangling several metres above it, dropped again, disappearing beneath the surface, then rose again and stopped, bouncing up and down, looking utterly petri-fied.

On the video, Meg could hear screams.

Cold terror squirmed inside her.

She could see, too far away to hear any sound, Cassie dangling like a fish.

She was being wound, slowly, jerkily, back up. After what seemed an eternity, she landed on the safety of a platform and was immediately grabbed by two men, who freed her from the harness.

The burner phone rang.

'Hello?'

The familiar, calm, male voice. 'Not a nice video, is it, Meg? Such a relief to see your daughter's friend safe.'

'You bastard, did you cause this? What are you trying to do?'

'Please don't worry, Cassie is fine, just a little shaken. She's been taken to hospital, accompanied by your daughter, suffering from shock. She'll be fine. We just need you to understand what we are capable of – treat this as a little reminder.'

'You don't have to do this. They are lovely, innocent people. You've already made your point; I understand what I have to do.'

'I'm sure, Meg. But we just don't want you getting too complacent. It was a better day in court, today, but there are a lot more witnesses to come. You've got your work cut out. The next video I send you might not have such a happy outcome for Laura, if you get my drift.'

'Your drift?'

'You know what I'm saying.'

'Please, I'm doing everything I can.'

'Oh, we know that, Meg. And we are right with you,

doing everything we can, too. You do have a friend on the jury.'

'Friend, or someone else like me who you are threatening?'

He sounded hurt. 'We are helping them just like we are helping you.'

'Helping me? Really?'

'Trust me, Meg, we are looking after your daughter in a dangerous country. You've seen how easily an accident can happen. Look upon me as your daughter's guardian angel on this trip of a lifetime that I know you are worried about. And you will see tomorrow how we are helping you in other ways, too. We have made your life easier, but so much is still down to you.'

'How have you made my life easier?'

'Wait until the morning, Meg. You'll know then.'

He ended the call.

59

Meg sat down at the kitchen table, unsteady. Had those bastards tampered with the zip wire? And if so, what else could they tamper with?

Poor, poor Cassie.

The next video I send you might not have such a happy outcome for Laura, if you get my drift.

Bastards. Bastards. But what should she do? What could she do? What if that had been Laura?

Until the zip wire, she had seriously been considering calling the man's bluff and sending a note to the judge. Now she didn't dare. How could she get Laura out of danger? How could she persuade her to come home? But would even that take her out of danger?

She wondered, momentarily, if she should tell Cassie's parents what was going on. They would go crazy if they knew. But she couldn't. She couldn't tell anyone; she did not dare.

She dialled Laura and heard the flat monotone of the overseas dialling tone. To her relief, she answered after just three rings.

'Hey, Mum!'

Meg thought she could detect the stress in her voice. But she couldn't let on she knew what had happened.

'Darling, how did it go? Did you do the zip-wire thing – was it fun?'

She felt the hesitation in her daughter's voice, desperately wanting to reach out to her but acutely aware her conversation was almost certainly being monitored.

'Actually, Mum, it was a bit shit.'

'Oh?'

Laura recited what had happened. Meg gave no indication that she already knew.

'God, how is Cassie?' Meg asked, desperately.

'Yeah, she's OK – she was pretty freaked out – they've given her something for shock and she's asleep. They want to keep her here in hospital until tomorrow.'

'What are you going to do?'

'They're cool with me staying with her here – in the room. Sorry I hadn't messaged you yet, it's all been a bit crazy.'

Meg desperately wanted to scream at her daughter, 'Come home! Come home now!' Instead she said, meekly, 'OK, my angel, that's so good of you to be so caring.'

'She would do the same for me.'

God, Meg thought, *please don't let that be necessary.*

'If anything else happens, anything at all, ring me day or night, and don't forget to keep an eye on your drinks when you are out.'

Ending the call, with Laura promising to message her in the morning with how Cassie was, Meg decided to watch *Twelve Angry Men* again. It was about the trial of a young black man accused of murdering his father. The evidence was compelling, especially to an all-white male jury back in 1957. One of the things that had resonated with her was a juror who reminded her of Gwen's protestations that she did not want to miss Royal Ascot. He was wanting a quick 'guilty' verdict, because he had tickets to a major baseball game.

Meg made herself some supper, then settled down in front of the television with a tray and a notebook and pen. As the film progressed, she repeatedly stopped it and noted down the arguments the actor, Henry Fonda, used to change the minds of one after another of the jury, until he had them all finally convinced.

She fell asleep as the end credits rolled.

60

At 8.30 a.m., Roy Grace sat with his team around the conference table in the Major Crime suite. A series of photographs were stuck to a fourth whiteboard behind him. They showed a replica set-up, outside the Starrs' Chichester house, of the crime scene that had been there the previous week. The cordons, scene guard, a high-visibility police vehicle and a number of police officers.

'One week on from the anniversary of when we believe Stuie Starr was murdered, we set up a facsimile of the scene,' he informed them. 'A team of officers were deployed to the area to stop and question all vehicle drivers and pedestrian passers-by, to establish if they had been there on the previous Wednesday and Thursday and had seen anything. DC Alldridge led the operation. What do you have to report, John?'

The DC replied, 'Boss, we spoke to a number of people who had been in the area, and logged their names and contact details, which I have here.' He tapped a document in front of him. 'Unfortunately, none of them were able to provide any useful information at this stage.'

Grace thanked him. 'I sat down with Alex Call last night and we've agreed a number of further submissions to the forensic lab, and hopefully we should get some results in the next few days. Nothing fresh has come up from the press and media appeal or house-to-house last week, nor from a CCTV and ANPR trawl. We've also drawn a blank on our drugs intelligence sweep. So, at the moment we are struggling to find any witnesses. But someone must have seen something. We believe at least two people carried out the attack. Someone must have seen them arrive and enter the property or leave it.'

At the end of the briefing, Grace returned to his office. Shortly after, Norman Potting appeared at his door.

'Brief update for you, chief,' Norman Potting said, walking into Roy Grace's office. 'About our one-eyed monster.'

The Surrey and Sussex Major Crime Team had moved buildings three times in as many years, firstly from Sussex House into a former dormitory building at Police HQ, and then to another building close by. At least, Grace thought gratefully, he now had his own desk, in his own private room, and a conference table, albeit one that could just about fit four very slim people around it. 'One-eyed monster? You've lost me, Norman.' He sipped his second strong coffee of the morning, although it was only just after 9 a.m.

'Dr Crisp.'

'Ah.' Grace understood now. 'Tell me? But first, how are you?' Grace realized he hadn't spoken to him since he had finished his treatment for prostate cancer.

Potting waggled a finger in the air. 'All working ticketyboo – the winky action! Just need a new lady in my life now, and I think I may have found her.'

'Really?'

Sitting down, Potting said, 'I've met this fantastic lady and I think I might be in love again, Roy.'

'That's great news!' Grace smiled, albeit a little dubious. During the ten years he had worked with Norman, he had come to greatly respect his abilities as a homicide detective, but somewhat less so as a man able to judge potential life partners – with one tragic exception, a wonderful detective on his team who was just the kind of down-to-earth, caring person Norman deserved. But she had died, heroically but tragically, whilst off-duty, when she had gone into a blazing building to attempt to rescue a trapped girl and a dog.

Before her, much of Norman Potting's love life had, in Grace's opinion, been a total train crash, due to his choosing completely the wrong women. The worst of them was a Thai con artist the detective had met online, who had rinsed him. But he was glad to hear him sounding so happy – Norman had been grieving for a long while and it was good he was now able to move forward. 'Tell me about her?'

Norman Potting gave him a dreamy look. 'She's Swedish, Roy. Her name is Kerstin Svenson and she's gorgeous and very witty. Amazing, I never thought at my age I'd meet someone like her!'

'And she's how old?'

'Twenty-eight.'

'Punching above your weight, aren't you?' Roy asked him, quizzically.

Potting beamed. 'Maybe just a little!'

'How many times have you been out with her?'

Potting shook his head and reddened a fraction. 'Well, it's a bit difficult because she lives in Sweden – a town called Sundsvall.'

'Where did you meet her?'

'Ah.' Potting suddenly looked evasive and reddened again. 'Well, we haven't actually met yet, Roy – I mean physically.'

'So, who introduced you?'

'We met online.'

'On a dating site?'

Potting looked sheepish. 'Yes.'

Alarm bells were clanging inside Grace's head. 'OK, when are you going to physically meet?'

Again, Potting looked uncomfortable. 'Well, we should have met last Friday – she was coming over to see me – but she was in a car crash on her way to the airport – some senile idiot pulled out in front of her. It's made a pretty good mess of her car, apparently.'

'Really?' Grace was doing his best not to sound sceptical, but it was hard. 'So, the car belongs to her elderly mother and it's her only means of transport? And Kerstin discovered she's not on the insurance policy, right?'

'It's not like that, chief.'

'WAKEY WAKEY, NORMAN!' His voice was so loud it startled the DS. 'Operation Lisbon? Does that ring any bells?'

Potting looked at him. 'Last October, the internet romance fraudsters we busted, you mean?'

'Yep.'

'This is different, honestly. Kerstin's the real deal. I'm not Johnny Fordwater.'

Potting was referring to a former army major who he had been sent to see at Gatwick Airport. The man, a widower in his late fifties, was in the Arrivals lounge, waiting for the love of his life, a German woman, to come through after landing from Munich. Potting had had to break the news to the man that this woman did not actually exist. Tragically, Fordwater had sent her over £400,000, every penny he had in the world.

'Really?'

'Really, chief. Even if she asked, which she hasn't, I

wouldn't lend her one penny until we've met. She's flying over this weekend.'

Grace looked at him in despair. 'Fine, good luck. But just stick to your guns and don't send her a penny until you've met her and made sure. OK?'

Potting agreed, but with the dreamy eyes of a man besotted.

'So, you said you have news about our *one-eyed monster*?'

'Yes. The officers at Lewes Prison thought it was a fellow inmate who'd stabbed him in the eye, but the inmate's denying that vigorously, and now they've got CCTV to back that up. Crisp attacked the man himself, for no good reason, and at some point during the fight, Crisp pulled out a ball-point pen and stabbed himself in the eye with it.'

Grace frowned. 'Has he gone mental or something?'

Potting shook his head. 'I don't think so. There's been talk of moving him to a maximum-security prison. If he'd got wind of that, knowing his past history as an escape artist, I'm guessing this is all part of a plan. I understand they want to keep him in hospital in London until the end of this week, at least. My suggestion is that we should increase the guard on him.'

Grace nodded. 'Good thinking, Norman.' He grinned, mischievously. 'Tell you what, you go and put that request to ACC Pewe.'

'Would you suggest I do that, chief?'

'Definitely.'

Potting glanced at his watch. 'Got to go now, chief, got to ring my Swedish lady.' He hurried from the room, closing the door behind him. Leaving Grace shaking his head in bewilderment and drawing a large intake of breath.

No more than a few seconds later the door burst open and he saw a huge beaming smile on Norman's face. 'By the way, chief, I'm only joking about Kerstin . . . she's not my next lover! I'm working with her on a romance fraud case that the Swedish police are dealing with. You should've seen your face, I had you going there for a minute, didn't I!'

Roy picked up a magazine and hurled it at him as Potting ducked behind the door and slammed it shut.

61

The jury bailiff, Jacobi Whyte, peered around the jury room, checking everyone was there and in place, before announcing, 'Very regrettably, one member of the jury is indisposed. I'm informed the lady in question apparently came off her bicycle on her way home from court yesterday evening. I understand she was found lying in a hedge, unconscious, with very serious injuries.

'The judge is now speaking to counsel, which is why you are remaining here for the moment.'

It was quite wrong, Meg knew, not to have much sympathy for her, but she wondered how many of the other jurors felt the same. Everyone in the jury room earlier had been commenting on Gwendoline Smythson's no-show, and they'd all presumed she must have been delayed by a puncture or some other problem with her bike – or, as Mike Roberts had suggested, perhaps she had been unavoidably detained by her own self-importance. And it was ironic how the woman had told them, the first time they'd all been together, that cycling here was the best solution to the parking problem in Lewes.

Then her mind went back to the phone call she'd had at home last night.

Please, I'm doing everything I can.

Oh, we know that, Meg. And we are right with you, doing everything we can . . . You will see tomorrow how we are helping you in other ways, too. We have made your life easier, but so much is still down to you.

Was this bastard behind what had happened to the woman? It seemed just too coincidental. And how easy would it be to knock someone off on a country lane?

OK, so she and Gwen hadn't exactly become instant buddies, but she didn't wish her any ill. And if these evil people were capable of causing this accident, did they have no limits?

The eleven of them remained in the jury room. Some of them sat at the table, others stood to help themselves to drinks.

Meg poured herself some coffee, then sat back down, looking around, thinking back to the words of her caller last night.

You do have a friend on the jury.

Which of you, she wondered?

'Anyone have any views on what we heard yesterday?' Mike Roberts asked.

'Yes,' Meg said. 'It seems we might have a huge disagreement as to whether Starr actually met Gready that day.'

'I agree with our foreperson,' Hugo Pink concurred.

Toby DeWinter chipped in. 'Perhaps we should all be a lot more concerned about Gwen's accident. She was the one who wanted us to cut short the trial and come to a "guilty" verdict – and now she's off the jury. Doesn't that worry any of you? It worries me!'

'What are you saying?' Mike Roberts looked at him. 'That her accident wasn't an *accident*? Are you worried that if we came to a "guilty" verdict you – and others on this jury – might also meet with an *accident*?'

'Just saying . . .'

'Just saying what?' Roberts pressed.

Again, the words of her caller came back to Meg.

We have made your life easier, but so much is still down to you.

How have you made my life easier?

Wait until the morning, Meg. You'll know then.

By eliminating Gwen from the jury?

Maisy Waller suddenly spoke, absently playing with her cross. 'Don't you think we should take a more forgiving attitude?'

All the other jurors looked at her.

'Forgiving what, exactly, Maisy?' Roberts asked.

'We seem to be jumping to a lot of conclusions, before we've heard all the evidence from both sides,' Waller said. 'Should we not be considering the Christian attitude of forgiveness here at all?'

'What period of Christianity are you referring to?' asked Edmond O'Reilly Hyland, looking at her darkly. 'The period in history where they went on *trial by ordeal*? Plunging the accused's hand into a vat of boiling water and, if it came out fine, they were innocent?'

'Please,' Meg said. 'I think we're all getting far too emotional. Maisy is right, we are still in the very early stages of this trial and it is far too soon to jump to any conclusions. We need to hear all the evidence from both sides before we can have an informed discussion.'

'I agree,' Harold Trout said.

'So do I,' said Pink. 'I don't think our judgement should be affected in any way just because a silly, arrogant woman fell off her bicycle.'

'Excuse me!' Meg interrupted them, loudly and firmly. 'A man is on trial for immensely serious offences, which could not only deprive him of his freedom for many years, if we come to a "guilty" verdict, but also destroy his standing in his community and end his career.'

'Very well said,' O'Reilly Hyland interjected. 'We are all sorry this lady had an accident, whether we liked her or not. But we need to focus on the evidence being put to this court, and from what we have heard so far I do think we need to be concerned about the strength of the prosecution's evidence on this point.'

'And not the defence's integrity?' Roberts queried.

'That, too,' O'Reilly Hyland conceded.

62

The atmosphere in Richard Jupp's chambers was tense.

The judge sat at the conference table annexed to his desk, opposite Stephen Cork and Primrose Brown.

'We are one juror down. I have considered whether to discharge this jury and we start over – probably in three months' time, which is about the soonest we could get everyone back together. That would be unfortunate for Terence Gready who will not be released on bail in the interim due to the severity of the case against him, not to mention time and money wasted for the State.'

Cork and Brown looked at each other. Then Primrose looked back at the judge. 'After this trial, Your Honour, I'm due to start a very complex case which could last several months. I would rather proceed.'

Stephen Cork nodded. 'I agree.'

'Good,' Jupp said and added, with only minor sarcasm, 'We're all on the same page, how nice.'

The two barristers left the room.

Richard Jupp wondered, privately, about the juror's accident. Was there anything sinister behind it? In any major trial like this, judges needed to be aware of the possibility of jury nobbling. There was some history of that happening, particularly when big-time mobsters were involved. And this trial was, without doubt, high stakes. If the prosecution case was correct, Terence Gready would have more than ample resources to pay for anything he needed to secure his freedom. And he would, undoubtedly, resort to all means at his disposal. Although Gready was solely on trial for drugs offences, there were plenty of allegations floating around about his not being afraid to use violence.

But at this moment, however, he had no actual evidence to give him any grounds for suspicion. Accidents happened. He felt happy to move on.

63

Five minutes later, the hearing resumed.

Richard Jupp leaned across and addressed the jury: 'I have made the decision, as we are now advanced with this trial, that we will continue with a jury of just eleven people. I'm sure everyone here in this court wishes the absent juror well, especially you, her fellow jurors, who will have got to know her by this time.'

Then he turned to Stephen Cork. 'You may continue with your next witness.'

Cork stood. 'I would now like to call Detective Sergeant Jack Alexander. He has confirmed that at the time of the arrest he was working as part of the Surrey and Sussex Major Crime Team, and acted as Supervisor on the raid on the defendant's home on Saturday December 1st last year, and subsequently on his office premises.'

A tall, slim man in his late twenties, carrying a bundle of documents and a small laptop, entered the witness box and took the oath. He had a calm and composed manner, and looked around the room, giving the jurors a polite, warm smile as he stated his name, rank and station.

At that moment, Meg noticed Gready staring directly at her, as if fixing her with his gaze. She looked away, hastily and uncomfortably.

Jack Alexander gave his evidence, describing how he had gone to the home address in the early hours of the morning on the date in question under the terms of a warrant issued by a local magistrate. He went into some detail telling the jury what had happened when they had arrived at the defendant's home.

'Now, Detective Sergeant, would you please tell this court what you found there?' Cork asked.

The DS spoke with a clear, educated voice. 'Yes, the first items of significance, which a search officer discovered concealed inside a bedpost in a spare bedroom, were an SD card and a number of phones.' He held up his bundle. 'I have here the detailed report from Aiden Gilbert of the Sussex Police Digital Forensics Unit on what was recovered. The burner phones had never been used, and the contents of the SD card have been analysed thoroughly. To summarize briefly – the full details are in the documents that both the defence and the jury have copies of – they include email communications with a company called Schafft-Steinmetz based in Düsseldorf, Germany, and receipts from this company for the work they carried out.'

'And what was the nature of this work, Detective Sergeant?' Cork asked.

'It was to build, as inexpensively as possible, a replica – or perhaps a more accurate description would be a *facsimile* – 1962 Ferrari 250 SWB.'

'And was this in order to try to pass off this fake car as the real thing and to sell it?'

'No, the instructions to Schafft-Steinmetz were to provide as many voids within the chassis, frame, doors and roof as possible.'

'And did the company at any time question the reasons for this?' Cork asked.

'Yes, they did. They were informed that they had a client who wished to use the vehicle for long-distance endurance rallies, and the spaces were for storage of fuel and provisions.'

Cork nodded. 'I see. And was anything else discovered on this SD card?'

'There was,' Alexander replied. 'Over the past five years, there were instructions to this same company to construct four previous facsimile classic sports cars with a similar specification of voids. An AC Cobra, another similar Ferrari, an Aston Martin DB5 and a French car, the marque of which is now defunct, a Facel Vega.'

'And where were all these vehicles destined?'

'To LH Classics of Chichester, which the Financial Investigation Unit have established is owned, through a convoluted chain of offshore companies, by the defendant.'

Cork nodded again. 'I see – and to your knowledge were any of these previous cars entered into any endurance rallies?'

'Not that I have been able to establish, no.'

Cork went on. 'Detective Sergeant Alexander, during your raid on the defendant's home, did you discover anything else of interest?'

'We did, yes. We discovered a number of prepaid travel cards, to countries that tallied with the offshore chain of companies that LH Classics is owned through, which include Panama and the Cayman Islands. The total amount of credit on these cards was just under £200k. We also found in a safe in the house a cash amount of £62,500 sterling, a further £87,000 in US dollars and a further £320,000 in euros.'

'Well,' said Cork, 'don't we all put a bit of cash aside for our holidays?'

The remark made someone in the court laugh out loud, and Cork milked it for all he was worth, dramatically pausing before addressing the detective again. 'Was there anything else, apart from the defendant's – ah – holiday fund – that you found during this raid?'

Jack Alexander nodded. 'Yes, we discovered an amount of cocaine, which the defendant said was for his personal use. But more significantly, we found a key, very cleverly concealed in the false bottom of an aerosol fly spray canister in the garden shed. It ultimately led, after several months of investigative work, to a private safety deposit box on the premises of a company, Safe Box Co, on the Hollingbury Industrial Estate.'

'Oh? Did you manage to take a look inside?'

'We did, it was opened under warrant. It contained more foreign currency, for the countries I have already mentioned, totalling £392,000, along with six USB memory sticks.'

'DS Alexander, can you tell us what was found on these memory sticks?' Cork questioned.

The DS replied, 'Further information relating to the movement of high-value cars in and out of the country that did not contain drugs and were part of appearing to maintain a genuine business front. There was also significant information relating to LH Classics and the company's bank accounts overseas.'

Cork addressed the DS once more. 'I am now going to ask you to tell the jury and the court in more detail about the information you have just summarized.'

Jack Alexander then spent the next two hours going through in detail the information found on the USB sticks. As he finished sharing the information, Cork asked the officer to wait and invited Primrose Brown to proceed.

Primrose Brown got to her feet. 'Officer, you mentioned

earlier in your evidence information relating to a German company, Schafft-Steinmetz. Can you confirm that at no time progressing these enquiries is my client's name mentioned?'

Alexander replied, 'That is correct.'

Brown continued. 'In relation to the instructions regarding specifically the four classic sports cars, can you again confirm that my client's name was not found anywhere on that paperwork?'

'That is correct,' said Alexander.

Primrose Brown persisted. 'Detective Sergeant, did you find anything untoward about these four previous cars, other than them being replicas?'

He shook his head. 'No, I did not. But, of course, they have never been examined.'

'Would you consider yourself an expert in the field of classic vehicles?'

'Other than my father owning a vintage Harley Davidson motorbike, no, probably not.'

She nodded. 'I understand there is a large and legitimate market in replica models of classic cars. Many of these are exhibited and raced at classic car events in the full knowledge they are replicas. So, you would not be aware of this?'

'No,' Alexander admitted.

'You have also just said that LH Classics of Chichester is owned by the defendant through a chain of offshore companies, as if you were casting aspersions on such a thing. Many highly reputable companies operating out of the UK are in fact owned by companies registered abroad, either for tax mitigation or for other equally legitimate purposes. Do you have any reason to suppose my client had a nefarious reason for having this company registered offshore, if indeed he did? Our case is that he had no connection with this company.'

'Beyond masking the ownership of the Ferrari seized at Newhaven Port, no,' he conceded.

Brown then spent the next hour running through the evidence that Alexander had given but was unable to sway his evidence or gain any advantage from what he had said to the court that would help her client.

She paused for a moment. 'One more question, officer. Is it possible that someone who visited the house could have placed these items in the post of my client's bed? Can you discount that?'

He replied, 'No, I cannot.'

'Thank you,' she said and sat down.

Cork then rose to his feet. 'Officer, how likely is it that the scenario my learned friend has just raised might have happened?'

'It is of course possible,' Alexander said, 'but due to the nature of where these items had been hidden, I think it extremely unlikely.'

'Thank you, officer, I have no more questions.'

Alexander left the courtroom.

64

Thursday 16 May

It felt like the defence had hit a brick wall, Meg thought, despondently, reflecting on today's proceedings. She was in Laura's bedroom, giving the daily treats to the rodents, as per the very precise list of instructions her daughter had left. A handful of dandelions for Horace the guinea pig, which he scoffed in seconds. She stroked him with her finger before moving on, hand-feeding some cucumber and pumpkin seeds to the gerbils. She did a quick spot clean to keep things fresh in between the deep clean she was instructed to do each week, then topped up the water in each cage. This whole process made her feel sad and worried. Laura cared for the welfare of each and every creature she kept and now, there she was, in danger, unaware and far, far away.

She stared at a purple cushion with a large L embroidered on it, on the bed. Then glanced around the room with a wistful smile. Her daughter's string of fairy lights; her stack of boxes that contained her precious, different-coloured trainers; the large map of the world; the clutter of her make-up and hair products on her dressing table; the fluffy rug; framed inspirational quotes dotted around the walls.

IF I WAS ORGANIZED, I'D BE DANGEROUS!

THE ONLY KIND OF SHIP THAT CAN NEVER
SINK IS FRIEND-SHIP!

IF YOU GO ON DOING WHAT YOU'VE ALWAYS
DONE, YOU'LL ALWAYS DO WHAT YOU'VE
ALWAYS DONE!

Then the photograph on the bookshelf. Taken just months before that fatal day. All four of them doing a family fun run in Reigate, which they'd done with Nick's brother and his family for charity.

The memory twinged, painfully. She turned and looked out of the window at the rear garden. A thrush was washing itself in the birdbath. It was a gloriously warm evening. Just five weeks shy of the longest day. Normally she loved this time of year. Normally. But nothing was normal any more. It never had been since Nick and Will had died. The day her world had skewed sideways. And had remained sideways until last week when it had skewed again, this time completely upside down.

It was 6.20 p.m. A long, light evening stretched out ahead. She should sit out in the garden and read a book, but she had barely read a single page since that first phone call last Saturday evening. Nor could she focus on anything much on television. Alison had been telling her for ages about a series called *Succession.* She'd tried the first episode a few nights ago in her attempt to switch off from all the horror of her predicament, but within seconds her mind had wandered.

A drugs gang was watching her – and had invaded her home. Her daughter, thousands of miles away, was being followed around the clock and they had threatened to kill her if there was anything other than a 'not guilty' verdict. She was breaking the law and risked going to prison herself – not to mention trying to help a major criminal evade justice.

The spinning wheel in the gerbil cage began squeaking; one of them was inside, turning it increasingly quickly, as if at some point, if he got fast enough, it would stop simply rotating and actually lead him somewhere – perhaps Mongolia, where most of them originated from, Meg thought with a faint smile. At first when Laura had given her the list, she'd viewed looking after these creatures as a chore, but now she found them comforting; grounding.

She was so damned wound up. A run would do her good, she knew, realizing she hadn't done any exercise for almost a week. Overwhelmed, suddenly, by everything, she sat down on the soft bed, feeling utter despair.

God, she so desperately needed to talk to someone. But she didn't dare.

She had a *friend on the jury* – but who was it? The evidence against Gready today from that officer, DS Alexander, was pretty damning. Although, if she was honest, Meg had lost track a little as he'd detailed, throughout the long afternoon, the chain of overseas companies and how they connected. She'd tried hard to follow, but it had done her head in – as it had for some of the other jurors, too, she could tell.

All that stuff before, about whether or not Terence Gready had been in his office when the man who had driven the vehicle into Newhaven, Michael Starr, had been there, too. That did not seem to have played well with the jurors. During a brief afternoon recess, Mike Roberts, sounding more like a cop than ever, had said he found the evidence so far to be strong and, in his view, the defence was squirming. He was backed up by Maisy, who seemed to have changed her mind, Toby, Edmond, Sophie, Mark and Harold. The ones who had kept quiet were Hari Singh, Rory O'Brien and Hugo Pink.

The man had very definitely said *a friend.*

Who? Hugo Pink was one possibility, she suspected. He wasn't accepting any of the negative evidence. Rory O'Brien was possibly another, but she couldn't be sure, he was difficult to read.

She'd looked up online to see if, with a jury reduced to eleven, a judge could still convict on a 9–2 verdict. They could.

If, however, more than two jurors were unconvinced of his guilt then that would simply result in a hung jury, and the judge would likely go for a retrial. And that wasn't acceptable. It had already been made very plain to her what was needed. Those two words. Nothing less.

'Not guilty' had started to become a mantra inside her head.

Not guilty, not guilty, not guilty.

She'd woken yesterday actually saying it out loud.

She sniffed, went into the bathroom and dried her eyes with the towel hanging there. But as she did so, she began sobbing again. Her phone rang. She hurried over to the bed where she'd left it and answered.

'Has the judge put his black cap on yet?'

She smiled, despite her tears, at the sound of her friend's voice. 'Hey, Ali.'

'Hey.'

For a moment, for the first time ever in their years of friendship, Meg couldn't think of anything to say.

'Megs, are you OK?'

'Yes.' Meg was struggling to hold it together.

'You don't sound OK. What's happened?'

Suddenly, she couldn't help it, the dam burst and the tears flooded again.

'Megs, I'm coming straight over, be there in fifteen.'

'N-n-n-no. No.' Meg thought frantically. Not here. Too dangerous. 'Why don't we go to the beach, have a drink in that bar there?'

'Sure, OK. Actually, tell you what, it's such a glorious evening, why don't I bring a bottle and a couple of glasses and we'll go sit on the beach. Usual place?'

'Yes, thanks, that would be good.'

'I've got a lovely chilled rosé in the fridge. OK?'

'Anything, Ali, so long as it's a big bottle. Like, a really big bottle. Maybe even two bottles!'

'You're sounding better already!'

65

'Look, look, look!' Cleo said excitedly as Roy Grace arrived home at a few minutes to 7 p.m. She leaned forward to kiss him then showed him the box in her hands.

'Eggs?'

She nodded vigorously. 'Well done. You should be a detective – oh, I forgot, you are one!' she said, playfully.

He grinned, closing the door behind him and giving Humphrey a quick stroke. 'Something special about these eggs?'

'There is, open it, something special about both of them!'

'Both of them?' He peered inside. 'OK, they are blue. Any significance?'

'Nope.'

'They're organic, free range and cost a fortune?' he ventured.

She shook her head. 'They're organic, free range and *free*.'

'Free?'

'Those things we have in the big run in the garden. The feathered creatures that make a clucking noise?'

His eyes widened with delight as he finally understood. 'These are from them?'

'Yes, our very first blue eggs!'

'Wow, amazing!' He felt a real buzz of excitement. 'Which ones did they come from?'

'It must be the new hens – Dorothy and Bessie – we've not had this colour before. I'll have to ask Bruno. I've put him in charge of them and he's now responsible for keeping them clean, feeding them and collecting the eggs. I think it will do him good and get him out of that damned bedroom. And I've told him if there are any eggs left over, he can sell them and pocket the money.'

'I like it. Good parenting! I'd actually given up on them ever laying,' he said.

She shook her head. 'The guy at Wishing Wells Farm said it could be a while before they started laying and he was right. I've been checking the nesting boxes every day and so has Bruno, so we know they're freshly laid.'

'Great, let's hope we get a few more quickly and we can make a meal out of them!'

'Definitely! One of your omelettes?'

'*Bien sur!*' he said, with a French accent. '*Oeufs Grace?* A little grated cheese, chopped chilli, spring onion, red peppers and tomato, madame?'

'You're making me hungry!'

'So tell them to lay some more, quick!'

'I will pass on your instructions.'

'How was your day?' he asked, following her through to the kitchen, slackening his tie and slinging his jacket on the back of a chair.

'OK, quiet at the mortuary – only two new admissions.'

'Signed the guest book, did they?'

'Their hands were a bit stiff.'

He grinned again.

'And Kaitlynn said Noah's got a cold and been pretty grumpy. He's asleep now.'

'Where's Bruno?'

'Where do you think? In his boy cave, the very one I'm trying to find ways of getting him out of!'

Roy stood behind Cleo, putting his arms round her waist, and pulled her in towards him. 'I'm glad it was quiet at work for you, we need to wrap you in cotton wool. I'm grateful every day that you're OK now.'

'Me too. I think about it constantly. It was around now we lost the baby last time.'

'I know you're worried, but you are fit and healthy and the doctor's said there's no reason why everything shouldn't be fine. And, of course, now I'm back in Sussex I can wait on my beautiful bride hand and foot.'

She laughed. 'As if! That will stop the first time you get called out. But I do know you've made a big sacrifice not staying on in the Met – I know how much that meant to you. '

He went to the fridge. 'It was the right decision. I'm good with it. Sussex is where I belong, and where I want to be. For sure my time on the streets in London has opened my eyes, and it'll help me here. And maybe I've made a tiny difference.'

She looked at him. 'Do you think you're ever going to win the war on drugs? Are you ever going to be able to stop the suppliers?'

'I don't think so.' He shook his head. 'I didn't tell you about the kid we stopped in Newham, fourteen years old, acting suspicious. He had a knife on him and nine wraps of heroin. When we nicked him, I said, "Shouldn't you be in school, why are you doing this?" He just smiled at me and said, "I make two grand a week – that's more than you make."' Roy shrugged. 'How do I argue against that?'

Cleo smiled. She had no answer.

'Can I get you anything to drink?'

She pointed at a mug on the table. 'I'm sipping my infusion. My pregnancy special!'

'Nice?'

She screwed up her face. 'It smells like molten tarmac and tastes like mildew.'

'Sounds like it could catch on.'

'It has – either very clever online marketing, or there are millions of pregnant women out there on social media who have different taste buds to mine.'

'Maybe your taste buds got altered by your pregnancy – that happened with you before.' He walked over, picked up the brew and sniffed it.

'Yecccccch!' He put the mug straight back down. 'That is vile.'

'I'm taking it for the team.'

'Our baby had better damned well appreciate it!'

'I'll be reminding him – or her – for the rest of its life.'

Humphrey trotted into the room and over to Roy.

He patted the dog. 'OK, boy, in a little while, I'll take you for a nice walk. Yeah, you want to go walkies?' Normally, Humphrey would have been jumping and pestering, but instead he sloped off under the table.

'Well, that's just weird, isn't it?'

'What, Roy?'

'I said the magic *walkies* word and Humph has taken himself off under the table. Look at him just lying there obsessively cleaning his feet!'

'Maybe he's embarrassed because I really told him off earlier – he was growling at Noah. He's probably gone under there in shame.'

'Growling? He's normally a big softy. What's happened?'

She shrugged. 'Perhaps he knows there's going to be

another baby in the house and is getting jealous. I hope
Bruno hasn't been teasing him. I often see him winding him
up, maybe that's it?'

'Bruno? Bruno is great with him. Don't start thinking
bad of him. It's one of his positive traits.'

'All I'm saying is we'll need to keep a very close eye on
the dog when he's with Noah and the new arrival. If he
shows any aggression—' Cleo held back from saying something she might regret.

'Hey, come on, darling, you're always telling people a dog
is not just for Christmas, it's for life. We'll watch him and, if
we need to, we can separate them. I'm sure it's nothing.'

'Let's hope so,' she said, flatly.

'I hear what you're saying, OK. Come on, let's not get
annoyed about something that hasn't even happened! I'll
be all over Humphrey, watching him like a hawk, and he
won't do anything to any of the children. I promise.
Remember, I'm a detective, so you have to believe me!' he
said, trying to lighten up the conversation a little.

'Good. OK, detective, how was the rest of your day?' she
asked.

'I've been going through the paperwork for Dr Crisp's
trial with Glenn and our legal team.'

'Slippery Dr Crisp. Who nearly blew your leg off. But it's
not personal, is it, for you?'

He grinned. 'Personal, *moi*? A nice, kind family doctor
who has a penchant for raping and killing young women
and who shot me in the leg with a twelve-bore, so I'm still
limping a little eighteen months on – why should it be
personal?' He grinned again. 'He was just doing his job and
I was doing mine.'

Cleo gave him a strange look, as if unsure for an instant
whether he was joking or not.

'The bastard is scheming to escape, I know it, and I want extra security – hospitals are easy for a man of Crisp's ingenuity, but idiot Pewe won't hear of it. He refuses to liaise with the Met Police on this, because of costs coming back to us. Can you believe it?'

'How did Pewe ever get to be where he is?' she asked. 'Who on earth promoted him in the first place?'

'The Peter Principle,' Grace replied.

'The *what*?'

'A guy back in the 1960s – I think he was a sociologist called Peter something – came up with the theory that in every organization, sooner or later people get promoted to the level of their incompetence.'

'That fits,' she replied. 'Guess you'd better make sure you don't get promoted again.' She grinned.

'Thanks a lot!' He gave her a friendly punch on the shoulder then shook his head. 'The problem with Pewe is no one ever knows where they are with him. I'm only just back from the Met and I've seen him a couple of times and he's been fine, almost friendly. In fact, he's going to support my application for the Chief Superintendent process in Sussex. But this Crisp business is taking him back to his old self.' He shook his head. 'You know, I'm almost wishing that he would bloody escape, just to piss off Pewe!'

His job phone rang, interrupting him. It was Norman Potting.

Roy Grace got his wish. Crisp had escaped.

66

Thursday 16 May

7.30 p.m. and it felt as hot as mid-afternoon in the still air. Dozens of people were on the beach, soaking up the last of the day's rays, and the tide was far out, exposing a vast area of mud. Closer in, just beyond the pebbles, two toddlers in sun hats, under the scrutiny of their parents, were busy digging with their plastic spades, creating a lopsided castle. A detectorist in a combat jacket and safari hat worked his way across the expanse, sweeping his scanner in arcs, occasionally stopping and digging with his trowel, and a short distance beyond the lazy surf, a paddleboarder moved serenely along. There was a tempting smell of barbecuing wafting in the air.

Alison and Meg found a quiet spot by a breakwater and settled down. Alison was someone who always seemed to Meg to be happy in her skin. She had a good marriage with Archie, a gentle giant of a man, a former bodybuilder who owned a couple of small health clubs in the city, and whom Meg liked a lot. Alison was a partner in a local advertising agency, a job she enjoyed, and she had the knack of always dressing appropriately for any occasion. This evening she wore a baseball cap over her long brown hair, fashionably large Dior sunnies, a short, floral smock and diamanté-studded sandals. She dug into her beach bag, produced a

310

bottle of wine in a cool bag, a corkscrew and two large glasses.

'I've got a spare in here, in case,' she said, tapping the bag with a smile. She worked the cork out, then filled both glasses halfway and handed Meg one. 'Cheers!'

'Cheers.' Meg was wearing a large straw hat and one of Nick's shirts over a bikini, in case for some mad reason they went in for a swim, and flip-flops.

They clinked glasses and each sipped a little.

'Right,' Alison said. 'So, talk to me.'

Further out to sea a jet-ski rasped along, trailed by a plume of spray. Meg sat in silence, staring at her glass, turning it round in her hands. She'd left the phone behind, deliberately, despite what they had told her, in case there was a listening device of some kind implanted in it by the bastards. She looked around, warily. Had anyone followed her here? Was anyone in earshot? The nearest people were two young canoodling lovers, a good fifty yards away. She took another sip; it tasted good, cold and crisp. Then another for courage.

'God, Ali,' she said, leaning forward and peering down into her glass again. Thinking. She'd recently watched an episode of an American spy drama where someone had used a directional mic to pick up a conversation hundreds of yards away. And another episode of the same series where two operatives held a conversation in a hotel washroom, where they ran a tap to muffle the sound and prevent any eavesdropping. 'Want to go and paddle in the surf?' she said.

Alison looked surprised. 'OK, sure.'

'We can take our glasses!'

Alison topped them both up. They walked across to the edge of the pebbles, kicked off their shoes and headed out towards the water, Meg enjoying the cooling sensation of the moist muddy sand. Making the pace, she led them knee-high into the icy surf then stopped and clinked glasses with her friend again. 'Thanks for coming, Ali.'

They stood in silence for some moments. Meg watched the tall structures of the wind farm some way out to sea, then turned back, looking at the shore.

'So, Megs, what is it, what's going on?'

'This may sound crazy, but I'm scared to tell you.'

Alison frowned. 'What do you mean? Scared to tell me what?'

Meg desperately wanted to check across the beach and beyond, to see if she could spot the glint of binocular lenses. But that would be a giveaway, she thought. 'I don't want to put you in danger,' she said, quietly, barely above a whisper.

'Danger?'

'Oh God, Ali, I'm living a nightmare. I went to hell and back after Nick and Will died and now I'm back in hell again.'

'What do you mean? What is it, what on earth has happened?'

'I'm scared to tell you. They – he – said they would kill anyone I told.'

'I can look after myself, and anyhow, I've got Archie to protect me too, Megs. He's been a bouncer and a bodyguard and in his teens he was once a bare-knuckle cage fighter – if you need someone sorting out, he'll do it!'

Meg smiled and shook her head. 'Thanks, but these people – I just have a feeling they are seriously dangerous. I don't think their threats are idle.'

'What people? Who are you talking about? Please tell me.'

'Alison, listen to me carefully.' Meg made and held eye contact with her, speaking quietly. 'I'm being watched.'

'What?'

'Ssshhhh, I'm serious, don't react. Mine and Laura's lives depend on this. When I tell you what I'm about to, act as if we are just chatting normally, try not to give anything away with your body language, and don't look around. It's really, really important, OK?'

'Yes, OK,' she replied, dubiously.

Meg took a few further paces into the sea until the water was above the bottom of her shirt. No one was around. In addition to the breaking waves behind them, the jet-ski was buzzing back in the opposite direction. No one, she was sure, could eavesdrop on them here. She told her friend the full story.

'Oh God, this is awful,' Alison said when she had finished. 'If you could find out who this bastard is, Archie would go and find him and break every bone in his body.'

'I wish. But that's not going to stop it, Ali, that's not going to protect Laura. He's probably just some hired gun. From all I've heard in court, this is a major and totally ruthless mob. Like – a kind of English Mafia.'

'Megs, they might think they're above the law but, ulti-mately, no one is.'

'Maybe, but I can't risk Laura's life. If anything happened to her, I – I just—' Her voice cracked.

'Can I give you a hug?'

Meg nodded. Alison put an arm around her. 'We're not going to let anything happen to her, OK?' She kissed her on the cheek.

Meg smiled then shook her head. 'I don't think there is anything you can do, Ali, I have to sort this out myself. I have to get the jury to deliver that "not guilty" verdict. Somehow.'

'What, and let this guy go free?'

'I don't have a choice, Alison, I *have* to.'

'Against all the damning evidence you've just told me? On the face of it, anyway, it sounds like these people are going to have to find something on the judge if you're to have a hope in hell.'

Meg nodded, despondently. 'That's how it's looking – after today, anyway.'

The pair stood in silence, watching the jet-skier whine back again, then turn in a wide arc, heeling over.

'I know someone,' Alison said, quietly. 'Someone I've become friendly with through my Open University course. She's married to a very high-up cop.'

Meg shook her head, alarmed. 'You mustn't tell anyone, please, for Laura's sake and your own safety.'

'Screw that, I'm not having these bastards get away with treating you like this.'

Meg touched her arm. 'Ali, please. I've told you this in confidence, you mustn't tell anyone. You *mustn't*. Please. Promise me?'

Alison was quiet for a short while then she said, 'Have you thought about it rationally, Meg – thought it through? OK, so they are blackmailing you to coerce the jury with threats to Laura. But let's say it does end up with a "guilty" verdict – then it's game over for them. What would be the point in them then going and killing Laura? It's not going to change the verdict. Maybe it's all just bluster?'

'I've thought that through a thousand times, Ali. Maybe you're right, but what if not?'

Alison shook her head. 'I can't believe this is happening. Not now, not in this day and age.'

'It's real,' Meg replied, bleakly. 'I don't even know who I can trust on the jury and who I can't.'

'I've an idea,' Alison said. 'What about an anonymous phone call or note to the judge, telling him that two members of the jury have been nobbled, required to coerce the rest into a "not guilty" verdict? He would have to take that seriously.'

'If he believed it.'

'Could he afford not to?'

Meg's mind went back to the phone call she'd had last night.

You do have a friend on the jury.

Friend, or someone else like me who you are threatening?

We are helping them just like we are helping you.

And she realized why he'd given her those details about the other juror, whoever it was. Both of them needed him. They weren't going to be stupid enough to give the game away.

Her blackmailer would know, without any doubt, that any informant would have to be one of them.

She shook her head and explained her reasons.

'I understand,' Alison said. 'God, what a predicament. You are truly stuck between a rock and a hard place. But there has to be a way through this. There always is.'

'Really? I'm all ears.'

Alison smiled. 'Could you throw a sickie? Feign appendicitis or something and get taken off the jury? Have something happen that's obviously not your doing?'

'Like falling off my bike and ending up in hospital?'

Alison shrugged. 'Well, maybe not so dramatic. And you don't have a bike, do you?'

Meg smiled. 'No, that's a bit of a problem right there!'

Alison suddenly looked very serious. 'There's a whole other aspect to this I hope you're aware of.'

'Which is?'

'What you are doing must be completely illegal. Influencing – coercing – your fellow jurors. Do you know what would happen if you were found out?'

Meg nodded. 'I do.'

She was well aware that she was about to break the law, but until now she'd been pushing that knowledge aside. Confronted with it starkly, out in the open, by her best friend, the true enormity suddenly rose up, engulfing her in a cloud of fear. 'I do know, Ali. But I don't have any choice. What's that quote?'

Alison frowned. 'Quote?'

Meg nodded. 'Something like, *If I had to choose between betraying my country and betraying my friend, I hope I'd have the courage to betray my country.*'

67

It was growing dark when Meg finally made her way home, a little unsteadily, from the beach. The bottle and three-quarters of wine they'd drunk between them was making her feel a lot more optimistic. As Ali said, *there has to be a way through this.* Her parting words, as they hugged on the seafront, were, 'Courage is knowing what not to fear.'

Someone in her street was having a barbecue and the smell made her even hungrier. She heard music and laughter coming from behind the house where the smoke was rising as she passed it and felt a pang of envy – and sadness. Nick loved doing barbecues with Will, their *man-thing*. Burgers, veggie burgers, steaks, lamb cutlets, chicken wings, corn on the cob, baked potatoes, king prawns and, on occasion, when he was feeling extravagant, lobsters.

She rarely ate meat any more, but what wouldn't she give for a big seared burger slathered in mustard and ketchup, with fried onions and a gherkin squashed inside a soft bap?

Ali's words were ringing in her head as she fumbled with the key, dropped it and bent down to pick it up. But as she entered the house, her focus switched back to food; she was starving and trying to think what she had to make a quick supper. There was a stash of microwavable dishes in the freezer, as well as a couple of vegetarian pies she'd bought on a whim recently, during an extravagant excursion to Waitrose.

In her rush to get indoors, she tripped over the front step and almost fell, face-first, into the hall. She went inside, closing the door behind her and securing the chain, and hurried through into the kitchen. Daphne was sitting on top of the tall fridge.

'What are you doing up there, you daft thing?' she said.

The cat was often up there, or sitting on top of the antique Welsh dresser, seemingly enjoying the commanding views it gave her.

Meg glanced at the phones, checking there were no messages, emails or a WhatsApp from Laura, then pulled open the freezer section of the fridge and rummaged through the contents of the drawers. She spotted to her delight a packet of *No Bull* veggie burgers from Iceland. *Perfect!* She'd have her own faux barbecue: the burgers, a microwaved baked potato and beans.

She removed the packet and was reading the instructions when the burner phone rang.

'Hello?' she answered and an instant later, to her dread, heard the familiar male voice.

'So, you had a nice time on the beach tonight with your friend, Alison, Meg. But very indiscreet of you – not to mention disobedient – to tell her so much,' he chided. 'Don't you remember the warning I gave you? About what would happen to any friend you told?'

How the hell did he know where she had been this evening?

'I didn't tell her a thing about – you know.'

'Really, Meg? Do you think I rode into town in the back of a truck? Come on, get real! I know what you were talking about.'

'We were just chatting about stuff. I didn't say anything about – you know.'

'Really? How about this, let me read it out to you. This is what your friend said, pretty much: *What about an anonymous phone call or note to the judge, telling him that two members of the jury have been nobbled, required to coerce the rest into a "not guilty" verdict? He would have to take that seriously.*'

Meg felt a rush of cold blood in her stomach. 'You – you couldn't – that's bullshit.'

'But you know it isn't, don't you, Meg? I mean, your *No Bull* burger might be bullshit, but not what Alison said.'

A prickle of fear crawled down her back. She looked up. Around. He was watching her. Inside her own home.

Courage is knowing what not to fear.

'Fuck you!' she said and killed the call.

She stood, shaking in terror, her eyes darting everywhere. Where the hell was the camera? In one of the downlighters? Heating vents? The phone rang again. She let it ring, once, twice, three times. Then answered.

'I really don't advise hanging up on me, Meg, there could be consequences. Let me tell you how your conversation on the beach with Alison – or rather *Ali* – started: *So, Megs, what is it, what's going on?* And you said: *This may sound crazy, but I'm scared to tell you.* I am correct, am I not?' he said.

How? Meg was wondering frantically. *How did he know?*

'You are curious, aren't you, Meg? You took precautions, paddling into the surf, very clever – I wonder where you got that idea from. You were absolutely right to do that, because running water of any kind masks conversation. But you overlooked something.'

'Oh, really?' The alcohol was giving her the courage to be angry. To be reckless.

'Technology may be fine for many purposes, but sometimes a more old-fashioned technique of surveillance works better. You checked everyone on the beach, looking for binoculars and directional mics, didn't you?'

She said nothing.

'Let me tell you something. You live in an historic city. Brighton and Hove have beautiful buildings, but so many have shops on the ground floor and they distract us. We forget to look up, at the beautiful architecture above them. Have you ever been to Chichester, Meg?'

'Chichester? What does that have to do with anything?'

'It's a beautiful cathedral city, Meg. Chichester has one of the prettiest high streets in England, but only if you look up. If you only look at eye level, you will just see the same shops as every other high street in the country. But raise your eyes and you see such lovely architecture. It's the same with Brighton and Hove. If you had just looked up at the apartment building above Marrocco's restaurant on King's Esplanade, you might have spotted a glint of glass. A telescope, Meg, through which a profoundly deaf gentleman was watching you and your friend, *Ali*. This gentleman is able to lip-read and picked up large chunks and the gist of your conversation. I'm so sorry to be the bearer of bad news, Meg.'

'You bastard.'

'Tut, tut, there is no need for bad language.' He sounded genuinely hurt. 'I'm doing all I can to protect Laura and you are not making my job easy. You do understand that I have to report everything back to my boss, don't you?'

The icy edge to his voice cut through her soul like a knife.

'I'm sorry,' she said, meekly. 'I – OK – I shouldn't have done what I did.'

'No, you shouldn't. I have already tried to warn you about *consequences*. Is that not fair to say?'

'Yes.' Still meek.

'Are you going to give me your assurances this won't happen again?'

'It won't happen again.'

'How would you feel about your friend *Ali* meeting with a fatal accident?'

'Please, leave her alone. Please. This is nothing to do with her, she's just a kind friend concerned about me. I won't say another word to her. I'll do whatever you want from now on. I really will.'

'Yes.' Menace returned to his voice. 'Yes, you will, Meg. You've got someone else involved now, well done. Now you have put another life at risk. You'd better get back to her and warn her not to say a word to anyone. Take this as a lesson. There is nothing you can do that we can't see or hear. Don't leave our phone at home again. Wherever you are. However clever you might think you are, however much drinking wine might give you false courage, all you are doing is putting Laura into very real danger. Do I need to remind you that she is not safe and never will be until this trial is over and you have delivered? You are going to deliver, aren't you?'

'I – I'm – doing – doing my best,' she stammered.

'Oh no, Meg. You and I – we both know how badly this trial is going for the defendant, don't we? You are going to have to do more than just your best. Much more. You don't get any prize for coming second, unless of course you consider Laura being unloaded from a plane in a coffin to be a prize.'

68

Shit. Meg sat in the jury box on top of an almost sleepless night of worrying about everything, on top of a large hangover. She'd swallowed paracetamols and drunk copious quantities of water during the night and again just now in the jury room. Her mind was all over the place, thinking back to the phone call last night, the threats, the knowledge that she really was being watched and listened to 24/7.

You do have a friend on the jury.

Who? This morning, as before in the jury room, opinions had been expressed. Hugo Pink, despite all they had heard yesterday, was adamant that Terence Gready was an innocent man, fitted up by the police because he was a solicitor who had made a career out of defending criminals. The former Detective Superintendent, Mike Roberts, seemed to be supporting him on that point.

One of them? She drifted fleetingly at the thought. Then she winced again as her headache cut like a cheese wire through her brain. Somehow, she was going to have to hold it together today, suffer in silence and keep focused, clocking anything she might see as a weakness in the prosecution's unfolding evidence. But she felt utterly exhausted from lack of sleep. Yesterday she had found herself nodding off many times – she was going to have to try even harder today to stay alert.

Alison's words came back. *Courage is knowing what not to fear.* She liked those words. But. A massive but. How could she know what not to fear? Was her mystery caller exaggerating about Laura? He knew where her daughter was, the photographs showed that. Then there was the zip-wire accident. He had definitely been involved in that. And what he had told her last night, relaying back to her parts of her conversation with Alison. Or *Ali* as he had correctly identified. Just what lengths would they go to to protect Gready? Where would this end? What price for their lives?

Her thoughts were interrupted by the prosecuting barrister standing. 'I would now like to call my next witness, Emily Denyer, from the Sussex Police Financial Investigation Unit.'

A woman in her early thirties, with sharply styled dark hair, dressed in a smart black-and-white herringbone-patterned suit and white blouse, holding a laptop and folder of documents, took the stand, gave her name and was sworn in. Meg watched her closely. She couldn't put her finger on it, but something about her worried Meg. Was it her confidence?

'Ms Denyer, you are employed in a civilian capacity by Sussex Police, in the role of Financial Investigator – is that correct?' Cork asked.

'It is sir, yes,' she said. Her voice sounded firm and assured.

'Would I be correct in saying that since the defendant's arrest on Saturday December 1st of last year, you have been leading the financial investigation into Terence Gready's background?'

Denyer agreed.

PETER JAMES

'And is it your opinion that the defendant is a so-called county lines mastermind?' Cork asked her.

'It is, yes.'

'And you are going to tell us the evidence you have for this?'

'I am.'

Cork removed his glasses once more and appeared to study them before continuing. 'Ms Denyer, before we go into your detailed investigations into these drug dealings, I believe you have also been running a wholly separate investigation into the ownership of a classic car dealership in Sussex, LH Classics. Is that correct?'

'That is correct.'

Cork accepted a document handed up to him by his junior, Williams, and put his glasses on to look at it, briefly, before continuing. 'Ms Denyer, this document, an Excel spreadsheet which I'm holding, was prepared by you and your Financial Investigation Unit team?'

'It was.'

He turned to the jury. 'You will find this in Tab Q in your documentation.' He paused to give them time to locate it, before turning back to the Financial Investigator.

'The shareholdings and directors of LH Classics seem to me to be quite complicated?' he said.

Denyer replied, 'If I have understood the chain correctly, the shares are 100 per cent owned by a Seychelles-registered company with nominee directors, which is in turn 100 per cent owned by a Panamanian-registered company, also with nominee directors, and which is in turn wholly owned by a Liechtenstein company, also with nominee directors.'

Cork smiled. 'That's pretty convoluted, wouldn't you say?'

'Extremely,' she replied.

He nodded, thoughtfully. 'If I may take a step sideways for a moment, Ms Denyer. How long have you been a Financial Investigator for Sussex Police?'

'Coming up to eleven years.'

'Eleven years. So, it would be fair to say you are experienced in these matters, wouldn't it?'

She smiled. 'You could say that.'

'And in all your experience, what would be the likely reasons for a company based in Sussex – and ostensibly trading in Sussex – to have a convoluted ownership via a sequence of overseas shell companies?'

Brown jumped up. 'Your Honour, the witness is being asked to speculate.'

Jupp nodded. 'I agree.' He turned to Cork. 'Please rephrase that question.'

'I apologize, Your Honour,' Cork said. 'Ms Denyer, to your knowledge, are many Sussex businesses owned through chains of offshore shell companies with nominee directors?'

'Not many, in my experience.'

'But some?'

'Yes, very definitely.'

'Ms Denyer, are there any advantages or disadvantages to having an arrangement of shell companies and nominee directors? Perhaps you could explain both?'

'Well, the disadvantages would be the cost and complexity of setting these up. The advantages could be in very substantial tax savings. Or in a number of other ways,' she added.

Meg sat up with a start. She suddenly realized she had missed several minutes of what had been going on. She saw Gready looking at her – had he seen her eyes shut? Had anyone? Somehow, she had to stay awake – her daughter's life was at stake.

'A number of other ways?' Cork prompted. 'What *other* ways?'

'I've seen this kind of set-up used for money laundering, for example. And by large-scale drug trafficking operations.'

The defence QC was on her feet again. 'Your Honour, this is casting aspersions on my client.'

Jupp shook his head. 'I disagree, the witness has given a straightforward answer to a question.'

The prosecutor turned back to Emily Denyer. 'You have told us you have been running an investigation into the defendant's finances for the past eighteen months. That I'm sure is a major time and resource commitment. Could you tell us what made Sussex Police decide to instigate this?'

'I was briefed as part of a confidential investigation that the name LH Classics had come up during an Interpol inquiry into a major international drugs supply chain, operating from Eastern Europe and also from Colombia and Ecuador in South America.'

Emily Denyer spent some time giving her evidence, sharing the accounts and information she had accumulated against the defendant, Terence Gready. There were multiple spreadsheets she went through in detail, showing regular large transfers of money into bank accounts, a number linked to LH Classics. She had established that during the last five years there had been four separate payments of over £5 million passing through the LH Classics account. These transfers coincided with the approximate dates listed on the details of the offence. They also matched the evidence DS Alexander had given in relation to other large importations of drugs via Newhaven Port using classic cars destined for LH Classics.

At the end of this evidence, the prosecutor briefly turned to the jury, to make them feel included, then back to his witness. 'So, in your capacity as a Financial Investigator, you drilled deeply into the complex international chain of shell companies and nominee directors of LH Classics. Did you discover, as result, who the real beneficial owner is?'

'I did,' she said.

'Could you tell us that person's name?'

She glanced almost disdainfully towards the dock and nodded. 'It is the defendant.' She hesitated, as if unsure whether to say what she wanted to next, but she did anyway. 'We actually had a code name for him in the office.'

'A code name for the defendant? Would you like to share it with the court?'

Instantly Primrose Brown was on her feet. 'Your Honour, this is not relevant.'

'I believe it is material, Your Honour,' Cork responded.

Jupp smiled. 'I'm curious. You may answer the question,' he directed Emily Denyer.

All eyes were on her and she played to the audience with gusto and a wry smile. 'We called him *The Iceberg*, because he had so very little showing above the surface.'

69

Despite the seriousness of the situation, of having a highly
dangerous, clever and unpredictable serial killer at large,
Roy Grace had to stop himself smiling as he sat in ACC
Cassian Pewe's office, watching his boss's apoplectic face
on the far side of his far-too-big desk.

'Heads are going to roll, Roy,' Pewe said.

Yes, Grace thought. *And the first one that should roll is
yours!*

'This is unbelievable. U N B E L I E V A B L E.' Pewe said
the word again, slowly, as if spelling it out loud. 'How on
earth has this happened, can you tell me?'

With pleasure, Grace thought. 'A consultant surgeon
went into Dr Crisp's private room to check on the wound
in his eye. It appears that Crisp took him by surprise, over-
powered him, rendered him unconscious and switched
clothing, putting him in the bed instead of himself. I understand the room was dark to ease the pain for Crisp's eye
– he was claiming that bright light hurt it. As a result, no
one was aware of what had happened for several hours,
until the consultant regained consciousness.'

Pewe, with his tensions rising, opened and shut his
mouth several times, looking like a cat trying to cough up
a hairball, before speaking. 'There was meant to be a police

guard, twenty-four-seven, outside Crisp's door – what were they doing – ordering their online shopping?'

'Guarding,' Grace said, and then waited for Pewe's response.

'I mean, honestly, Roy, how – how could they have let this happen?'

'I'm afraid it's very simple, sir. Shortly before the consultant visited on his rounds, the previous police guard went off shift and was replaced by another PC who had never seen Dr Crisp. The consultant was, apparently, wearing scrubs, with a cap and a mask hanging loose over his chin. The new PC hadn't taken a close look at him. When Crisp came out, some minutes later, dressed in this kit, he had no reason to question him.'

'I'm holding you personally responsible for Dr Crisp's escape, Roy,' Pewe said.

Despite Pewe's currently senior rank, Grace jabbed a finger at him. 'No, sir, you're the one responsible. I emailed you, after we'd learned his injury was self-inflicted, that this might be an escape plan and recommended that we should ask the Metropolitan Police to double up on his guard, which you rejected for cost reasons knowing that they would recharge Sussex Police.'

Pewe narrowed his eyes. 'Roy, you've been the SIO all along on the Crisp case. It's your responsibility to make sure your prisoner is properly guarded until he is brought to justice and – if there is any justice – sentenced. You've failed abjectly. I suggest you buddy up with the Met Police PDQ and recapture the doctor. A man wandering the streets of London in surgical scrubs shouldn't be too hard to find, even for an incompetent like you.'

Grace bristled at the insult. 'I'm sorry, sir, I'm not going to take that crap from you.'

'No? Well, maybe you'll take this, instead: get Crisp back under lock and key within the next forty-eight hours or I'm reassigning you from Major Crime. We could be looking at suspension here because of the way you are reacting to this.'

Grace responded. 'This is typical of you. You know you are wrong, so you pull rank, just like a bully.'

Pewe hesitated a moment, mouth opening and closing again as if trying to find the right words. 'Well, perhaps suspension isn't appropriate here.'

'That's very generous of you,' Grace retorted. 'But if you take me off Major Crime – assuming you even have the authority to do that – I would go straight back to the Met in a Commander role, where I have the ear of the Deputy Assistant Commissioner. And my first recommendation to her would be that you are flushed down a fucking toilet into the Thames estuary. But before I do that, I will be sending a full report to the Chief Constable and to the Police and Crime Commissioner on my recommendations to you on how Dr Crisp should have been guarded. And how you rejected them. I wrote them in my Policy Book along with a note about your bullying conduct.'

Pewe winced at Roy's words, raising a conciliatory hand. 'Perhaps we are both getting a little bit heated, Roy.'

'Not me, sir. I'm a cucumber.'

'Cucumber?'

'Cool as.'

'Very well. Look – let's forget our differences, shall we?'

Grace stared him in the eye, saying nothing.

The ACC blinked first. 'You and I, we go back a long way.'

Unfortunately, Grace thought.

'I've said it to you before and I'll say it again now. We may never be best friends. But we have a common purpose, don't we? To try to make this world a better place.'

Yes, thought Grace, *and it would be a much better place without assholes like you.*

70

In a small interview room in the cell corridor under the courts in Lewes' Crown Court building, Nick Fox looked at his client. This was the first time the two men had been alone without Primrose Brown or her junior present since Stuie's death.

Terence Gready sat opposite him, hunched and with a worried expression, looking small and vulnerable. Fox thought he already looked like a crushed man. Except, of course, as Fox well knew, the man was a consummate actor and even more consummate manipulator.

'What the fuck went wrong with Stuie? I told you to have him roughed up a bit, not to kill him. You've lost the one hold we have over Starr, our best bargaining chip.'

'We can't turn the clock back now, Terry, what's done is done. Let's focus on the trial.'

'How do you think it's going then, Nick?'

Both men kept their voices low, aware of the watchful eye of an officer standing a short distance away.

'So far, Terry, if you want my honest opinion, you're the filling in a triple-shit sandwich.' He smiled. 'But all we've been hearing so far is the prosecution. Cork's good – but so is Primrose. Once she gets going it's all going to swing your way – trust me. And, we have our Plan B!'

Both men smiled. Then Gready said, 'You are confident in Plan B?'

'Oh, yes.' The dapper, unflappable Nick Fox smiled, then frowned. 'But we have a potential fly in the ointment we need to sort.'

'Who or what?'

'Michael Starr.'

'Mickey? Why do you say that, I trust him – despite him pleading guilty to get a softer sentence – I understood his reasons for doing that, his responsibility for his brother, Stuie. Fair play to him.'

Fox shook his head. 'Not any more.'

Gready suddenly adjusted his position and sat more upright, leaning forward. 'What do you mean?'

His solicitor tapped the side of his own head. 'It may just be the rumour mill, Terry, but I don't think so. As a result of what happened to his brother, I've heard from a good source that Starr, through another solicitor – obviously – is exploring what kind of a deal he could cut for grassing you up.'

In all the years Fox had worked for Terence Gready, he could never remember seeing the man angry – until now. Gready always took everything calmly, in his stride. But now he looked like the Devil himself was inside his head. 'Grassing me up?'

'That's what I've heard.'

'He's exploring what kind of a deal he could get by doing that?'

'Yes, Terry.'

'I just can't believe he'd do this.'

'When people are desperate, they do things differently. He's a very hurt and angry man because of Stuie.'

Gready sat in silence for some while, thinking. *Lucky*

Mickey had the ability to sink him. If he started giving evidence for the prosecution it was going to take more than the current tampering with the jurors, it was going to take a miracle. 'Mickey doted on his brother. Has he forgotten how much I've helped him over the years? Everything I paid for? Now he's looking to make a deal by grassing me up? What happened to loyalty, Nick?'

'They say that when a Black Mamba bites you on the end of your dick, you find out who your true friends are.'

Gready, absorbed in his thoughts, didn't react. 'I can't believe Mickey could do this.'

'Well, you'd better, and you're going to have to move fast if you want to stop him. The way the prosecution case is going, they'll finish next week so they'll have to call him then.'

'Witness for the *prosecution*? Fuck, he's one of our key *defence* witnesses.'

'Maybe not any more.'

Gready was thinking hard. 'Just let him try. I'll tear his other sodding arm off and fuck his other eye up, and the only job he'll ever be fit for again after I'm done with him will be as a fucking paperweight.'

Fox stared across the little divide at him, expressionless.

'Loyalty, right?' Gready said, bitterly.

'It is what it is.'

'I hate that expression.' Gready was silent for some moments then said, 'No. I'm not having this. This isn't what it is at all.'

Fox nodded.

Gready was perking up. 'I've thought of a way we can get to him. Mickey needs to be given a reality check.'

'What kind of *reality check*?'

Looking around cautiously before he spoke, Gready replied, 'A permanent fix. Know what I'm saying?'

Fox nodded. 'I know what you're saying, Terry, but are you sure? It's one thing threatening Mickey, but this is taking it to another level. I'm not sure I want to be involved.'

'We all have to do things we don't like sometimes.' Gready stared at him. 'That's what I pay you for. Nothing's *easy*, Nick, if it was, I wouldn't need you. My wife and my kids are up in the public gallery watching every day. They're expecting to see me acquitted because they know I'm an honest man. And that's what you're going to deliver. Is that clear enough?'

Nick Fox shrugged then smiled. 'The King of the Jungle's always delivered, Terry, you know it. I just don't think this is a clever thing.'

Gready looked at him. 'Perhaps the *King of the Jungle*'s going soft in his old age? Or perhaps the *King of the Jungle* is just too plain warm and cuddly? Maybe I need a wolf instead?' His voice was hardening as he spoke and Fox frowned, uncomfortably.

'Just remember this, Nick,' Gready said. 'A lion may be the king of the jungle, but a wolf doesn't perform in a circus.'

71

Roy Grace finally left his office at Sussex Police HQ at 7.30 p.m. He'd spent the past hour on the phone with Detective Superintendent Ross Shepherd at the Met, who was co-ordinating the lockdown of the hospital, in case Edward Crisp was hiding in there, as well as a manhunt across London. They both well knew, with Crisp's past form, their chance of a result was slim. He could be anywhere, including out of the country, by now.

Grace had suggested – and not in jest – they focus on sewers. The seemingly mild-mannered family GP had used sewers as an escape route previously. Did he have a particular reason for wounding himself in the eye – was it to end up at Moorfields Hospital, either because of its location in the east of London, or because of its relatively low security?

As he drove his Alfa out of the car park, he was reflecting on his difficult day, especially with Pewe, as well as the knowledge that he would be spending much of the weekend ahead back at his office. But with Cleo pregnant again, there was at least something to be really positive about.

Turning into the residential street outside the HQ, he drove home in a slightly better mood, but his mind still churning with all that had happened today. And, mostly, his fury at Cassian Pewe. He tried to calm his anger by thinking of a Buddhist saying Cleo loved: *Everyone you meet is fighting a battle of their own you know nothing about. Be kind to everyone.*

Even to Pewe?

72

Twenty-five minutes later, Roy Grace drove along the track and pulled up outside his cottage. As he climbed out of his car into bright daylight, the sun still high in the sky, he heard the familiar bleating of sheep on the hill behind their house, but was surprised he couldn't hear Humphrey. Normally the dog would be at the front door, barking his head off in greeting. Cleo was at home today. She was using the time to finish off her final modules and dissertation in order to complete her OU philosophy degree course.

He lifted his laptop bag off the rear seat and walked up the path, past the riot of flowers in their front garden, unlocked the front door and went in. No sign of the dog. 'Hi!' he called out, across the open-plan living-dining area. Cleo's course papers were spread out across one of the sofas and the coffee table. Noah's playthings were strewn around the floor.

'Hi, darling!' she replied, coming down the stairs, wearing a loose dress over her small baby bump.

He went over and kissed her as she reached the bottom, then asked, 'Where's Humphrey?'

As if in response, he heard the dog barking from somewhere at the rear of the house. 'I've put him in the utility room.'

He frowned. 'What's happened?'

'He started growling at Noah, again.'

'What?'

'Earlier this afternoon, Noah was playing in here quite happily. Then he stood up and toddled over to Humphrey, and as he tried to stroke him, Humphrey snarled at him. Like, a really menacing *keep away* snarl.'

'Shit. He loves Noah.'

She nodded. 'I thought so, too. They often rough and tumble together and I've always felt we could completely trust him with Noah. But this afternoon I was really scared he was going to go for him.'

'Did Noah try to take his food or something?'

'No. It was really weird. I put him straight into the utility room and left him there. It's odd, Roy. It's just so out of character. And he's still got that limp, but I can't work out which leg it is. I don't want him near the kids when he's like this. This is all we need right now, a problem dog.'

Grace frowned. 'He's not a problem dog, come on, there might be something up with him. I'll get him to the vet and see what she says about the limp.'

'Monday is the earliest appointment. Can you take him for 5.30 p.m.?'

'You're two steps ahead! I'll happily take him, but we can't keep them separated until then.'

'We have to, Roy, I'm not risking it. Once we find out what is up then we can help him. Or . . .'

'Or what? What were you going to say?' Roy said, guardedly.

'Well, I am just saying that we can't have a dog who keeps growling and scaring our kids.' She looked down and took a deep breath before carrying on. 'Kaitlynn and Jack have just adopted Buster, that Yorkshire terrier who belonged to that poor lady found murdered in her home in Hove – Suzy Driver?'

'Yes, what's your point?'

'Well, maybe they want a friend for Buster too?'

Roy stood, aghast. 'No, no, no! Whatever's up with Humphrey, we will sort it. We are not rehoming him. I thought you loved him?'

'I do, Roy, but we have to think about the kids too. You weren't here when he was growling.'

'Let me sort it. Honestly. End of.'

Cleo looked closely at Roy. 'OK, I'll leave it with you, Mr Fixit. It's been making me really stressed. And I do love him too.'

'I need a drink.'

'Go and sit down, I'll get you something. You look shattered.'

'It's OK, I'll get it.'

'Is it Cassian Pewe again?'

'Yep.'

'You want a Martini? I'll mix you one. Grey Goose, four olives?'

He smiled. 'I can't, I'm on call. I'll have a sparkling water – a strong one,' he said with a grin. 'Anyhow, I always feel guilty when I have a drink and you can't.'

She shook her head with a teasing smile. 'You're such a martyr – if it helps your guilt, after the baby is born and weaned, I'm damned well going to make up for it!'

He held her in his arms. 'I'll get Humphrey sorted, so stop stressing and focus back on you and bump two, OK?'

'OK.' She gave him a tight hug.

'You know you can depend on me,' he said.

She pursed her lips. 'I actually quite like you, too. Now loosen your tie, take your jacket off, sit down, chill, and help me chill! A Detective Superintendent Grace special glass of sparkling water is on its way. Extra strong.'

He complied, untying and kicking off his shoes as well, then flopped down on the sofa opposite hers. Humphrey continued to bark. Moments later, Cleo let him in; he bounded over and jumped straight onto his lap.

Roy stroked him. 'What's all this about you growling at Noah?' he asked, staring him in the eye.

Humphrey nuzzled up to him, the very picture of sweet innocence. Other than the arrival of the postman, which always set him off into a fury of barking, Roy Grace had never seen an ounce of aggression in the dog.

A few minutes later, Cleo handed him the glass and sat down beside him. 'Just as Humphrey's master likes it, I hope,' she said, giving Humphrey a pat. 'So, good day – bad day? Any update on charming Dr Crisp?'

Grace told her then added, 'To be honest, and I really should not be saying this – or feeling it – much though I want to see this monster behind bars for the rest of his life, all the time he's at large, I'm loving Cassian Pewe's pain!'

'Until Dr Crisp murders another young woman,' she said.

Grace shook his head. 'He's going to be too busy saving his skin. He'll know that every police officer in the UK has his photograph – and every Border Force officer. Any documents he has on him will either be stolen or forged. Unless he has a very clever Plan B, he's going to be picked up within a few days.'

'I hope you're right.'

'He's in the last-chance saloon. He's under arrest on charges that will ensure he'll never see the outside of a prison wall again. He's probably taken the view he has nothing to lose – but equally knows that he has little to gain.

Unless he has a hidden stash of money or credit cards some-where, he's going to be stymied for money – without stealing it. He's just having a laugh, a final fling, his last hurrah.'

'I hope you're right,' Cleo said, dubiously.

'So do I.' He leaned across the dog to reach his glass. 'So other than Humphrey snarling at Noah, how was your day?'

'It started well with a lovely pregnancy massage at Sarah Hurst's down in Brighton. The best massage ever! I think you could do with some massages to de-stress.'

'Yep, but I'm not pregnant.'

She tried to hold back a smile and failed. 'They do other types. I'm sure they have a *stressed copper* one.'

'I could do with that.'

'Oh, before I totally forget, I need to ask you something. I was chatting online on my class forum this morning. There's a fellow student, nice lady who I've met a few times, *Alison Stevens*. She DM'd me because she wanted some advice for her daughter who's doing a dissertation about jury service.'

'Go on,' he said, interested.

'Well, she knows I'm married to a very important senior police officer,' she said, buttering him up. 'She needs to know how someone could nobble a jury. I said I'd ask you what you know.'

'Yeah, I'd be happy to have a chat with her, if she wants. It won't be for at least a couple of weeks as I'm tied up on this murder investigation.'

'Fine, I'll let her know.'

'Jury nobbling does go on but not as often as people think. It's pretty rare, these days.'

73

Meg sat in the jury box, trying to follow the Financial Investigator, Emily Denyer, as she continued to give her complicated evidence. For the second day, she was talking the jury through a mountain of spreadsheets, detailing transactions through an increasingly complex network of offshore bank accounts. She listed dates of transactions, amounts, what credits and debits had occurred, and highlighted ones that she considered to be of specific interest.

In truth, Meg was completely lost, and she could see from the expressions of some of her fellow jurors that they were, too. She was struggling to remain focused. There had been no word over the weekend from Laura. Her daughter usually responded to her calls or messages within a few hours. She decided if she hadn't heard by the end of the court session, she would try to call Cassie. She really didn't want to bring Cassie's parents into this yet – that would not be a good move in the eyes of the people watching her.

On top of that, she was deeply worried that she'd said too much to Alison on Thursday night and by what the man had threatened. They'd met for a coffee yesterday morning and Ali had assured her she was keeping everything to herself. *Trust me*, she'd said.

Meg had to; she had no choice.

This morning, before the hearing had recommenced, several of her fellow jurors seemed to have made up their minds that Gready was guilty, based on the Financial Investigator's evidence on Friday. Meg was becoming increasingly anxious about what was now seeming an impossible task. She noticed Gready staring intently at the jury box, and in her direction. At her? She fleetingly caught his eye and detected the flicker of a nod. She glanced quickly away, with a shock, as if she had touched an electric fence.

74

Throughout his career, Roy Grace had always found it helpful to revisit crime scenes a week or two later and look at them with fresh eyes.

It was now nearly two weeks since Stuie Starr's murder. As Norman Potting pulled up the car right in front of the house, the area seemed back to normal. A handful of vehicles were on the forecourt of the garage opposite, some refuelling with petrol or diesel and one that looked like it was plugged into a charger.

He climbed out and looked at the small, bland, red-brick house. It was a fine summer's day, with a clear blue sky and the promise of fine weather to come. But, as always in this job, a cloud hung over him. This particular one was called Cassian Pewe. The murder of a Down's Syndrome man had caused a wave of revulsion which had ripples well beyond just the county of Sussex. The pressure on him to solve it was even greater than ever.

But at this moment he had no bone to throw to his ACC.

As he looked again at the house, and then at the constant stream of passing traffic, he wondered how it was possible that the offenders had arrived, parked, done their horrible deed and left, without a single person noticing them.

Above him, high in the sky, he heard an engine. He

looked up and saw a small aeroplane. And remembered something. Sandy, his now dead former wife, had loved cars. Several times, they'd been to the Goodwood Revival race meeting. The race circuit was around the perimeter of the Goodwood Aero Club, just a couple of miles from here. He turned to Potting.

'Norman, I've an action for you. This is probably a total long-shot but have someone check out Goodwood Airport – and any flying or gliding clubs nearby. Just in case anyone flew over this area on the day Stuie Starr was killed – they might have seen something.'

Potting nodded. 'Right away, chief!'

75

Monday 20 May

Like several other members of the jury, Meg had taken to bringing her own lunch in, rather than having to go out during the recess. She'd have preferred to have taken a walk around Lewes and got some fresh air, particularly on this glorious, sunny early afternoon, after the stuffy atmosphere of the court, but it gave her the opportunity to talk to any of the jurors doing the same as herself. Today there were just three other jurors in the room. Good, she thought, a chance to speak one to one.

Hari Singh had a wonderful-smelling picnic box, from which he again pulled samosas and proffered them to his colleagues. Maisy Waller looked at the one handed to her, dubiously, and nibbled the edge like a mouse at a piece of cheese which it knows is a trap.

Harold Trout declined with the excuse that spicy food gave him indigestion.

Meg gobbled hers down and could happily have had another. 'So, what do you think so far, Hari?' she asked.

Ever jolly, he said, 'Well, you see, I really don't know if I should be on this jury at all. I am just not a person who can easily sit in judgement of my fellow human beings.'

'But that's why you are,' said Trout, sourly and pedantically. 'That is precisely what doing jury service is.'

Singh nodded. 'Oh yes, Harold, you are absolutely quite right to make this point. But you see I am having this problem because of my beliefs.'

'You're a Buddhist, you told us, is that correct?' Trout said the word 'Buddhist' with a faint hint of distaste – not overtly disapproving, but making clear his dyed-in-the-wool mistrust of anything alien to his own culture and belief system.

'Indeed I am!' Singh replied with pride.

'So, forgive my ignorance,' Trout said. 'What does being a Buddhist have to do with deciding whether the defendant is guilty or innocent? Surely the law is the law, and right and wrong are the same, regardless of anyone's beliefs?'

Singh nodded, still smiling, and Meg watched, loving the way he stood up to the dull old fart.

'Well, sir, you are quite right. But what you need to understand is that the Buddha teaches kindness and under-standing.'

Trout frowned at him. 'Are you suggesting that slimy creep – that monster – in the dock who has clearly destroyed countless lives through the drugs he sells – deserves any kindness?'

Singh rose to his own defence. 'What I am saying, sir, with much respectfulness, is that until today, we have heard only from the prosecution. At this moment the defendant, Mr Gready, is charged with offences relating to drugs, but these do not mean he is a drug dealer. That will only happen if we, the jury, decide that he is guilty. Surely you will respect the opinion of the people called as witnesses, both for the prosecution and the defence?'

'Well, yes, of course,' Trout said, with some hesitation. 'Are you saying you doubt the quite overwhelming evidence we have all heard to date against the defendant?'

'No, sir, that is not at all what I am saying. But you need to understand that my duties as a juror are in conflict with my own personal conduct as a Buddhist.'

'So, what are you actually saying?' Trout quizzed, his voice laden with doubt. 'I'm a little confused.'

'What I am saying is I am not very comfortable to be sitting in judgement of a fellow human being.'

Trout stared at the man. Meg could see the contempt in his face. She could almost read his mind. All the prejudices Trout probably had about any race, or culture, different to his own were showing in the twitches in the corners of his mouth. Sure, Singh's views, in terms of reaching a verdict, were not the kind of tick-box that Trout would understand. But she was very happy to take Singh as another potential ally.

A loud sneeze from Maisy Waller interrupted her thoughts. Maisy sat at the table, sipping herbal tea and eating a particularly bland-looking cheese sandwich. She sneezed intermittently, having sniffed all the way through this morning's proceedings, to Pink's especial annoyance. During a brief recess earlier in the morning he had rounded on her, telling her in no uncertain terms that she should be home in bed before she infected the entire jury.

To Meg's surprise, Maisy had argued back robustly, telling him it was a summer cold that was doing the rounds, and it wasn't going to prevent her from performing her duty. But it probably explained, Meg thought, why there were fewer people in here eating their lunch than there had been last week.

As she bit into a falafel wrap she'd picked up from a deli on her way in that morning, she began eagerly reading a long WhatsApp message from Laura that had just come in, to her relief after the long silence, telling her their plans and itinerary for their visit to the Galapagos. Meg calculated the current time difference from the time stamp on the message and worked out that Laura must have been up and compos mentis at 7 a.m. today. If there was one positive about her daughter's trip, Meg thought, it had at least cured her – even if only temporarily – of her ability to sleep all morning.

'Looking pretty open and shut to me,' Trout said, suddenly, in his monotone Yorkshire accent, turning away from Singh and looking at Maisy Waller. He had all the spreadsheets open in front of him.

'I'd certainly have to agree with you on that one at the moment,' Maisy said and sneezed again.

Meg looked up and saw Trout pop the lid off a plastic lunch box, remove a stick of carrot and crunch on it with small, sharp-looking incisors. She noticed, for the first time, what a very small mouth the man had, as well as virtually no chin at all. He was rather odd-looking altogether, thin and angular, with a greying comb-over, glasses perched on a beak of a nose and a bobbing, protruding Adam's apple above the collar of his checked shirt which was at least one size too big for him. He wore a drab tweed jacket, a lichen-coloured tie, grey flannels and sandals over socks. He reminded her of one of Laura's rodents.

'Well,' Meg said, calmly but defensively. 'I think it's a bit early to start forming any judgements. The prosecution hasn't finished giving evidence and we haven't yet heard any of the defence witnesses.'

Trout tapped the pile of spreadsheets. 'It's all here, all we need to know. That Financial Investigator lady is pretty sharp. *The Iceberg*, she called him.' He gave a rather smug smile. 'I'd say that is a pretty accurate description. So much so very cleverly concealed.'

To Meg's surprise, Maisy suddenly interjected. 'I think we need to bear in mind that the defendant is a criminal solicitor – a specialist in legal aid cases. I once worked for a legal aid law firm and, I can tell you, they are very poorly paid, for what they do. They are decent, dedicated people who really struggle financially.'

'And your point is?' Trout said, rather petulantly.

'In my experience, the police hate lawyers – certainly criminal ones, and legal aid ones. They don't like the idea of them defending people they believe are clearly guilty. We need to consider whether this case against Mr Gready could be a police conspiracy – a vendetta. We've seen a long history of falsified or unsafe evidence given by police in the past. The Birmingham Six is one. The recent enquiry into the Met Police investigation of high-profile sexual abuse accusations is another. Who's to say this is not yet another case of trumped-up evidence?'

Good for you! Meg thought. Maisy seemed to change her mind a lot.

Trout tapped the spreadsheets again. 'These, madam. These are irrefutable, in my humble opinion.'

'I'm a payroll clerk,' Maisy said. 'And I've been studying these spreadsheets carefully myself. I agree with our fore-person.' She nodded at Meg. 'It is certainly a convoluted trail of shell companies and bank accounts, but I've not yet seen anything that comes anywhere near to estab-lishing *beyond doubt* any link between the defendant and these companies.'

Trout removed another carrot and crunched on it, noisily, looking miffed. When he had finished, he said, 'Clearly, the man is devilishly clever, I will concede that.'

'And since when,' Maisy Waller asked, 'has being *devil-ishly clever* been a crime?'

76

'Hi, Paul,' Roy Grace said. He nodded to Glenn and put the phone on loudspeaker. 'How are you? Missing me already?'

The Inspector replied, sounding serious. 'Actually, yes, guv, we all are. Got to figure out a way to tempt you back to the Met. But that's not why I'm calling. It's about Dr Crisp.'

'Our happy fugitive!'

'Yep, well, I'm afraid he's not such a happy bunny now.'

'Tell me?'

'He was identified on CCTV by one of the Met Super Recognizer Unit, walking along the Thames Embankment in the direction of Waterloo Bridge earlier today. Three cars and the helicopter were deployed – two cars on the south of the bridge and one to the north. As he reached the bridge the two officers in the car to the north approached him. He did a runner across it. When he saw the car blocking off the south exit, he jumped over the parapet into the river.'

'Shit. Did he get away again?'

'Not this time, Roy. People underestimate the current in the Thames. If you jumped off the north bank at Waterloo at certain times, you'd be carried down to the Albert Bridge long before you reached the south bank. The River Police pulled him out a mile east of Kew Bridge. Dead. Drowned.'

Grace heard the last few words in numb silence. *Dead. Drowned.*

It took him some moments to process this. 'You're absolutely sure it is him, Paul?' He caught Branson's shocked expression.

'We've had fingerprint identification and we've sent DNA off, but it's him, Roy, I'm certain – and there's a very obvious eye injury. I'll send you a couple of photographs.'

Roy Grace didn't know whether to be happy or to cry. The monster had escaped justice – in a way. In doing so, Crisp had denied the families of the victims, as well as his last intended victim, the closure of seeing him brought to justice.

Roy Grace was not a religious man. But there were times in his life when he envied those who did have faith. Those who believed in the afterlife.

His mind dwelled for a moment on the concept of the Akashic Records – a theory that, after you died, you were held to account. The Akashic Records replayed every thought, emotion and intent you ever had throughout your life on earth and you had to explain what exactly you had done with your time – just how you had used the amazing privilege of life that you had been granted.

And to be punished accordingly.

It was at times like this he so wished the idea were true. That Dr Edward Crisp, instead of rapid oblivion in the dark, cold current of the Thames, would be made to stand up and squirm as all the horrors he had inflicted on fellow human beings were replayed to him.

'Very obliging of him, Paul,' he said. 'Too bad he didn't drown in a sewer, which would have been more fitting.'

'From what I know about him,' the Met Inspector said, 'he'd have polluted any sewer.'

Glenn Branson grinned. Grace smiled too, thinking fast. Suddenly, a whole chunk of his workload had gone. No Crisp trial.

Ending the call, he said, 'I'd better tell our dear ACC.'

'Please let me listen in!' Branson said.

'Be my guest!' Grace dialled, and felt smugly pleased when he answered, almost immediately. It wasn't often that Roy Grace actually looked forward to talking to Cassian Pewe. This was one of those rare occasions.

'Yes, Roy?'

'I thought you'd appreciate an update on Dr Crisp.'

'What do you have?'

Grace informed him what he had been told by Inspector Davey. When he had finished, Pewe was uncharacteristically silent for some moments. Then he retorted, 'At least this resolves the budget issues, Roy.'

'Actually, sir, I have good news for you on your budget front.' He winked at Glenn Branson.

'You do?' Pewe said, suspiciously.

'Very good news indeed.'

'Are you going to keep me in permanent suspense or tell me?'

'As he died in London, all costs of his postmortem and disposal of his body are down to the Met. I thought you'd be pleased to hear that, sir.'

'I'd be a lot more pleased if he'd never escaped in the first place.'

'He wouldn't have, sir, if you'd allocated the funds for the guard on him I'd recommended.'

Pewe's response was to slam down the phone on him.

Grace turned to Branson. 'Good to know Sussex Police have another happy customer!'

'You need to watch it, matey, one day that bastard's going to have your arse.'

'He loves me. He just doesn't know it.'

'Or show it,' Branson cautioned.

'I feel the love!'

'In your dreams.'

Grace smiled. Then his thoughts became serious. He shouldn't be glad about Crisp, but he was. Perhaps because the man had once tried to kill him and had failed. All he really felt was a twofold relief, firstly that there was one monster less in the world, and secondly, that Crisp's early departure had left him free to concentrate on catching up on everything he had missed during these past six months.

But his hopes of that were dashed by the next call that came in.

It was from Sussex Police Inspector Mark Evans, the duty Oscar-1.

'Hi, guv,' he said, very polite as always. 'Welcome back to Sussex!'

'Thanks, good to be back.'

'We all missed you. Am I right you're the on-call SIO this week?'

'Yes, I am, Mark, what's up?'

Evans told him.

77

Ending the call from Mark Evans, Roy Grace immediately asked Norman Potting and John Alldridge to come to his office.

As soon as they were all seated around his conference table, he relayed the information he'd just received. 'Hampshire Police have two men in custody. They were arrested following a police pursuit from the scene of an attempted burglary at a residence in Havant.' With a grin, he added, 'I'm sure from your encyclopaedic knowledge of South Coast geography, you know Havant is just ten miles from Chichester.'

'I was a bit rubbish at geography at school, guv,' Potting said. 'Alleuvian plains and all that.'

'*Alluvial*, I think you mean, Norman,' Grace corrected him.

The DS nodded, almost wistfully. 'Like I said, I was a bit rubbish at—'

'Thank you, Norman,' he said, firmly.

'Sorry, guv,' Potting said, looking sheepish at the reprimand. 'Was just thinking it would be harder for me to get on in the force today, especially with having to compete with fast-track grad schemes.'

'Me too, Norman,' Grace said.

'And me,' Alldridge added. 'Still, be their loss, eh?'

Grace smiled and continued. 'When the officers searched the car, they found property from other burglaries in Chichester, from which cash, jewellery and electrical equipment had been stolen. All of it was recovered in the BMW vehicle in which they were travelling – and which had also been stolen some hours earlier.'

'They're clearly not the sharpest tacks in the box, are they, chief?' Potting said.

'Must be the ones that your geography teacher used to pin up his maps, Norman!' Alldridge retorted.

Ignoring him, Grace actioned them. 'I want you both to go straight over to Havant now and liaise with the Hampshire Police. Tell them these two suspects they have in custody are persons of interest to us in our murder enquiry, and see if they can establish their whereabouts and movements during the time we believe Stuie Starr was murdered.' Then he added, with a grin, 'Use your satnav, Norman, if that helps make up for your geography deficiency.'

Potting gave him a sheepish look.

'Or if you get lost,' Grace couldn't help adding, cheekily, 'ask a policeman.'

78

Mickey Starr's previous cellmate, Charles Nelson, had been transferred to another prison, and to his dismay, Mickey had been moved to a different cell on the remand wing of Lewes Prison. He was now sharing with a tattooed, unfriendly and intimidating hulk of an Albanian body-builder called Lorik Vusaj, who was on a murder charge.

The tiny cell, as the one before, but even smaller, consisted of two bunk beds, one above the other, and a toilet and washbasin screened off by a plastic shower curtain. There wasn't enough room to swing a mouse, let alone a cat.

By dint of the fact that Vusaj was here before him, the beefcake controlled the remote. Which meant Mickey had to endure an endless diet of football games, during which the Albanian shouted, constantly and loudly, at the screen, at pretty much every move every player – on either side – made.

Ever since the news of Stuie's death, Mickey had been desperate for some peace and quiet. To mourn his brother, but also to study the law, partly as a distraction. It was for these reasons, at 5 p.m. on Tuesday, he was grateful that the Albanian, with his minimal grasp of English, had fucked off to do some weight training.

It left him free to concentrate on his research, both on the laws around drugs importation and around sentence reductions through pleading guilty and turning Queen's Evidence – a posh description for grassing someone up.

His solicitor, Anu Vasanth, had left him several thick books on the law, at his request, with relevant chapters and pages helpfully highlighted with yellow Post-it stickers. But even so, he was struggling to get his head around the legal jargon.

Suddenly it felt like the sun had gone behind a cloud. Except there was no sunlight in this cell. He looked up to see the bald head and muscular physique of another Eastern European man he'd vaguely noticed on this wing, who had a teardrop tattoo below his right eye. It signified he might have killed someone.

'Got a message for you, Mickey. From your good friend Terry.'

Starr looked up.

'You're not going to be giving evidence tomorrow.'

An instant later, his throat was gripped by a hand as powerful as the jaws of a bulldozer. Then he saw a plastic blade inches from his left eye.

Mickey's throat was crushed even tighter. So tight he was struggling to breathe.

He looked into the eyes of his attacker. Eyes that were as dark and empty as the deepest well in the universe. The blade came closer. The pressure increased around his throat. He could not breathe. The blade touched his good eye, cold, a shining blur.

Then, suddenly, the grip on his throat was gone.

He heard a grunt, then a crashing thud. All the light was momentarily blotted out. He saw his assailant fly back and strike his head against the side of the cell door. An instant later the man was on the ground with Starr's Albanian cell-mate, Lorik, on top of him. Holding the weapon.

'You going to blind my friend? I'll cut your ears off, then I cut your dick and balls off and stuff them down your throat if you ever come near him again. We understand each other?'

Mickey's assailant nodded. Then screamed as the Albanian sliced through his right ear, which fell to the ground, leaving blood spurting out of the side of his head.

'You lucky man. Today I just take one ear. You come near my friend again, ever, I take your other. Now go fuck yourself.'

Starr's assailant scrambled, clumsily and unsteadily, to his feet, clamping his hand to his head, and made for the door. Lorik kicked him hard in the backside, sending him forward through the doorway and crashing face down onto the floor, blood still pouring. The Albanian threw the ear after him, then kicked the door shut.

'Thanks, pal,' Mickey said.

Lorik patted him on the shoulder. 'You my friend.'

79

Meg, waiting to go back into court, reread the message she'd received from Laura late last night.

> Hi Mum, Galapagos – amazing! Did a budget boat trip where we were like inches from blue-footed boobies, so close! And red-footed ones. And iguanas everywhere. And we saw all these red crabs – a gazillion! And did I tell u that really creepy guy who's stalking us is here too? He's everywhere we've been and we're sure he keeps taking photos of us. Well, we've taken a photo of him – attached! Cassie went over to him, he said his name was Jorge and said he wasn't taking photos of us. But don't worry, we're big and ugly enough to sort him out!
> Miss you. X

Back in court, Emily Denyer had finished giving her evidence after 4 p.m. on the afternoon of the previous day and due to the lateness of the hour the judge agreed that the cross-examination by the defence could begin this morning promptly at 10 a.m.

The defence counsel was on her feet.

'Ms Denyer, would I be correct in saying you are unable

to specify where this cash deposit of three point five million euros has actually come from?'

For the first time since she had begun giving her evidence, last Friday, Emily Denyer looked a little nervous.

'Yes,' she said. 'But if we go back to Spreadsheet 11 in your bundle of documents, you will see an equivalent amount transferred from the Cayman Island Elstrom Bank account, which tallies with the amount deposited into the Seychelles Neubank account on the same day.'

'Can you tell us beyond any doubt that this amount deposited into the Seychelles Neubank account came from the Cayman Islands Elstrom Bank account?' Brown asked.

Denyer shook her head. 'Not beyond all doubt, no.'

'Are you aware that there are many hundreds of transactional deposits daily into the Seychelles Neubank account, many of which are for large amounts?' Brown pressed.

'It was not necessary as part of my investigation to look at every deposit made. What I have told the court in my evidence is the electronic information that shows the large movement of monies into the relevant accounts,' the Financial Investigator conceded.

'Really?' Brown said. 'But I put it to you that this was just a fishing exercise, hoping you would find my client's name on one of these accounts. Is it correct that you did not find the name of my client on any of these overseas accounts?'

Denyer replied, 'There was no trace of a specific name but that's what I would have expected to find. The whole purpose of creating these types of accounts overseas is to conceal identities.'

Meg felt a flutter of hope.

Brown spent the next hour asking Denyer numerous

questions regarding her evidence in chief, but it appeared to Meg that the QC was making very little, if any, progress in discrediting any of it.

Brown continued. 'Ms Denyer, my client is facing extremely serious allegations, it is important that the jury is aware of exactly what you are saying, you understand that?'

'Yes, of course.'

'Ms Denyer, let's be very clear, there is nothing linking these two transactions except that they are of the same amount, that's right, isn't it? There's no name, company details, nothing whatsoever beyond the cash amount, is there?'

Denyer countered her. 'That, and the account numbers match.'

'So, your conclusion is based solely on coincidence?'

Denyer started to respond but, before she could, Brown added, 'That's pretty desperate, isn't it?'

Cork immediately stood up and said to the judge, 'I object to my learned colleague's last comment, Your Honour.'

'I agree,' said Jupp, and instructed the jury to ignore it.

'I have nothing further for this witness,' Brown responded, and sat down.

You are good! Meg thought, privately. But then she worried, *Or am I just clutching at straws in desperation?*

Cork got to his feet. 'I have only one more question, Your Honour. My learned friend suggests your conclusion is based solely on coincidence but how would you describe the evidence?'

Emily Denyer replied, 'Strong circumstantial evidence.'

'Thank you,' said Cork. 'I have no more questions.'

The prosecution case against Terence Gready had been

due to finish around mid-morning and all the jurors had been eagerly anticipating the start of the defence, which would commence soon after Emily Denyer had finished giving her evidence. And there was anxiety among some of the jurors that although they'd been told the trial was expected to last a couple of weeks, there was now every indication it might run longer.

Their anxiety was compounded by Stephen Cork making a surprise announcement that he had a new prosecution witness – someone who had formerly been lined up as a defence witness. Primrose Brown had immediately requested an adjournment to give her team time to prepare their cross-examination. Richard Jupp had given her short shrift. 'You are well aware there is no property in a witness,' he said, sternly. 'You know this person, you know what evidence he has. I'll give you fifteen minutes – time to let the jurors have a quick coffee break.' He glanced at the clock. 'Court is adjourned. We reconvene at 11.35.'

In the jury room, while everyone else discussed Emily Denyer's financial evidence, Meg again read the WhatsApp message from her daughter, and stared at the attached photograph, the first one she had seen of the man that Laura said was following and photographing them.

She had been anticipating some swarthy slimeball with greased hair and slick sunglasses. But what she saw was a guy in his early thirties, with South American looks and close-cropped curly hair, casually dressed in a jogging top over jeans and trainers. He looked harmless, the kind of guy who could blend into any crowd. Which, presumably, was the intention.

Jorge.

Had the photographs which had been put on her kitchen table been taken by this man?

'The financial evidence is utterly compelling,' droned the voice of Harold Trout. 'I don't see how anyone could think otherwise.'

'Well, I can,' Toby DeWinter announced. 'I am completely and utterly lost – and I didn't like that woman anyway, she's trying to bamboozle us with figures, IMHOP.'

'Imhop?' queried Maisy Waller.

DeWinter shook his head. 'In my humble opinion,' he translated.

'Ah.'

'Absolute nonsense,' Trout retorted. 'If you were concentrating, you'd have found it all very clear.'

DeWinter bristled. 'There's a big difference between *following* and *understanding*. That *woman*,' he said, with contempt, 'that *Financial Investigator* is nothing more than a prosecution puppet. She's spent God knows how many hours trotting out links between shell companies, board members and bank accounts all around the world, but in all these bloody spreadsheets is there one mention of the defendant's actual name on any board of directors or on any bank account?'

'Well, of course not,' Trout replied, his Adam's apple bobbing up and down frantically, his voice rising. 'That was the whole point – total obfuscation.'

'Hey!' Meg interrupted. 'Can we all keep our tempers, please? Getting angry with each other is not going to get us very far. We're not a bunch of squabbling school children. Please remember, Harold, that everyone is entitled to their own opinion, whether you agree with them or not.'

In the moment of awkward silence that followed, Meg did wonder whether she should have let the argument continue. If it had broken into a fight, what would have happened? Two jurors who couldn't be in the same room together – would that be enough for a retrial with a fresh jury – and a safe solution for her and Laura?

Then she heard the pompous voice of Hugo Pink. 'I'm with Toby on this one,' he said. 'We've been shown very fancy financial shenanigans, I'll grant you. But I've not yet seen any conclusive link to the defendant.'

There was a rap on the door and the jury bailiff entered, announcing they were required back in.

80

Wednesday 22 May

As they were getting ready to file into the court, Harold Trout, right in front of Meg, suddenly stopped, holding back for a second. He pointed at the back of DeWinter's bleached blond head and leaned over to whisper in her ear. 'If that man's IQ was any lower, we'd have to water him every day.'

She smiled and rolled her eyes. They entered the court and took their seats. The judge, already seated, addressed the jurors. 'As you heard, a new, last-minute witness for the prosecution has just come forward. It looks likely that this trial will now go into a third week and I realize this will be an inconvenience to some of you. But I'm sure you all appreciate the gravity of the allegations against the defendant and I'm asking you to please understand the need for this extra time in the interests of giving the defendant a fair trial.'

He nodded to Cork. 'Please proceed.'

'I now call my next witness,' the prosecutor said.

Meg watched a pugilistic-looking man in his forties, escorted by a security officer, make his way through the well of the court and into the witness box. He had a misshapen nose, gold ear stud and wore a battered leather jacket over a denim shirt and jeans. He had an awkward swing of his right arm.

'Please state your name,' the clerk asked.

'Michael Starr,' he said, nervously but clearly, then took the oath on the Bible.

'Is it correct, Mr Starr, that you have pleaded guilty to all the counts that the defendant is currently being tried for before this court?' Cork asked.

'Yes, at the first opportunity.'

'Mr Starr,' Cork asked him in a friendly, gentle tone, 'is it true you have made a full statement admitting your guilt and giving details of your criminal activities over the last fifteen years to the police?'

'Yes, the other day.'

'Do you know a man called Terence Gready?'

'Yes, I do. He is sitting over there,' Starr said, pointing at the defendant in the dock.

Cork continued. 'How long have you known him?'

'About eighteen years.'

Meg watched Gready. He was staring ahead, impassively. Then suddenly he glanced fleetingly at the jury – at her. Making eye contact with her, holding it for a moment too long.

Meg's mind was in turmoil. She was already convinced of his guilt, and that Harold Trout was right. How many thousands of lives had been ruined by the drugs Gready had supplied? Yet here she was fighting for him to walk out of this court a free man.

The more evidence she heard against him, the more her hopes were fading of an acquittal. Sure, they'd not yet heard any defence witnesses and maybe his legal team was going to pull a rabbit out of a hat. But on what she'd heard so far it wasn't looking good for Gready. Which meant she was going to have her work cut out with the jury.

No question Harold Trout would be voting guilty. He

was the only one she was absolutely certain would, at this stage. Hugo seemed to be genially disposed towards the defendant. She was increasingly convinced he was the one who was her *friend*, but she dared not approach him to ask.

Toby DeWinter was a wild card. Highly opinionated, so far he had not liked any of the prosecution witnesses, nor the prosecutor himself. But he did seem to like her. With him and Hugo on-side, she had enough to prevent a 'guilty' verdict. But a hung jury would simply mean a retrial.

'Mr Starr, have you and the defendant ever met?' Cork asked.

'Yes, we have.'

'And what was the occasion?'

'The first time was about eighteen years ago; I had been arrested on a charge of possession and dealing in cannabis. My then brief introduced me over the phone and Terry – Terence – said he could get me acquitted.'

'Really? And what happened?'

'He succeeded.'

'So he acted for you then?'

'No, not in any official capacity.'

Cork looked, theatrically, at the jury. 'Not in any *official* capacity? Can you explain what you mean by that?'

'Not really, no – he wasn't my solicitor. But suddenly my appeal was successful, and it was Mr Gready, I was told, who was responsible for securing it.'

Cork continued looking at the jury, making eye contact with some of them pointedly. Meg felt the glimmer of humour in his expression as her eyes met his.

'Were you grateful to Mr Gready at the time?'

'I was, yes. Very.'

Cork nodded. 'And did you repay this gratitude?'

'I did, yes.'

Meg glanced at Gready. He was staring rigidly ahead, his face betraying no emotion.

'Can you tell us how, exactly?' The prosecutor's eyes danced over each juror, as if to say, *Watch and listen, you are in for a treat!*

'I've worked for him ever since.'

Cork paused for a long time to let this sink in for everyone in the court. Sounding quite astonished, he said, with considerable emphasis, 'You have worked for him *ever since*? For how many years, exactly?'

'For fifteen or sixteen years now.'

'And in what capacity have you been working for him?'

'He owns a classic car dealership, which he uses as a front for importing drugs into England in high-value classic sports cars.'

Cork counted to five to let this bombshell sink in too. 'Such as the dubious Ferrari you were bringing into Newhaven Port in November last year?'

Primrose Brown sprang to her feet. 'Your Honour, this is not admissible evidence.'

Richard Jupp spoke up. 'I don't agree.' He turned back to Cork. 'Continue with your witness.'

'Thank you, Your Honour.' Cork addressed Starr once again. 'Between the time when you believe the defendant was instrumental in winning your appeal and the present time, can you tell us the nature of your involvement with this business?'

'I have been its General Manager since 2004.'

'And what has that involved?'

Cork's expression, thought Meg, was almost unbearably smug.

'Well, basically, running it.'

'You and how many other employees?'

'Just me, mostly. We do have a couple of part-time workers and a full-time mechanic. Most mechanical work and cleaning I farmed out to independent contractors, as well as bookkeeping and secretarial services.'

'So what have been your duties in this role of General Manager?'

'I've been responsible for the regular purchase and resale of various classic sports cars, often selling them at a loss, to provide turnover and to give the impression of this being a legitimate business. I have also from time to time taken in high-value cars for clients, putting them on display to try to sell them on their behalf.'

'So, during your time as General Manager of LH Classics, would you consider yourself to have become something of an expert in classic sports cars, Mr Starr?'

He smiled. 'You could say that.'

Cork paused, nodding with a profound air. 'With all of these years of trading in what you describe as *classic sports cars*, have you learned to identify those that are real and those that are fakes?'

'I hope so.'

Playing to the jury again, Cork said, 'And I would imagine your customers would hope so, too?'

Again, Starr smiled. 'Trust is very important.'

'Indeed, so I can imagine. Tell me, what is the most expensive car that LH Classics has sold in your time there?'

'Last year we sold a 1961 Ferrari 250 GT, Short Wheelbase for eight point five million pounds.'

'And you made a nice profit on that?'

'We take a ten per cent premium on any car we sell for a client.'

'I'm not a brilliant mathematician,' Cork said. 'Eight hundred and fifty thousand pounds profit?'

'Yes.'

'And is that less profitable than the importation of drugs?'

'Of course it is,' Starr replied.

'Mr Starr,' the prosecutor continued, 'this 1961 Ferrari – were you certain it was genuine?'

'I was, yes. We had its full history and were satisfied with its provenance. I have to say that the sale of that car was an exception, we didn't make anywhere near that sort of money on the majority of the cars that went through the business.'

'So, with your expertise, you would have been able to distinguish this venerable Ferrari from the fake that you transported into Newhaven on November 26th last year?'

'Yes, without doubt.'

'How are you able to be so certain?'

'Because I was charged with overseeing the construction of the fake Ferrari I brought into Newhaven,' he replied.

'On whose instructions were you doing this?'

Starr pointed at the dock. 'On his, my boss's.'

Cork paused again to let this sink in. 'So, just to be clear, the defendant instructed you to oversee the construction, in Düsseldorf, Germany, of a fake Ferrari?'

'Yes.'

'For what purpose? Was it to dupe a potential buyer?'

'No, it was to bring in drugs to England concealed in the vehicle. In the belief that it wouldn't be questioned by Customs.'

'What led to such a belief?'

'We'd got away with it before.'

'Can you explain what you mean by that?'

Starr nodded. 'To begin with we restored genuine cars and constructed replicas which we sold on. It was a good way of money laundering. Five years ago we moved into drug importation ourselves, and since that time we have packed those replica imports with drugs from our workshop in Germany.'

'Always on the instruction of the defendant?'

'Correct.'

'And what did you do with these cars once they arrived at your premises?'

'I removed the drugs, then arranged the sales of the vehicles.'

'You had accomplices?'

'I worked alone. None of the mechanics were aware of what I was actually doing.'

'We won't delve into the other employees of LH Classics for now. What do you estimate was the street value of the average shipment of Class-A drugs that came into this country concealed in these fake cars?'

Starr shook his head. 'Hard to say. I would estimate around three million pounds for the first one and then between five and six million for all the others, including the Ferrari.'

'Can you confirm how many times a year you would have brought these shipments in?'

Starr shrugged. 'As I said, we started five years ago. The one I got caught with was the fifth time we'd done it.'

Cork feigned astonishment. 'Five times – and four with approximately five million pounds of drugs each time? Over twenty million pounds' worth of Class-A drugs in five years? Quite a sum, isn't it?'

'Yes, if you put it like that.'

'Is there some other way I should put it?'

Starr blushed, and said nothing.

'Mr Starr, what I would like to establish is the true nature of your work for the defendant. Was it to sell cars or was there some other – perhaps nefarious – work that you carried out?'

'I suppose you could say I was his courier and general fixer.'

'Courier and general fixer?'

'Yes. I've worked as a courier for him, regularly bringing in drugs from continental Europe, mostly on yachts and small planes. I also distributed his drugs within the UK. I'm not proud of it, but I'd had to look after my kid brother who had Down's Syndrome. I did it to try to pay for a decent life for him. To ensure he had a decent home. So I could take him on trips, like to Florida, to Disneyworld. I knew what I was doing was wrong, but I'd made a promise to our mum that I would always take care of him.'

Cork was still looking at the jury with the conviction of a man who knows he has them with him. 'Mr Starr, you are a man whom the defendant has been claiming he has never met. Yet you say you worked as both General Manager for a company owned by him and as a courier and general fixer for him. Can you recall the last time you did meet?'

'Yes, it was sometime before November 26th of last year.'

'Might it have been Wednesday November 21st?'

Starr paused. 'It might have been. If we was allowed our phones, I could tell you.'

There was a small ripple of smiles at his reply, before the court became deadly serious again.

'Are you certain he knew it was you, yourself, who was acting in the roles of General Manager, and courier and fixer?'

There was a brief silence in which the entire court could have heard the proverbial pin drop.

'Well, how could he not have, he's known me all these years?'

Cork paused. 'Mr Starr, you have yourself pleaded guilty to all six counts that Gready faces – are you aware that you face a long prison sentence for your part?'

'Yes, I am aware.'

'Can you fully describe the nature of your relationship with the defendant? And expand on your other responsibilities?'

'I would say I was his lieutenant.'

'Lieutenant?' Cork repeated.

'Yes, I acted for him as his eyes, ears and authority. Whilst he remained out of sight, to the whole world a good and dutiful citizen, running his law practice, I was the person both bringing in the majority of his drugs and running his county lines empire for him.'

All pleasant and calm, Cork asked him, 'Can you tell this court just what your duties entailed – and could I ask you also to explain to the court just what exactly the extent of this so-called *county lines* empire was – and how it operated?'

Mickey Starr spent some time giving chapter and verse on Terence Gready's operation.

Cork then said, 'In summary, Mr Starr, you have told the court that you were actively involved not only in a conspiracy to import drugs but also to distribute them, and your actions have been driven by the defendant Terence Gready.'

'That is correct, sir.'

It was nearly 3 p.m. when a clearly dispirited Primrose Brown stood up to cross-examine the witness.

'Mr Starr, you are lying, aren't you?'

'No, I'm telling the truth.'

'You are trying to reduce your sentence, aren't you?'

'That's not true, he was my boss.'

'Well, let's talk about the truth for a moment, shall we? You say that you first met my client when he intervened in a case when you were starting out on your criminal career, eighteen years ago?'

'Yes.'

'And that since then you have been involved in the drugs trade, yes?'

'For him, yes.'

'Please answer the question that is asked. For the past eighteen years you have been involved in the drugs trade, yes?'

'Yes.'

'Making you a seasoned drug trafficker, yes, and this culminated in your arrest at the port with six million pounds' worth of Class-A drugs concealed in a car?'

Starr hesitated. 'Well . . .'

Brown interjected. 'Answer the question, please.'

He replied, 'Yes.'

'And when cornered, you assaulted a Border Force official, kidnapped an innocent member of the public, stole his car and drove like a maniac on public roads, before being forcibly stopped by police officers. You continued to resist arrest until you were restrained. Mr Starr, you are just making it up as you go along, aren't you?'

'No, I've told the truth.'

'But you must appreciate, Mr Starr, that the jury simply cannot believe a word you say given your criminal history, can they?'

'Yes, they can.'

'But why, Mr Starr, when you are plainly only turning on my client in the hope that your story will be believed, and you may receive a reduced sentence? You are a drug dealer, who has previously lied to the police, who has been involved in importing drugs for years, without a care in the world about the damage this trade does. As I've just said and I will now repeat, the jury cannot believe a word you say, can they?'

'I'm telling the truth.'

Brown picked up a document from the desk in front of her. 'Can I show you this statement that was taken from you by one of my team, back in February?'

She then handed the statement to the usher, who gave it to Starr.

'Did you make this statement?' Brown asked.

'Yes, I did,' replied Starr.

'Can you tell the court about its content?'

'I basically say that I have not been involved with Terence Gready in any sort of drug dealing or importation of drugs.'

'That statement is true, isn't it?'

'No, I was only saying it to help him get off the charges.'

'So you were lying?'

'In that statement I gave to your team, yes, but I'm telling the truth now.'

'How can anyone believe what you say now when you have just admitted lying in a witness statement?'

'The circumstances are different now, I'm telling the truth.'

Primrose Brown, now she had him on the ropes, spent the next hour challenging the evidence Starr had given, addressing the content of his witness statement and highlighting discrepancies, tormenting him with them.

When she finally stopped, Starr blurted out, suddenly and emotionally, 'My brother has been murdered and I strongly believe that this case has something to do with it.'

Richard Jupp immediately interjected. 'Mr Starr, I understand that you are grieving for your brother, but this court is neither the time nor the place to make this sort of accusation. Please confine yourself to answering the questions you are asked.'

Jupp then turned to Ms Brown. 'Do you have any further questions?'

'No, Your Honour.'

Cork rose to his feet. 'Just to be absolutely sure, Mr Starr, you stand by your evidence that you have told the court today, not only about the drugs but also your knowledge that the defendant used the classic car company as a front for his drug dealing?'

'Yes, that is correct.'

'Finally, you spoke about your knowledge of the evidence found at the defendant's house and in a safety deposit box.'

'Yes, he always told me he kept the information regarding his deals in a place no one would find them and it meant that although his name would not be found on the bank accounts, he would be able to keep track of the money.'

Cork and Brown had no further questions, and the judge then instructed the court security staff to escort the witness out of the court.

Cork addressed the court. 'I would now like to call my final witness, Senior Investigating Officer Detective Inspector Glenn Branson.'

Branson entered the courtroom, took the oath and began giving his evidence, walking the court through the key points of the investigation, how and when it had started.

He outlined his monitoring and supervision of Emily Denyer, and told the court that, in his opinion, she had conducted a very comprehensive and efficient investigation of the financial details, 'chasing the money'. He also confirmed the evidence found on the USB sticks, which contained details of the cars involved, and the relevant dates, which matched large deposits being paid in to overseas bank accounts.

He further confirmed the numerous other sums that were deposited in the same accounts.

He concluded that his team had obtained sufficient evidence to indicate large-scale drug dealing and importation, together with money laundering. Finally, he reaffirmed to the court that Gready had maintained *no comment* interviews throughout his time in custody, when he had been questioned at some length about the allegations and his involvement.

Primrose Brown stood. 'As you know, my client says he is innocent of these allegations and that the police have fitted him up?'

'That is not true, the evidence we have found as part of the investigation indicates that he is guilty of drug dealing on a huge scale. He has not been fitted up in any way, shape or form.'

Brown continued with her questions, suggesting that her client had been framed, which Branson denied.

'You have told the court that my client was responsible for so-called county lines drug dealing within Sussex. From what I have been able to establish, these activities have continued despite my client and his alleged conspirator being locked up. How do you explain that?'

'The reality is that whenever the police are able to cut off one supply or take out one drug dealer, there are many lining up to take their place, which is what has happened within Sussex.'

'So there are any number of people who are involved in the county lines drug dealing?' she asked.

PETER JAMES

'Yes.'

'Are any of them solicitors?'

'No,' Branson answered.

'Do any of them defend those accused of serious crimes?'

'No.'

'I have one more question,' Primrose Brown said. 'My client believes that you have been taken in by Michael Starr, who has lied throughout to help himself and reduce his sentence. That is a possibility, isn't it?'

Branson replied, 'Absolutely not, there is clear evidence of your client's involvement.'

'So whatever is suggested to you, you cannot even entertain the thought that my client is being cleverly accused of crimes he did not commit?'

Branson stared at her, unsure of how to respond. Before he could, she nodded once and said, 'I have no more questions, Your Honour.'

Cork confirmed he had no re-examination and that the prosecution case was complete.

Richard Jupp said that the trial was now adjourned for the day and they would recommence tomorrow at 10 a.m., when they would hear from the defence.

As soon as the judge had left the court and the jurors headed back to their room to collect their things, Meg scrambled past the others, just making it to the toilet in time. She locked the door behind her, lifted the lid and threw up.

81

Wednesday 22 May

Just after 5 p.m., Primrose Brown, her junior counsel, Crispin Sykes, and Nick Fox sat once more with Terence Gready in an interview room at Lewes Crown Court.

To all three of them, Gready was looking shell-shocked, as if all the fight had gone from him. He sat, hunched over the metal table, defeat in his eyes. 'What the fuck happened?' he said, quietly, almost as if he was talking to himself.

'Terry, you tell us,' Fox said. 'Michael Starr was meant to be our prime witness. He was going to swear on the Holy Bible in the witness box that he had never met you before in his life and was acting alone. What the hell happened?'

Gready looked up at him, haplessly. 'Someone must have got to him. Who and why? This has got to do with the murder of his brother. That's what's behind this – he thinks I'm responsible. OK, so I did—'

Fox raised a hand, calling him up short. 'Terry, be very careful what you say.' He nodded at the two barristers. Gready heeded the warning. He knew that if he gave any hint that he might have been involved in any way, his defence counsel would be compromised and no longer able to act for him.

Primrose Brown, notebook in front of her, looked across the table at him, very seriously. 'Terry, I'm afraid that evidence from Michael Starr has holed you below the water-line. It is very damning, and I could see that the jury were with him. In all my years at the bar, I honestly cannot remember many more convincingly damning witnesses.'

He looked at her with fury. 'You're a top criminal brief and you're throwing me under a bus on the evidence of one total shit who's switched allegiance?'

'I'm not throwing you under any bus, Terry. I'm just suggesting we need to reconsider our strategy. We've hung a big part of our entire defence around you and Starr never having met – on your assurances.'

'I'll fucking kill—' He halted in mid-sentence, realizing that anger wasn't going to get him anywhere. He looked at the three of them and didn't like what he saw in their faces.

'Let's just review everything calmly, Terry,' Nick Fox said. 'That Financial Investigator is smart, and Starr was pretty convincing. We're not in a good place right now.'

'Really, Nick? It doesn't take a rocket scientist to work that one out,' he retorted, bitterly.

After an uncomfortable silence Brown said, 'Nick is right, Terry. On what we've heard so far, to be brutally honest, we're going to struggle to get an acquittal. Your best bet might be to change your plea.'

'Change my plea? To guilty?'

She nodded. 'I'm afraid we are looking at the likelihood of a long custodial sentence, but we might be able to work on the tariff, using your previously good character to reduce the length of sentence.' She picked up her pen and unscrewed the top. 'Let's start with all the charities you support.'

Gready shook his head. 'No way, Primrose, you are wrong. You are being defeatists – all of you. We're not rolling over, paws-up. We are going on the attack!' He caught Fox's eye. Nick knew something neither Primrose nor her junior did, nor anyone else in the courtroom apart from themselves: that they had two jurors in the bag, including the foreperson.

Gready continued. 'I've been watching the jury, and I think a lot are on my side. That Financial Investigator hasn't been able to link me conclusively to any of those offshore shell companies, nor to LH Classics. She has delivered a credible circumstantial story of sorts, she might have convinced some of the jurors, but by her own admission under your cross-examination, she admitted she doesn't have hard facts. And as for Starr, he's nothing more than a crafty but not-very-bright opportunist who's tried to fit me up. Well, he's not succeeding. Put me on the stand. I know how to handle myself. I know what to say, trust me, I'll have the jury eating out of my hand.'

It was an eternal dilemma that defence counsels had. Whether or not to put the accused into the witness stand. If they didn't, in anything other than an open-and-shut case, the jury would wonder why the defendant was being kept silent. But if they did, the client might say something stupid under cross-examination and all but convict themselves. It was a risky tactic either way.

For days and maybe weeks on end, the jurors would listen to the evidence, with the defendant silent in the dock, unable to speak. Someone who was at the same time both the fulcrum of the trial and an inanimate third party. Putting the defendant on the witness stand was the defence's one opportunity to show the jury that, contrary to the monster painted by the prosecution, this was actually a decent, caring fellow human being. But it could backfire terribly on your case if that person came across as cold, or arrogant, or pretty much conceded their guilt under cross-examination by a cunning barrister.

Originally, in Primrose Brown's defence plan, she had been relying on Mickey Starr to deny any association with Terence Gready, and she had been certain that with his testimony, she would have put sufficient doubt into the jurors' minds that they would have to acquit. Now it was a wholly different scenario. Starr had been devastatingly convincing. And she wasn't sure that Terence Gready, despite all his professional experience, would be able to do anything more than dig his hole even deeper if he went into the witness box.

But then again, what did she have to lose? The evidence against him, despite his protestations, was overwhelming. He might knock a few years off his potential sentence by changing his plea, but he was still going to be an old man when he came out, if he came out at all. She could tell from the look of distaste on the judge's face. No one in the legal profession liked one of their brethren gone rogue. There was little chance of any leniency from Jupp, even if Gready did roll over. What the hell.

'Go for it,' she said.

82

At 6 p.m., Roy Grace sat at the head of the conference room table in the Major Crime suite, with his full team assembled. He had in front of him, as always, his briefing notes and his Policy Book, with the whiteboards behind him.

'OK,' he said. 'This is the update briefing on Operation Canoe, the investigation into the murder of Stuie Starr. Firstly, I have no new information from the public to report, to date, following our press appeal and the widespread press and media publicity that followed. There were a few calls in the days immediately following and all the leads were pursued, but they didn't take us any further forward. In the past few days it has been quiet, with only a handful of calls, most of which were cranks.' He glanced at his notes.

'One of our lines of enquiry is that his murder was a burglary that went wrong. Two suspects were arrested in Hampshire a few days ago – serial burglars, in a stolen vehicle – after attempting to break into a house in Havant, and Hampshire police found property in the vehicle that was subsequently identified as having been taken from a house near Chichester that same day. Norman and John will now give us an update.' He nodded at the two detectives, who were sitting next to each other. Alldridge's massive six-foot-four-inch frame dwarfed Potting, reminding Grace of *The Two Ronnies.*

'The Hampshire detectives we met with were extremely helpful,' Norman Potting said. 'They gave us a list of the property recovered in the stolen vehicle, a BMW X5, which included silverware, a number of expensive watches and other jewellery, around £10k cash, laptops, iPads and phones. They were able to confirm all of these items were stolen from a house near Chichester approximately three hours before their arrest, following a pursuit, in Emsworth, Hampshire.'

All of the team looked up, expectantly, sensing a possible breakthrough.

'But I'm afraid,' Potting said, dashing their hopes, 'there is bad news. Although these scrotes looked initially like good suspects for Stuie's murder, they'd only been released from prison the day before they committed this car theft and burglary. They were both in prison, in HMP Winchester, at the time of Stuie's murder. John and I have double-checked with the Governor there to make sure.'

Roy Grace thanked the two detectives for their diligence, then continued. 'We are still waiting on forensic updates, but so far we have nothing from the labs to give us any further leads. Something which may well be of significance – and which I believe most of you are aware – is that Stuie Starr's brother, Michael, has surprised the Terence Gready trial by giving evidence for the prosecution. It is possible his motivation for doing this might be Stuie's death.'

'Meaning what, exactly, sir?' EJ Boutwood asked.

Grace chose his words carefully. 'Meaning it is possible that Michael Starr believed that Terence Gready was behind his brother's death.'

'Why would Gready want that, boss?' Alldridge asked.

'That doesn't seem to make any sense. Are you suggesting it was to silence his brother? But would he have made a credible witness?'

'I'm with you, John,' Grace replied. 'At the moment it makes no sense. But when you hear the sound of hooves, think horses, not zebras. We have a man on trial for his freedom for pretty much the rest of his life, and Starr's brother, on whom he doted and with whom he lived, murdered. There is, surely, a high chance the two are connected.'

'But how?' EJ asked.

'I don't know, EJ, but I have a feeling there is a connection. If we find it, we'll solve the case.' He shrugged. 'Are there any updates from any of you following other lines of enquiry?'

Potting raised a hand. 'Chief, DC Alldridge and I went to Goodwood Aero Club and spoke to the secretary and a number of pilots, to see on the off-chance if any of them had been up in the air around the time of Stuie's murder. I left some Op Canoe leaflets with them. Then I did the same with a local gliding club. But nothing positive to report – so far.'

'Good work, guys,' Grace said. 'As I see it, we have two current significant lines of enquiry. The first is Terence Gready and the drugs world. The second is still the possibility this was a burglary gone badly wrong. Keep going. *Dissi u surici a nuci, dammi tempo ca ti perciu.*'

His team looked at him blankly. He looked at Potting. 'So Italian didn't feature in your studies, Norman, alongside geography?'

Potting shook his head.

'I'll translate,' Grace said. 'A mouse tells a walnut, *Just wait, I'll crack you eventually.*'

83

It was gone 8 p.m., but it was still full daylight outside. Roy Grace sat alone in his office, sifting through copies of some of the documents for the Terence Gready prosecution, seeing if any of the evidence linked in any way to Stuie Starr. Laid out on his desk was a thick wad of paper, a printout of all calls made from the offices of TG Law going back to four weeks prior to the arrest of Mickey Starr in November last year.

He had the analysis by Aiden Gilbert's Digital Forensics Team of the calls made from the mobile phone dropped by Mickey Starr at Newhaven Port. Additionally, there was a further printout of regular calls from the Lewes Prison phone log to the brother's phone.

Grace rubbed his eyes and took a swig from his bottle of water. This was not getting him anywhere. Nothing in the past twenty-four hours had taken the investigation further. No useful information back from house-to-house enquiries, no vehicles of interest picked up on CCTV or on ANPR cameras. He still had just the three hypotheses written in his Policy Book. The weakest one was kids targeting the brother because of who he was, then going too far. Sadly, it did happen in these sick times. But he preferred the other possibilities, which were stronger. The most likely was that it was a warning to Starr from Gready not to grass him up, which had gone wrong. But he had no evidence and the prime suspect, on that hypothesis, was in jail and had been at the time of the attack. The other hypothesis was the burglary which was either genuine or had been set up.

His phone rang.

He answered a little irritably, not welcoming the interruption, but instantly changed his tone to polite respect when he recognized the voice of the Chief Constable, Lesley Manning.

'Ma'am, good evening.' He was surprised to hear from her, she very rarely called him, and usually only when there was a major investigation that she wanted an update on.

'I hope I'm not disturbing you, Roy?' she asked, pleasantly, although he sensed an edge to her normally assured voice.

'Not at all, ma'am – I'm just going through a long phone log on Operation Canoe.'

'That poor man who was murdered – he had Down's Syndrome?'

'Yes, very sad – and a particularly brutal attack.'

'How's it going?'

He sensed from the tone of her voice this wasn't the reason for her call. 'Slowly, but we'll get there.'

'I've every confidence you will.'

'Thank you, ma'am.'

There was a brief silence, then she said, her tone suddenly both sympathetic and a little awkward, 'Roy, I wanted to let you know myself that unfortunately you haven't been put forward for the Chief Superintendent's promotion boards.'

It took an instant for the words to register. Then it felt as if the floor had been pulled away from under him. Before he could comment, she went on.

'I know this will come as a disappointment to you, Roy; there have been limited vacancies and I'm afraid ACC Pewe has chosen other candidates as opposed to you.'

'I see,' he said, blankly, feeling stunned. Inside he was seething, but he knew better than to vent his anger at her. 'Well, I really appreciate your telling me, ma'am.'

'I hope you will apply again in the future, Roy.'

'Yes,' he said, lamely. 'Thank you. Maybe.'

'I hope more than *maybe*, Roy.'

He said nothing.

'But I do have a little bit of good news for you,' she went on. 'It has been approved that you will be receiving the Queen's Gallantry Medal for your actions when rescuing the drowning hostage on your recent kidnap case, Operation Replay.'

The award was one of the highest honours a police officer could receive. Under any normal circumstances he would have been elated. But at this moment, it felt like he had been handed a tarnished trophy that no one had bothered to polish. 'Thank you, ma'am,' he said, trying to sound as enthusiastic as he could.

'I thought you'd also be pleased to hear that we are ready for the delayed award to be presented to your late colleague, DS Bella Moy. I know how much you valued and respected her, and just how upset you were by her death – just as we all were.'

'I'm very pleased to hear that, ma'am. And I think DS Potting will be very grateful for this recognition.'

'They were engaged to be married, weren't they?'

'Yes. I had been so happy for them both.'

'Well, I'm very pleased to tell you the decision's been made that both medals will be awarded at a ceremony in London, where they will be presented by HRH the Prince of Wales accompanied by HRH the Duchess of Cornwall – the date will be advised.'

'Thank you, ma'am, it is very gratifying news.'

'Perhaps DS Potting may wish to accept the medal on DS Moy's behalf. Does she have any other close relatives?'

'Her mother. I know she's not been in good health, but I'm sure she will want to accompany Norman.'

'Will you make the approaches?'

'I will, ma'am. And thank you.'

As soon as the call ended, Grace sat, staring at his phone, all joy about the medal eclipsed by his fury at Pewe. *That lying shit*, he thought. His first reaction, which he reined in, was to call him and shout at him.

Then he thought, *What the hell am I doing sitting in my office at 8 p.m. working for a boss who is a total wanker and a liar?*

He left everything as it was, stormed out, slamming the door behind him and went down to the car park. As he fired up the Alfa's engine, he had just one angry thought.

I will get even with you, Cassian. I promise you.

84

Thursday 23 May

Richard Jupp, robed and regal, entered as normal, carrying his laptop and several folders, and took his commanding position in his chair. The jury filed in and took their seats. The judge peered at the jury, as if counting and checking they were all present and correct, then addressed the defence counsel below him in the well of the court. 'Please proceed.'

Primrose Brown stood up. 'I call my first witness, the defendant, Terence Gready.'

Accompanied by a security guard, Gready momentarily disappeared from the glass-fronted dock before emerging from the rear. The guard left him to make his own way to the witness box, under the watchful eye of everyone in the court. Wearing a navy suit, white shirt and plain tie, and with an upright, but not too proud posture, as rehearsed with his team, he took the stand with a respectful air, already looking more a victim than a perpetrator.

Not remotely a believer, despite his former regular churchgoing with his wife to keep up appearances, Gready held the Bible and swore on it with true, passionate reverence to tell the truth, the whole truth and nothing but the truth.

Meg stared at him with both surprise and contempt.

Seeing him walk to the witness box, she realized how small he seemed, in every way. Five foot five at most, thin, with dark little eyes behind his tortoiseshell glasses and tiny, delicate hands. His lank, thinning hair, still mostly black, was neat and he was clean-shaven. Other than his glasses, he could have been a travelling sales representative or perhaps a ticket clerk. Neither ugly nor handsome, he was truly nondescript, Meg thought, although he did definitely have an attitude, an expression on his face that said: *Don't misread me, I'm not anyone's pushover.*

She was about to see how true that was.

Primrose Brown asked him, 'Mr Gready, you are indicted on a number of counts relating to the importation of Class-A drugs and conspiracy to supply these drugs. Can you tell us your reaction to these allegations when they were first put to you?'

Gready seemed, in front of Meg's eyes, both to grow in stature and at the same time let his demeanour soften into a warm, approachable man. He smiled politely, first at his defence counsel, then at the jury, clocking in particular the good-looking woman in the front row who was absolutely on his side but always avoided eye contact with him, then with the corpulent businessman in the row behind her, whom he was saving from bankruptcy.

He began speaking, addressing the jury as if they were the only people in the world he cared about. His voice was sincere, his tone that of a genuinely wounded innocent. 'It was complete astonishment.' He gave a derisory little laugh. 'I mean, I thought it was mistaken identity – that they couldn't possibly be charging *me*.'

Brown probed. 'Anything else?'

Still totally zeroed-in on the jury, he opened his arms out. 'I have been in court so many times, I'm a firm upholder of the law. It is what I have made my career in. I believe in the justice system and want every person to have their chance for justice.'

'What do you say about the evidence you have heard over the last few days?'

'Over the past ten days you've heard a litany of very convincing evidence against me, painting me as a complete monster. If I were any one of you jurors, based on what I'd heard to date, I would be wanting to lock me up and throw away the key. No question!'

His barrister cut him short. 'Mr Gready, could you get to the point, please.'

He continued. 'But what you have heard during these past ten days is a very elaborate and cleverly planned and orchestrated tissue of malicious lies.'

'Can you tell us your reasons for believing this?' Brown coaxed.

'Yes, I can. These are lies perpetrated by someone – or some group – out to destroy my reputation, in order to further their commercial gains in the vile world of drugs importation and distribution they inhabit.'

'But why you, Mr Gready?'

'Unfortunately, as a criminal lawyer one makes a great number of enemies throughout one's career. Some of these are people you have defended unsuccessfully, however hard you have tried. And of course, sadly, we legal aid solicitors all too frequently incur the wrath of the police themselves, who consider we are simply playing a game and that we do not care for the truth or for justice.'

'You want the jury to believe the police are fitting you up?'

'During the course of my career I have on many occasions after doing my duty, trying to ensure fair play for a suspect, had police officers tell me to my face that *they are going to get me one day.'*

He paused to let this sink in. 'One police officer just a couple of years ago told me that, if anyone appears in court charged with an offence, it is because they are guilty – that the Crown Prosecution Service won't charge anyone who is *not* guilty as hell – in his words. I'd just got a suspect, whom he'd arrested, acquitted. The officer was waiting for me outside the court and called me a money-grabbing little parasite.'

'The point you are trying to make, Mr Gready, is what exactly?'

'I'm not saying this because I have anything at all against the police. They do a vital job. I'm telling you this because I need you to understand the hatred some officers have for lawyers like myself.'

He paused to make eye contact with the jury. 'I've no doubt you have been amazed at some of the things you've heard during this trial. Frankly, so am I. The internet today is highly dangerous. Anyone can make it seem that someone else is doing something wrong. Anyone with the right skills – or with the money to hire those skills – can alter phone records, bank accounts and any kind of personal record held on a database.'

'And how is that relevant here, Mr Gready?'

He glanced at his notes. 'Any of you, any *one* of you on this jury, with just the most basic of computer skills, could gain access to the phones and computers of almost anyone you choose and doctor their records – even those of one of your fellow jurors, if you really wanted to. You could give your best friend a criminal record, you could plant all kinds of incriminating evidence in their computer files without their knowledge.'

Brown signalled to him. 'Do go on.'

He looked at them imploringly. 'I'm just like you – like any of you. What has happened to me could happen to any of us. Someone sees an opportunity to frame a totally innocent person.' He paused, as if having trouble with his emotions, his voice quavering. 'But in my case, they have taken it even further, they have done something utterly disgusting, utterly depraved, something almost beyond human comprehension in their efforts to put me on trial for offences I have never committed. Something that threatens the whole life I've built with my wife and children, who have been here in court every day supporting me – it's as though I am being punished for no other offence than trying to be a decent, upright citizen in a world that is becoming increasingly violent and crooked.'

He paused for a moment, looking around the court as if to ensure he had everyone's attention. He needn't have worried. Continuing calmly, he was sounding every inch the rational man.

Meg was battling with her own emotions. She so sorely wanted to stand up and expose the creep for the liar he was. She wanted to demand, in front of this entire court, why he was threatening to murder her daughter if he was so damned innocent? But she kept quiet, seething inside as he went on, sounding increasingly pious.

Gready's QC interjected. 'Mr Gready, can you tell the court why you think Michael Starr is doing this to you?'

'I can't tell you whether Michael Starr is a man operating on his own or is the front for a criminal syndicate – the latter, I strongly suspect. But if you believe me, and I sincerely hope you will, as my whole future life and reputation depend on it, I'm going to tell you something that I know you all will find utterly shocking, utterly vile and almost beyond comprehension.'

He paused, looking dreadfully hurt. 'I believe it is very probable that Stuie was murdered by someone in an attempt both to implicate me and to give credence to the quite astonishing and incredibly inventive pack of lies that you heard from Mr Starr yesterday.'

Primrose Brown again interjected. 'Mr Gready, the court has already heard that Mr Starr has admitted his guilt. Can you explain that?'

'Yes, he's a desperate man with nothing to lose, facing a very long prison sentence.'

He fell silent for a few seconds before speaking again with the utmost sincerity in his voice. 'I would like to take this opportunity now to offer my condolences over Stuie Starr's tragic death.'

He then spent the next two hours denying anything at all to do with the financial records and maintained he had no links to the overseas accounts. He told the court he had not been involved in any importation of drugs, using classic cars or distributing drugs within Sussex.

Brown turned to him. 'Finally, you believe you have been framed by Starr and his associates?'

'I am a completely innocent man being framed by the police, Starr and others.'

He went on to inform the court that the reason he had answered *no comment* in his police interviews was that the charges were nothing to do with him and were part of the overall conspiracy to frame him.

'Finally, Mr Gready, why should the jury believe you?' Primrose Brown asked.

'I have sworn on oath to tell the truth, I am a legal professional and the prosecution has produced no compelling evidence to show I'm guilty of what they allege. I am an innocent family man, and I would ask every member of the jury to believe what I have just shared. I am an innocent man.'

'Please wait there,' Brown said to her client.

Cork rose to his feet. 'Mr Gready, you are positing a somewhat hard to believe theory as to who might have murdered Stuie Starr. You suggest that Michael Starr gave evidence against you because he thinks it is you who killed his brother.'

'That is the truth he would like this court to believe,' Gready responded calmly. 'A *truth* that is a very elaborately planned and executed fiction.'

'We heard yesterday,' Cork continued, 'Mr Starr is claiming to have been the General Manager of your classic car dealership. And we have evidence from the SD card and USB sticks showing your relationship, drug dealing and foreign account activity over many years. Yet you are maintaining that you never met him and that he never worked for you?'

'That is correct.'

'And beyond the occasion, some eighteen years ago now, when you used your – ah – influence in some way to get him acquitted, you are maintaining you have never had any dealings or communications with Mr Starr?'

'That is correct.'

'You have suggested to this court that if any calls had originated from Michael Starr, they would have been connected to your role as a solicitor and nothing more sinister. And yet, you also say you have never met the man.'

Gready made no comment.

Cork persisted. 'Is this correct?'

'I believe there were some calls to the office from Starr many years ago. Back at the time when I was able to get the case against him quashed, I subsequently became very uncomfortable, believing he had not told me the truth. As you would well know from your days as a defence barrister, if you have reasons to doubt the veracity of a client you are obliged by the Law Society to cease acting for that person. This was my situation, which Mr Starr refused to accept, and he did hound me with calls for a time – calls which my office deflected.'

'In that case, Mr Gready, why, when there are dozens and dozens of solicitors like yourself practising criminal law, did Mr Starr not just approach another firm?'

'It's very simple,' Gready said with poker-faced confidence. 'Because everyone knows I'm the best.'

There were some smiles around the court. Only the judge sat stony-faced.

'Let us now address the issue of the safety deposit box in your name, Mr Gready. As we heard from evidence given by DS Alexander, a key was discovered very cleverly concealed in the false bottom of a spray canister in the garden shed of your home in Onslow Road, Hove. This key was for a private safety deposit box, in your name, on the premises of a company, Safe Box Co, on the Hollingbury Industrial Estate. It was opened under warrant and found to contain foreign currency totalling £392,000, along with six USB memory sticks. You accept that, don't you?'

'I believe that is what they say.'

'Well then, where did this substantial sum come from?'

Gready shook his head. 'I'm afraid it must have been all part of Mr Starr's clever plot to frame me. I can only assume he planted the key in the shed and the money in the deposit box. If I had that substantial sum I can assure you I would have treated my wife and family to something considerably more exotic than our annual fortnight's holiday in a time-share cottage in Appledore in Devon.'

Cork paused, frowned and said, 'Do I have this right? You are suggesting Mr Starr opened a safety deposit box in your name, hid a huge sum of cash, together with damning evidence against you, inside it, then placed the key in an aerosol inside a shed on your property, on the off-chance that if caught he could point the finger at you?'

'Yes, he must have,' Gready replied.

'Are there fairies at the bottom of your garden as well?' Cork challenged.

Jupp immediately instructed the court to disregard the previous comment and said, 'Mr Cork, you should know better than that.'

'Of course, I'm sorry, Your Honour.' The prosecuting counsel paused and then continued. 'You refused to answer questions from the police about the details of the information found?'

'I was under no obligation to answer any questions. They have nothing to do with me.'

'Interestingly, that content showed details of four further importations through Newhaven Port using classic cars involving large quantities of drugs. These runs coincided with large deposits being made through LH Classics into the overseas bank accounts.'

'They are nothing to do with me. You should be asking Michael Starr. He's the drug baron, not me. He's admitted it to this court!'

Cork persevered. 'I suggest to you, Mr Gready, you refused to answer any questions because you had no plausible reason for having this damning evidence which shows your criminality, and this is something for the jury to take into account.'

'I knew I was being set up so decided to keep quiet at that stage. I have explained to the court this morning that I am innocent and had nothing to do with any of this.'

Stephen Cork continued to question him at length, but the defendant steadfastly maintained his innocence.

'Finally, Mr Gready,' Cork said pointedly, 'I put it to you that you are a thoroughly dishonest drug-dealing criminal and have made millions of pounds from the misery you inflict. You have been careful to hide your involvement but of course you didn't consider that your loyal colleague, Michael Starr, would turn against you.'

'The jury know I'm telling the truth,' Gready said, confidently and directly.

Primrose Brown stood up, adjusting her gown. 'My learned friend, Mr Cork, asked you about a key to the deposit box in your name and you denied owning it, is that correct?'

'Yes, nothing to do with me. The key was found in my garden shed and it would be easy for anyone to access it.'

'I would like you to look at the prosecutions exhibit JA/17, the form that was completed at the time the safety deposit box was rented back in 2004. I have copied the document for the benefit of the court.' She then handed a bundle of copies to the court usher, David Rowland, for distribution.

'Mr Gready, is that your signature on the document?'

'It looks like mine and it is signed Terence Gready, but it is definitely not my signature. As I have said before, I know nothing about the deposit box.'

Brown then addressed the court. 'No more questions, Your Honour, thank you.'

Terence Gready was escorted back to the dock.

Brown proceeded to hand a document to the prosecution counsel. 'You have heard evidence from the defendant that he believes he has been framed by Mr Starr. My next witness will be a person recognized as the UK's leading forensic handwriting expert, Professor Geoff Shaw of Magdalene College, Cambridge.'

Cork jumped up. 'Your Honour, this is the first time I have heard about this witness, I must object.'

Jupp considered this for some moments before turning to Brown. 'Why was this not passed to the prosecution before now?'

'I apologize, Your Honour, but this evidence was only obtained this week when Starr unexpectedly gave evidence for the prosecution.'

'Court is adjourned for twenty minutes,' Jupp announced. Then he looked, irascibly, at the two lead counsels. 'Come to my chambers immediately.'

85

In the jury room, Harold Trout, seated, said, 'What the defendant is saying is utterly preposterous. The man is cornered in the last chance saloon and is clearly lying through his teeth. Are we really expected to swallow such arrant nonsense?'

Mike Roberts, spooning coffee into a mug by the kettle, said, 'Well, during my last two years with the police I'm afraid I saw some quite astonishing cases involving falsified documents and records created by cyber criminals. I think he is making a valid point about what we can and can't trust these days.'

'My nan was swindled out of £12,000 by online fraudsters just two months ago,' Toby DeWinter concurred. 'They are extremely clever and sophisticated. She showed me the email purportedly from her bank and it really did look genuine.'

'We've had to engage a computer expert full-time in my business to protect us and our clients against cyber fraud,' Hugo Pink added. 'What the defendant says is completely plausible.'

'Would he lie under oath?' Maisy Waller questioned.

'With respect, Maisy, when someone's back is to the wall, they will say anything,' Trout said, dismissively.

'I wasn't sure earlier, despite all the evidence against Mr Gready,' Maisy Waller persisted. 'But after listening to him, I have to say I really don't like him – and I don't trust him.'

'I'm with you, Maisy, and with you, Harold,' Mark Adams said. He looked around at his fellow jurors, all now seated at the table. 'Do we really need to run into a third week just to hear a bunch more lies? I've got to earn money for my family and for the mortgage, and it's tough enough losing two weeks as it is. Surely we've heard enough – do we need to hear any more?'

'Any more what, exactly?' Meg said, sternly rounding on him. 'That we don't need to hear any more from the defence? Is that your idea of justice? You'd like to see a kangaroo court convict this man regardless of the facts so you can get back behind the wheel of your Uber?'

He glared back at her. 'I don't know if you and I have been sitting in the same court, but it's blatantly clear to me that, as Harold has just said, the defendant is in the last chance saloon. He's guilty as hell. A child of three could see through the baloney he's just spouted at us. Does he think we're a bunch of idiots sitting around playing pass the brain cell?'

86

In his chambers, Jupp turned to Brown. 'Primrose, can you tell me what is going on here?'

She replied, 'As I said in court, Your Honour, as a result of Starr giving evidence on behalf of the prosecution, a matter that I was going to bring up with him required me to seek a further opinion from a handwriting expert. My expert, Professor Shaw, has only just turned up having rushed here from another court appearance. I apologize to my learned friend, but I think it would be helpful to the court to hear his evidence. Mr Cork will be able to cross-examine him and I accept that he may, if not happy, ask you for a short adjournment to instruct his own witness, but I don't believe that will be necessary. I appreciate that he can reserve that right.'

Jupp turned to Cork. 'Your thoughts, Stephen?'

'In the ideal world, of course, I'd like to have seen this evidence before, had time to consider it and make a judgement about instructing my own expert. I am mindful of where we are with the case at the moment and if I think I can deal with it today, I will, but I do reserve my prerogative of instructing my own witness if necessary.'

Jupp considered what he had heard for a few moments. 'If that is your view, I would rather deal with this witness today, but that should not prevent you from making a proper evaluation of the handwriting evidence and you are right to take it further if necessary.'

The three of them returned to court.

87

Thursday 23 May

'Let's have the jury back,' Jupp said to the jury bailiff after he had taken his seat.

The jury returned and took up their positions.

The judge turned to Primrose Brown. 'You may proceed.'

'Thank you, Your Honour.'

She stood. 'I am calling Cambridge handwriting expert, Professor Geoff Shaw.'

A bright-eyed man in his forties, with a mane of wild, greying hair, stood in the witness box, exuding confidence.

First, the QC established the professor's credentials as a leading handwriting authority, which included listing a number of fraud trials in which evidence he had given was a major factor in securing convictions.

Shaw, speaking with an infectious enthusiasm, began by giving evidence regarding the alleged signature of Terence Gready on the Safe Box Co document. He referred to a series of slides on the monitor next to the judge. Each was of the signature, some showing it in its entirety, some enlarged details of one part of it.

He clicked a remote control. After a short delay the signature appeared on the monitor, *Terence Gready*, upright, with a separation between the first and last name, above the printed name SAFE BOX CO.

'In the interests of brevity, I will explain to you the key points to look at, without going through all the minutiae of detail. All of you will be given a copy to study later. The first area to look at is the starting strokes, which you can see clearly highlighted in yellow on the first image,' he said, checking against the document but keeping his main focus on eye contact with the jury. 'Next, again highlighted, is a pen lift and the appearance of a tremor, indicative of hesitation and a lack of confidence.'

The third image now appeared. There were four yellow circles on different parts of the signature. 'This is the most telling of all the three images, as it shows clear evidence of *patching*. For those of you unfamiliar with graphology language, patching is the term for *touching up* a piece of handwriting. There are four instances of such patching on this signature, each indicated by a yellow circle.'

Shaw paused, looking thoughtfully at the jury. 'I don't know if any of you ever make corrections to your own signature when you've just signed something, but I certainly don't – and have never done so.' He could see from their expressions they agreed.

Shaw continued. 'My point is that each time you sign a document, your signature does not have to be an exact replica of any previous signature, it is simply your personal mark. So, I would ask you all to think very carefully about something: if this really was Terence Gready signing his name, why would he have subsequently touched up his signature so meticulously – in *four* different places?'

Brown said to the witness, 'It is the defence's submission that this account was not opened by my client, and this is not the signature of my client.'

Shaw replied, 'It is my professional opinion that there are a number of anomalies with the signature, and it is not consistent with the defendant's handwriting signature samples that I was provided with.'

Brown shuffled her papers, paused for a moment and then sat down.

Cork stood up and turned to Shaw. 'Is it correct you have only had signatures to work on and no other handwriting samples?'

'That is correct,' Shaw replied.

'Am I also correct in saying that where signatures are involved you are only able to say that it is more likely or less likely to have been signed by a particular individual?'

'In many cases that is correct. It is always difficult when you are only working with signatures. But you are able to look and comment on similarities and construction of letters and words.'

'The point I make, Professor Shaw,' Cork said, 'is that because you only have signatures to work with, the weight of this evidence is limited.'

Shaw paused for a moment. 'What I am able to tell the court is that there is a possibility the defendant did not make this signature mark, and I can say its construction is unusual.'

'One last question, Professor Shaw. Is it possible that somebody who was seeking to throw doubt on the originality of a signature could have done so in this way – could that person have deliberately made the signature look questionable?'

'It is possible. I can say that this signature purported to have been made by Mr Gready is not consistent to others that I have seen from him. He may have signed it, but there again someone else may have signed it attempting to forge his signature.'

'No more questions.' Cork sat down.

Primrose Brown rose. 'Professor Shaw, is it fair to say from your evidence that your conclusion is that it would be highly unusual for someone to sign their own habitual signature in this way?'

'Yes.'

'Thank you, no more questions.'

'We will break for lunch,' Jupp said.

88

It was pelting with rain outside and most of the jurors, mindful of the forecast of heavy rain all day, had brought their lunch in with them. The few that didn't had made a quick dash outside to get food and had brought it back with them. By 12.30 p.m. they were all seated around the table.

Meg's hopes had been lifted by the defence QC's handling of the handwriting evidence. No one could argue against what they had all just heard, could they? As she removed her egg and tomato sandwich from Laura's lunch box, which had animals all over it, she was starting to feel increasingly optimistic. She put it down and made a note on the pad she'd been carrying in her handbag since the start of the trial: *Safety deposit box signature.*

It was one more piece of evidence in Gready's favour as there was some doubt as to its authenticity. As strong as the earlier challenges to the Financial Investigator's evidence. There was nothing linking Terence Gready to any of the overseas bank accounts and transactions, other than *circumstantial* evidence. Until Michael Starr's evidence – which Meg knew she would have to work on to discredit its validity – there was no evidence of him and Gready ever having met.

She glanced back through some of her notes. Some very

strong arguments to put to her fellow jurors. Maybe, just maybe, she was going to be able to pull this off.

God, please.

'You know something,' Mark Adams said. 'If that bloody windbag defence woman doesn't wrap it up soon, I'm going to vote guilty just to piss her off.'

'Don't you think we need to put emotions aside, Mark?' Harold Trout reprimanded. 'We are here to do our civic duty and judge a man on the facts – this is not about tactical voting because we like or do not like the person defending him.'

'Yes, well, my *civic duty* is to put food on my family's table. I'm already struggling to do that with all the competition out there these days without losing two weeks' income – running into a third might suit a retired person like yourself, living on your fat pension, but it would be a bloody disaster for me.'

'And me, too,' responded Singh.

'And me,' chipped in Toby. 'The daily amount we're getting paid is a joke. I'm facing missing an audition that could give me a part in a series that would offer me six months' lucrative work I badly need.'

'And a man facing years in prison isn't important?' Meg asked, her sandwich still untouched. 'We're all sitting here having to decide whether a fellow human being is guilty or innocent. Just take a moment to think what that means. Imagine he is innocent – are you willing to make possibly a wrong judgement, one that might destroy his life forever, just so you can get out of here?' Her anger was rising as she went on.

'Any one of us could be in a dock, accused of an offence we haven't committed. How would one of you feel knowing the jurors there to decide your fate were more interested in getting the trial over than actually coming to the right verdict?' She looked at them and waited. From their expressions, her point had hit home.

'Mark, you are anxious to get back to earning money as an Uber driver. And you, Toby, are worried about missing an audition. Well, I'm in the same boat, OK? I'm out of work having been made redundant – thank you for asking. I've got a job interview which I should be attending on Monday. I'm prepared to sacrifice that interview, and the chance of a really good job that would put food on the table for myself and my daughter, out of my civic duty. So, I suggest everyone calms down and accepts the situation for what it is. Several of us may suffer financially, temporarily, but I for one know that if I do make that sacrifice, at least I will be able to sleep easily for the rest of my life knowing I did the right thing. Do you want it on your conscience that you may, possibly, have ruined someone else's life for your own gain?'

There was a long silence.

Mike Roberts broke it. 'Very well said, Meg.' He picked up the thick bunch of trial documents and opened them at a page he had bookmarked. Then he looked at Mark Adams. 'This lady you have described as a *windbag*, Primrose Brown, is an eminent criminal barrister. She will call more witnesses this afternoon. When she has finished with those, we will then have the closing speech from the prosecution, followed by the closing speech from defence. After that we will have the judge's summing up, before we are sent out for our deliberations. It is highly unlikely you will get your wish of the trial ending this week, so as our foreperson has eloquently said, you'd better get over it.'

'If I had one shred of doubt about the defendant's guilt, then yes,' Adams said, defensively. 'But can you really, honestly, say you have, Meg?'

'Yes,' she replied. 'I can. There are already plenty of arguments for *reasonable doubt* – and we still have more witnesses to come.'

'I'm sorry, you just have to look at Terence Gready's body language to see he is guilty,' Toby DeWinter said.

'Really?' Meg quizzed. 'You're an expert on body language?'

'Actually, yes. I'm an actor. Body language is part of what I do.'

Hari Singh chipped in. 'There's a saying we should all be aware of. *Before you judge any man, first walk ten miles in his shoes.*'

'Isn't that an old Groucho Marx joke?' said Pink. '*Before you judge a man, first walk ten miles in his shoes. Then you'll be ten miles away and you'll have his shoes.*'

The tension in the room was broken by some laughter and smiles, except for Meg, who sat thinking.

'I suggest,' she said, tartly, 'before we judge the defendant, we do what we are here to do, the thing we are sworn in to do, and that is to listen to all the evidence. The time to do our judging is after that.'

Rory O'Brien, the geek who had remained silent since they had entered the room, looked up from one of the stacks of spreadsheets in the bundle he had open in front of him and said, quietly, 'I agree with our foreperson. We should hear all the evidence before we start coming to conclusions.' He returned his focus to the spreadsheet.

Perhaps because O'Brien had barely spoken since the trial had begun, what he had to say had an oddly calming effect on the room.

89

The first defence witness of the afternoon was a forensic financial analyst in her early fifties called Carolyn Herring. Primrose Brown began by coaxing her credentials out of her. Having worked for some years in a senior position in the fraud detection department of the Inland Revenue, she was now employed in a similar role in the private banking sector.

With a few skilful questions, the QC established for the benefit of the jury that this woman was a very much more experienced and qualified forensic financial analyst than the prosecution witness put forward by the CPS, Emily Denyer. Then slowly, item by item, she went through the spreadsheets produced by Denyer, totally losing Meg – and she sensed quite a few of the other jurors – in the process.

Quite apart from being baffled by the figures, Meg was struggling to concentrate, because she was so distracted by her fear for Laura, and the challenges some of the jury presented. Who could she count on, at this moment, for a 'not guilty' verdict?

She looked surreptitiously down at the list on the tiny notepad she kept in her handbag. So far those she hoped were on her side were Maisy Waller, Hugo Pink and Hari Singh, who, with his Buddhist views, she was increasingly sure wouldn't give a 'guilty' verdict. Including herself, that was just four out of eleven – so far. Enough for a hung jury, but not remotely enough for the verdict she had to deliver.

Shit.

And now the QC, plodding through these spreadsheets with her witness, in agonizing detail, was going to antagonize some of the jurors even further, for sure. It was gone 2.30 p.m., over an hour, but they were coming towards the end.

Suddenly, as if sensing the mood of the jury in a moment when the analyst had paused, Brown said, 'Ms Herring, I don't wish to go back over all these transactions and the complexity of the inter-account trading. I'm sure some members of the jury, like myself, struggle when we see columns of figures.' She smiled as she glanced at the jury. 'Are you able to summarize what you have found during your exhaustive analysis?'

Herring turned to the jury. 'Everything that you have heard from Emily Denyer is circumstantial. In all the transactions, between bank accounts across seven different countries, not once does the name Terence Gready appear, nor do any of the transactions link back to any accounts pertaining either to him or to his firm in Brighton. In my opinion, I can see no evidence of any financial benefit to him in any of them.'

Meg's spirits rose at this.

'Undoubtedly, there is a very clever mastermind behind all of these transactions, but could anyone say *beyond reasonable doubt* that the mastermind is Mr Gready? There is no direct evidence to show this.'

Primrose Brown addressed her witness. 'To be sure I have this right, your conclusion, from reviewing the prosecution's case, is that there is not one shred of evidence that would link Terence Gready to any of the financial transactions?'

Herring shook her head.

Jupp leaned forward. 'Could you please say that aloud, for the benefit of the recording.'

'No,' Carolyn Herring said, very definitely. 'I could find no link connecting Terence Gready to any of these transactions or bank accounts.'

'Thank you,' Brown said. 'I have no further questions for my witness.'

Cork stood. 'Ms Herring, one thing you have not addressed is the Rolex wristwatch, valued at approximately £55,000, purportedly given to the defendant by his wife, Barbara, as – ah – a supposed *Christmas present* some five years ago. This lady is a renowned worldwide authority on orchids, who regularly performs the function of judge in orchid competitions and had an orchid cultivation business, but is there anything to suggest she could have made sufficient money to make such a purchase?'

The financial expert answered him with barely a moment's hesitation. 'The defendant's wife, Barbara Gready, from my careful study of the family's financial affairs – and prudency – had inherited the sum of £284,000 net of tax from the estate of her late mother.'

'Still quite an extravagant amount – close to twenty per cent of her inheritance on a gift for her husband – would you not say?'

Primrose Brown addressed the judge. 'Your Honour, this is misleading. A rare watch of the kind Mrs Gready acquired is an investment, with a proven track record of rising in value. I would say, in our uncertain times, perhaps a better investment than having the money in some banks.'

Jupp nodded. 'It is a fair point.'

Cork went on. 'Ms Herring, in your experience, is it usual to find with this type of investigation that it is hard to connect actual people to these types of overseas bank accounts?'

Carolyn replied, 'Yes.'

'When you worked for the Inland Revenue, were you faced with the same issues?'

'Yes.'

'Would you agree that there are links between these accounts and LH Classics?'

'Yes.'

'So all you can say really is that you have not found the defendant's name anywhere?'

'Correct.'

'Do you agree that someone has gone to great lengths to hide the origin of the monies in the accounts and the source of the large value deposits? Someone who could be the defendant, Mr Gready?'

'Yes, but I found no trace of the defendant's details.'

'But then you would not expect to, would you?'

'Not necessarily, no.'

Cork paused for a moment. 'You placed great importance in your evidence that all the details Ms Denyer referred to were merely circumstantial evidence. However, circumstantial evidence is still evidence that the court can take into account, is that not true?'

She replied reluctantly, 'Yes.'

He continued. 'And in this case the court has heard there are substantial amounts of circumstantial evidence from the financial transactions, is that correct, Ms Herring?'

She muttered a response.

'Sorry I don't think the court caught your last answer, would you mind repeating it?'

She replied, 'Yes, it is fair to say there is substantial circumstantial evidence in this case.'

'Thank you, no further questions.'

'I have no re-examination,' Brown said.

The usher escorted Carolyn Herring from the witness stand.

'I would now like to call my next witness,' Primrose Brown said. 'Mr Arthur Mason-Taylor.'

A lean man in his fifties, with brush-cut grey hair and a suit he was clearly unused to wearing, was escorted in, gave his name and took the oath.

'Can you please tell us your profession?' Brown said to him.

'I'm a mechanical engineer and worked full-time at LH Classics with a couple of part-timers.'

'Do you have a particular speciality?'

'Yes, restoring classic racing cars.'

'Were you employed by LH Classics between the years of 2005 and 2018?' she asked.

'I was.'

'And what were your duties during that time?'

'Working on preparing cars acquired by the company, for sale.'

'What kind of cars?'

'Ferraris, Aston Martins, Jaguar E-Types, Chevrolet Corvettes, AC Cobras, Austin Healeys – among others.'

Brown nodded. 'Who was your boss during the time you worked for LH Classics?'

'The General Manager, Mr Starr.'

'Would that be Michael – Mickey – Starr? Sometimes known as *Lucky*?'

'Yes.'

'Can you tell me, during these thirteen years, did you ever see Terence Gready on the premises?'

He frowned. 'Terence Gready?'

She pointed at the dock. 'That man, there, the defendant?'

Mason-Taylor looked at Gready, then shook his head. 'No, never.'

'Did you see his name on any paperwork? Documentation?'

'Terence Gready?'

'Yes.'

'No, never.'

'You are certain?'

Mason-Taylor smiled. 'It's not the kind of name you'd easily forget. No, I never saw it or heard it.'

'Thank you,' she said.

The prosecutor asked, 'Mr Mason-Taylor, during your time with LH Classics, were you ever involved in the construction of fake – or rather *replica* cars?'

'A number of times, yes. There is a very legitimate market for replicas of certain models.'

'A number of times? And did the construction of any of these replicas differ from the originals by having cavities built into them, which would not have been there in the originals?'

'Yes,' he said, positively. 'Quite regularly.'

'Did you query what the purpose of these were?'

'No, I knew.'

Cork feigned astonishment. 'You *knew*? Really. What exactly did you know?'

Mason-Taylor shrugged. 'The motor racing world is full of cheats – it always has been – and the world of classic car racing is one of the worst offenders. I always assumed these cavities were about weight loss, to make the vehicles more competitive in races.'

'Did it ever occur to you,' Cork continued, 'that there might be another purpose for these cavities?'

'Why should it?' Mason-Taylor responded with genuine innocence. 'What other purpose do you mean?'

'The smuggling of drugs.'

The mechanic's astonished expression was all the response he needed. But he went on. 'I'm sorry, but that really is absurd. My work for LH was to carry out restoration work on cars intended for sale, and to prepare cars for clients for races.'

'Even though you knew you were helping some to cheat?'

'With respect,' Mason-Taylor replied, 'you clearly have no understanding about motor racing. All cars go through a rigorous scrutineering before any competitive event. That includes weighing the vehicles. My job was to make cars as competitive as possible – but always within the rules.'

Realizing he was holding a losing ticket, Cork sat down. Brown rose again.

'So, to your knowledge, Mr Mason-Taylor, none of the cars belonging to LH Classics were ever built or used for the purposes of importing drugs?' she asked.

'Absolutely no way, madam.'

'No further questions,' she said.

The QC was about to call her final defence witness, Barbara Gready, when her junior counsel whispered in her ear.

Brown turned to the judge. 'I have a very urgent matter that I need to make you aware of, Your Honour, but without the jury present.'

Jupp addressed the jury. 'Members of the jury, I must now ask you to leave the court while I speak to my learned friend, Ms Brown.'

After the jury left, Jupp instructed Brown to continue.

421

'It has just been brought to my attention that my next witness, Barbara Gready, who is at the back of the court, has changed her mind about appearing as a defence witness, Your Honour. I need time to speak to her.'

Terence Gready looked shell-shocked.

His wife stepped forward and started shouting at him. She had tears streaming down her face and was sobbing uncontrollably. 'You, you lying bastard, you've broken our family. How could I have been such a fool – you've lied to me, you've lied to your children, and I've been sitting there listening to you lying to the court. If you think I'm going to speak up for you, you are sadly mistaken.'

Gready looked ashen-faced. 'Barbara! I'm not lying, they're making it up. They've fitted me up, can't you see that?'

'It's lies, Terence, it's all lies. How did you think your little story could convince anyone – you can't even convince me?'

Jupp raised his voice, sternly. 'This is not the time or the place for this sort of behaviour to continue, this is a court of law. I'm now adjourning this court sitting for this issue to be resolved.'

Primrose Brown turned to Barbara Gready. 'Let's go outside where I can talk to you privately.'

'Don't waste your time. I'm through with this. He's a loser, he deserves everything he gets. They can throw the book at him for all I care.' She turned, still crying, and stormed out of the court.

Well aware that this could be grounds for appeal, the judge looked around sternly at those present in the court and up in the public gallery. 'I am instructing all of you to disregard what you have just heard. If any of you mentions it in or outside of this court, you are in contempt and you will be dealt with severely.'

Twenty minutes later the hearing resumed, with the jury back in place, unaware of the drama that had just unfolded in the court. Jupp looked at Ms Brown. 'Do you have any further defence witnesses?'

There was a moment of awkward silence.

Brown got up. 'No, Your Honour, that concludes the case for the defence.'

Jupp looked at the clock, which read 4.18 p.m., then turned to the jury. 'Thank you all for your patience today – you have a lot to consider. We have now heard from all the witnesses for both the prosecution and defence. Tomorrow we will hear the closing speeches from the prosecution followed by the defence. When these are finished, I will sum up for you, after which I will send you out to commence your deliberations. I would like to remind you again that you must speak to no one about what you have heard during this trial, nor must you attempt to look up anything related to it on the internet.'

Then, addressing the whole room, he said, 'Court is adjourned. We meet back here at 10 a.m. tomorrow.'

90

Rain was still pelting down an hour after Meg had left the court. She sat in her car in the Hove station car park, engine running, demister on full blast, trying to clear the windscreen. Rain pounded the roof and thoughts pounded her brain. The trial today, how had it really gone?

The defence counsel had scored some points and all her witnesses had been robust. How much would that prosecutor twist everything in his closing speech tomorrow? How would she respond? How would the judge direct the jury – impartially, she hoped? Richard Jupp had been hard to read all along.

A text pinged. It was from Ali, suggesting they meet for a coffee or a drink on Saturday and saying they were having a barbecue on Sunday, if the weather was better. Then she noted a WhatsApp had come in from Laura some hours ago – it must have been while her phone was on silent when she had gone into court.

She opened it immediately, scared what might be there. Scared, suddenly, now the trial was almost at an end, that she might have been abducted and this was going to be yet another threat. To her relief, she saw a happy Laura, in a floppy hat and sunglasses, standing on a rock in front of a massive sea lion that almost dwarfed her.

Mum, he barks like a dog! XXXXX

Meg smiled. *God, I need to get a message to you. To warn you to disappear if it goes badly tomorrow. How?*

How?

I love, love, love you so much. My precious angel. I'm going to keep you safe, whatever it takes, somehow, I promise you.

As she drove home, she continued churning over the day's events in her mind. It had been a good day for the defence, no question. But how good? Enough to convince the disparate jurors?

Good enough to save her daughter's life?

A quarter of an hour later, entering her house as warily as always now, she was greeted by a stench from Daphne's litter tray. But there was another, fainter smell. As if someone had been cooking. Meg frowned. She had made herself an omelette and fried tomatoes for breakfast – and burnt some of the tomatoes in the process. But it seemed strange the smell still lingered.

Daphne suddenly gave a pitiful *miaowww*. Meg knelt and stroked her neck. 'You want food, right? Of course you do, when didn't you?'

She stuck her umbrella in the Victorian coat stand, hung up her wet cagoule and went through to the kitchen. As she tore open a packet of cat food, Daphne vaulted up onto the work surface and began eating ravenously, once she'd tipped the contents into her bowl.

She cleaned up the litter tray, then went upstairs to check Laura's rodents had water. As she reached the landing, she heard the familiar *squeak-squeak-squeak* of the gerbils on their spinning wheels. She switched on the light and entered her daughter's bedroom.

She peered into their cage. They looked up, twitchily, on their hind legs. They had plenty of water. She moved on to Horace.

And stared, puzzled. The cage was empty.

She opened the door, put her hand in and lifted up the tiny little covered area at the back where he sometimes slept on his bed of straw. It was empty.

Had the little bugger escaped? How? She felt panic.

'Horace!' she called out. 'Horace!'

Useless, she knew, he had never responded to his name. She checked all around the room, looking under the bed, Laura's chair and in every other nook and cranny where he might possibly be. Then she returned to the cage, checking it carefully.

Could she have left the door open this morning, after feeding him and filling up his water, she wondered? And had she left the bedroom door open or closed? If closed, he must be in here. If not, he could be anywhere in the house. What would she tell Laura if she couldn't find him? She doted on this dumb little creature above all her other pets.

Exhausting every possible hiding place in the room, and feeling increasingly anxious, she searched every room in the house. Had he gone through a hole into one of the cavities? Or out of the house somehow? Her best hope, she thought, was that he would get hungry and head back to what he knew as his food source. And, despite all her anxieties, she was hungry too, she realized.

She propped his cage door open and went back down into the kitchen, trying to remember what quick meals she had in the freezer. Bending down, she opened the door of the freezer compartment and pulled the top drawer out.

And stared in numb horror at what lay there, with a handwritten note beside it.

91

Brown in parts, blackened in others, shrivelled and covered in flecks of ice, was a skinned, cooked creature the size of Horace.

Her worst fears were confirmed as she shakily picked up the note and read it.

> *A welcome home gift for Laura – you can surprise her with the national dish of Ecuador, roasted guinea pig! Or not, of course, if the next time you see her is on a tray pulled out of a mortuary freezer. The choice is yours, Meg.*

She turned away, staggered over to the sink and retched into it. The burner, which she'd left on the kitchen table, rang.

'Hello?' she answered. And heard the calm, horribly familiar man's voice.

'Big day tomorrow, Meg.'

'You bastard,' she said. 'You fucking bastard.'

'Oh, come on, Meg,' he said with infuriating calm and charm. 'I just thought you'd like to surprise Laura with a little taste of Ecuador when she and Cassie come home – of course, that is, *if* they come home.'

'You are sick.'

'They are very tasty, I'm told. A bit like chicken, but sweeter and more tender.'

'Laura is a vegetarian, in case you weren't aware,' she snapped. 'You seem to know everything else about her.'

'Pop it in the microwave, two minutes on full power, and it'll make a tasty supper for you tonight. Help you build up your strength for tomorrow.'

'Fuck you. Seriously. FUCK YOU.' She killed the call and stood, shaking.

The phone rang again. She hesitated, debating whether to answer or not. But she had to speak to him, try to talk reason with him. She answered.

'Meg, hanging up on me isn't going to save your daughter's life. There is only one thing that will, and you know what that is, don't you?'

He let the question hang in the air, then went on. 'Now, don't panic if you don't hear from Laura for the next day or two. Very unfortunately she and her friend Cassie were pickpocketed earlier today. They've lost their phones and all their money. But don't worry, my friend Jorge – Laura may have mentioned his name – he's going to take care of them. You won't hear from Laura again until after the verdict – after you have gone into the court and said those two words. Repeatedly. On each charge. You do know what they are, don't you? You haven't forgotten? Shall I remind you?'

She held the phone to her ear, stonily saying nothing. Daphne jumped onto the table and walked towards her. Almost unconsciously, she stroked her.

'Beautiful cat,' he said. 'So affectionate.'

His words hit her like an electric shock. Her eyes darted around the room, up at the ceiling, into all corners, desperately wondering where the cameras were. She felt utterly helpless. There didn't seem anything she could do without jeopardizing the girls' safety in Ecuador. Sadly, she had no other choice.

'Don't worry, Meg, don't try to find where I'm looking at you, conserve your energies for tomorrow. You are going to need every ounce of strength.'

Then silence.

He was gone.

Immediately, she dialled Laura's number. It went straight to voicemail.

In desperation, she dialled again. Then again. Then again. The same each time. Cassie's number also went to voicemail.

She sank down in a chair and put her head in her hands, tears of desperation streaming down her face.

92

'What do you think, matey?' Roy Grace asked Glenn Branson.

The two detectives sat on adjoining chairs in the communal hallway of Lewes Crown Court, at 9.30 a.m. on Friday morning, sipping bitter vending-machine coffee. People streamed in past them. The unexpected cancellation of the Crisp trial had given Grace a welcome respite in his workload, which had rapidly been filled by the murder enquiry on Stuie Starr. But Glenn had asked him to attend court today, to hear what he hoped might be the final day of speeches and summing-up in the Terence Gready trial, and Grace was intrigued to hear the comments in one of the biggest drugs trials ever to be heard in Sussex.

'I can't call it,' Branson said. 'Gready's guilty as shit, but as you'd expect from a weasel of a legal aid solicitor, he's got himself a top brief and team. I've been watching the jury and they're hard to read. The judge is on our side, I think. But it's in the lap of the gods. How are you doing with the Stuie Starr murder?'

Grace shrugged. 'Nothing much to go on, so far. We're widening the search area of CCTV and ANPR cameras. There was no forced entry, which means Stuie may have let his killers in.'

'Some bastards beat him to death?' Branson asked.

'Yes.'

'And took nothing?'

'We don't know for sure. There's electrical items and possibly a large amount of cash unaccounted for.'

'Is Pewe on your back over it?'

'Of course. My regular phone buddy.' As he talked, Grace watched the people filing into Court 3. Suddenly, he saw the *Argus*'s crime reporter – and Glenn's fiancée – Siobhan Sheldrake. She blew a kiss at Glenn as she passed and he responded with a kiss back, followed by a soppy grin.

'Know her, do you?' Grace ribbed.

'Haha. Written your best man's speech yet?'

'No, still digging up the dirt on you.' Grace was looking forward to his best man's role.

'Don't waste your time, there isn't any.'

Grace looked at his friend and colleague. 'Really? Short memory, have you?'

Branson suddenly looked alarmed. 'What are you going to say?'

'Top Surrey and Sussex homicide detective fraternizing with the enemy? Nuff said?'

'Siobhan is so not the enemy – I love her independent mind.'

Grace nodded. 'Fair play to you for that. But going back to your trial, Gready is an evil piece of shit, who's downright guilty. You and I both know that. The evidence, from what you've told me, is overwhelming.'

Branson was shaking his head. 'That's why I wanted you here today. We have a strong case, but have we done enough to convince a jury? At the start of the trial, I thought it was a slam-dunk. Now, I'm really not so sure.'

'Great news,' Grace said sarcastically. 'I'm not sure about anything at the moment.'

Branson looked at him. 'You're down, aren't you? I understand. Bummer. But Pewe's not going to be here forever.'

'Maybe I won't be either.'

'This is your home, Roy. This is where you live and where you belong. Don't let that two-faced creep drive you out and back to the Met. You got rid of him once before, surely you can do it again?'

Grace smiled thinly. 'I wish.'

'Karma.'

'Karma?'

Branson nodded. 'People like Cassian Pewe, who go through life pissing people off, always get their comeuppance in the end. That's how karma works.'

'Nice thought, Glenn, but with everything that's going on in my life at the moment I'm staying in Sussex anyhow.'

'I understand that, mate, and don't forget there are people above him who know just how good you are. The Police and Crime Commissioner for one.'

'Maybe.'

Branson shook his head. 'Steve Curry, ex-District Commander at Hastings, he's now working in her office. He had a drink with a friend of mine – Dan Hiles – the other day.'

'I remember Dan when he was a probationer.'

'He's now an Inspector at Brighton nick. Steve told him that the PCC considers you future Chief Constable material.'

Grace gave him a pat on the shoulder. 'Good to hear, but I wouldn't want that job. I like being a hands-on copper. Detective Chief Superintendent is as high as I want to get. I don't want to run the force, I want to catch criminals and put them behind bars. That's what I signed up for. Not dealing with bureaucratic shit and taking the flak for everything that goes wrong, all day long.'

Glenn Branson nodded. 'I get it. Why not go after Pewe? Find some dirt on him for a change and stuff him.'

Grace gave him a wan smile. 'Easier said than done.'

He didn't know it, but just such an opportunity was not very far away.

93

Friday 24 May

Meg was not sure – about anything. After a totally sleepless night, she was struggling to think clearly – on the very day she needed, more than ever before in her life, to have complete clarity.

'All rise.'

When the judge and everyone in the court was seated, Jupp leaned forward and addressed the jury in a serious tone, but as if they were all his friends. 'You are about to hear the closing speeches from first the prosecution counsel and then the defence. It is for you the jury alone to assess the reliability and importance of the evidence; to decide what conclusions should be drawn from the evidence that you accept, but to avoid speculation, and thus to decide what are the true facts of the case. You must do this assessing the evidence of all witnesses, for the prosecution and the defence, with the same impartial standards. All witnesses start equal. How they end up is a matter for you when you have assessed all the evidence. You do not have to decide every point that has been raised; only such matters as will enable you to say whether a charge against a defendant has been proved.'

He paused, before continuing. 'You must decide this case only on the evidence that has been placed before you.

You are entitled to draw inferences, that is to say, to come to logical conclusions based on the evidence which you accept, but what you must not do is speculate about what evidence there might have been, speculate about why any witness has not given evidence, or allow yourselves to be drawn into speculation in any way. Speculation is just another word for guesswork.'

He smiled. 'Do not be influenced by any emotion, sympathy or prejudice. What is needed is a calm appraisal of the evidence. You are entitled, however, to use your collective common sense and knowledge of the world and the people in it. You do not leave that outside the door of the jury room and decide this case on some sanitized approach to the evidence, you take it into the jury room with you and use it in assessing the evidence. Most importantly, do not be daunted by your task. Juries up and down the country every working day of the week are trying serious cases with complex issues.' He took a sip of water.

'The law is for me, ladies and gentlemen, and I am now going to give you directions as to the law that applies in this case. You must accept these directions and follow them. In this first part of my summing-up, I will explain to you what the prosecution has to prove before you can convict. I will give the second part of my summing-up after you have heard both speeches from counsel, when I will give you an overview of the prosecution and defence cases and I will remind you of the prominent features of the evidence. It is important for you to understand that the speeches you will hear are not evidence – they are simply the arguments each advocate puts forward as to how you should view the evidence. As the facts are a matter entirely for you, you do not have to accept any of the arguments you hear in the speeches. I hope this is clear?'

Meg, unsure whether the jurors were expected to respond, gave a slight nod of her head.

Jupp continued. 'When you weigh up the evidence, you will need to form a view about the witnesses you have heard from as to who you believe and who you disbelieve. It will be for you to decide what you accept and what you reject. I have heard it said, by many past witnesses in other cases, that to stand in the witness box is to be standing in the loneliest and most daunting place on earth. You will no doubt want to take into account the nervousness of witnesses when assessing their evidence.' He paused and, once more, Meg nodded.

'If you conclude a witness is being truthful on the issues you have to decide, you also have to ask yourselves whether the witness is reliable. A witness may be telling the truth as they genuinely recollect it, but that recollection might not be accurate. People's perception and recollection of events may genuinely differ. Therefore, when you assess each witness, you will wish to form a view as to their reliability. You might wish to consider whether the witness was balanced and fair? Did the witness make concessions or accept the limitations of their evidence, or accept they may have made a mistake about a particular point? You might consider this reflects an attempt to convey a fair account of what occurred.'

He took another sip of water before going on. 'When considering the evidence of Mr Starr, you should bear in mind that he has already pleaded guilty to the offences with which Mr Gready is charged, and given evidence which implicated Mr Gready after formally agreeing to help the prosecution by doing so. Mr Starr did this hoping to get a lesser sentence as a result. Because this is the situation, you should approach Mr Starr's evidence with caution, knowing that Mr Starr has an obvious incentive to give evidence which implicates Mr Gready. You should ask yourselves whether Mr Starr has, or may have, tailored his evidence to implicate Mr Gready falsely or whether you can be sure, despite the potential benefit to Mr Starr of giving evidence against Mr Gready, that what Mr Starr has told you is the truth.'

Jupp paused again, to allow his words to sink in, then turned to Stephen Cork. 'You may proceed.'

Cork stood and addressed the jury with the consummate charm of a favourite uncle, neither speaking down or up to them. Instead, his voice was gently conversational, as if he was just chatting to a few mates in his local pub.

He began by talking about the discovery of the drugs in the Ferrari in the trailer at Newhaven Port, Michael Starr's subsequent arrest, escape and rearrest. The raid on Terence Gready's home and the items found there. He recapped on the evidence from Haydn Kelly regarding the CCTV footage showing Starr entering the offices of TG Law, then the evidence from DS Alexander on the items concealed in the bedpost and on the safety deposit box key found hidden in a canister in Gready's garden shed. He followed that with a detailed summary of the key points of Emily Denyer's evidence.

He concluded by saying, 'You have heard the most damning evidence of all from Mr Michael Starr. This is a man who, despite the defendant's quite ludicrous assertions that they have never met, is clearly both the defendant's colleague, lieutenant and co-conspirator. Over many years Mr Starr has played an instrumental role in helping the defendant develop a vast and highly lucrative drugs empire. I would remind you that Mr Starr has already confessed to his crimes by pleading guilty to all counts on which he is charged. The defendant's assertion that Mr Starr has in some highly elaborate way framed him as a scapegoat is, I put to you, like a drowning man grasping at driftwood.'

Cork continued, 'It is always the case when producing evidence relating to shell companies, nominee directors and offshore bank accounts that much of the evidence is going to be circumstantial. But when you add all of that to the rest of the totally damning evidence against Mr Gready, which we have heard during the course of this trial, can you the jury really come to any conclusion other than that the defendant is guilty on all the counts he faces?'

He felt a sudden, overwhelming wave of revulsion against the defendant. In his mind, Gready was a despicable man, a traitor to his profession.

'Drugs, as you will know from your own life experience, are a scourge of our society. They destroy people, even kill people, yes, but have other destructive impacts. Some estimates suggest they cause the vast majority of thefts, robberies and burglaries in our towns and cities. The addicts turn to these crimes to fund their habits. It is easy to judge those people, but without the addiction that has them in its grip, they would not act in that way. No one sober would choose such a life, had they options. None of this is in issue, nor that, without the suppliers, there is no trade.

'What is in issue is whether the defendant is what he claims to be, a simple solicitor, or whether he is what the bank statements, the drives concealed in bedposts, the safety deposit key hidden in a shed, and the compelling evidence of Mr Starr say he is. A man who is at the top of the drugs supply chain, insulated by people like Mr Starr, who himself had few options for making a living and providing for his brother. This is not to excuse Mr Starr's actions. But the prosecution say that, without Mr Gready, there would be no Mr Starr.

'What they share, the prosecution say, is a complete and utter disregard for the misery this trade causes. The trade relies on those who import these drugs in bulk. Why do they do it? The answer is easy to understand. The rewards are astronomical, as you have heard.

'Most cases that come to court involve dealers far below the level of Mr Gready. Take one street dealer out of action and another will pop up within hours. There may seem to be nothing anyone can do, that we are powerless. But a street dealer does not have the guile or resources of those higher up the food chain, does he?

'This case has not been straightforward, and I thank you for your attention throughout. The prosecution, as the learned judge will direct you, has to make you sure of the defendant's guilt.

'Conspiracy theories are often raised as an alternative explanation, but here you do not have to rely on a theory. Here you have cold facts of what was found in his house, the assets recovered, the financial links to the shell companies and, most damning of all, the voluntary evidence of his former associate, who had the courage to stand before you and tell the truth, even if doing so painted him in a terrible light.

'If you find the defendant guilty, it will be as the prosecution has set out, as a kingpin in the supply of class-A drugs in this country. You, and you alone, have an extraordinary power in your hands. It is your decision and I urge you to use it wisely, and convict.'

After he had finally sat down, some two hours later, Jupp adjourned the court for lunch.

94

Meg left the court building, needing to get away and think. It was a fine, warm day, after the torrential rain of yesterday. She negotiated the steps, through a gaggle of press photographers and news crews, and made her way down the steep High Street towards the river. She was deeply dispirited by Cork's closing speech, which made the evidence against Gready seem even more overwhelming than before. And she was further discouraged by some of the comments she heard from jurors leaving the court.

She decided to keep her powder dry for the moment rather than try to argue against the prosecution counsel's impressive rhetoric – at this stage. She needed to wait and see what ammunition Primrose Brown hopefully delivered in her speech this afternoon. She wondered how the judge's summing-up would be, and what directions he might give to the jury. She'd found him impossible to read.

She wasn't hungry, but having eaten nothing last night, and just a yoghurt for breakfast, she knew she needed something to keep her strength up. She bought a prawn baguette, a chocolate bar and a Diet Coke and carried them along the towpath until she found an empty bench.

As soon as she had sat down, she checked her phone, in the forlorn hope there might be a WhatsApp from Laura.

But there was nothing. She dialled her number yet again. Then Cassie's. Voicemail. Her nerves were all over the place.

Last night she had buried the unfortunate guinea pig.

Had that bastard been lying again, telling her that Laura and Cassie had been pickpocketed, or was the truth – as she felt more likely – that the two girls had been kidnapped and were now being held captive pending the verdict?

It was terrible fear that had kept her awake throughout the night. And the shock of the dead creature. And guilt. If anything happened to Cassie because of all this, it would be her fault. Why the hell hadn't she told Laura and Cassie to go to the police or the British Embassy the moment she'd received that very first call? And informed the judge, to hell with the consequences?

But she knew the answer. She had been too scared then and she was too scared now. She knew she should say something to Cassie's parents, but she was too scared of losing Laura. She felt so utterly helpless and hated that feeling. Hated the knowledge there was nothing she could do until the jury retired, when she would have to use every ounce of ingenuity she had to somehow sway them.

And how was she going to do that when she knew, in her heart, in her soul, that Terence Gready deserved to be behind bars until he was too old to ever again, as the prosecuting counsel had said, *resume his evil trade*?

She thought back to the nightmare, five years ago, that had seemed as if it would never end. She had tried to put it out of her mind, but at this stage in the trial those thoughts came flooding back. The week in hospital with two busted ribs, a lacerated liver, a broken ankle, a broken finger, a torn wrist and whiplash. Laura in the next bed with a dislocated collarbone, bruised spleen, broken arm and also severe whiplash.

Arranging the death certificates of her husband and son. Attending their funerals in a wheelchair. Endless meetings with lawyers. The inquest in Northampton being adjourned by the Coroner only a few minutes after it had started because the police were bringing charges against the van driver. Months of physiotherapy. Then sitting in the public gallery of Northampton Crown Court, listening to the evidence given against the plumber who had killed her husband and son, and very nearly herself and Laura, too. He'd tried to lie his way out of the fact that he had been texting his girlfriend whilst driving down the M1 motorway and hadn't noticed their camper van at a tailback for a contraflow system. His defence was that the brakes on his van had failed – something later disproved by the police Collision Investigation Unit.

She had hated that man with every fibre of her body. Just as she hated Terence Gready – and his sinister, creepy accomplice who tormented her over the phone.

Her husband and son dead. Will would have been twenty now if he'd lived. So much he might have gone on to achieve.

The plumber got an eighteen-month suspended sentence, an £800 fine and a five-year driving ban. And she got a life sentence. The sense of injustice had never left her. And now it was on the verge of happening again.

Her mind was all over the place. If – and it was a big *if* – she somehow succeeded in delivering that 'not guilty' verdict, Laura would be safe – so, at least, she had been assured. But at what price to the community at large? How many lives would be destroyed, as Cork had pointed out, by Gready going free?

She took a bite of her baguette and chewed. But if it wasn't Gready, she rationalized, it would be others. The supply of drugs wouldn't stop because one man was removed from the chain. Dozens more would step in to fill the breach.

She remembered something she had read, years ago, in a book, the title of which she couldn't recall. Something to do with icebergs? What had that Financial Investigator's nickname for Gready been? *The Iceberg*. And now she remembered – it wasn't icebergs, it was glaciers. Wars were like glaciers, they would just keep on coming. Wasn't it the same with drugs? Weren't drug dealers like glaciers, too? Unstoppable. Relentless.

If Terence Gready went to jail, his shoes would be filled in an instant. But nothing, ever, could replace Laura. If anything happened to her, Meg wasn't sure she would want to go on living – or even be capable of it.

95

Richard Jupp swept into court with a spring in his step, and shortly afterwards the jury followed.

After he was seated, he addressed them. 'You are now going to hear the defence counsel's closing words. Following that I will be giving you my summing-up – don't worry if you think you might have missed anything, as I will give a very thorough recap.' He turned to Primrose Brown. 'Please proceed.'

Primrose Brown now stood and faced the jury. 'I would like firstly to thank you for your patience and diligence during this trial. You've heard a great deal of evidence from both sides, some of it extremely factual, some of it highly emotional and some of it – I'm referring to the financial evidence – at times deeply baffling!' She grinned and several jurors smiled back, nodding their agreement.

'My learned friend has outlined the prosecution evidence that he relies on, at times in considerable detail. But in my view this evidence you have heard is at best circumstantial. Despite what my learned friend would imply, there is, firstly and very crucially, not one shred of evidence you can rely on which puts the two men, the defendant, Mr Gready, and his *purported* colleague, Mr Michael Starr, together at any time.'

444

She went on at length to challenge all the evidence that had been presented that the two men had met, including a detailed attack on the testimony provided by the Forensic Gait Analyst, before moving on.

'The links to the financial evidence are not as strong as the Crown's Financial Investigator would have you believe, and as you have heard, my client has offered an explanation for the computer evidence that has been found, allegedly created by him. As I have previously said, there is no evidence at all that my client has received one penny from this elaborate network of offshore companies and bank accounts. He has told you himself that he believes he is the victim of a plot to frame him, perhaps aided and abetted by vengeful police officers out to get back at him for being a highly successful defence lawyer.'

She let the jurors digest this before continuing. 'A key witness that Mr Cork highlighted is Mickey Starr. You have heard that he can be relied on and that his evidence is strong and clearly shows the defendant is a drug dealer. I challenge that assertion and would ask you to do the same. Starr admitted in court, in front of you, that he lied in a statement that he made regarding these proceedings. How can we be sure about if and when he is telling the truth? It suits his purpose to blame Terence Gready as being the mastermind, but I suggest he is a lying, conniving individual who is looking after his own interests and is prepared to say anything.'

As the QC looked at her notes, Meg checked the time. It was past 3 p.m. The trial would, for sure, be running into next week. Which meant, she thought bleakly, somehow getting through the long weekend.

Brown resumed her speech. 'You have heard eloquently from my client, a solicitor who deals with facts, not fiction.

He has explained to you that he is not a powerful drug dealer with international connections and hidden fortunes around the world, but a family man, a man of devout religious faith, with strong ties to his local community. I'm sure you are all familiar with the old expression, "If it walks like a duck, quacks like a duck and looks like a duck, then it probably is a duck"?'

She paused and smiled again. 'My point being that I'm sure all of you have at times seen images of big-time drug dealers in films, in television series and in newspaper photographs. These tend to be swaggering characters, with fancy clothes, loud jewellery, flashy cars and bold as brass.' She pointed at the dock. 'I ask you, does the defendant resemble such an image? I put it to you that he does not in any way at all. Terence Gready is a truly honourable man who has worked hard throughout his life. He has built a highly respected law practice dedicated to helping the less fortunate members of society who require legal aid to help them achieve fair trials for their alleged misdemeanours.'

She cast her friendly eyes across the two rows of jurors. 'Successful drug dealers live in swanky homes, often owning big yachts and private jets. I doubt any take their annual holiday as a fortnight in a timeshare cottage in a coastal Devon village. I doubt any live in modest four-bedroom houses in quiet residential streets, such as the Gready family does, or drive nice but medium-priced little saloons and people carriers, again as Mr Gready does. I very much doubt that any criminal masterminds, drug barons or organized crime overlords – all of which the defendant has been called during the course of this trial – would serve as a school governor, as Mr Gready has done for over a decade. And I also very much doubt that any such people I have mentioned would work so tirelessly for local charities as Mr and Mrs

Gready do.' She was relieved as hell that the jury had not heard Barbara Gready's outburst in court.

Meg glanced at Gready. There were creases around his eyes as he gave a modest smile. He was the very picture of an upright citizen, seemingly oblivious to his wife's damning outburst.

The QC repeated Stephen Cork's technique of engaging eye contact with the jury, smiling at each of them, before speaking again. 'It is my view that the prosecution has failed to establish that my client is guilty of any of the charges against him. It is now your duty to consider the evidence and come to the only possible conclusion – find my client not guilty.'

She sat down. She was pleased with the timing and the fact the jury were going home for the weekend with her words ringing in their ears.

Richard Jupp said, 'It is now 4.10 p.m. We will resume at 10 a.m. on Tuesday morning, after the bank holiday.' Addressing the jury, he said, 'I will leave you with the reminder that you must not speak to anyone about what you have heard during this trial, not to your husbands, wives, lovers, friends or family or any members of the public, nor must you attempt to google or use any internet search engine to look up anything related to it. On leaving this building you may find you are accosted outside by members of the press and media. Do not respond to any of them or you will find yourselves in contempt of court and seeing very little of this weekend's forecast sunshine. Court is adjourned.'

'All rise.'

96

Friday 24 May

Roy Grace had promised to take Bruno deep-sea fishing tomorrow and had chartered a small boat out of the marina for the day, with a skipper. As he walked from court back towards Police HQ, Glenn Branson strode along beside him, phone to his ear, talking to the CPS solicitor handling the Gready – and Starr – prosecutions.

Grace checked the weekend's weather on his phone. The judge had been right, the forecast was sunny, but it was the shipping forecast that Roy was most interested in at the moment. Last time he'd gone on a fishing trip had been with a group of colleagues a few years ago, and the sea had been unpleasantly choppy. The smell of the freshly caught fish lying on the deck, exhaust fumes and the heavy swell had combined to sandbag him. After throwing up, he'd spent the next six hours on a bunk down below, his brain feeling like it was rolling around inside his skull, pretty much wishing he was dead. His only consolation had been former Detective Superintendent Nick Sloan, cheerfully telling him not to worry, that Lord Nelson used to get seasick, too.

But, despite the horrific memory, he was delighted Bruno actually wanted to do something with him – and something different from being holed-up in his bedroom playing computer games all weekend. So he had pre-armed himself with seasick tablets and a wristband that supposedly helped and was now praying for light wind, or preferably no wind at all.

To his relief, the forecast was benign. Light to moderate decreasing light; sea state calm.

'He's happy,' Branson said, shoving his phone into his pocket.

'CPS?'

'Yep. Reckons the jury is with Cork.'

'I thought that QC put up a spirited closing.'

Branson shrugged as they walked in past the visitors' reception. 'Yeah, well, these briefs have to say something to justify the money they charge,' he quipped.

Grace smiled.

'You off home, Roy? Fancy a quick jar?'

'Would have loved to, but I've got a briefing on Op Canoe at 6 p.m. and I need to get up to speed on anything that's happened today – although from the lack of traffic on my phone, it doesn't seem much.'

'That's because you don't have me as the SIO.'

Grace smiled again. 'You're full of it, aren't you?'

'Yeah, I'm in a good mood. I scent blood, we're going to win!'

Grace gave him a sideways glance as they headed up the hill of the sprawling Police HQ campus. 'Just remember, it ain't over until it's over.'

'Hopefully the judge'll hammer the final nail into Gready's coffin when he sums up on Tuesday.'

'I don't want to piss on your parade, matey, but two things to bear in mind while you're all loved up with Siobhan over the weekend. First is that judges aren't allowed to direct juries to convict – and if they are not utterly impartial, it gives the defence grounds for an appeal. Second is something you'll learn from time in this game – juries are totally unpredictable.'

'Want to have a bet on the result?' Glenn asked. 'A friendly fiver?'

As they walked in the entrance to the Major Crime suite Grace shook his head. 'Nah, don't want to take sweeties off a child.'

'Yeah yeah!'

'Have a good weekend.' Grace bounded up the stairs, followed by Branson.

'You know what you are?' Branson called out. 'You're a born pessimist!'

Grace paused in the corridor at the top of the stairs. 'Know the definition of a pessimist?'

Branson shook his head.

'It's an optimist with experience.'

Grace entered his office, logged on to his computer and stared at the screen, quickly glancing through his emails, then the day's serials of all crimes logged, in case there was anything of significance. There wasn't. He entered the password-protected evidence file on Operation Canoe, the investigation into the murder of Stuie Starr, and began viewing the video taken of the exterior and interior of the Starrs' house by the CSI. He'd viewed it all before but now wanted to look at it again, to see if he could have missed anything.

First, he studied the exterior, looking at all doors and windows on both floors, as the camera tracked 360 degrees. Next was a slow panoramic sweep showing the busy main road in front of the house and the garage opposite. Cars and other vehicles streamed by. From the pathologist's estimate and other factors, it appeared Stuie had been killed in the daytime. Someone *must* have seen something. Maybe a passing car – or even a cyclist – had caught something on a dash or helmet camera? But it would be a near-impossible task to find every car that had passed during the window of time in which Stuie's killers might have been entering or leaving the house, and it would require immense resources and manpower. He made a note in his Policy Book, all the same, not wanting to rule this out. If someone had seen them, they might remember them. No matter how hard-nosed any killer was, in the immediate aftermath of having committed their crime all villains, in his experience, would be in an agitated state as they left the scene – the *red mist*, police called it.

But despite a public appeal by the local press and media, and his own plea for members of the public to come forward at the press conference he had given two weeks ago, so far there was nothing – and traffic coming down this road could have come from four different directions.

Next he looked at the video footage of the interior of the house. Gartrell had made a careful video record of the downstairs of the house, showing all the possible entry and exit routes. But he knew there was no sign of any forced entry.

He next viewed the sickening scene in Stuie's bedroom. The Home Office pathologist had identified kicks to Stuie's body made by two different-sized shoes. It was impossible to tell from the chaotic mess and destruction whether it was the work of two or even more people. He froze the image repeatedly on the wide sweep and then the different angles of close-ups and the crime scene markers laid down. He was interrupted by his phone ringing. It was Cassian Pewe.

'Just calling for an update on Operation Canoe, Roy. Any good news for me, for the weekend?'

Grace was sorely tempted to lash into him over the promotions board, but at this point he wasn't supposed to know that the ACC had failed to support him despite his promise. So instead he kept calm and studiously polite.

'I'll be able to give you more after our next briefing at 6 p.m., sir, I hope.'

'Hope?'

'Yes, sir.'

'Hope doesn't interest me, Roy. Come to my office at 9 a.m. tomorrow and we'll do a complete review of the case and investigation to date.'

Grace's heart momentarily sank. Then he decided to stand firm. 'I'm afraid I'm taking my son fishing tomorrow, sir,' he replied.

'Fishing?'

'Yes.'

'You are the SIO of a murder enquiry and you're taking time out to go fishing?'

'I am, yes,' Grace replied, calmly. 'I will ask Acting Detective Inspector Potting, who I've appointed to be SIO in my absence, to meet you at 9 a.m. tomorrow and he will fully brief you.'

'Isn't it about time Potting was pensioned off? He's long past his sell-by date.'

'If you want to get rid of one of the best detectives we have, then yes, sir.'

'He's yesterday's man.'

'I don't agree.'

'Fishing, when you are running a murder enquiry. I think this is very bad, Roy. Not setting a good example at all.'

'There is some good news,' Grace replied, mischievously.

'There is?'

'Yes, the forecast is good.'

'I don't think that's funny. Call me when you have some proper good news.' He ended the call abruptly.

That won't be possible, thought Grace. *Because the good news will be when I can hold a press conference announcing your sudden and tragic death.*

97

Meg, fighting a yawn, sat along with her fellow jurors and everyone else in Court 3. She had so badly wanted – needed – to be rested and fresh for today. Ready for the biggest and most terrifying challenge she'd ever had to face in her life. Instead she felt terrible, her eyes raw, her brain a porridge of leaden, tangled thoughts.

A bag of nerves over the long weekend, which seemed longer than ever, she'd wandered around the house like a zombie, spending the entire three days alone, despite invitations from friends. She didn't want to see anyone, that way she could avoid difficult conversations. She'd tried to watch *Twelve Angry Men* again, but her mind kept drifting. Thinking about Laura – and dear Cassie. What had happened to them? Were they safe? How could she trust her caller? What if they were already – God forbid . . .

She pushed that thought away, just as she had done repeatedly since the nightmare began. They weren't dead. Her captor knew full well that if she succeeded in delivering the right verdict and then she found out something had happened to Laura, she would go straight to the police and tell them everything. There would then be a retrial, and from the research she had done, in cases where there was a real danger of tampering with a jury, the case could be heard by a judge alone, without a jury. In that scenario, from what evidence she had heard against Gready, he wouldn't stand a cat in hell's chance of going free.

She'd excused herself from meeting Alison on Saturday, mindful they would be watched and their every word recorded, and she hadn't felt up to attending the barbecue at their house on Sunday. A couple of other friends had phoned to see how she was, and she hadn't picked up, letting their calls go to voicemail.

Throughout the weekend she had repeatedly tried to contact Laura and Cassie. With no response. A late glass of wine on Saturday night had helped her fall asleep, but only to wake at 2 a.m. with a dull stomach ache, pins and needles in her fingers, and her scalp feeling like a rat was clawing its way over it.

Meg had felt briefly better after a long run along the seafront on Monday morning, but the endorphin high had long worn off by the afternoon. She had planned to do a very early run this morning, too, but she'd felt too tired when the alarm went off. Now she was having to go into battle to save her daughter's life after another totally sleepless night. And it seemed, from the talk in the jury room just now, that most of the jurors had already made up their minds to convict.

Addressing the jury, the judge went straight into his summing-up, walking them through detail by detail of the evidence they had heard from both sides. He took particular care to refer back to his earlier caveat about Michael Starr's motives when recounting all the points that Starr had made against Gready, and reminded the jury again that he had already pleaded guilty to all of the counts that Gready faced.

Meg made copious notes, underlining all the points

that would be most helpful to her, glad for the seeming impartiality of the judge. But then, to her dismay, his tone suddenly changed.

'You have heard from the defence QC about the respectability of her client. That Mr Gready is a school governor, a tireless supporter of local charities, a good and well-respected employer, a modest man who lives a modest life, one unencumbered by the trappings of vast wealth. In every respect he appears a thoroughly decent man, worthy of every citizen's respect. One could indeed say he is a model citizen! All these qualities are to be admired.'

He went on. 'Members of the jury, I'm sure you have indeed been impressed by all the fine work the defendant and his wife have done. And you have been made aware of the relatively modest lives they have lived. But before I send you to your deliberations, there are a couple of thoughts I would like to leave you with, which I feel are relevant.'

Meg's heart was sinking.

'You need to consider your own life experience and that things are not always as they appear. It is up to you to decide whether the defendant's good character makes it less likely that he committed the offence. My point is, very simply, that not all crime overlords, in real life or in fiction, fit the stereotype picture that has been painted to you by the defence. This is not to cast aspersions on the defendant, in any way, but you should in your deliberations consider only the facts of the evidence presented to you, rather than be influenced by the fact that Mr Gready appears to be a jolly good guy.'

Shortly after 1 p.m. Jupp finished his summing-up. 'Members of the jury, you have heard the evidence of both sides. It is now your job to retire to the jury room and debate all the facts that you have heard during the course of this trial and to reach a verdict. Is the defendant guilty or not guilty on the matters for which he is accused? It is my view, from all that we have heard over the past weeks, that there is sufficient evidence for you to make an informed decision. I will now leave it to your sound judgement.'

98

There had been speculation in the jury room earlier this morning that the judge's summing-up might take several days. The reality was, according to Meg's watch, just under three hours.

It left her in panic, she wasn't prepared for this. She had hoped for at least a night clear to study her notes and get her arguments ready for the jurors.

Bleakly, thinking hard, she followed her colleagues back into the jury room and took her place at the head of the table. As she sat, she decided her best chance was to be assertive and take immediate control. She also needed to buy herself more thinking time.

'As it is now lunchtime,' she announced, 'may I suggest we take a short break? Some sandwiches and drinks have been provided for us. Let's resume with clear heads in half an hour's time.'

Her suggestion was greeted by universal assent and to her relief everyone found their own space around the room. She got straight on with her plan, scanning through all of her notes and numbering them in a sequence she felt might work best for her – just her hunch. Her tiredness was long forgotten. She felt alert and increasingly optimistic the further she read through her notes.

She could do this, she realized, it was no longer an impossible task – she actually could pull this off.

99

It was half an hour later, after everyone was ready in the jury room, had made themselves drinks and sat back at the table, when Meg put the first part of her plan into place.

'Right, I'd like each of you to write down on a piece of paper your initial verdict on each or all of the counts. It would be useful to see where everyone stands before we begin our discussions. Do please write down, also, if you are undecided.'

They all dutifully complied, passing the various-sized folded scraps of paper into the middle of the table, which were then pushed up to her. They arrived in too much of a jumble for Meg to figure out who had written which.

The handwriting gave her few further clues, although she knew for sure that Harold Trout would have been a 'guilty', and one of those 'guilty' votes had shaky, old-person handwriting. His?

Nine of her ten fellow jurors were looking at her, expectantly. One, the geeky Rory O'Brien at the far end of the table, was poring through a stack of spreadsheets in front of him and scribbling notes.

'OK,' Meg said. 'We have five "guilty", three "undecided" and two "not guilty".'

'Meg,' Toby said in his pained voice, 'are you going to tell us what *you* think?'

She decided on a tactical bluff. 'Well, from all I've heard, I think he's guilty.'

'But can you really say that for sure, Meg?' asked Hugo Pink, coming to her rescue.

She sat, pretending to weigh this up for some moments, thinking hard. Maybe the way she could win this would be by appearing to lose, she thought. 'Fair point, Hugo. I understand why you say that, and I'm struggling to process it all myself. To be *sure* is the essence, the most important factor. Are we satisfied on the evidence to be sure of the defendant's guilt?'

She looked around at her fellow jurors. 'What I suggest we do now, in the interests of being fair to the defendant, and complying with the judge's directions, is to review all the evidence from both sides.'

'Do we really need to?' asked Trout. 'The man is so obviously guilty. In my view the prosecution has made it an open-and-shut case.'

'Actually, Harold,' Hugo rounded on him, 'we do. Of course the prosecution wants him to be guilty, they've invested a large amount of time and money in bringing this case – they would have very red faces if Terence Gready walked free. Which is precisely why we need a proper discussion.'

'I don't believe he is guilty,' Hari Singh said. 'He has a kind face.'

'What?' Trout said. 'He has a kind face, ergo he is innocent?'

'Can you trust all of the people on both sides who gave evidence?' Singh asked him. 'Tell me honestly. You believed and trusted every word?'

Trout shrugged. 'Maybe not every single word. But pretty much most of it.'

'Are you sure?' Meg quizzed.

Trout dug a finger into his ear and twiddled it. His face flushed slightly, showing some emotion for the first time since the trial had started. 'Well, yes, I suppose so.'

'You *suppose so*?' she pounced. 'You'd sleep easily knowing he had been put behind bars for maybe fifteen years because you *suppose* he is guilty? Are you saying you are not one hundred per cent sure?'

'One hundred per cent certainty on anything is very hard to achieve, Meg,' he said, defensively.

And now she knew she had him on the ropes. 'Please correct me if I'm wrong – your job was assessing the risks of everything your company insured?'

'I had to assess the risks of loss at sea of both ships and their cargoes.'

She nodded. 'All right, let's imagine the hypothetical situation in which your company had been asked to insure Terence Gready for ten million pounds against the risk of going to prison. How would you have calculated the premium?'

'That is pretty much an impossible question,' he said, affably.

'You must have had a model on which to calculate your premiums? A ratio of risk to reward?'

'Ah, I see. You want me to give the percentage chance of a "guilty" or "not guilty" verdict?'

'Based on the hard facts of the evidence. Without the spin put on it by the prosecution or defence counsels.'

He pouted his lips. 'With my insurance hat on, I would put it at around eighty per cent probability of guilt on all counts.'

'So a twenty per cent chance he is innocent?'

After a moment he responded with a reluctant, 'Yes.'

She looked at him hard. 'Could you say that a horse in a race, given odds of eight to one, would, for sure, fail to win that race?'

'Of course not,' he replied, petulantly. 'There are too many variables in a horse race.'

'But you would be prepared to send a man to prison on the same odds?'

His Adam's apple was bobbing up and down and a few beads of perspiration popped on his brow. 'I don't think we can compare the defendant's guilt or innocence with either a shipping insurance risk assessment or a horse race.'

'Really? Why not? Are you not admitting you have some doubts – a one in five chance that the defendant might actually be innocent?'

Trout found an itch on his threadbare dome, which he began to attack vigorously. 'Well,' he conceded, with clear reluctance. 'You do have a point, I suppose.'

'Thank you.'

Meg returned to her notes. 'We have heard a wide amount of argument about whether the defendant did or did not ever actually meet the man purporting to have been his so-called *lieutenant*: Michael Starr. This man, who has already pleaded guilty to all of the offences, is clearly, as we have all heard, a highly dubious and untrust-worthy character. It is very much his word against the defendant's. As we have also heard, he has much to gain, in terms of a reduced sentence, by implicating Mr Gready. Can we really trust what he has said? I, for one, am not comfortable with it.'

'Oh, for God's sake,' Sophie Eaton exclaimed. 'We all heard the evidence from that expert witness, the forensic podiatrist Kelly. We saw the video footage, which was compelling, of Mr Starr entering the premises of TG Law.'

'We did,' Mike Roberts said. 'But to be fair, we heard the evidence of Gready's employees – and in particular that of his secretary – who I thought was quite convincing. There is nothing any of them said from which we could infer Mr Gready and Mr Starr met on that day – or any other.'

Meg watched the retired police officer with interest. Was he on her side?

'I agree,' Maisy Waller suddenly butted in. 'That mechanic, Arthur Mason-Taylor, at LH Classics, looked a very honest man to me. He said that he had never seen Mr Gready – and had never heard his name. If Mr Gready, as Mr Starr suggested, owned LH Classics, surely it is odd that the chief mechanic there had never seen him?'

'Well, I've worked at the hospital for nine years and I've never met the chief executive of it,' Sophie piped up.

'But what reason would a man like Arthur Mason-Taylor have for lying?' Hugo said. 'That makes no sense to me at all.'

'It comes back again to the judge's direction to us,' Meg said. '*You must be satisfied of the defendant's guilt.* Can any of us here say that the defendant and Mr Starr ever met – for certain?'

She looked around the table. Only Toby raised his hand.

'Really, Toby? You are certain, are you?'

'Yes.'

'OK. It is very important that we all give our honest opinions. But let's again remind everyone of the judge's comments about Michael Starr, which I wrote down. He said we need to bear in mind that Starr had given evidence implicating Terence Gready in the hope of getting a lesser sentence.' She looked down at her notes. 'The judge instructed us to – in his words – *approach Mr Starr's evidence with caution.* He also went on to say, and I think this is very important for us to consider, *you should ask yourselves whether Mr Starr has, or may have, tailored his evidence to implicate Mr Gready falsely.'*

She looked up again. 'To me, that is pretty unequivocal – I think the judge was going as far as he dared to warn us not to trust Starr.'

Trout shook his head. 'I think you might be reading too much into those words, Meg. My interpretation is that undoubtedly he is doing the right thing in warning us of the possibility that Starr could be lying for his own gain, but I don't interpret that as a thinly veiled instruction to use from the judge.'

'I disagree with you,' she replied and noticed enough nods around the table to indicate she had most of the jury with her on this.

'Well, we'll have to agree to disagree on this, won't we!' Trout retorted, with irritating smugness.

Meg fleetingly wondered what living with this man must be like. She was sorely tempted to snap back, *I was told always to allow other people to be right, it consoles them for not being anything else.* But instead she decided it was best to change the subject.

'Let's move on to the evidence given by Emily Denyer. I have to say that by the time she had finished, I was almost certain that Mr Gready had to be the mastermind behind all the banking and financial shenanigans. But then we heard from Carolyn Herring. A person with impressive credentials from her former senior role in the Fraud Prevention Department of the Inland Revenue. After she had given her evidence it made me think.'

To Meg's relief, there were several nods of agreement

around the table. 'Can we,' she said, 'be sure, again, that it was Mr Gready behind all the banking and financial transactions? I wouldn't be comfortable saying it was.'

There were several murmurs of assent. But to her slight consternation, there was no reaction from Rory O'Brien, who had, for the past hour or so of their discussions, been totally focused on the spreadsheets. She wasn't even sure if he was listening, but then again, he hardly ever spoke. For the moment, though, she didn't mind, she was on fire, adrenaline coursing through her. She really sensed this was going her way.

'Let's now discuss the evidence given by Michael Starr, which on the surface is highly damaging,' she said. 'But as we have just discussed, can we trust this person? We have heard he is a man of extremely dubious character and, having already pleaded guilty, has nothing to lose. I would add that he came across to me as an extremely bitter man.'

Sophie Eaton, Hari Singh and Maisy Waller all nodded. She went on.

'Starr told the court he believes Mr Gready was responsible for his brother's murder. But it is hard to see how he could have been involved, since he was in prison at the time of the very sad murder of Mr Starr's brother,' Meg added.

'I would have to disagree with you there,' Roberts said. 'In my experience as a police officer, prisoners with influence have plenty of access to the outside world – much of it through smuggled phones, as well as corrupt prison officers. An inmate with Gready's alleged credentials and criminal contacts would have no problem arranging a hit on someone, anywhere.'

'Point taken,' Meg replied. 'But can any of us around this table say, again, with complete certainty, that the evidence given against the defendant by Mr Starr is the truth? Please raise your hands if you believe this.'

No one did.

Meg's heart was thumping, she really was on a roll. 'Let's finally consider the evidence given by the defendant himself. As we have all heard, Terence Gready believes he is a victim of a perfect storm of events and that he has been framed by a bitter would-be client whom he refused to take on, on moral grounds. And he believes Starr has been assisted by a police officer – perhaps more than one – who bears a grudge against Gready for the mere fact that he defends criminals the police have arrested, and often gets them off.' She paused and took a sip of water. Her mouth was dry.

'We know Starr to be a highly untrustworthy person, who has already admitted that he is both a smuggler of Class-A drugs and a major player in a substantial county lines drugs distribution network. Do any of us believe, with certainty, that the evidence from this person, implicating the defendant, Mr Gready, is the truth? Please, again, give me a show of hands.' She hammered home the message, remembering from her sales training days that a sales message needed to be seen or heard three times before it would start to be effective.

No one raised a hand.

She was beginning to feel elated. She had them eating out of her palm! 'Can I now ask you all, please, to write down on a piece of paper your verdicts? Guilty, not guilty, or don't know.'

A couple of minutes later she scooped up the scraps and then looked at each. She moved the 'not guilty' votes to the right, 'guilty' to the left.

Two 'guilty'. Seven 'not guilty' – eight, including herself.

If she could get just one more 'not guilty', she would be home free, if the judge allowed a majority verdict.

The missing vote and unknown quantity was O'Brien, still preoccupied with his spreadsheets.

'Rory,' she prompted. 'Could you let me have your decision?'

'I'm sorry,' he said, 'not yet, no. I'm going to need more time.'

'How much more?' she asked, politely, not wanting to put him under pressure.

'Several hours at least,' he replied.

'What!' Mark Adams exclaimed, furious. 'This is ridiculous! Surely we've all heard enough to make a decision about the defendant's guilt. Do we have to drag this out for yet another day?'

Meg turned to the jury bailiff. 'I think you need to let the judge know that we will not be reaching a decision today.'

Toby exclaimed, 'Don't say we are all now going to be sequestered in some bloody shabby hotel. What a nightmare!'

'That happens in films, Toby,' Roberts said. 'It only happens in real life if a judge has concerns there might be an attempt to interfere with the jurors.'

Meg felt her face smarting and hoped it didn't show. If Roberts was her mystery friend, he was keeping up a remarkable poker face.

The bailiff suddenly made an announcement. 'His Honour would like you all back in court, please.'

When they were seated in the jury box, Jupp addressed them. 'Have you elected a foreperson? If so, will that person please stand.'

Meg stood, suddenly a bag of nerves.

'I understand you are still making your deliberations?'

'That's right, Your Honour.'

'No problem, you can continue tomorrow but I intend to adjourn the court for today. You may all go home, but I will remind you that you must discuss neither this case, nor your deliberations, with anyone, not even your loved ones and closest family. It is also important that you don't talk to each other about this case either or undertake any research. This includes when you come back to court tomorrow morning and may find yourselves in the retiring room together. Discussions cannot continue until you go back to the room with the jury bailiff. Court is adjourned until 10 a.m. tomorrow.'

100

It had been a great fishing trip on Saturday, with the sea almost flat calm. Bruno had reeled in a ton of mackerel when they hit a shoal on the way out, and later hooked a fine bass, several good-sized mullet and a Dover sole. They'd taken some of the catch home and Bruno had eagerly helped cleaning and filleting the fish, which they'd then barbecued on Sunday. Bruno seemed in his element, and happier than Roy and Cleo had ever seen him. Humphrey had gobbled down his leftovers, too, and it did seem he might be turning a corner. The vet had referred him for myotherapy treatment at the Galen Centre, where he had started on a course.

To Roy and Cleo's relief, the therapist believed through her assessment that the dog wasn't becoming aggressive but was being grumpy towards Noah as a consequence of being in pain with his muscles. This also explained his occasional reluctance to go for walks and the continual licking of his paws. There was still a way to go with the treatment, but they were happy with the early signs and news that he could be helped back to health with some more sessions. Roy was relieved that Humphrey's grumpy moods and uncharacteristic bouts of being aggressive had nothing to do with Bruno. He'd never really considered it that seriously, but it was often Cleo's first thought when Humphrey acted strangely that it must have something to do with his elder son perhaps tormenting him.

But now, coming up to the 6 p.m. briefing of Operation Canoe, Roy Grace was less happy with the team's progress in the case. They were still no further along with any clues as to Stuie Starr's killers, and Norman Potting had warned him earlier in the day, as if he didn't already know it, that Cassian Pewe was even more on his back than ever.

Suddenly his door burst open and a beaming Potting lumbered in, holding something in his outstretched hand. Before Grace had a chance to rebuke him for not knocking first, the DS said, 'We have a breakthrough, chief!'

'Yes? Tell me?'

Triumphantly, the DS plonked a small black memory stick on his desk. 'Take a look at this!'

Grace frowned. 'What's on it?'

'Take a look!' he beamed.

Grace inserted the USB, then clicked the image that appeared on his screen to open it and saw the start button for a video. He clicked on that and immediately there was an aerial view of lush, rolling countryside. The video was silent, slowly moving across the landscape, and very steady. Was it from a drone, he wondered?

Shortly, Grace could see a housing estate, and near it a cluster of industrial buildings. The landscape changed, rapidly, to an urban one – the edge of a town or city. He always found aerial views took a while to figure out, everything looked different and distant. But it was starting to look a little familiar as they passed over a large church or cathedral.

'Recognize that?' Potting exclaimed, his excitement palpable.

'Chichester?'

'Yes! Look at the date and time, top right on the screen!'
It read: Wednesday 8 May 3.24 p.m.

Grace felt a beat of excitement. This was the day before Stuie Starr's body was discovered by his carer. The day on which, according to the pathologist, Stuie might have died. It fitted.

'Keep watching, chief!'

More of the city appeared as the camera tracked over it. Then, suddenly, the image froze. It began zooming in on a particular area below, before it started moving again.

'I've had Digital Forensics work on this all day, enhancing it,' Potting said.

Grace could now see a garage, with a housing estate opposite. As the image was enlarged even further, he could make out what he was pretty sure was the Starrs' house. A lone car was parked further down the road and, after the camera zoomed in further still, he could recognize the marque, a Mercedes, dark-coloured – either a C or E-class, he wasn't sure.

Two figures, in hoodies, suddenly ran out of the house, sprinting away to the car. They looked furtively around, then jumped into the Mercedes and drove off at speed.

'Norman, this is bloody brilliant! How did you get it?'

'We didn't have any luck from the aerodrome, but whilst I was out I passed a park in Chichester and saw people flying their drones. I went over and spoke to them and asked if any of them had been flying them on the 8th of May. They said they hadn't but would mention it to other drone enthusiasts that they knew. One of them contacted me earlier today and produced this video. Sheer luck, chief.'

'Excellent work, Norman.'

The video continued moving away from the house, in the opposite direction to the car, across the city, circling out over the harbour and the sea. Grace stopped and replayed the earlier part.

'A local dealer's confirmed the model as a current E-Class,' Potting said. 'I've had the ANPR team check all cameras in the Chichester area for an hour either side of 3.24 p.m. The gods are smiling on us, it was relatively light traffic. Just five of that particular model had pinged any cameras and only two of them dark-coloured. And here's the bit you are really going to like, chief – one of them has a Sussex Police marker on it as being linked to a suspected armed drug dealer. Name of Conor Drewett.'

'That's a familiar name.' Grace smiled. 'I nicked him a while back in a drugs bust.'

'Yep, well, he's still around and still a nasty piece of work. I had the pleasure of being bitten on the nose by him about ten years ago and then ending up with a dislocated thumb as I put him on the ground. We have his address. With your permission, chief, I'd like to arrange some of our guys and the local team to pay him a visit early tomorrow.'

Grace grinned. 'What a shame to spoil his beauty sleep.' He shook his head. 'Driving a known car and parking it in the same road. I often think how lucky for us that some villains are not the whole enchilada.'

'The whole enchilada? You've been away in the smoke for too long. Know what I mean?!'

'Six months in the Met, you pick up their jargon, but I'm back home now.'

'He could be a candidate for the Darwin Awards,' Potting said.

Grace frowned. 'The what?'

'It's a spoof award, given annually to the person who by the nature of their stupidity has contributed the most towards Darwin's theory of natural selection. Mostly they're awarded posthumously for editing themselves out of the gene pool.'

Grace smiled. 'Love it. Any idea who the other person with him is?'

The DS shook his head. 'No doubt one of our finer citizens, chief. If we arrest Drewett, maybe he'll squeal, or we'll find some DNA in the Mercedes.'

'Whatever, nice work, Norman.' His phone rang. Grace answered and listened to the call, intently. The moment he ended it he turned to Potting. 'That was the lab – it shows that good detective work will always produce results. The lab has found DNA material in the drain-hole contents in the shower tray, belonging to Conor Drewett. My hunch about the towels on the floor has come up trumps. I had a feeling that with all that blood at the crime scene, one of them may have taken a shower.'

As soon as the DS had left his office, Grace dialled Cassian Pewe's number. *Long past his sell-by date* Pewe had said, dismissively, about Norman Potting.

He waited, eagerly, for the ACC to answer.

101

Meg had slept better. Certainly her first reasonably decent night's sleep since the nightmare of the trial had begun. Yesterday had been tedious, with Rory not saying a word, just poring over the spreadsheets and making endless notes. The rest of them had spent the day deliberating, and using the time to look through the exhibits. Finally, towards the end of the day, Rory had told Meg he was fairly confident he would be able to give her his decision this morning. He just needed to do some thinking at home.

Eight of the jury, including herself, were ready to deliver a 'not guilty' decision. She just needed one more to get a 9–2 verdict, once the judge had said he would accept a majority verdict.

Hopefully, after his night of thinking over the spreadsheets, geeky oddball Rory O'Brien would have arrived at the same conclusions as the majority of them – and Laura would be safe.

And if O'Brien didn't, she was confident she could work on him and on the other two who had voted 'guilty', one of whom had to be Harold Trout.

She made sure she arrived early, and was already seated by 9.30 a.m. The rest of the jurors filed in over the next twenty minutes, and there was a relaxed, end-of-term feeling in the room.

At 10 a.m., there was just one absentee. Rory O'Brien.

Where was he, Meg wondered? Five minutes later he had still not appeared, and a dark thought crossed her mind. Had something happened to him? Surely there would have been nothing to gain by Gready's henchmen doing anything to him?

A couple of minutes later, the geek hurried in, muttering an apology, something about a change in the bus timetable.

With all eyes on him, he took a while to settle down and find his place in the bundle of documents he had left in situ from yesterday. He then apologized again, to Meg, for his tardy arrival.

'No problem, Rory,' she said in an encouraging tone.

The jury were summoned to the courtroom for a short time before being escorted back to the jury room by the bailiff, as before, to continue their deliberations.

102

'Have you arrived at your own verdict?' Meg asked the young man.

'Yes,' he said. 'I'm there. But I don't think you are going to like this.'

Meg looked at O'Brien and felt, suddenly, very scared. There was something about the calm way he had spoken that unnerved her. His words ground into her brain like the whine of a chainsaw.

I don't think you are going to like this.

She held her breath for a moment then said, 'Tell us your thoughts, Rory?'

The man looked nervous, as if unused to having an audience. He stammered a little. 'Well – um – the thing – the thing is – the d-d-d-dates – this is what I find in-in-interesting.'

He fell silent.

'Dates of what, Rory?' Meg asked, maintaining her gently inquisitive tone.

'I've checked the dates of the classic car importations and also the large deposit transfers involving the overseas accounts and the classic car company. From these dates provided I've discovered that, if Mr Starr is to be believed, Mrs Gready was very conveniently abroad, judging orchids in international competitions, on each of those dates. All the competition dates were in the document bundle.'

'And your point is?' Meg asked.

O'Brien responded, 'Well, it's very simple. Is it beyond coincidence that on all twenty-seven occasions that Mrs Gready has been abroad, engaged in her judging, that a classic car, packed with Class-A drugs, has entered a British port, or a large cash deposit has been moved through the LH Classics account? I don't think so. I would say that to consider this a series of coincidences is pretty far-fetched.'

'You're suggesting Gready deliberately chose the dates for when his wife would be out of the country?' Roberts asked.

'Yes.'

Meg felt deep, growing anxiety.

The former detective looked thoughtful. 'That does make a lot of sense. These quantities of drugs and cash movements are enormous by any standard. If Gready was involved – indeed, the mastermind – then in the immediate hours and days following the arrivals of the shipments he would have been busy, probably around the clock, inundated with calls on burners. He might have had a problem explaining to his wife quite what the hell he was up to. Much better if she was conveniently out of the country.'

There was a palpable silence in the room.

Meg was thinking hard and fast. 'It could simply be coincidence,' she replied. But the moment she had spoken, she realized just how lame that sounded.

So, it seemed, from the change of atmosphere in the room, did everyone else.

'Twenty-seven coincidences,' Roberts said. 'With respect, Meg, do you really think that is plausible?'

There was a long silence, during which Meg was struggling to come up with a response. Suddenly, from feeling in control, she was staring up at a seemingly impenetrable wall. 'On the face of it, no,' she was forced to admit. 'But there may be another blindingly obvious explanation.'

'Which is?' said Harold Trout.

She felt her face reddening. Part with embarrassment and part in anger at the look of smug triumph on his face.

Pressing his perceived advantage, Trout said, in a condescending voice which angered her even further, 'You have demonstrated that you are clearly a highly intelligent lady, Meg. Do you really expect any of us to accept that on each of the twenty-seven times that Mr Gready's wife has been abroad, judging these competitions, it is entirely coincidental that major drug deals, allegedly by her husband, took place? Does that extraordinarily high number in any way fit the issue of innocence? I'm afraid it doesn't for me.'

'Nor me,' said Mark Adams.

'Doesn't do it for me either,' said Toby.

'I'm afraid that much though I want to believe Mr Gready is indeed a nice man, this does change the landscape for me,' Hari Singh said.

Edmond O'Reilly Hyland had been quiet for some while, but now chipped in. 'As well as this, we need to remember the evidence found at Gready's house and in the deposit box. In my opinion it's inconceivable that Gready would have told anyone else about the hollowed-out bedpost. To me, his suggesting that Starr was behind this is total nonsense.'

Meg looked bleakly around the solemn faces and felt tears welling, but needed to be strong and not let it show. Only Hugo Pink met her eye, and he gave her a reluctant *chin up* grimace.

The jury continued with their deliberations until lunch-time, when it became apparent they would not be able to reach agreement. Meg turned to the jury bailiff. 'Can we return to the court to let the judge know we are not close, or likely to be unanimous?'

A short time later, with all parties back in court, the judge turned to the jury. 'I understand that you are unable to reach a unanimous verdict on the counts and that there is no likelihood of you doing so. As we are reduced to eleven members, I am able to accept a majority verdict of 10–1 or 9–2 from you. This is in accordance with section 17 (1) b Juries Act 1974.'

He then asked the jury bailiff, Jacobi Whyte, to take the jury back to their room to continue their discussions.

103

Thursday 30 May

Forty-five minutes later the jury followed their bailiff back into court and took their places in the box. Meg was shaking, her brain almost frozen by despair and terror. She could scarcely believe the events of the morning, just how quickly the panel had turned.

She looked around the court. There was utter silence. No one was moving. It was as if she had entered a tableau at Madame Tussauds. Terence Gready was seated, neatly dressed, staring dead ahead, as motionless as a statue. All the legal counsel in their grey wigs and dark garb were static, the public gallery filled with people as motionless as cardboard cut-outs and the full press gallery equally frozen.

Time had stopped.

She felt as if she might faint.

The imposing figure of Judge Richard Jupp dominated the courtroom. The clerk of court, Maureen Sapsed, stood and faced the jury. Looking directly at Meg, her tone friendly, but stiffer and more formal than previously, she said, 'Will the foreperson please stand.'

Meg rose, trembling even more, gripping a sheet of paper. She was terrified she would throw up at any moment.

'I understand you have reached your verdict.'

'Yes.' She stared, fearfully, back at the judge. Her voice

481

was trapped inside her throat. She was conscious that every single pair of eyes in the court was focused on her. Utter silence. A drop of perspiration trickled down the back of her neck. She began to hear a drumming in her ears. The pounding of her heart.

Sapsed continued. 'On the first count, do you find the defendant guilty or not guilty of the charge?'

'Guilty, Your Honour,' she managed to say, finally.

There was an audible gasp throughout the court. A woman up in the public gallery shouted, 'Oh my God, no!'

The judge looked up, with clear annoyance, and waited for silence. The court clerk addressed Meg again. 'Is that the verdict of you all?'

She glanced at the sheet of paper for reassurance. 'It is a majority verdict, Your Honour, 10–1.'

Meg continued to read the verdicts of the jury for the other five counts against Gready. Each verdict was guilty by a majority of 10–1.

Sapsed cast her eye over the entire jury. 'Your verdict, by a 10–1 majority, is that the defendant is guilty on all counts.' The jurors looked back at her, a couple nodding.

Meg shot a glance at the dock. Gready was still staring dead ahead, impassive.

The judge told Meg she could sit down, then turned to Gready. 'Terence Gready, you have been found guilty on all the counts you faced. Tomorrow morning, I will sentence both you and your co-defendant, Michael Starr.' He switched focus to the two guards behind him. 'Please take the defendant down.'

After Gready was gone from the dock, Jupp turned again to the jury. 'You have given diligent and dutiful service throughout what has been a challenging and at times extremely complex trial. I appreciate some of you will have suffered both inconvenience and financial loss due to the trial running into a third week. Tomorrow morning at 10 a.m. I will be sentencing both defendants. There is no obligation on you to attend, as your duties have now been discharged, but should you wish to attend, you will be most welcome.' He paused before continuing.

'It just remains for me to thank you for your service. You may like to know, if you do not already, that juries date back to the twelfth century, to Henry the Second, who set up a system to resolve land disputes. A jury of twelve free men were assigned to arbitrate in these disputes. Members of the jury, you will be pleased to know that juries have consisted of female and male jurors as far back as the thirteenth century. Ahead of their time maybe. In my opinion, they have served the model of justice, on which this country can rightly pride itself, well. I thank you for maintaining that tradition.'

'All rise.'

104

Throughout her train journey back to Hove, fighting off tears, Meg repeatedly tried to get in touch with Laura. No response.

A vortex of thoughts raged inside her head. What to do? What could she do? She had failed. What would she say to her tormentor when he called, as he undoubtedly would?

Now she had nothing to lose, should she go straight to the police and tell them the whole story? But would that put her into legal trouble? Perjury? Perverting the course of justice? None of that would matter if they got Laura back, she didn't care if she ended up in prison so long as she was safe. But would they get her back? Could they? How? By contacting the police in Ecuador? And saying what? It was a vast country, she didn't even know if Laura and Cassie were still in the Galapagos – or even in Ecuador at all. They could be anywhere in South America.

She thought back to the tumultuous events of the past hour and a half. At least it was a 10-1 verdict. Not unanimous. Could the evil bastard at least give her some benefit of the doubt? Could he not recognize this was a majority verdict?

When she arrived home, she sorted out all the animals. All the time waiting for the call.

She occupied herself with every possible distraction, first turning on the television news. But her mind was jumping all over the place, she couldn't focus – she didn't care about the news, all she cared about was Laura. Laura had to be safe. Nothing else, nothing in the world, ever, would matter again if anything happened to her.

Call, please call. Darling Laura.

Please call, you evil bastard.

She planned that when – if – he did ring, she would emphasize how hard she had tried, against what had become increasingly impossible odds. She would throw herself at his mercy, appealing to his better nature.

But he did not ring.

105

Friday 31 May

Harold Trout was there, of course, he would be, Meg thought. A retired man with time on his hands, well able to turn up today and no doubt smugly looking forward to seeing justice meted out. Justice he had the satisfaction of playing a part in.

And so had she.

When the chips were down, she had decided she had to be true to her conscience and had voted guilty.

Trout sat at the table in the jury room reading a copy of the *Argus* newspaper. Not very subtly, as he noticed Meg enter, he shifted his position slightly so she could not fail to see the front-page headline.

BRIGHTON SOLICITOR GUILTY!

Sick with fear for Laura, she gave him a brief nod, in no mood for conversation, certainly not to listen to him gloating, and made herself a strong coffee.

In a parallel universe she, too, would have looked forward to seeing Terence Gready get the sentence he deserved. But twenty minutes later, as she entered the court and took her place in the strangely half-empty jury box, she was still hoping – praying – for a miracle.

It was something her thoughts had returned to frequently during the long night. Occasional snatches of sleep freed her from the prison of her mind, but each time she woke, back to the reality, her terror worsened. In the end, sometime around 3 a.m., she'd given up altogether, gone down into the kitchen, made a mug of tea then sat at her computer. She was completely alone. She hadn't heard from Laura in what seemed like an eternity.

On Death Row in prisons in America, appeals went on for years, didn't they? Wouldn't Primrose Brown stand up the moment the judge entered and say she was appealing? Was that how it worked? She had repeatedly tried googling the appeals process, but whether she was too tired, or unable to concentrate with her brain jumping all over the place, she kept, annoyingly, ending up on American websites, aware the legal system there differed in numerous aspects from the UK.

And every few minutes during the night, she'd picked up her phone, checking to make sure there wasn't a voice-mail from Laura from a call she'd somehow missed, or a text, or a WhatsApp. And each time after she'd done that she'd tried calling again.

Where was Laura? And, of course, Cassie? And what about Cassie's parents? How was she going to explain things to them?

Where were they?

Where were the bastards keeping them?

She was startled by a voice whispering in her ear, accompanied by a sudden whiff of halitosis. 'I hope he gets what he deserves.'

It was Maisy Waller, and she was nodding at Meg. Again, whispering, she said, 'I know you did your best to make it a fair debate for us all, but it's the right verdict. I think we all know that, don't we?'

Meg gave her a wan smile and returned to her thoughts. She looked at the defence QC and her junior barrister, Sykes, and at Gready's tall, silver-haired solicitor seated behind, along with two others who were, presumably, his assistants. The trio had been busy throughout the trial, passing notes between themselves, conferring, then whispering or passing notes either to Primrose Brown or her junior. She wondered what the solicitor was thinking. He looked a sly, hard man – was he going to pull a rabbit out of a hat at the last minute before sentencing? If he was, he gave no clue. He was leaning back in his chair, looking too relaxed for her liking, as if he were a member of the audience in a theatre, contentedly waiting for the curtain to rise on a show he was going to enjoy.

Perhaps it was like that for lawyers, she thought. Win or lose, they got their fees, it was just a game for them. She looked up at the public gallery, which, unlike the jury box, was rammed. She saw Barbara Gready and her son and daughters, who were there to see the outcome of the trial. Then she noticed a man with slightly Latino looks who was staring down at the jury box. At her?

She glanced away, towards the empty dock, then back. He was still looking, but his face gave nothing away; it was as if he was studying an exhibit in a museum.

Was it him, she wondered?

He was dressed in a smart, casual jacket over a white open-neck shirt and his dark hair was shiny. She tried to engage eye contact, but he just looked elsewhere. Then, the moment she turned away, she could feel his eyes back on her. She shot him a sudden glance and saw she was right.

She shivered. *What game are you playing with me?*

Looking away again, she noticed another wigged and

gowned barrister in the court today, with what was presumably a solicitor or junior seated behind him. Was this Michael Starr's legal team?

Judge Jupp entered the courtroom, turning to the dock officers. 'You can bring the defendants up now.'

A sudden murmur went around the court, and people started turning towards the dock. Terence Gready and Michael Starr entered, with two dock officers standing behind them. Both defendants wore suits. Gready looked quite at home in his regular attire, while Starr looked like he'd put on a hand-me-down. The jacket hung loosely over his shoulders and the sleeves came halfway down his hands. His shirt, by contrast, looked too small for the top button to be done up, and the collar was held partially clamped by his tie. He looked uncomfortable and agitated.

Hardly surprising, Meg thought.

Neither man glanced at the other. They stood like two strangers who had never met, just as Gready had claimed in his defence.

106

The clerk told the defendants to sit down. The judge then entered into a lengthy discussion with both defence barristers about the sentencing guidelines.

Meg was surprised, she had thought it would all be over in minutes. Instead, the barristers and judge engaged in what sounded like a cross between a verbal sparring match and a horse trade, as each referred to past cases and judgements, citing varying lengths of sentences. Reference books were produced, with Jupp thumbing for some minutes through one before he found what Brown had asked him to read.

All the time, Meg was distracted by the Latino who still seemed to be playing games with her. Watching her, looking away, watching her.

Who the hell are you, damn you? Are you signalling to me – telling me something about Laura? Telling me I had my chance and I blew it?

'The starting tariff for that would be fourteen years,' she heard Jupp say. 'But that is just the starting tariff, and the scale of this particular offence warrants a sentence towards the higher end on that particular charge. You are aware the maximum sentence I could impose on this charge is life, aren't you?'

Meg felt the silent vibration of her phone, in her jeans pocket. Laura? At last? *God, please, please, please.* She pulled it out quickly, scared it would ring off, and glanced down surreptitiously. To her disappointment, it was only a message from the recruitment agency she had joined. She would read it later.

As she slipped the phone back, she heard Jupp say to both barristers, 'Before I make my final decision, are there any mitigating circumstances you wish me to be aware of?'

Starr's barrister, Michael Footitt QC, a striking-looking man in his late forties who kept nodding his head, replied, 'Your Honour, my client promised to take care of his younger brother, Stuie. Mr Starr has fulfilled this promise in an exemplary manner, by having Stuie live with him ever since his mother died, until his incarceration. Mr Starr has been in a state of deep anxiety for many months now, ever since being remanded, because Stuie, right up until his dreadful murder, had difficulty understanding why his brother could not come home.'

'Well, Mr Footitt,' interrupted Jupp, 'perhaps your client might have considered the risks of going to prison and the impact it would have on his promise before committing the crimes he did.'

More frantic nodding by the barrister. 'Yes, of course, Your Honour, my client does realize that and wishes to apologize to the court for his misdemeanours.'

Jupp frowned. 'Misdemeanours? You are calling the importation and supplying of drugs, to the value of many tens of millions of pounds, *misdemeanours*? How many people have died from overdoses or other conditions resulting from taking drugs imported and supplied by your client? How many families have been destroyed, how many lives ruined? How many innocent people have been the victims of crime, from drug users needing cash for their next fix breaking into their cars, their homes, and taking things or mugging them on the streets for their phones or handbags? *Misdemeanours?* Your client is not a schoolboy who has nicked a few chocolate bars from a corner shop.' The judge was now glaring at him in undisguised fury. 'Mr Footitt, I'm not at all clear on the point you are making, regarding mitigation. The length of sentence I impose will make no difference at all to the care of the defendant's brother, since he is tragically deceased.'

'No, Your Honour, the point I wanted to make is to show aspects of my client's good character that have perhaps not been brought to your attention.' He then pointed out that Starr had pleaded guilty at the first opportunity and that he had given evidence for the prosecution which had helped convict his co-defendant. At the conclusion of his mitigation Jupp responded with a terse, 'Thank you.'

The judge then turned to Primrose Brown. 'Do you have anything you want to say on behalf of your client that I should take into account before I pass sentence?'

'I would like to call a character witness,' Brown replied.

'Go ahead.'

The Reverend Ish Smale, vicar of the Good Shepherd, Hove, entered the box.

With his silver, shoulder-length hair, the vicar looked more like an old rocker than a member of the clergy. But he delivered to the court a portrait of a man deserving of a royal gong. He talked about Terence and Barbara Gready's devout Christianity, evidenced through their regular attendance in church. As well as their ceaseless work for Brighton and Hove charities and their generosity to them. The couple were, in his eyes, examples to the community, examples which, if we all followed, would truly make the world a better place.

The judge thanked him for attending court.

Brown then spoke briefly, accepting that, as he had been found guilty after a trial, her client could not expect his sentence to be reduced. However, she once again stressed his good character and standing in the local community.

The judge pondered for a few moments and then looked at the dock and the men sitting there. 'Stand up, please,' he said authoritatively. 'Michael Starr, you are an evil drug dealer who has made millions of pounds over many years peddling death. I take into account that you pleaded guilty at the first opportunity and that you assisted the prosecution by giving evidence against your co-defendant. For those factors I will give you credit. My normal starting point for these offences would be to send you down for twenty-seven years, but the appropriate sentence, I believe, is a term of imprisonment on each of the counts of twelve years, to run concurrently. You will, of course, be subject to the Proceeds of Crimes Act procedures.'

He then turned to Starr's co-defendant. 'Terence Gready, you have brought shame on the legal profession with your drug-dealing activities and by exploiting your knowledge and position as a person of trust. Your conduct is abhorrent. You've thought you are above the law, despite being one of its practitioners. You've let your family down with your tissue of lies that you even convince yourself with. You have maintained the facade of being a pillar of the community whilst profiting from poisoning vast numbers of it. You only had one motivation. Greed. You have contested these matters since the day of your arrest, never having the courage to accept your criminal conduct. Now you will suffer the consequences of that. I can give you no credit for pleading guilty and therefore my sentence will be severe. I would normally be looking as the appropriate sentence for these matters to be one of life imprisonment, but having heard about your charitable work, which I am taking into account, I have decided the correct sentence is one of twenty-seven years' imprisonment, concurrent for each charge.'

Meg was about to glance up again at the Latino, when she saw a strange movement in the dock. With his left hand, Michael Starr appeared to be pulling hard at his right hand. An instant later his prosthetic right forearm came free of his jacket sleeve. She just had time to notice the spike protruding several inches from its base, before Starr shouted, 'You might not be giving him life, your nibs, but I will! He fucking killed my brother!'

As he shouted, he plunged the spike twice into Gready's chest and then several more times, in a frenzy, into his neck, before the dock officers realized what was happening and lunged forward. Blood jetted onto the dock glass and onto the security guards. People were screaming. Pandemonium. Everyone in the court staggered to their feet. More security people came rushing in.

A klaxon began ringing outside.

Jupp was staring, frozen in utter disbelief.

Gready's hand, covered in blood, was clutching at his throat as blood spurted from it in uneven squirts. He was making gurgling noises, as if struggling to breathe and pleading for help at the same time. The guards wrestled with Starr. Two more rushed into the dock as well as a police officer, the detective Glenn Branson.

The last thing Meg saw of Gready, as he sank down and became blocked from her view by the guards and police officer, was the look of utter helplessness and terror in his eyes.

107

Five minutes later, as the court was emptied, Meg stumbled out into the corridor in a complete daze, into a scene of utter chaos. She heard the wail of sirens approaching, emergency vehicles were arriving. Someone was crying and someone else was screaming.

She'd just seen a man stabbed, many times, in the chest and the neck. It looked like his throat had been ripped open, an artery severed. It was almost all she could see, those few seconds replaying on an endless loop in her mind.

Her head was throbbing, her body shaking. As she was jostled down the steps, she felt limp, like a rag doll. The look of terror in Gready's eyes was burned into her brain. Someone bumped into her from behind, unbalancing her and sending her lurching into the back of a bulky man in front of her. A voice behind called out an apology. She was pushed from the side. Left, then right. Someone stood, painfully, on her foot.

Suddenly, to her surprise, she felt a hand gripping hers. A strong, coarse, reassuring, masculine hand. Stealthily pressing something soft and crinkly into her palm. It felt like a banknote.

In an instant, the hand was gone.

Gripping whatever it was tightly, she looked around in

astonishment. She saw one of the court ushers she recognized, hemming her in to the right, and a young Chinese guy, who looked like a student, to her left. She turned and behind her stood a tall, tweedy woman. As she caught Meg's eyes she asked, 'Do you know what has happened? Why are they clearing the building, is there a terrorist bomb?'

Meg looked away, hunting with her eyes through the melee for the Latino man. Then she thought she saw the top of his head, his dark shiny hair, some distance over to her right. Frantically, she barged her way through, forcing a path, yelling, 'Excuse me, excuse me, excuse me!'

Then finally she was clear of the crowd. She stopped and looked around. He was nowhere to be seen. Panting from the exertion, her heart thumping, she carefully opened up her clenched right hand and looked at what had been pressed into it, as more people swarmed around her.

A small scrap of paper, torn from a ring binder, and folded several times. She opened it out; in neat handwriting in blue ballpoint, were written some words, with a row of digits below.

> *You did your best.*
> *Call this number.*

After all she had been through in the last three weeks, she couldn't believe what she had just read.

108

Terrified of losing the scrap of paper, Meg tried to tap the number into her phone, but her hands were shaking too much. Suddenly the note fell from her trembling hands onto the ground and immediately disappeared under several pairs of feet. In complete panic, she fell to her knees, trying to grasp it. She ducked down and retrieved it, then from somewhere, as she stood up again, she found the presence of mind to photograph it, for safety.

She stared at it. The prefix was for Ecuador, she recognized. But the number was unfamiliar. Who the hell was it?

Call this number.

Laura?

An authoritative voice called out. 'Will everyone who was in Court 3 please remain in the building!'

Too much noise, impossible to speak here. She eased away from the crowd and headed towards the toilets. As soon as she was far enough away from the din, she leaned against a wall, and with fingers that seemed to be in total disconnect from her brain, she struggled for a good minute or more before she finally got the correct number entered.

00 593 112 679483

She hit dial, lifted the phone to her ear and waited. There was silence, for what seemed an eternity, almost drowned out by her panting, the thudding of her heart and the drumming in her ears.

Then an overseas ring tone. Whine – silence – whine – silence – whine – silence.

A click.

Then to her utter joy, she heard the sleepy voice of her daughter.

'Hrrrullo?'

It was midday here, which meant if she was still in the Galapagos, or over that side of Ecuador, it was a six-hour time difference – 6 a.m. 'Laura! Laura, darling?'

'Mum!'

Oh my God, she thought. *Oh my God, you are alive!* She closed her eyes, crushing away tears of relief. 'My darling, have I woken you?'

'Yrrrr, but that's OK. S'good to hear you.' She was talking quietly, as if she didn't want to wake anyone up. She sounded fine, relaxed, normal.

'Where are you, are you OK? Are you safe?'

Laura sounded surprised. 'Safe? Yes, we're in a hostel, back in Guayaquil.'

A tidal wave of relief surged through Meg. 'I've been going out of my mind with worry. I haven't been able to get hold of you.'

'Yrrrr, sorry about that, Mum. Cassie and I got pickpocketed – can you believe it, in a queue for the toilets. Bastards took our phones, purses and passports. It's been a bloody nightmare, we couldn't pay for anything. We phoned the British Embassy in Quito – they're going to help with new passports. Then we bumped into that weird guy – remember we told you about him – Jorge – who we thought was stalking us. He's turned out to be our saviour!' She was sounding increasingly animated. 'We bumped into him right outside the hostel in the Galapagos – such a coincidence! He lent us some cash – I told him you'd pay him back, hope you don't mind?'

'Of course not.'

'He found a phone place and bought Cassie and me a phone each – so amazing of him. But I couldn't call you – we can't call out internationally on them. He said he would get a message to you to call us!'

Meg said nothing. She didn't believe Jorge was the saviour her daughter thought. But more importantly at this moment, she couldn't believe she was talking to Laura again, how normal she sounded. How relaxed.

Had she been spoofed all along about the threat to her life?

'How are you, Mum? How's the trial going?'

'Interesting,' was all Meg could think to say at this moment, she was too concerned about her daughter. 'Listen, you've lost your passports and your purses, with your cards?'

'Jorge has bought us air tickets to Quito. I'm getting my credit card sorted.'

'Do you need me to wire you money now, darling?'

'No, it's OK, Jorge is giving us what we need. I told him you'll pay him back. You don't mind, do you, Mum?' Laura often repeated herself when she was excited, she always had.

'My angel, absolutely I do not mind!'

'I miss you,' she said suddenly. 'Like I really miss you. You'd love it here, Mum, it's just – totally awesome. I'm really hacked off though, cos all my cash has been taken by those bastards. We were planning to fly to Argentina to see the

Iguazu Falls. Cassie says her parents might lend her the cash – would you, too? And could you let them have her number if I give it to you?'

'Of course. But how about if I pay for you both – for your flights there – if I came with you?'

Laura sounded elated. 'If you come too? No way, wicked! Are you serious?'

'Very serious. I could get a flight out to Quito and meet you both there! If Cassie's OK with that?'

'She'll love it! Unreal. You are the best mum in the world!'

Meg grinned, all the horror of the past hour – and the days before it – temporarily forgotten. 'I know.'

'Seriously?' Laura said. 'You'll come?'

'If you really want me to? If you don't mind an old person tagging along?'

'Don't worry about that,' Laura said. 'We'll sort out wheelchair-friendly transport for you.'

Ending the call, Meg felt utterly elated. She was about to call her travel agent, when she suddenly remembered the text that had come in, from the recruitment agency. She read it.

> **Meg, we have a very exciting job interview for you from a major pharmaceutical company. Can you give me a couple of dates/times you could do an interview? They seem really keen on you!**

Meg replied,

> **Just off to South America – a couple of weeks?**

A response came back almost instantly.

> **I'm sure they will wait. You have exactly the background they need!**

Despite all the horror in court just a short while ago, she felt a sudden burst of optimism. She'd not felt like this ever since the accident. For the past five years she had been living her life in survival mode, more like existing than living, being there for Laura. This was the first time she felt a real frisson of excitement about the future. Going to see Laura! Laura was safe, she was fine. Possibly a new and really good job when she got back!

Had she ever actually been in danger or were they just using Laura as a bargaining chip and a threat? Should she now go to the police, she wondered? But tell them what? And what would that achieve? She would simply be implicating herself and, at the end of the day, she hadn't really done anything wrong – she'd made the right moral decision in finding Gready guilty. It was now time to move on. Hopefully, they no longer viewed her as useful to them. But would she ever feel really safe again? Only time would tell, but there was no point worrying about things she couldn't change.

The real excitement at this moment was reuniting with her daughter. There was just one cloud on the horizon – telling Laura about Horace. She'd been trying to think of ways to cushion it.

Guinea pigs had a lifespan of around five years. Poor Horace had been close to that, she calculated. She'd bought him for Laura as a coming-home-from-hospital companion after the accident. Maybe she would tell her he'd died peacefully in his sleep, slipped away in his old age.

After all the lies she'd heard in court over the past few weeks, this seemed a pretty tame one.

109

'Dead?' Roy Grace said, in near disbelief. 'Stabbed by his co-defendant, in the dock, in broad daylight?'

It was just gone 2 p.m. Glenn Branson stood in front of him in his office, nodding. 'Yep.'

Grace shook his head.

'You all right, Roy, you seem very distracted recently?'

He waved a hand, dismissively. 'More grief about Bruno. Cleo had a call from the school this morning, he was really rude to a teacher. Anyhow, we'll deal with that later. So, tell me. How the hell did he get a weapon in through court security?'

'Did I tell you Starr has a prosthetic right arm? He must have spent hours – days – on it, turning it into a weapon – a shank. It was plastic so wouldn't have been picked up by the metal detector.'

'Doesn't sound like Terence Gready is a big loss to the human race but, shit, I've never heard of that happening, ever.'

'No doubt Cassian Pewe will find a way to hold you responsible, boss,' Branson said with a sardonic smile.

'No doubt.' He shrugged. 'So, talk me through what exactly happened.'

Branson gave him chapter and verse. When he had

finished, Roy Grace was pensive. 'So, first Starr pleads guilty, to get a reduction in his tariff. Next, his brother, Stuie, his raison d'être for his "guilty" plea, is murdered. Then, in court, he negates his potential reduced tariff by murdering his co-defendant in cold blood. Why?'

'Anger?' Glenn ventured.

'He must have planned the attack on Gready for at least several days. He would have known it would have blown out his reduced tariff – and given him a much longer sentence. What triggered him to do that?' Grace was pensive for some moments. 'In my view, he must have suspected Gready was behind his brother's murder. Perhaps, as was mooted earlier, Gready had ordered Stuie to be beaten up, as a warning to Starr to keep schtum. And the beating went too far?'

'What about if there was an ulterior motive?'

Grace frowned. 'Such as?'

Branson smiled. 'Bear with me. That shit, Conor Drewett – who the Mercedes was registered to and who we nicked yesterday morning – squealed pretty quickly on his accomplice when we offered to tell the judge he'd been a good boy. The accomplice was totally wasted when we picked him up. Derren Skinner. Before he was even interviewed, in the car on the way to the custody centre, he'd told the arresting officers who'd hired him and Drewett. Probably because he was shitfaced on something.'

'Grassed him up?'

Branson nodded. 'Perhaps *ratted* on him would be a better word for Skinner – horrible little creep.'

'So, who was behind it – tell me?'

Glenn Branson spun the chair in front of Grace's desk, sitting down on it the wrong way round, placed his arms over the backrest and leaned forward, a big grin pushing across his face. 'I think you are going to like this. I mean, *really* like it! You've told me before that we can do all the planning in the world, be as professional as all our training has taught us, but that one elusive thing we can't count on is luck. I think we just got lucky.' He smiled. 'Like, very seriously lucky!'

110

Nick Fox was feeling very seriously lucky.

He was sitting at his desk in the deserted Hoxton offices of his law practice, shortly after 7.30 a.m. He liked to be in well before the rest of the team, whenever he wasn't attending a trial or client meeting out of town. And while the Gready trial had been in progress, he'd barely been in the office at all, which meant he had a mountain of catching-up to do. But that was fine. Today, everything was fine!

And it wasn't going to be for much longer that he had to put up with the never-ending criminal scumbags he had to deal with. Truth was, much though he put on a smiling, positive facade, he mostly despised his clients. Whining lowlifes, protesting their innocence, swearing blind they'd been *fitted up* by the police – or as many of them called them, *the filth.*

Throughout his career, he'd kept his eye out for opportunities. Playing the long game had always been his tactic. And he had been playing a lot of different clients – all in the criminal arena. Just like that old Biblical parable: *Some fell by the wayside; some fell on stony ground; some fell among thorns. But others fell on good ground and brought forth fruit.*

And with one, he had struck gold. His client Terence

Gready. Over the past twenty-five years, Gready had brought forth so much fruit. And some of it truly low-hanging.

Fox knew he had been lucky – lucky that Gready trusted him implicitly, lucky that, with Gready's scheming mind, the Brighton solicitor had, all those years ago, set a trap, miscalculating the risk that it might one day backfire and help to ensnare him. Just like himself, Gready played the long game, too, always carefully covering his back. But, Fox knew, almost everyone, at some point, makes a mistake, even the cleverest people. The safety deposit box account was Gready's first mistake and where it had all started to unravel.

As a hedge against ever getting investigated, Terence Gready had made sure it was always going to be Mickey Starr who took the fall, not him. With the deposit box, he'd made it look as if Starr had forged his signature. He'd also left the key in the shed, which could have been accessible to Starr or someone else. He'd been scrupulously careful not to be seen together with Mickey, and all contact they had was either by burner phone or where they would not be seen. By not having cameras and alarms at his house there was always the chance that someone, possibly Starr, could have planted the evidence that the police found. This concoction he always felt would be enough to distance himself if he was ever to be part of a police investigation.

Like so many successful criminals before him, Gready had become complacent. For many years, his network of drug distribution and, more recently, his system of importing drugs concealed in high-end classic sports cars, had worked brilliantly. Complacency had been his second mistake. He thought he could easily manipulate a jury. His third had been to entrust so much to Mickey Starr, who had a vulnerability. Stuie.

His fourth mistake, Nick Fox thought, very happily, had been to hire him as his trusted solicitor, and to confide in him over these many years. Fox knew where all the bodies were buried – or rather, in this case, where all the cash was stashed. And Gready had given him unique access to it.

With Gready now dead, there was no one standing in his way. He held all the bank account numbers, and the equally important codes to them, to access over £35 million that Terence Gready had carefully squirrelled away around the world.

All it had needed for that money to become his was one piece of luck. And that had come in the form of Mickey Starr's love for his brother, Stuie.

When Gready had told him to find someone to 'rough Stuie up a little', as a warning to Mickey not to attempt to grass him up for a sentence reduction, Fox had seen his chance. All he needed to do was find a couple of thugs from his client base and offer them a massive financial incentive to kill Stuie, while making it look like a roughing-up gone too far.

He tapped on his keyboard, entering a serial number, followed by the password for one of Terence Gready's accounts – at a bank in the Cayman Islands.

$750,578.02 on deposit.

All his now.

Luck had smiled on him. Not that luck was chance, it was something you worked at. Like his golf pro once told him after holing-in-one at a pro-am tournament, 'Nick, I find the harder I practise, the luckier I get!'

That was kind of how he felt right now. Subtly feeding the information to Mickey Starr that it had been Terence Gready who had ordered Stuie's death had done the trick. Producing a better result than he could have imagined!

Shame about the kid brother, but shit happened.

He smiled, cynically.

He was now rich. Properly rich. Beyond what would once have been his wildest dreams. All he needed to do, publicly, was to continue playing the long game. Be just like Terence Gready had always been, Mr Respectable. Just until everything died down. And then, a quickie divorce and vamoose! Off shore and out of sight. With his new girlfriend – well, not so new, three years and counting – not that Marion, his wife, suspected a thing.

His reveries were interrupted by a knock on his door, and his loyal secretary entered.

'Sorry to interrupt you, Nick. There are two police officers – detectives – asking if they could have a word with you?'

'Police – where from?'

'I believe they are from Sussex.'

'Show them in,' he said, confidently.

A stocky, suited man in his mid-fifties with a shaven head and a smart tie entered his office, holding out a sheet of paper in one hand and his warrant card in the other. He was followed by a tall, equally sharp-suited younger man.

'Acting Detective Inspector Norman Potting and Detective Sergeant Jack Alexander from Surrey and Sussex Major Crime Team,' he announced. 'You are Nicholas Fox?'

'I am,' he said, pleasantly. 'How can I help you, officers?'

'Nicholas Gordon Fox, I have a warrant for your arrest on the charge of conspiracy to commit murder.'

Fox stared at them in sudden, utter panic, bewildered. What the hell was going on? For an instant, he wondered if he should make a dash for it. But Alexander, behind the DI, was blocking the doorway. 'Arrest?' he said, instead. 'What do you mean?'

Potting started to caution him.

Fox held up his hand, interrupting him. 'Yadda, yadda, yadda. I'm a solicitor, OK? Spare me the fucking pre-take-off crap. I know how to put on a life vest and blow the whistle.'

Ignoring him, the DI continued with the caution.

'Which way exactly do the straps go around my chest?' Fox asked, facetiously. 'And you haven't pointed out the emergency exits.'

111

Roy Grace let himself and Humphrey into the garden after a morning walk, went over to the hen house and lifted the lid of the first of the three nesting boxes, trying to ignore the sour reek. Two eggs of different sizes, one brown and one blue, nestled in the straw.

'Good girls! I'll tell your keeper, Bruno!' he called out to them, gently lifting each egg out and placing them in a bowl. He retrieved a further three from the next two boxes and headed back towards the house with the triumph of a crusader returning home laden with booty.

Strolling in shorts and flip-flops across the freshly mown lawn, he felt, suddenly, an almost intoxicating happiness. It was moments like this when he wished he could freeze time and hold them in his mind forever. He stopped and stood, looking at their cottage and the hill, dotted with sheep, that rose up behind. It was coming up to 9 a.m. and the clear, cobalt sky looked set to deliver the forecaster's promise of a fine weekend. There was just one major cloud and it wasn't in the sky.

Cassian Pewe.

Even when he'd given the ACC the news that poor Stuie Starr's murder was pretty much cleared up, there was no thank you, simply an admonishment that two murders in

Sussex within such a short period of time did not make good headlines. A litany of anger from him then followed, blaming Grace for failing his team by not anticipating Starr's attack on Gready.

Maybe Pewe was right, he reflected, perhaps as the leader he should have done. But how? Police officers had been described by a former Met Commissioner as 'ordinary people doing extraordinary things'. True sometimes, Grace thought. But we're not *superhuman*.

He was at a loss how to deal with Pewe. The ACC had welcomed him back from his secondment to the Met with open arms, only to immediately stab him in the back and return to his former hostile attitude. A few years ago, when they'd been on equal rank, Grace had risked his life to save Pewe's, when the front of his car had gone over the edge of a cliff and the vehicle hung precariously. There had been little more than grudging gratitude afterwards.

Was there something in psychology, he wondered, some innate pride perhaps, that could turn people against those who had saved their lives?

It hadn't helped their relationship that he subsequently found a discrepancy that nearly resulted in Pewe being investigated by Professional Standards, and which had sent him fleeing back to the Met, from where he had originated, with his tail between his legs.

Grace had scarcely been able to believe it when he was told by the Chief Constable less than a year later that Pewe was returning, and in a senior rank. The Chief told Roy that Pewe had assured him he felt no animosity towards him. How wrong that had turned out to be.

He decided to try to put Pewe from his mind for now and enjoy the weekend with his family. Bruno had asked him to cook French toast today and that's what he planned to do. Then they were going to take a picnic to the beach.

A sudden squawking and clucking behind him made him turn and look at the chicken enclosure. Anna was pecking Isobel furiously, before strutting off in what looked like a huff. He smiled, fascinated by their little world. He loved watching how busy they were, rushing around in short bursts, eyeing the ground beadily for a speck of corn or mixed seed they might have missed.

After the endless daily horrors of human violence, in the papers, on television and, all too often, like poor Stuie Starr, on a tray in the mortuary, the simple act of walking Humphrey over fields, or picking an egg out of a nesting box, he found incredibly grounding and calming.

Not that he was starry-eyed or naive about hens, or any other aspects of Mother Nature. Chickens could be as vicious as any humans, with domestic violence – as he had just witnessed – an almost daily occurrence in the enclosure. People said violence was just human nature, but it wasn't, it was all nature – and you didn't have to go far to see it. The local wood half a mile away was, in its densest part, a war zone of plants and trees trying to strangle each other.

As he walked in through the kitchen patio doors he heard the sound of a vehicle, and an instant later Humphrey, barking furiously, catapulted himself across and through the living area. They'd sealed up the letter box a while ago, as the dog would rip everything that came through to shreds.

Cleo, seated at the breakfast bar, eating a bowl of cereal, was studying her course work. Noah lay on the floor watching a cartoon on television and giggling intermittently.

'I think that was Mr Postie,' she said.

'I'll go check.'

'No wait, I need to speak to you quickly about that call

from Bruno's headmaster. I really think we should be pro-active. Let's get him properly assessed by the psychologist for everybody's peace of mind, they might be able to help integrate him better. We don't want the school ringing us up every five minutes about him.'

He nodded. 'Look, darling, I know where you are coming from, but he's not a bad kid and maybe the school is being oversensitive.' He paused, thoughtfully. 'Or maybe I'm just protective of him. If it helps us move forward, let's do it.'

'Thanks, it would. Oh, just a thought, now your investigation is over, will you have a chance to call my OU mate Alison and chat with her daughter – you know, she wanted to learn about jury service and nobbling for her dissertation?'

'It's on my list! I'm sure there's not much I can tell her that she couldn't find out online. As I said, it hardly ever happens. I've never had a case, but of course I'll ring her.'

Humphrey continued barking. Roy put the eggs on the table, walked to the front door and calmed the dog down. He heard a vehicle driving away and opened the door a crack, not wanting Humphrey to race out and chase it. The lid of the free-standing mail box was raised and he saw that a couple of the motoring magazines he subscribed to had been delivered, along with some letters held together by a rubber band.

He carried the letters back and plonked them on the kitchen table, then took a knife from a drawer and began sliding the envelopes open.

'Anything interesting?' Cleo asked.

He was about to say there wasn't, when he picked up a small, flimsy envelope that was hand-addressed. It reminded him, darkly, of one he'd had some years back, containing a death threat from a particularly nasty drug dealer he'd put away. He slit it open and removed the equally flimsy folded sheet of paper.

At the top was written,

HMP Ford. Prisoner No 768904

He frowned again, then realized, even before he read the signature, who it was from. His former friend and colleague Guy Batchelor.

Last year Guy had panicked when a woman with whom he was having an affair threatened to go public. She'd ended up dead in a bathtub, and Guy hadn't exactly helped his claim that it was an accident when he'd tried to cover his tracks and later escape arrest. But all the same, and despite his loathing of any cop who brought the force into disrepute, Grace couldn't help feeling some sympathy for the man. He had a lovely wife, an equally lovely daughter, he'd been on a rising career path and he'd had everything going for him. Prison was not a good place for a police officer to be. In terms of prisoner loathing, they didn't rank far above paedophiles.

He read the letter. It was brief. Guy's handwriting was, as ever, neat.

> *Roy,*
>
> *Hope this finds you well. Not much to report here, other than waiting for the appeal hearing against the length of my sentence. Other prisoners haven't been as nasty to me as I feared – so far, anyway.*
>
> *I'm writing because I may have something of interest about our mutual friend. No names mentioned because all these letters are read, but I know you were interested in doing something with*

that church bench. I may be able to help you.
Perhaps you could come over – I can promise you
it won't be a wasted journey.

All my best to you and all the team – hey,
I miss you all.

Guy

'From a secret admirer?' Cleo asked with a grin. 'Not very classy taste in headed paper.'

'I don't think they have Harrods stationery departments in British prisons,' he said and handed her the letter.

She read it then frowned. 'All very cryptic – what is he talking about? What church bench?'

'I've no idea, I'm trying to figure it out.'

She gave him a sideways look and grinned. 'Pew?'

He raised a finger. 'Genius! Of course!'

'I thought you were supposed to be the detective.'

'Yep, well, it's my weekend off!'

'So what's his reference to Pewe, exactly, meaning?'

Grace smiled. 'It may be he has found out something – got the goods on him. He's always known the crap I've had to take from him. I will definitely pay Guy a visit, next week if I can.' He smiled again. 'The weekend just got even better! Something to look forward to afterwards – I'm very nicely intrigued!'

'Perhaps we could go to church tomorrow – we haven't been to a normal service since before we got married. Might be good to take Noah and Bruno?'

'Really? I don't want to get in the way of a thunderbolt aimed at our little Antichrist upstairs.'

She punched him. 'You are terrible!'

'And I can just about cope with one Pewe – don't want to spend my Sunday surrounded by dozens of them.'

'Stop it!'

He went over to a cupboard and removed a jar of coffee. 'Any tea or coffee, darling?'

She shook her head. 'Thanks, I'm fine. So, tell me, do you think Gready's wife was in the know?'

He shrugged. 'Honestly, I've no idea. She refused to give evidence and abandoned him during the trial – she seemed to have made her mind up that he was guilty. It's the age-old question, was the partner really innocent? I've heard that she has made a substantial donation to the Down's Syndrome Association. Interesting to know when she had this epiphany – blood money?' Roy said cynically.

'What about the rest of the money, surely she doesn't get to keep it?'

'She won't lose anything under the Proceeds of Crime Act because he is dead, but there might well be civil action – Customs and Excise, the police, that sort of thing.'

'Imagine if she didn't know, Roy? First, she's lost her husband, now she stands to lose her reputation.'

He nodded. 'Twenty years ago, I might have imagined that she genuinely didn't know. But less so these days.'

'Because twenty years as a copper has turned you into a sceptical bastard?' she said, with a teasing smile.

'No, life's about making choices. She chose a wrong 'un.'

'And what about me?' Cleo asked. 'What did I choose?'

He grinned back at her. 'I'm far too modest to say.'

GLOSSARY

ANPR – Automatic Number Plate Recognition. Roadside or mobile cameras that automatically capture the registration number of all cars that pass. It can be used to historically track which cars went past a certain camera, and can also create a signal for cars which are stolen, have no insurance or have an alert attached to them.

CID – Criminal Investigation Department. Usually refers to the divisional detectives rather than the specialist squads.

CPS – Crown Prosecution Service.

CSI – Was SOCO. Crime Scene Investigators (Scenes of Crime Officers). They are the people who attend crime scenes to search for fingerprints, DNA samples etc.

CSM – Crime Scene Manager.

DIGITAL FORENSICS – The unit which examines and investigates computers and other digital devices.

FLO – Family Liaison Officer.

HOLMES – Home Office Large Major Enquiry System. The national computer database used on all murders. It provides a repository of all messages, actions, decisions and statements, allowing the analysis of intelligence and the tracking and auditing of the whole enquiry. Can enable enquiries to be linked across force areas where necessary.

IOPC – Independent Office for Police Conduct.

OSCAR-1 – The call sign of the Force Control Duty Inspector, who has oversight and command of all critical incidents in the initial stages.

PM – Postmortem.

POLSA – Police Search Adviser.

RSOCU – Regional Serious & Organized Crime Unit.

SIO – Senior Investigating Officer. Usually a Detective Chief Inspector who is in overall charge of the investigation of a major crime such as murder, kidnap or rape.

FIND THEM DEAD

CHART OF POLICE RANKS

Police ranks are consistent across all disciplines and the addition of prefixes such as 'detective' (e.g. detective constable) does not affect seniority relative to others of the same rank (e.g. police constable).

ACKNOWLEDGEMENTS

With every novel I write, I'm always overwhelmed by the kindness of so many people who help me get the facts and descriptions of their professions and worlds accurate. I'm a stickler for accuracy in my research, so if I have got anything wrong please forgive me – and I'm sure you'll let me know!

It's always difficult to single out any particular person or group of people who have given me the most help, but I have found to my good fortune that with every novel, I seem to stumble, by luck or synchronicity, into either one person or, in this case, a small group of people, who have helped me beyond and above anything I have any right to expect.

In *Find Them Dead*, for the first time I've entered the world of a major court case, which has entirely its own language, culture and procedures. I am very deeply indebted to Resident Judge Her Honour Christine Laing QC, Judge Paul Tain QC, and Crown Advocate Richard Pedley, all of whom have tirelessly read the manuscript and made corrections, as well as happily taking my numerous calls on so many aspects of legal procedure. I honestly could not have written this novel without them. Nor without the immensely generous help of Juliet Smith JP, former High Sheriff of East Sussex, who opened so many doors for me.

Further invaluable legal help came from Anthony Burton CBE, Richard Cherrill, Moira Sofaer, Clive Sofaer, His Honour Paul Worsley QC, and also from staff at Lewes Crown Court, with particular thanks to Sally Burr, Lynda Pennicard-Nicholls and Denise Stonell.

Equally crucial for me is getting all aspects of policing accurate, and for this novel I'm indebted to both Sussex and the London Metropolitan Police. For many years I have had the immensely kind and generous support of Sussex Police and Crime Commissioner Katy Bourne, and the Sussex Chief Constable Giles York QPM, and many officers and support staff serving under them. I'm listing them, as well as Surrey and Sussex Major Crime Team officers and Met officers, in alphabetic order (and please forgive any omissions):

Sgt Peter Barnes, Chief Superintendent Lisa Bell, Inspector James Biggs, PC Matt Colburn, PC Ana Dark, Inspector Paul Davey, Financial Investigator Emily Denyer, DC Jenny Dunn, PC Philip Edwards, Inspector Mark Evans, CSI James Gartrell, Aiden Gilbert in Digital Forensics, DCI Rich Haycock, Inspector Dan Hiles, PC Dave Horton, Joseph Langford, DC Martin Light, Superintendent Paula Light, Chief Superintendent Nick May, Chief Constable of Kent Alan Pughlsey QPM, DCI Andy Richardson, Acting Inspector Andy Saville, Detective Superintendent Nick Sloan, James Stather in Forensic Services, DS Phil Taylor, Detective Superintendent Jason Tingley, PC Richard Trundle, and DI Bill Warner. And Beth Durham, Sue Heard, Jill Pedersen and Katie Perkin of Sussex Police Corporate Communications.

A big thank you, also, to Theresa Adams, Martin Allen, Graham Bartlett, Alan Bowles, Nick Cameron, Clare Davis, Sam Dawson, Peter Dean, Sean Didcott, Martin and Jane Diplock, Simon Drabble, Jonathan Gready (whose name I 'borrowed' for one of the main characters!), Anna Hancock, Ron Harrison, James Hodge, Terry Hooper, Claire Horne, Haydn Kelly, Rob Kempson, Gary and Rachel Kenchington, Paul Khan, Gerry Maye, Adrian Noon, Ray Packham, Julia Richardson of Galen Myotherapy, Kit Robinson (role model for Noah Grace!), Alan Setterington, Helen Shenston, Dick Smith, Orlando Trujillo, Mark Tuckwell, and Coroner's Officer Michelle Websdale.

A very special thank you also to my mentor Geoff Duffield, my amazing editor, Wayne Brookes, and the team at Pan Macmillan – to name just a few: Jonathan Atkins; Sarah Arratoon, Anna Bond, Lara Borlenghi, Emily Bromfield, Stuart Dwyer, Claire Evans, Samantha Fletcher, Anthony Forbes Watson, Lucy Hine, Hollie Iglesias, Daniel Jenkins, Rebecca Kellaway, Neil Lang, Rebecca Lloyd, Sara Lloyd, James Long, James Luscombe, Holly Martin, Guy Raphael, Alex Saunders, Jade Tolley, Kate Tolley, Jeremy Trevathan, Charlotte Williams and Natalie Young.

And everyone at my fabulous UK literary agency, Blake Friedmann: Lizzy Attree, Isobel Dixon, Sian Ellis-Martin, Julian Friedmann, Hana Murrell, James Pusey, Conrad Williams and Daisy Way. My US agent, Mitch Hoffman, at the Aaron M. Priest Literary Agency. And a very special shout-out to my fabulously gifted UK PR team at Riot Communications: Preena Gadher, Caitlin Allen and Emily Souders.

I'm blessed with a very close-knit and creative team around me, whom I jokingly – and perhaps not so jokingly – call Team James! Susan Ansell, Dani Brown, Mark and Debbie Brown, Kate Blazeby, Linda Buckley, Chris Diplock, David Gaylor, Lara James, Sarah Middle, Amy Robinson, Mark Tuckwell and Chris Webb.

I do often wonder if I'd not have the good fortune to meet a young DI, David Gaylor, back in 1997 (who rose to become Detective Chief Superintendent), whether Roy Grace would ever have happened. We work together closely on the planning and every stage of the development of each book. He's not quite my slave driver but he never lets me slacken the pace!

Last, but first of all, my beloved wife Lara. She is the first person to read every word I write, and she has judgement I completely trust, not just on how the story is going, but on how I'm portraying anything of a sensitive nature. She supports me and the team tirelessly, and with endless enthusiasm and wisdom. Even in my toughest moments with each book – and there are always some – she never lets my spirits flag.

As I write this, we are in dark times with the daily, growing nightmare of the Covid-19 pandemic. The one thing that always keeps me grounded, and puts a smile on my face despite almost any adversity, is being with our adorable menagerie of animals who are – so we think at any rate! – blissfully unaware of the horrors of the wider world. Thank you to all of you furry and feathered creatures! Our dogs, Oscar, Spooky and Wally, our cats, Madame Woo and Willy, our alpacas, Alpacino, Fortescue, Jean-Luc, Boris and Keith, our emus, Spike and Wolfie, our pigmie goats, Bouscaut, Margaux, Ted and Norman, and our miracle Indian Runner duck, Mickey Magic, that we hatched in an incubator in our home.

And a very special thank you to you, my readers – I owe you so much for your support. Do keep your communications coming; the whole team loves hearing from you by email, Twitter, Facebook, Instagram, YouTube – and even occasionally by post. I've learned so much from hearing what you like and what you don't, and when I occasionally make a slip-up. Above all, stay safe.

contact@peterjames.com

www.peterjames.com

You Tube peterjamesPJTV

f peterjames.roygrace

@peterjamesuk

@peterjamesuk

@peterjamesukpets

@mickeymagicandfriends

COMING 2021

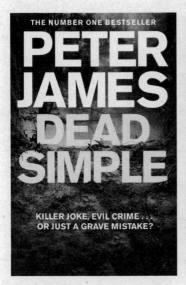

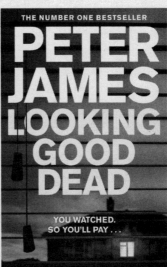

Peter James's first two books in the Detective Superintendent Roy Grace series, *Dead Simple* and *Looking Good Dead*, have been commissioned by ITV. They are being adapted for television by screenwriter Russell Lewis and will star John Simm as Roy Grace.

OUT NOW

I FOLLOW YOU

By Peter James

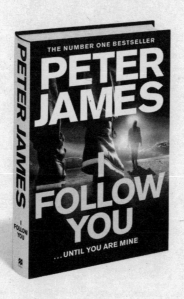

Turn the page to read an extract now . . .

1

Timing is everything.

Marcus Valentine lived by those words. They were his mantra. He was always scrupulously punctual and, equally, punctilious in all that he did, starting with his attire. It was important to him to be appropriately dressed for every occasion, with each item of his clothing immaculately clean and pressed, whether the business suits he wore to work, his golfing kit, or the cardigan, polo shirts and chinos he favoured when at home.

With his greying hair groomed immaculately, straight but prominent nose and piercing grey eyes, his perfect upright posture making his corpulent figure look closer to six foot than he actually was, he had the demeanour at times of a bird of prey, studying everything and everyone a little too sharply. Legions of his patients adored him, although a few of the hospital staff found him a tad arrogant. But they put up with it because he was good – in truth, more than just good, brilliant. Regardless of his particular field of expertise, he was the consultant many medics in the hospital would go to as first port of call for advice on any issue with a patient that concerned them.

In his mid-forties, he was at the top of his game. He had to admit he lapped up the attention, but he'd worked hard to get there, sacrificing much of his social and family life for years. So now was the time to enjoy it.

Today, though, had started badly. He was late. So late. He had overslept. He knew it shouldn't stress him out, but it did. He glanced at his watch, then at the car clock, checking their times. Late. So late. All his timings for the day now out of sync.

His wife, Claire, had told him mockingly more than once that the words *Timing is Everything* would be carved on his gravestone. Marcus knew he was a little obsessive, but to him timing was a matter of life and death. It was crucial, in his profession, in the calculation of due dates of the babies of expectant mothers, and equally so during those critical moments of delivery. It mattered in pretty much every aspect of his life. Of everyone's life.

Claire's job, as an executive coach, was much more flexible, and she worked it around her schedule – something he could never do. He always wanted to be early for a train, a flight, even for his golf. He'd be at a concert for doors opening and at the cinema for the trailers, whereas Claire constantly drove him nuts by leaving everything to the very last minute. But then again, she'd arrived into this world three weeks overdue so maybe that had something to do with it.

And this morning, at 8.40 a.m., squinting against the low, bright sun and reaching out with his left hand for his Ray-Bans, speeding in the rush-hour traffic along Victoria Avenue on his daily commute to the Jersey General Hospital, timing was about to matter more than he could have imagined.

As he pulled on his glasses, he didn't know it but the next sixty seconds were about to change his life forever.

Well, forty-seven seconds, actually, if he had checked.

2

Friday 7 December

Timing wasn't happening.

Georgie Maclean's sports watch had frozen. The lights at the pedestrian crossing she took most mornings over the busy road to the seafront were red, against her, as they usually were. But for some moments she was fixated on her watch. She'd been running fast, on course for a personal best – and then the damned watch crashed.

No, don't do this to me!

These lights were the slowest in the world. They took forever to change. They messed up her times for her run when she missed them, forcing her to wait, jogging on the spot to keep warm in the freezing early-morning air, with traffic streaming past too fast to risk a dash between the vehicles, almost all of them way exceeding the speed limit.

She stared at her fancy new running watch, silently pleading with it, the all-singing, all-dancing, top-of-the-range model that seemed to do everything but tell the time, and which wasn't doing any of those other things either. Right now, it was a useless big shiny red-and-black bracelet on her wrist.

All she had wanted was something to replace her trusted old sports watch that had died, something that had a heart-rate function and GPS that would connect her to the app

RunMaster. The salesman in the sports shop had assured her this one had more computing power in it than NASA when they put the first man on the moon. 'Seriously, do I need that just for a running watch?' she'd asked him. 'Seriously, you do,' he'd assured her, solemnly.

Now she was seriously pissed off. As she finally got a green and ran out into the road, she noticed too late the black Porsche. The driver hadn't seen the lights were now red, against the traffic. The driver with fancy sunglasses who wasn't even looking at the road.

She froze. Flung her arms, protectively, around the tiny bump growing inside her.

3

Friday 7 December

Marcus Valentine was irritated by what part of *I have to go, I have an emergency operation,* Claire didn't understand.

He'd been besotted with her the very first time he'd seen her. It was when he'd attended management development training she'd delivered at the hospital, the year after he'd moved to this island to start his new life as a consultant gynae-oncologist. She was tall, willowy, beautiful and always smiling. Although blonde, she'd reminded him so much of the girl he'd been infatuated with as a teenager – Lynette.

He would always remember the first time he'd seen Lynette on that perfect mid-summer Saturday afternoon. He was sixteen, lying in long grass behind a bush, out of sight of teachers, smoking illicitly with a bunch of school-mates, all of them skiving off from cricket. Jason Donovan had been playing on a radio one of them had brought along. 'Sealed With a Kiss'.

When an apparition had appeared across the field.

Impossibly long legs, flowing red hair, dark glasses, in a tantalizingly short white dress that clung to the contours of her body. She'd walked over, introduced herself, bummed a cigarette, then sat and flirted with them all, asking their names. Each had done their best to chat her up, before she'd left, striding away and blowing a kiss, then giving a coy wave of her hand.

At him, he was certain.

'You're in there, Marcus!' one of his friends had said. 'She liked you – dunno why she'd like a spotty fatso like you.'

'She was probably blind – that's why she wore those glasses!' said another.

Ignoring the comments and jeers, Marcus stood up and hurried after her. She gave him an inviting sideways glance and stopped. And right there, in full sight of his now incredulous – and incredibly jealous – friends, had snogged him, long and hard.

They'd met three times over the next few days, very briefly, just a short conversation then a deep French kiss each time. Nothing else as she always had to rush off. Marcus was becoming crazy for her.

'When can I see you again?' he'd blurted on the third meeting, barely able to believe his luck.

'Same time, same place, tomorrow?' she'd replied. 'Without your mates?'

Marcus had barely slept all night, thinking about her. At 3 p.m. the following afternoon, half an hour before she was due, having ducked out of a cross-country run, he'd positioned himself behind the bushes. She'd arrived on the dot and he signalled her over, standing up to meet her.

This time they'd kissed instantly, before they'd spoken a word. To his astonishment she'd slid her hand down inside the front of his shorts and gripped his penis.

Smiling into his eyes, and working her hand up and down, she'd said, 'Wow, you're big, do you think it would fit me?'

He was gasping, unable to speak, and seconds later he came.

'Nice?' she asked, still gripping him.

'Oh my God!'

She looked into his eyes again. 'Let's do it properly. Next Saturday, same time?'

'Next Saturday.' He couldn't wait to tell all his friends. But equally he didn't want them spying on him. 'Next Saturday, yes, definitely!'

'Bring some rubbers.'

'Rubbers?'

'Protection.'

It had taken him most of the rest of the week, during which again he'd barely slept, to pluck up the courage to go along to the local town, which was little more than a large village, enter the chemist and ask for a packet of Durex. He'd been served, his face burning, by a girl only a few years older than himself, while he looked furtively around in case there were any teachers from his school in there.

To his dismay, it had pelted with rain through the Saturday morning. And he realized he didn't know Lynette's number – nor even her last name. Lynette was all he had. By 3 p.m. the rain had eased to a light summer drizzle. With the condoms safely in his blazer pocket, trembling with excitement, reeking of aftershave and his teeth freshly brushed, he walked out across the field towards the bushes. He held his parka folded under his arm to keep it dry. They could lie on it, he planned.

3.30 p.m. passed, then 4 p.m., then 4.30. His heart steadily sank. At 5 p.m. he traipsed, sodden and forlorn, back to his school house. Maybe she'd come tomorrow if the weather was better, he hoped, desperately, his heart all twisted up.

Sunday was a glorious sunny day. He again waited all afternoon, but she never appeared. Nor the following weekend.

It had been three agonizingly long weeks before Marcus

saw Lynette again. Three weeks in which he'd fantasized over her, constantly. Three weeks in which she was never out of his thoughts or his dreams, distracting him hopelessly from his studies. On the Saturday morning, after class, he'd changed into shorts and a T-shirt and mooched down into the town, hoping against hope that he might find her there shopping.

Then to his excitement he saw her! At last! Outside a bikers' cafe. She'd dismounted, right in front of him, from the rear of a motorcycle pillion. The guy she was with was a bearded, tattooed hulk, in brass-studded leathers.

Marcus stopped dead and stared as she removed her helmet and shook out the long strands of her hair, tossing her head like a wild, beautiful free spirit.

'Hi, Lynette!' he said.

She didn't even look at him as she put her arm around her hulk and kissed him. Holding their helmets, they strode towards the cafe.

'Lynette!' he called out. 'Hi, Lynette!'

As he hurried towards her, she shot him a disdainful, withering glance and strutted on.

The biker stopped and blocked him. 'You got a problem, fatty?' He held up a tattooed fist glinting with big rings. 'Want a smack in the mouth?'

'I – I just wanted to say hello to Lynette!'

She had stopped and stared at him, then turned away, dismissively.

Marcus had watched as, arm in arm, they'd entered the cafe.

But he had never really stopped thinking about her. Sure, she wasn't part of his everyday thoughts, but at milestones – like both his wedding days – he had to admit to himself she did come into his mind. Wondering. Wondering what if it had been Lynette he was marrying? After he'd graduated from Guy's Hospital medical school he'd taken a post at the Bristol Royal Infirmary where he'd met and married his first wife, Elaine. The marriage had been a disaster. Within months, as he was working round the clock to build his career, Elaine, to his dismay, had fallen pregnant. But she'd had a miscarriage. In the aftermath, with Elaine in emotional turmoil and him working even harder, the marriage had disintegrated into an acrimonious divorce.

It was while the proceedings were going on that he'd seen the post in Jersey advertised and had successfully applied for it.

Then, working at the General Hospital in Jersey, he'd met Claire, and all the memories of that blissful summer's day with the Jason Donovan song playing had come flooding back.

Marrying Claire had made him feel whole. Those first two years in their beautiful hilltop home in St Brelade, with its striking sea view, they'd been so close. So very comfortable with each other that there had been moments – when he'd had perhaps a drink too many – when he'd been tempted to share with her a dark secret from his childhood that he'd harboured for years. But, always, he'd held back.

Then the twins had come along, and their relationship had inevitably changed. Even more so when their next baby had arrived. Unlike in his previous marriage, he had now been ready for children. They completed him as a family man, but he didn't like the feeling of being relegated to fourth place in Claire's affections, behind the children.

Claire kept her humour even though she was stuck in the house for much of the time with needy three-year-old twins, Rhys and Amelia, and an even needier nine-month-old baby boy, Cormac – the 'Vomit Comet'. In hindsight, three children under five was hugely stressful and had taken a toll on their relationship. He could only hope it would improve as the kids got older. But despite his misgivings, to the outside world he was the proud, happy father.

He'd seen so many friends grow apart when their children came along, and, Christ, his own parents had hardly been a shining example. He'd come to realize over the years that, far from being the glue that held relationships together, children could easily become the catalyst for their disintegration. Yet, though parents blamed the children, he knew the truth, that it was the other way around. Just like the words of that poem about your parents fucking you up.

Would he and Claire break the mould?

Not if this morning was anything to go by. She'd been so distracted by the twins fighting, she'd given Cormac milk that was far too hot. On top of that she'd begun firing questions at Marcus, blocking him from leaving the front door. A human barrier, as tall as him, long fair hair a wild tangle around her face.

When are we putting up the Christmas tree?

Who's coming?

What outside lights shall we put up?

When are you going to give me a list of what you want for Christmas? And shall we get the twins the same presents or different? We've got to get them soon or they'll all be gone.

'I've got to go – later, please, Claire. OK? Friday's my morning in theatre – and I have an emergency ectopic – everyone will be gowned up and waiting, they know that I'm never late for knife to skin.'

'Come on, you always have an emergency something. Later isn't a time! Later is *never*! Is that what you tell your patients when they ask you when their baby is due? *Later?*' She shook her head. 'No, you say June 11th or July 16th. Or, knowing you, you probably say at 3.34 p.m. precisely.'

When he had finally left the house, he was eleven

minutes behind schedule. Time he was never going to make up on an eighteen-minute journey.

The joy of kids! All those pregnant women he would be seeing in his consulting room this afternoon. Smearing on the gel and moving the ultrasound scanner around their expectant bellies. Showing them the shadowy silhouette of the little lives inside them, on the screen.

Watching their happy faces. Their own worlds about to change.

Do you know what's ahead? Months of sleepless nights. And for some of you, the end of your life as you know it. All the sacrifices you'll both make over the years to come? Will you produce geniuses who'll change the world for the better or ungrateful little bastards who'll turn you into an anxious mess? The gamble of life. A good kid . . . or a waste of space? Nature, nurture; good parents, crap parents. You needed a licence to keep certain animals, but any irresponsible idiot could have kids.

He knew he should be more positive, change his mindset. But he couldn't help it, that was how he felt. Increasingly. Day by day. Working all hours in the hospital. Frequently on call, working weekends. He'd kept in touch with a few of his old friends from his time at boarding school. One had gone on to become an insanely rich hedge-fund manager, and was now a tanned, relaxed hedonist with his super-rich hedge-fund manager wife and retinue of white-suited acolytes. They proudly called themselves the TWATs – only working Tuesdays, Wednesdays and Thursdays. What a life!

Another old buddy seemed equally relaxed working as a sailing instructor. Marcus admired his choice to live modestly and still, at forty-five, to go on backpacking adventure holidays with his wife.

It seemed, some days, that he envied everyone else's life.

PETER JAMES

Sure, he made a good living, and he loved the kudos he got for his role at the hospital, but at times he couldn't help feeling he'd made the wrong life choices – including the wrong career. And possibly the wrong discipline within it. Sometimes he made people happy, but not this morning. His first operation was to remove the remaining fallopian tube of a thirty-nine-year-old woman who'd endured nine tough years of in vitro fertilization and whose final chance of a natural pregnancy was now gone. Her symptoms had been confirmed just over an hour and a half ago and he had little time to lose.

Cursing for being so late, he was now driving faster than the 40 mph speed limit along Victoria Avenue, his baseball cap pulled low over his forehead against the low, dazzlingly bright sunlight in his eyes. Over to his right, the tide in St Aubin's Bay was a long way out. Full moon. His own tide felt just as far out.

Snapping himself out of this mood, he hit the speed-dial button on his phone to call his assistant, Eileen, to give her his ETA.

Then he looked up and saw the red light.

Bearing down on it at speed.

A young woman, with Titian-red hair, in running kit, had stopped right in front of him. Staring at him in horror.

Frozen in her tracks.

Hands clamped over her midriff.

Shit, shit, shit.

He stamped the brake pedal to the floor.

The wheels locked. The car slithered. Yawed left, then right, then left again, the tyres scrubbing and smoking.

Oh Jesus.

Heading straight towards her. No longer driving his car, just a helpless passenger.

4

Friday 7 December

The Porsche stopped inches from Georgie. Like, *inches*. Another foot and it would have wiped her out.

She stood still, staring, momentarily rooted to the spot in shock. Through the windscreen the driver, in a baseball cap pulled low and sunglasses, also looked shocked. She shook her head and opened up her arms, mouthing an exasperated, *What?*

He put his window down and leaned out a fraction. Then froze as he saw her properly.

Lynette.

Was this Lynette, after all these years?

No, it couldn't be. Couldn't. Could it?

'It's a red light,' she said, tartly. 'Or are you colour blind?'

'I'm sorry,' he said. 'I'm—'

She shook her head and ran on.

Marcus sat staring after her, stunned. His mind flooded with emotions from the past.

She was exactly how he imagined Lynette might look now – some thirty years on. Handsomely beautiful, alluring, and in great shape.

God, how ironic if it really was Lynette and he'd run her over!

PETER JAMES

Could it be possible that it actually was her? A million-to-one coincidence?

Destiny?

He'd never made any attempt to find Lynette – he'd never even known her surname. And in any case, he was well aware it had only been a teenage obsession at best. But suddenly the sight of this woman had reminded him of that summer. That girl. Those fumbling, tantalizing moments when she had touched him, that he had replayed in his mind countless times. And still occasionally did when he was making love to Claire. All that Lynette had promised. And never delivered.

A horn blared behind him. A large white van.

The lights were now green.

He raised an apologetic hand and, as he drove on, shot the woman another quick glance.

Followed by a longer one.

Could it possibly be her?

He felt stirring in his groin. He was aroused.

5

Georgie Maclean finally got the watch restarted, although to her annoyance it had frozen again and not recorded all the details of the past two miles of her daily morning run. And, incredibly, given her current condition, just when she was sure she had smashed her previous five-mile time.

Whatever.

She was still shaking. Shit. That idiot in the Porsche. She patted her midriff again, where tiny life was just beginning, a few millimetres in size but growing daily.

At forty-one, she was only too aware her biological clock was ticking away crazily fast now, like it was on speed. Which was why it felt so very good to be pregnant, after years of yearning for a baby. She'd left it late, and hadn't even started trying until she was thirty-three, after she'd finally found Mr Right, the man she wanted to have a child with, back in London. Mike Chandler, a teacher at a tough comprehensive. She'd been working as a PE teacher back then. After years of no success, her gynaecologist discovered she had a tilted – retroverted – uterus but did not operate as he did not feel that should stop her falling pregnant. But still nothing had happened. Then Mike had been diagnosed as having a low sperm count. When that had been sorted, it was discovered she had hostile mucus.

543

She recalled going to see a sweet, elderly specialist up in Hampstead, who had helped a close friend with her fertility issues. As she'd lain in his reclining chair, feet up in stirrups, while he inspected her with a vaginal speculum, tut-tutting, she'd exclaimed in anger that she couldn't see how the hell anyone ever got pregnant. And always remembered his words, in his strong Scottish burr: 'You have to understand, Mrs Chandler, there is an awful lot of copulation that goes on in the world.'

Several years of infertility treatment had followed. Her menstrual cycle logged into her laptop and phone. Making love according to a date stipulated by an ovulation kit and an app. Followed by expensive and painful attempts at IVF. It sure had been a romance-buster. Finally, they'd separated, sadly and very painfully. Mike had quickly got together with a fellow teacher, who was now pregnant by him, and Georgie had gone back to her maiden name.

After a sudden bout of acid reflux, something that was occurring constantly at the moment, she ran down the side of the Old Station Cafe, crossed the cycle lane and turned left, following the curve of the bay towards St Helier. To her right, below on the beach, people were walking their dogs, some of which were bounding, free of their leads, across the vast expanse of wet sand left by the retreating sea. Further over, the rock outcrop to the east of the harbour, topped by Elizabeth Castle and separated from the mainland by a causeway, was now walkable with the far-receded tide.

To get away from the trauma of her marriage split, she'd come to Jersey for the summer at the invitation of an old girlfriend, Lucy, who she'd known since primary school. Lucy had moved to the island a while back with her sister, and Lucy herself was training to become a nutritionist.

Georgie loved her passion for this and for going back to study. They'd both made a big leap to change career well into their thirties and were a huge support to each other. In fact, whenever they met up, which was often, they were normally in tears of laughter within minutes. 'The Gigglers', as they had been known back when they were five years old. That had stuck, and they loved and cherished it.

Soon after Georgie's arrival on the island she'd had a short relationship with an estate agent, which hadn't worked out. She hadn't been ready to return to London and had really grown to love everything about Jersey – the calmer pace of life, the rugged landscapes and the beaches, and the feeling of safety that the island community offered. She'd decided she wanted to stay. She managed to get accepted as a Jersey resident and was making a life here, building a new career as a personal trainer. She called her company Fit For Purpose.

Although this island she now called home was small, just nine miles by five, it felt much larger. One of her clients, who had spent all her life in Jersey, had told her that it increased its land mass by one third when the tide was out. Not hard to believe, from the vast amount of beach she could see.

There were also hundreds of miles of lanes and roads, with stunning coastal views around almost every corner. Its only town, St Helier, which she was now heading towards, with its port, network of pedestrianized streets and vast array of shops and stores, felt substantial, almost a bonsai version of an English city.

The one oddity was St Helier's principal landmark, an incinerator chimney, and she always wondered why, with its inhabitants so keen on preserving the island's natural beauty, nothing had ever been done to somehow mask it.

But it hadn't spoiled her love of the place. And the one thing she loved more than anything was how safe she felt. The crime levels were so low that she felt completely secure running here, even at night, and she never bothered to lock her car.

As she ran on towards the Esplanade, where many of the banks were sited, passing a closed ice-cream kiosk, shading her eyes against the low winter sun, she didn't notice the Porsche which had now made a U-turn and was cruising back past her. Slowly. But not so slow that it was obvious.

6

Inside his car, Marcus was unsettled. And hard.

Lynette?

The slender woman on his left in the pink top, bright-blue shorts and compression socks, who he'd almost run over, was now heading in the opposite direction, grim determination on her face.

As he drove, he discreetly held up his phone and took a photograph of her. Then he did a quick mental calculation, wondering how Lynette would really look today – assuming she was still alive? Was she still beautiful like this running lady? Or was the Lynette of his dreams now fat, tattooed and living miserably with her bolshy biker husband? Her likeness was uncanny, although he knew that in reality it almost certainly wasn't her.

And yet?

The clock in the round white dial above the dash said 8.42. It was running sixteen seconds fast against the dial of his wristwatch and the imprecision angered him. The watch that received, each night, a radio signal from the US atomic clock in Colorado. It was accurate, every day, to within nano-seconds.

He was really late now, but at this moment did not care. He turned round at the first opportunity, catching one more glimpse of her from the other side of the dual carriageway, then drove on. He wanted to see her again. With a small population of around 107,000 on this island, you were constantly bumping into people you knew, or at least recognized. For sure, he would see her again.

Finally, he pulled into an underground parking space at the rear of the tired old granite buildings of Jersey General Hospital and hurried from his car. Still thinking about the woman.

Running.

He'd taken up the sport at medical school and after losing a lot of weight had become a useful runner himself, often winning cross-country races at county standard. He'd always loved the buzz, the competitive high. How long had it been since he'd stopped running seriously because of a ligament injury and just did the odd jog here and there? Three years? God, no, four. He felt his stomach. *I'm turning into a paunchy bastard. Just like I was once mocked for being a teenage fatty.*

Got to get back on it on a regular basis. Get a training regime set out. And maybe see her again?

With three young kids and a demanding career, where would he find the time – or the energy? But he needed to. His lack of exercise was already taking a toll on his health. At his last check-up, his GP had prescribed him statins, telling him he was overweight, his blood pressure wasn't great and that he was drinking too much – and he'd lied about his weekly alcohol units, which were double at least what he had told the quack. Oh, and he'd conveniently forgotten to tell him that he'd taken up smoking again. Not much, but enough for disapproval.

He knew he wasn't a great example to his patients, if they were to find out, as he told all of them to cut down their drinking and quit smoking.

Maybe he could try a longer jog over the weekend, see if he could stretch it to a run? For his birthday, a few months back, Claire had bought him a sports watch, which he'd only used a handful of times. Was it a hint, he wondered, that his changed physique and his increasing belly were turning her off? Did he care?

And hey, he knew his looks and charm were still there, even with those few extra pounds on him; some of his patients clearly fancied him – and, he thought, at least two of the staff members at the hospital – well, three actually.

He strode towards the main entrance. Twenty-two minutes late. Normally this would have stressed him, but not now that a plan was forming in his mind.

Start running again properly. Yes.

And maybe he'd see the redhead sometime, out on the promenade.

Although he did not know it, he *was* going to see her again. Very much sooner than he thought.